The Agent's Frustrated Prince

The Tales of Avalon Series

L. KALAJIAN

BALBOA.PRESS

A DIVISION OF HAY HOUSE

Balboa Press books may be ordered through booksellers or by contacting:

Balboa Press
A Division of Hay House
1663 Liberty Drive
Bloomington, IN 47403
www.balboapress.com
844-682-1282

Because of the dynamic nature of the Internet, any web addresses or links contained in this book may have changed since publication and may no longer be valid. The views expressed in this work are solely those of the author and do not necessarily reflect the views of the publisher, and the publisher hereby disclaims any responsibility for them.

The author of this book does not dispense medical advice or prescribe the use of any technique as a form of treatment for physical, emotional, or medical problems without the advice of a physician, either directly or indirectly. The intent of the author is only to offer information of a general nature to help you in your quest for emotional and spiritual well-being. In the event you use any of the information in this book for yourself, which is your constitutional right, the author and the publisher assume no responsibility for your actions.

Any people depicted in stock imagery provided by Getty Images are models, and such images are being used for illustrative purposes only. Certain stock imagery © Getty Images.

Cover art by J. E. Quinton

Print information available on the last page.

ISBN: 979-8-7652-5808-8 (sc)
ISBN: 979-8-7652-5807-1 (e)

Library of Congress Control Number: 2024925734

Balboa Press rev. date: 01/27/2025

For My Grammy Rose and My Grandma Shirley.

To the women who helped shape my life before and after I was born, no matter how long you're gone, I will remember the stories and lessons passed down to me...

Contents

Contents

Prologue: A Prince's Fate

14 May 2010...

Prince Arthur Evergreen Drago stood numb outside Westminster Abby. The weight of duty had settled around his shoulders like a heavy blanket. His dark suit jacket felt more like an anchor today than simply fabric. His title was still prince; according to a law passed a few years ago, Arthur couldn't be officially named and crowned king until he and his twin sister, Catherine Anastasia 'Anya' Evergreen-Drago, turned twenty-one.

Their *Tad* (Father), King Andros of England, had died ten days ago after being diagnosed with cancer. It had been a quick death after diagnosis, quicker than either he or Anya had hoped. They wanted more time with him, but Stepmonster kept them away. By the time they reached him, he had slipped into a coma. Uncle Aaron had rearranged everything on their jam-packed schedules in those last few days so they could stay with their father.

Arthur stood between his dark-blond sister and Great Uncle Aaron Black (Lord Black to everyone who wasn't family). Anya wore a knee-length black dress with black tights. They were both old enough that she was wearing chunk heels instead of flats. She also wore a black pillbox hat, which royal women wore in the modern-day instead of crowns outside official dinner parties.

Great Uncle Aaron was wearing one of his military uniforms, having never officially retired when he transitioned to being *Tad's* Lord Security and guardian. He just couldn't be sent overseas with his men on active duty. He had several medals pinned to his chest. Most of the medals had been given to him by *Tad*, but some were from their grandmother, Queen Eliza of England, a woman not even *Tad* would have remembered.

The three were waiting for a coffin draped in the royal standard to be placed on a cannon carriage adapted for Queen Victoria of Scotland's funeral. One of the treaties between England and Scotland in the last hundred years allowed the English Royal Family to use this cannon carriage. It was part of their shared history of the World believing that the Scottish Royal Family and the English Royal Family were the same...

Once the coffin was settled on the cart, the navy cadets started pulling the cart. Still numb, Arthur, the king-in-waiting, started moving with Anya and Uncle Aaron. Three others were walking behind them. Auncle Dylan decided to dress in a tasteful three-piece black suit, and they were behind their father, Great Uncle Aaron. Damian, who was dressed in a military uniform, was behind Arthur. Lord Liam Wales, who *Tad* referred to as Uncle Liam, was dressed in a three-piece suit but had his medals pinned to the left side of his chest. He had been retired from active duty for some time. He was behind Anya. All of them were doing their best not to show any emotion.

Two Rolls Royce slowly followed behind them. The first car carried Aunt Melanie, *Hennain* (Great Grandmother), and *Hen-daid* (Great Grandfather). They refused to be in the same enclosed space as the Murrian women, especially when they refused to follow any funeral protocol regarding clothes.

The second car carried the Murrian women: Kendra or 'Stepmonster', as Anya and Arthur refused to call her mother, Stepmonster's dreadful mother, and her horrible sister, Karen. The bright colours they chose to wear to a very public funeral that was being shown all over the world would be the one thing that would be talked about for days.

Arthur didn't like thinking about those horrid women. Morning colours were part of royal protocol. Even when travelling, he had to have a set of black clothes back just in case something like a ruling monarch died while being away from home. This was something that happened to Queen

Elizabeth II of Scotland when her father died. It was adopted into the English protocols for Grandmother Eliza, as she also was nowhere near home when King George VI of Scotland died and didn't have black clothing with her.

Arthur was pulled out of his thoughts as they came to a stop at Hyde Park. It was time to transfer the coffin from the cannon carriage to a specialised hearse with clear back windows. Damian had brushed against him slightly.

"Wh—..."

"Are you alright?" Damian asked quietly, "You're like on auto-pilot."

Arthur shook his head, "Just numb, and I might have taken something to keep my powers from acting up."

"Did Catherine take something, too?"

Arthur blinked as the world blurred as he started walking to a different car, "Maybe, I don't think she's flamed at anyone recently. Her firefighter guard had to go home for something that he couldn't be on hand to douse her with water. Why?"

"Because I'm not *singed* in any way," Damian replied dryly.

Arthur resisted the urge to smack his forehead. Damian opened the backdoor to the waiting Rolls Royce that he would share with Uncle Aaron, Aunt Melanie, and his great-grandparents. Arthur paused as Damian stayed on the other side of the door.

"Are you going to join us?"

Damian's bloodshot eyes widened, "Are you sure? I didn't think I was invited. I'm just the stepson."

"Who we like better than your mother!" Aunt Melanie called from somewhere inside the car.

"Melanie!" Uncle Aaron hissed, "Not now."

Damian grimaced, "It would be better to travel with them. I'll meet you at Windsor. This time should be for you and your immediate family."

Arthur nodded reluctantly before sliding into the car with

some family members. Damian closed the door as Arthur looked around, "Where's Anya and Auncle Dylan?"

Aunt Melanie and Uncle Aaron look at each other. Arthur missed *Hen-daid* shuttering as *Hennain* pulled him close. The windows in the back could darken when needed.

"There's not enough space," she assured, "They're with Matheo and *Lili*."

Arthur let himself relax in *Hennain's* arms. He felt safe to let tears roll down his cheeks. He felt it was alright to do so. His grandfather's side of the family was not big on maintaining protocol when they were finally behind closed doors.

✠ ✠ ✠

"*Arthur!*" Anya sharply whispered, jolting Arthur to the present with a nudge. "*You need to go.*"

Arthur blinked and refocused. He noticed the traditional sceptre and ball were no longer on the coffin. It was time to lay the camp colours... *Are we already at the end of the second ceremony in Windsor?*

"I... can't," he started, whispering, "I can't do it."

She remained silent for a moment. He saw her eyes darken. A tear rolled down her cheek.

"Let's do it together," she finally suggested.

Anya then stood, making him stand, too. They moved as one of the coffins before anyone could stop her. They each held a corner of the camp colours flag as they lifted it and draped it over the coffin where the sceptre and ball were moments ago. The Lord Chamberlain joined them and lifted his wand staff with both hands. He then snapped the staff in hand and placed the broken pieces on the coffin.

The royal twins and the Lord Chamberlain moved away from the coffin as Anya herded Arthur back to their seats. Off to the side, a bagpiper started playing as their father's coffin was lowered into the crypt below.

Anya had to nudge him again. This time, it was to get him to stand and leave. The others couldn't leave until he did. Numb and sick to his stomach, Arthur rose. As he passed, some were either bowing or deep curtsying.

When the twins got outside, Anya squeezed his hand and gently pushed him into a black Rolls Royce with the Royal Standard flying on the edge of the hood. Matthew Evers, his guard, nodded as he entered the car. The door closed behind him without her. Then, in the silence, with only the driver and Matthew, he realised his whole world would never be the same. He and Anya would not be allowed in the same car for a long time.

Chapter 1: That Fateful Trip

1 October 2010

With a heavy sigh, Arthur cast a miserable glance at his reflection in the mirror. He dressed far more formally than he would have preferred on the weekend, but the role of a to-be ruling monarch demanded such attire, even if his official coronation was yet to take place. His ensemble included a dark tie, a crisp white shirt, and dress pants; he planned to don the suit jacket just before he left.

However, the most crucial part of his outfit was his dress shoes. These were no ordinary footwear but a gift from his Spanish cousins, who shared his unique powers. Imported from Spain and crafted to harness his earth powers, the shoes granted him the ability to see rooms away through vibrations in the ground.

Arthur sighed again as he moved away from the mirror to the sitting room of his apartment in Buckingham Palace. He was mentally preparing himself for another mind-numbing day of duties. One of those duties was a newly scheduled meeting with Parliament and the House of Lords. With it being a Saturday, he had a vague idea having a meeting scheduled was not normal.

However, *'normal'* for Arthur went out the window five months ago, and those months had not been kind to him. He was seventeen years old, and under regular circumstances, he would not meet with them until he was twenty-one. They moved this *'important'* meeting he *'must'* attend to the weekend so it didn't interfere with school.

Meanwhile, the king-in-waiting still hadn't had his regal name approved. 'Arthur' hadn't been a common regal name among the kings before a long line of queens ruled. Historians were still debating if there should be 'II' after his name as there hasn't been any proven evidence that a *King Arthur* or even that *Camelot* existed out of stories, despite many claims of the English, Welsh, or Scottish Royal Families in the past.

Arthur knew that he would soon have to choose his place as a ruler of his people. His father, the late King Andros, had spent the short time he could actively train his children to be the next ruler. However, whoever was supposed to take over wasn't who the late king wanted to rule. Arthur didn't know that his father's will had been overridden by Parliament. Parliament was currently being ruled by the Royalist side of the Conservatives.

Arthur also knew that Anya would make a great queen. And, if he could find a way to prove that to the government, he would have done that by now. He felt like there was a rope tightening around his neck.

The month of October was always busy. He tried his best to help his subjects celebrate the holidays that were important to them, like Thanksgiving for some or Yom Kippur and Sukkot for others. The day that he liked the most was *Halloween*. Halloween, or All Hallows Eve, was the sweetest day for most kids under ten *(or those who were still kids at heart)*, especially for those who dressed up to get candy from different adults around the neighbourhoods. It also happened to be his and Anya's birthday.

However, for him and Anya, who was unfairly older than him by ten minutes, this meant an all-out celebration. Their birthday party was always in costume and mask. This happened without fail, even when, according to Stepmonster, they *'should have been too old for it'*.

October felt different to him this year. It even felt different from that first October after his mother and his little brother died in a flood, swept away in their car. He and Anya had spent ten birthdays without them. But now, this would be the first birthday since their father had passed. He didn't know why it felt more... *constricting* than in the past. But it did. A weight was slowly making him feel heavier, with both grief and guilt.

Unfortunately, Arthur couldn't show much grief. He would cry privately, either by himself or with Anya or their cousins, Antonio 'Tonio', William 'Wills', and Harry. He would never let anyone know about his guilt—guilt over both not being able to save his father and not wanting to be king. Quietly, he prayed an old law somewhere that said '*the oldest child*' and not '*oldest son*' was the next ruler.

Growing up, in general, just *sucked*, especially having powers that were influenced by emotions and hormones, causing them to go haywire. Objects tended to explode when Arthur lost his temper. He didn't know if he could consider his control slipping worse now than when he was a child. Not only did he try to process *Tad's* death, but he also had to deal with the bullying happening around him.

Arthur's heart hurt for his stepbrother, Damian, every time he overheard Stepmonster put the twenty-two-year-old down. She seemingly only claimed him as '*hers*' when he was '*useful*' to whatever scheme she believed he could help her with. Arthur knew that Damian just wanted Stepmonster's love like a family should, not as someone who could further her position in society.

He picked up his *iPhone*, which happened to have all the bells and whistles the phone company insisted were secure enough to make his head security guard, Matthew Evers, and Uncle Aaron happy, off the side table as he sat down in an armchair. He unlocked the screen and opened the picture app. He silently started scrolling through the photos, including the sneaky ones he'd taken. Damian would never know he had taken them. There was too much at stake for Arthur even to consider telling him about his crush.

This...*crush* Arthur had for the slightly older lord was forbidden in so many ways. The first reason was that they had been raised as stepbrothers for the last nine years. The other problem that he faced was that he was King of the English throne and eventually had to continue on the royal line. However, at the rate things were going, he might have to do what his cousin, King Edward VIII of Scotland, did and abdicate for love without any attempts at treason. Arthur also knew of the less drastic option of simply naming Anya's firstborn child as his heir if he didn't abdicate.

Arthur then switched to the new social media fad, *Facebook*. He didn't have control over the account, but he liked to see what his other 'friends' were up to. He liked to follow his favourite actors, actresses, and musicians under an assumed name that he had made up, being careful never to post any photos of himself, just of things that he enjoyed.

Usually, he wouldn't be scrolling this mindlessly. There was just no time to get pulled into a really good book, and it was too early to sneak off to the kitchens to help make lunch for the staff and his family.

However, he wasn't distracted enough with his phone to see a tall, dark-haired man, dressed in a dark suit quietly enter the private sitting room. The older man was carrying a package; Arthur had been waiting for this particular package for the past few days. He had ordered it with one of his fake names as he didn't want the fashion magazines to learn about this project until *after* the holidays.

Arthur overheard faint words coming over the older man's earpiece. He paused his scrolling and closed the *Facebook* app. The older man nodded to himself before coming closer.

"Hello, *your Majesty*," he greeted with a slight bow, "The car is ready for you."

"Thank you, Matthew," Arthur replied as he locked and pocketed his phone before standing, "You know that you can call me Arthur?"

The older man's blue eyes gleamed as he gave him a small smile, "But never in public, sir, which is where we are going."

"We're just going to see my *hen daid a nain!* (Great Grandparents!)" He protested.

"That is in a very public setting with Lord Murrian as a

4

new boss who could fire me on his mother's orders," Matthew continued dryly as they started walking through the palace halls, "We both know that Lord Murrian would have to do it."

Arthur made a face before hastily wiping his expression. He understood that they would force Damian to listen to Stepmonster and the other nobles, even if it hurt Arthur if they believed that there was too much familiarity between him and the staff. One of the things that Damian never wanted to do was hurt Arthur emotionally. The young king-in-waiting also didn't want to put Damian between a rock and a hard place when it came to his protection.

⊕ ⊕ ⊕

Arthur sighed again, slightly less miserable, as he looked out the tinted window of the SUV. The bustling London streets started to blur as his mind wandered. He quietly began going over what they had to accomplish today as they headed to one of his favourite things to do in the autumn months.

The Farmers Market was one of the few duties he never grew tired of doing. Sometimes, he'd go to explore and help attract customers for the small businesses. Other times, he would go just to visit *hen daid a nain*.

It was the added meeting with the squabbling Parliament and the House of Lords on a Saturday that he didn't like, being something important enough that the last-minute change left no time to switch, or he would have sent Anya in his place. She had to make an appearance at the Children's Hospital, which overlapped with his trip to the Farmer's Market. Switching was a normal occurrence for them; it just wasn't easy to do today.

He grunted as the driver hit the curb and pulled him back to the present.

"*Sorry, sir,*" the driver said from the front. "I didn't mean to do that."

"It's alright," Arthur replied as he straightened up, "Driving in London has always been a pain, even when I'm not doing it."

"Thank you, sir," the driver replied before looking forward.

Arthur felt Matthew's concerned eyes on him from the front passenger seat. He must have heard something in the young royal's voice.

"Are you sure you're alright?" Matthew asked quietly.

Arthur nodded as he took a deep breath and unbuckled his seatbelt, "Let's do this."

"Very well," Matthew tipped his head before unbuckling himself and exiting the car.

Per protocol, Arthur forced himself to wait for Matthew to open the door. One of the things he hated about being in public was feeling like he was being waited on hand and foot. While most nobles and other royals liked that feeling, *he* didn't. Arthur thought he would flourish working behind the scenes and away from crowds.

"*Sir?*" Matthew asked after he opened the back passenger door, holding out the package from earlier, "Would you like to carry this?"

Arthur mutely nodded as he slid out of the backseat. He hastily took the package as the crisp autumn air filled his lungs, carefully tucking it against his body as they walked toward the entrance.

Holding the package tight, the semi-permanent booths of the market became visible to Arthur as they approached. Heading toward *hen daid a nain's* booth, a sense of excitement surrounded them as the people he passed started taking out phones and digital cameras. He had another reason for coming to the Farmer's Market today; Arthur desperately needed their advice. They know the other vendors and crafters that come to the Farmer's Market regularly and could direct him to someone selling what he was searching for.

Typically, he would have bought the yarn and then asked his cousin, Tonio, for help. However, Arthur considered Tonio wouldn't help him this time since the project gift was for the one person everyone seemed to be at odds with.

Damian got the short end of the stick for the last nine years because of Stepmonster, otherwise known as Lady Kendra Murrian. She was seen by many as a conniving social climber who had wanted the throne long before Damian had been born.

Others unfairly grouped Damian in with the gaggle of Murrian women. These women have been trying to undermine everything since entering the English Royal family less than ten years ago. Only Arthur and his *hen ewythr* (Great Uncle), Lord Aaron Black, gave the young man the benefit of the doubt.

"*O, dyna chu, Arth Bach!*" (Oh, there you are, Little Bear) *Hennain* (Great Grandmother) excitedly greeted as Arthur approached the main table.

Hennain Black, dressed in black for the everlasting mourning of deceased family members, had her greying hair tied back into a bun at the base of her neck. She rounded the tables filled with handmade jewellery and practically tackled him. Arthur hastily put the package down on the table and braced himself. Though small in stature, she has knocked him over with her hugs in the past.

Hennain's arms wrapped around his waist; her head only came to his upper chest. She laid her ear against him as if to assure herself that his heart was still beating. Arthur missed the days when he was small enough to curl up in her lap and cry. Her radiating warmth had always been the same, seemingly to chase away the cold despite not having any fire powers.

"*Helo, Hennain,*" he greeted, settling his chin on her head. "*Sut wyt ti a Hen Daid hediw?*" (How are you and Great Grandfather today?)

She pulled away and had him bend a little so she could kiss his cheek. She then grabbed his hand and pulled him behind the table to work with them. Arthur started laughing; his tall *Hen Daid* shook his head with amusement, and his eyes shone with laughter.

"*Rwy'n siŵr bor ganddo bethau eraill i'w gwneud, Cariad,*" (I'm sure that he's got other things to do, Sweetheart) *Hen Daid's* thick, raspy voice washed over him. He remembered all the bedtime stories *Hen Daid* Black read to him and Anya when they were younger.

"*Mewn gwirionedd...*" (Actually) Arthur started as he kept *Hennain* from pulling him into the booth.

Hennain's happy expression dropped from her face, "*Wnest ti ddim dod i helpu?*" (You didn't come to help?)

"*Gallaf aros os oes angen mwy o draffig traed arnoch,*" (I can stay if you need more foot traffic) Arthur assured, knowing that many commoners couldn't ignore their curiosity about a royal family member being out and about. He would also have a legitimate reason to skip his meeting later. "*Des i yma oherwydd mae gen i'r ffabrig—*" (I came here because I have the fabric)

Hennain clapped, the smile returning to her face as he gestured to the package now on the table. "*Ni allaf aros i weld beth ddewisoch chi eleni!*" (I can't wait to see what you picked out this year!) She grabbed the package and examined it before looking him over. "*Ydych chi angen help gydag unrhyw beth arall?*" (Do you need help with anything else?)

"*Rwy'n ceisio cael anrheg i rywun arbennig,*" (I'm trying to get a gift for someone special) he admitted shyly.

Hennain squealed, nearly causing Arthur to wince, realising that was his mistake.

"*Pwy yw'r person lwcus?*" (Who is the lucky person?) She asked, happily, more open-minded than most women her age because her other *wyres* (grandchild) showed her that she needed to be open-minded.

"*Nawr, Isolde,*" (Now, Isolde) *Hen Daid* soothed before turning to Arthur, "*Does dim rhaid i chi ateb ynghylch pwy rydych chi'n ei hoffi. Rwyf am iddynt eich trin fel person, nid fel nwydd.*"(You don't have to answer about who you like. I want them to treat you as a person, not as a commodity)

"*Dydw i ddim hyd yn oed yn gwybod a yw'n fy hoffi i felly,*" (I don't even know if he likes me that way) Arthur shifted back and forth. "*Nid wyf ychwaith am ddweud unrhyw beth a allai ei gael i drafferth.*" (I also don't want to say anything that could get him into trouble)

"*Beth allai ei gael i drafferth?*" (What could get him into trouble?) *Hennain* asked, astonished, "*Rydych chi'n dywysog— Brenin, yr wyf yn ei olygu.*" (You're a prince— King, I mean)

"*Wel, mae'n hŷn na fi,*" (Well, he's older than me) Arthur rubbed the back of his neck, "*Ac mae ganddo deulu genedigol homoffobig iawn nad yw uwchlaw ei arestio am fod gyda rhywun dan oed, yn enwedig gan ei fod bellach yn gyfrifol am fy niogelwch, dim ond i ddysgu gwers iddo.*" (And he has a very homophobic birth family that isn't above getting him arrested for being with someone underage, especially since now he's in charge of my security, just to teach him a lesson.)

Hen Daid hummed as he nodded, "*Yna dwi'n gwybod pa fwth rydych chi'n edrych amdano.*" (Then I know which booth you're looking for.) He turned and gestured down the row and to the left. "*Parhewch i lawr y ffordd honno. Mae bwth PRIDE i lawr yno.*" (Just continue down that way. There's a PRIDE booth down there)

Arthur brightened, "*Diolch, Hen Daid! Plîs dywedwch helo wrth Wncwl Aaron i mi!*" (Thanks, Great Grandfather! Please say 'hi' to Uncle Aaron for me!)

He then kissed *Hennain's* cheek before bouncing away. As he left, he heard *Hen Daid* say, "*Nawr pam nad yw'r gwrthgyferbyniad dryslyd hwn a gafodd Aaron yn peri i ni beidio â gweithio nawr!*" (Why isn't this confounded contraption that Aaron got us not working now!)

Arthur twisted back, "*Hen Daid?*"

"*Mae gen i, Arth Fach,*" (I've got it, Little Bear) *Hen Daid* assured. "*Mae angen i chi fynd yn ôl i'r Palas cyn i'ch llysmonwr hwnnw ddarganfod eich bod chi dal i lawr yma.*" (You need to get back to the Palace before that Stepmonster of yours figures out that you're still down here)

Arthur nodded reluctantly, knowing that the older man was right. Stepmonster was the one who called the *'emergency'* meeting. She could understand being late for crowds of people but not visiting family or shopping at a PRIDE booth.

"Huh, my phone's not working either," a young man commenced from the next booth over as he passed.

Trying to keep moving, Arthur hoped it was just a coincidence that someone closer to his age was also having trouble with their phone. However, an uneasy feeling started to settle in the pit of his stomach as almost every booth he wandered past had similar experiences with misbehaving technology. He hoped they would figure out what was happening soon. The Farmer's Market would be opening to the public shortly; he knew the vendors would be using his presence to get potential shoppers to come down.

Slowly, he moved around the booths, making his way to a rainbow banner, declaring it to be an LGBTQ+ ally. He then suddenly felt a different set of vibrations through the earth, ones that he hadn't felt before.

The movements of three of his guards didn't feel right. It was as if they weren't used to the paths that they usually took when they visited the market in the past. Matthew, who had been with him since infancy, was the only one that felt normal to him.

Matthew had been following about a meter behind him since entering the market, not letting the young prince leave his line of sight. He had even nodded to *Hen Daid* as they had passed the booth. Matthew was also one of the few people outside of his family that knew the truth about Arthur's powers.

Arthur slowly made a small hand sign that only Matthew would understand: a three-finger salute with the sign language symbol 'D'. He'd developed this sign with Anya when they were little and shared it with Matthew. It was to indicate that something bad or dangerous was happening.

Normally, Matthew would include the other guards to get Arthur to safety. This meant using hand signs and spells to move him from one place to another without the enemy realising what was going on until it was too late.

However, that couldn't happen this time because of the guards' strange behaviour. It was as if the other guards didn't even know their way around a market Arthur had regularly attended in the past. The two slowly tried to make their way back to the Black booth without trying to let the other guards know that he was on to the guards.

Arthur seemed to be paying little attention to other people in the market except to the vendor he was passing. On the outside, he appeared to be looking through their wares, silently deciding if any of the items would work as holiday gifts for the family. The reality was that he was keeping an eye out for the compromised guards.

His powers were unique enough that he could *see* things through the ground, kind of like a sonar with vibrations. People give off different vibrations—a light, airy feeling meant the person walking past was friendly. A dark, heavier feeling meant the person walking past him didn't have the best intentions.

How was this possible? Well, his shoes were different. Everyone knew he had his shoes made for but him; they just didn't realise that the shoes were specially made to work with his powers and any other shoes would leave him 'blind'. He and *Hen Daid* learned from Spanish shoemakers to create these *'old man pointy shoes'*, as Anya has called them on more than one occasion. She would tease him and Tonio for having to wear them. Arthur was just grateful that he chose to put them on today.

Arthur went to the market enough to know that he and Matthew were being corralled into an alleyway at the end of the market. He just wished he could have gotten back to *Hen Daid*. The older man would have suggested springing the trap...

"You've been watching the new *Star Wars* trilogy too many times," Matthew grumbled.

Arthur groaned, "I said that out loud?"

"Yep, and we don't have enough backup for that," Matthew deadpanned.

"I know," Arthur muttered, "I should have stayed with *Hen Daid* and *Hennain*, Stepmonster be damned."

"That would have been a great help," Matthew agreed sarcastically, "Great-Grandfather Black trained Lord Wales and helped to train your grandfather and great-uncle."

They passed another booth where a vendor declared, "Stupid technology! How is this supposed to be helpful?!"

The vendor in question was closer to his age than *Hen Daid's* age. Arthur now knew the situation was dire, and Matthew's eyes widened.

"*Reveal,*" Matthew whispered, with power behind the word.

A faint light purple shone from Arthur's pocket and was closer to the vendors. It disappeared as quickly as it appeared. Arthur grimaced, knowing it meant nothing good. That was the damn pocket that his cell phone was in! He wanted to know how these *Fakes* got close enough to it to put such a disruptor spell on it.

"*Don't take it out!*" Matthew nearly hissed, "They will come get you faster, and these nice small business owners could get hurt in the process."

Arthur then gave him a slight nod, "I'm why everyone is having problems right now, aren't I?"

"And why none of your *'adoring fans'* haven't shown up yet either," Matthew suggested dryly, "No one could get the word out that you're here."

"How much further do you think we have to go?" Arthur

questioned humourlessly as they moved down the row of booths. "How didn't we catch this before we got here?"

Matthew breathed deeply to keep himself calm, "They went ahead of time to ensure everything was secure. They weren't supposed to leave their stations." He then glanced over his shoulder for a moment, where the impersonated guard was helping to corral the two of them.

"Reveal," Matthew whispered again.

The pretend guard's face and hair began flickering, almost like it couldn't decide if it wanted to stay on the fake identity being projected or to show the guard's true face. Matthew didn't put enough power behind the spell for the facade to fall away completely. However, it was adequate for Matthew to confirm the trickery and not send the vendors into a panic...*yet.*

"It's a powerful glamour spell," Matthew continued as the two slowly moved toward the alleyway, "They must have been planning this for weeks."

Suddenly, Arthur felt a shiver run down his spine. The vibration feedback was so bad that he visibly flinched, causing Matthew to look at him concerned.

"Your Majesty?" Matthew questioned, weary.

"I think the one that was supposed to replace you just got here," Arthur breathed, trying not to topple over. He hadn't felt that much anger rolling off someone in his life, "I think he's angry that he couldn't switch with you."

Matthew blinked, "When could that switch take place? I never go out with anyone that I work with. I'm their boss and have been working for your family longer than any of them."

Arthur could only shrug, "I don't think rational thoughts can be applied to these guys."

"Milord!" A panicked voice called, *"This way!"*

"Reveal," Matthew hastily whispered as they looked up to see another guard.

This was also a fake guard, as the flicking spell did not

allow them to see their true face. The fourth person must have made a new plan to get where they wanted. The switched guards were now working simultaneously to get Arthur and Matthew to the alleyway.

"Are you ready?" Matthew asked. *"They outnumber us."*

"They can't trick Uncle Aaron, Auncle Dylan, *or* Damian," Arthur insisted, as his left hand tightened into a fist. *"They picked the wrong king to mess with!"*

Then Arthur, a little too reckless for his own good, marched straight into the alleyway. Matthew trailed behind, resisting the urge to facepalm, muttering something that Arthur didn't hear clearly as his heart pounded in his ears.

As he hurried, he looked down briefly to see a subtle blue light settle on his clothing before dissipating. He knew another spell landed on him; he just didn't know *which* spell it was.

Arthur moved to enter the alleyway first. It was long and secluded but not dark. It would be more creepy at night. It was also the only way to the back vendor lot. Shadows kept him from seeing the far end of the alley where he could sense the hatred *rolling* off the fourth guard that wanted to replace Matthew...

The moment the two of them cleared the alleyway, everything started going wrong as predicted. Muffled protests behind caused Arthur to turn around in time to see three flickering guards holding onto Matthew.

"Guys?" He questioned, masking his anger with confusion, "What's going on?"

"This isn't who he says he is," the first 'guard' defended, trying to hold onto Matthew's right arm.

"And just *who* is he?" Arthur asked, trying to hide his rising panic and hoping to get to the bottom of this madness.

"He's been lying to you the whole trip!" The second 'guard' added. This one held Matthew's left arm, "He's the mad Wilhelm Rothbart!"

Arthur stared at the four of them for a moment before he let out a deep belly laugh at the ridiculous accusation, *"Yo...u th... ink that he's a hit...man for hire!"* Through breaths of laughter, he exclaimed, *"A man who's...been my gu...ard sin...ce the day I w...as bo...rn!"*

"This isn't funny!" The third 'guard' insisted, who somehow wrapped themselves around Matthew's legs, trying to keep him from kicking his way free, "You've been in danger from the moment you left Buckingham Palace today!"

Arthur snorted, no longer wanting to play this game, "Yeah, because of the three of *you!* Not the man that swore to my mother he would protect me with his dying breath."

"You're in danger and denial!" The first guard exclaimed, struggling to hold onto Matthew. They directed the next question to Matthew: "What spell did you put on him?!"

"And do you think I'm defenceless?" Arthur demanded before Matthew could respond. The young royal raised his arms to his chest, fingers curled into fists, "I know his every move; he's taught them all to me!"

"Please don't make us fight you!" The second one pleaded, "We know your every move."

Arthur snorted, "Fat chance of that–let's see who's lying. I bet you've never seen the inside of the practice gym!" *Oh, my gods! Since when do I resort to small talk to distract the enemy until backup comes?* He thought desperately, momentarily distracted as he started to feel a flare of panic on the other side of the twin connection he had with Anya. It was usually helpful when they needed to switch and not let anyone know. He hastily clamped down on his panic to keep her from feeling it, trying to refocus, but it was too late.

"I wouldn't be too sure about that," a voice said from behind him.

A sudden and sharp pain to the back of the head kept Arthur from turning around. What he saw as he fell to his knees, ears ringing, was Matthew's shocked face and the three 'guards' doing nothing about the damn coward that hit him from behind. The last thing Arthur heard was:

"Lights out, your bratness!"

⛨ ⛨ ⛨

The faint sound of screeching tyres and the pinging noise of phone notifications alerted Merfyn Black, *Hen Daid,* to the fact that something had happened. He couldn't shake the feeling that it was extremely wrong. His head snapped in the direction that he just sent *Arth Bath* and *Mathew.* The retired guard for the English Royal Family let his training kick in, searching the crowd for his *gor-wyr* (Great-Grandson), his *Arth Fach* (Little Bear).

He tossed the confounded smartphone that *Arawn* (Aaron) had given him to Isolde, *Hennain.* She caught it gracefully, used to random things being thrown in her direction.

"Cael Arawn ar y peth gwirion yna!" (Get Aaron on that stupid thing!) He commanded as he pulled a staff off a nearby hook. *"Dw i'n mynd am Arth Bach."* (I'm going for Little Bear)

She nodded as fear washed over her.

"Faint o aelodau o'r teulu fyddwn ni'n eu colli cyn i'r boen ddod i ben o'r diwedd?" (How many family members will we lose before the pain finally stops?) She whispered. *"Gwirodydd, os gwelwch yn dda eu hamddiffyn."* (Spirits, please protect them)

Clutching an angel-winged necklace she pulled from under her blouse in one hand, Isdole tried to call Aaron with the other as she helplessly waited while Merfyn stepped out onto the same path Arthur had just walked.

"Arthur!" Merfyn called, *"Arthur!"*

His voice grew more and more desperate every time he yelled, *"Arthur!"*

"The noises came from that way, sir!" A middle-aged woman nearby directed, pointing further down the path, "I can bring you there."

16

Merfyn nodded his thanks before following the vendor to where she last saw Arthur and Matthew. Murmurs of *"Technology is being weird"* and *"What's going on?"* continued to fly past him.

"Please don't go anywhere" and *"My son is on his way"* were some of the things Merfyn found himself repeating over and over as he passed the other vendors. The repetition was the only thing he could cling to. His fear grew with every step he took. This family couldn't afford to lose another member; they were barely hanging on from losing *Amlawdd* (Andros).

The vendor led Merfyn to the alleyway, which appeared to have seen more traffic within the last few minutes than it had in the last few months, if not years.

The closest thing to him and the market was a pile of glitter, and at the furthest end of the alleyway, something or *someone* lay on the ground and slowly began to move.

Merfyn approached, careful to avoid the glitter, knowing its importance.

"Are you okay?" he asked as he helped turn the moving figure and stared down into Matthew Evers's face. He hastily looked back to the glitter, confused.

Something wasn't right.

Chapter 2: Of Meetings
and Investigations

1 October 2010: 7 am...

Damian rolled over in his bed to grab his journal, an activity he'd consistently kept up on since he was a kid. This was his tenth journal, which hadn't changed much over that time either; it was just a simple brown leather journal that would make Mother overlook it.

Through bleary eyes, he flipped to a clean page. He wiped some sleep out of his eyes before grabbing a pen. He then began writing...

Papa Andros came to me in my dream today. He looked distraught, more worried than I had ever seen him when he was still alive. I thought the dead lost their worry once passing

He kept saying, "Protect him."

"Protect who?" I asked.

Only he kept responding with, "Protect him."

Knock, knock.

Damian looked to the door, startled.

"Milord, are you up?" One of the staff members asked from the other side.

Damian hastily hid his journal before responding, "Yes, I'm up. You can come in."

⊕ ⊕ ⊕

10:30 am...

"King Arthur is missing!" The staff exclaimed as they rushed past the young lord Damian as he walked down the hall, ignoring him, like usual.

Damian sighed; he wished his life wasn't like this. People ignored him his whole life, so he didn't know who his father was. Every time he tried to ask, he got a look that said, *'Don't bother me.'* This was one secret that Mother was planning to take with her to the grave. His aunt and grandmother couldn't or wouldn't help him either.

Mother, better known as Lady Kendra Murrian in most high society circles, has always been looking for something... more. When Damian was younger, he naively thought she was looking for love. But now, he wasn't sure. Looking back, there was no love between her and the man she married, the widower King of England, Andros the First.

Damian was excited when he learned his mother was marrying King Andros. He thought he wouldn't be so alone anymore because he was getting two new siblings. He just wanted someone to see him for him.

However, that was never going to happen with his stepsister. There was too much animosity between them. Then, there were too many *feelings* that were keeping him and his stepbrother from actually *being siblings*. The one thing that all three of them could agree on was detesting the Murrian women, even if Princess Catherine seemed to lump him in with them. He hasn't ever called her Anya the way that Arthur does. He hasn't been permitted to do so.

"Milord!"

Damian turned to find the dark-haired man who was both his mentor and his right-hand man, Jose Santos.

"Are you all right?" Jose asked, concerned.

Damian swallowed sharply. He nodded for a moment before shaking his head.

"What's going on in that head of your, milord?"

"Do you know that Arth… *the king* is missing?" Damian asked, resigned, as they rushed down the hall to his office.

Jose nodded tightly.

"I think *they* had everything to do with it," Damian continued tiredly, pushing the door open.

"Which side of this dysfunctional family?" Jose quietly asked as he entered the office first, trying not to be disrespectful by being too forward.

"Mine," Damian growled as he nearly slammed the door behind him, "But the Princess will think I had a hand in this."

The room wasn't as big as the office that Arthur inherited from his father or that Queen Elizabeth II of Scotland used when she was in residence. His office was a modest room big enough for a large, deep mahogany desk with two bookshelves and a filing cabinet behind it. In front of the desk, there were two comfortable armchairs. This is where Jose sat down, waiting for Damian to join him.

"You're in too deep this time," Jose suggested.

"Don't I know it," Damian muttered as he stepped to the other side of the desk and started sifting through paperwork.

"May I be frank with you?" Jose requested after a moment.

Damian's golden eyes momentarily zeroed in on the older man, "That's never stopped you before, hence why I asked for you to be in this role. It's refreshing to have someone saying the things that need to be said, not only something you think I wish to hear."

"Why don't you stand up to them?" Jose continued after a moment, "I've known you since we were ten; you want *nothing* to do with the Princess anyway…"

Damian shook his head, trying to interrupt, "The only time my biological family even glances in my general direction is when I can help them gain even more power than they already have. I'm useless to them if they knew I'm...well, *you know...*"

Jose sighed. They had been friends long enough to know that the young lord was right. "I bet that's also why you haven't told the Princess yet."

"Well, it doesn't help that she's hated me since my family entered her life," Damian confirmed, resigned, "Mother is a big part of that."

Jose looked at him sadly, "So, you're not telling either of them that you would rather be with the king?"

Damian paused as he dropped a file, startled for a moment before asking, "H... *how?*"

Jose chuckled dryly. "First, we've been friends for over ten years. Second, you stare at him the same way that I look at my Maria. All this means that finding him is at the top of your to-do list."

Damian nodded, "And proving that Mother is behind this," he said, which startled Jose.

"How are we going to do that?" He asked, dismayed, "Lord Black has been trying to prove that King Andros' death was more than cancer with kidney failure but keeps coming up short."

Damian gulped, knowing what the other man was talking about. Mother was willing to take the steps needed to gain the romantic interest of the grieving King Andros, something that he didn't learn until recently. Part of the rumours swarming around is that she wasn't willing to let the romance happen naturally, especially since the King had turned down her advances in the past.

Knock, knock.

They both look up toward the door, surprised.

"Were you expecting anyone?" Jose asked.

Damian shook his head before calling, "Come in!"

The door slowly opened as if a bomb would go off if it went any faster. Domain tried not to flinch under the grey-eyed gaze of Lord Aaron Black and instead forced himself to stand up, resisting the urge to curl into a ball.

The salt-and-pepper-haired man showed very little emotion across his face. However, he held his jaw tight and his eyes sincere. Only ever getting glimpses of the real 'Uncle Aaron' under the Lord Black mask he'd crafted over the years, Damian learned he must search for the emotions from the older man, even if they were still few and far between.

"Good morning, sir," Jose greeted as he stood. "How can we help you?"

"I suppose you both have heard what has happened by now," Lord Black commented as they nodded. "Then, may I speak to my step-nephew alone?"

"Of course, sir," Jose continued smoothly as he bowed to the older lord. "I should be running interference anyway."

Jose hastily moved past the other man and left the room. Lord Black made sure to close the door before approaching Damian, stopping in front of the desk where the young man was standing behind, and sighed.

"How do you know?" Lord Black asked tiredly.

"The staff has never been great at hiding their gossip or panic," Damian replied dryly.

"They never are," agreed Lord Black, sounding tired.

"I want to lead the investigation on our side," Damian requested before Lord Black could continue, "I *need* to be the one to do this."

Lord Black's eyes scanned the younger man briefly, assessing, "Are you sure?"

Damian nodded.

"Even if that meant arresting your mother, grandmother, or aunt?"

"Especially if it comes down to that," Damian replied, rubbing his face. He then sat heavily in the high-back computer

chair, "I know more about her dealings than she cares to admit. I just don't know how they all connect. However, I do know that Papa Andros has told you some of the secrets that I have told him over the last few years."

Lord Black looked grim, "I never thought I would have to start another investigation so soon. You'll need to keep your eyes, ears, and mind open. Things are happening around here that aren't what they seem."

Damian's eyes narrow, "What are you talking about?"

Bang!

The door suddenly slammed open with such force that the wall shook, interrupting Lord Black's answer. Damian hastily stood, bracing himself.

"Where the hell is my brother?!" Princess Catherine demanded as she battled her way through the doorway. Her blonde hair had turned to flames, and her typical grey-hued eyes gleamed red with anger.

Her loyal guard, Kaiden Woolf, trailed behind her with water around his wrists. He had been putting out the fires following the rampage, and it looked like he was put through the wringer. His long dark hair was braided but messy down his back, and his dark eyes constantly looked for threats.

"*Anya!*" Lord Black exclaimed as he tried to interfere.

"*Answer me!*" She demanded again, red in the face. Her fists were inflamed and crackling, waiting for her to use them.

"No one has read me into the situation yet," Damian replied, trying to stay as calm as possible and standing his ground. "I only know as much as the Staff gossips about."

This animosity between them stemmed from the Murrian women trying to control Anya's every move. Mother *hated* the fact the twins even existed, but they inherited the throne; Damian didn't know why she thought the throne would fall to her.

Then again, he wasn't allowed to know that information. Mother only ever acknowledged his existence when she needed him for something, which almost always benefited her and her regime.

"Princess Catherine," Damian finally continued after forcing himself to deal with the present. "What makes you think that *I* had something to do with this?"

"Aren't you the new *'Lord Security'?"* She nearly screeched as the temperature in the room went up another degree.

"Yes," Damian replied slowly, "I just took over today."

"Was it *you* who assigned three brand new hires to King Arthur's security detail?" Lord Black interrupted; the word *King* sounded forced as he tried to defuse the situation.

"What?" Damian's mouth dropped before shifting and grabbing a file off his desk. He hastily opened it, only to be filled with dread. The shimmering names and his signature were in red on a document that only used black ink. "I...I didn't sign off on these changes willingly."

"What does that even *mean?"* Princess Catherine almost growled.

Damian suppressed a flinch as he closed the folder without saying a word and passed it to Lord Black, who promptly retrieved a pair of glasses from his pocket and put them on before taking it. The Princess couldn't take it right now without accidentally turning it to ash in anger. The Black Lord reopened the folder and looked over the top document.

"There's magic on this document," Lord Black declared grimly, "Someone made the names appear differently to get them approved. Damian's signature would have remained black otherwise."

The temperature in the room finally went down a little as Princess Catherine tried to take in a few deep breaths. Her anger didn't disappear completely, but it was just enough that Kaiden visibly relaxed. However, he didn't put the water away, seeming to know that her temper could flare again at any moment.

"Isn't that supposed to be hard to do?" The princess asked, confused.

Lord Black nodded, looking concerned, "This would have to be an inside job."

Kaiden hastily shifted to blast the princess with water if her temper exploded again. Instead, she took in and let out a few more deep breaths. The fire didn't leave her hands altogether, but Damian didn't feel the need to duck behind his desk anymore.

"Did they take advantage of Lord Murrian entering the position, or was this supposed to be an attempt to get Uncle Aaron off the job early?"

Damian opened his mouth to protest as Lord Black pulled the document out of the folder, holding it to the light to inspect it closer. He hummed for a moment before handing the document to Damian. "Is that even *your* signature?"

Damian Murrian

"This is typed," Damian breathed.

"What?" Princess Catherine exclaimed, temperature rising again, the calm gone.

"Kaiden, why don't you take Anya to the gym," Lord Black hastily suggested, trying to defuse the situation, "I'll send Antonio to you when we have more information."

The princess silently debated, clenching and unclenching her fingers. Her fire was still ready and waiting to follow her every command. She clenched one more time.

"You promise?" The princess requested with a weary voice.

Lord Black nodded as he placed his right hand over his heart, "On my honour."

Returning the nod, the princess turned. Kaiden moved from in front of the doorway to keep her from knocking him over, and she hastily left the office, leaving behind a trail of fire in her footsteps. Kaiden rushed after her, putting out the firey prints along the way.

Lord Black then handed the folder back to Damian. The young man placed the document inside before moving around the desk, relieved that the princess had chosen to leave. He didn't want to be dodging flames or dealing with her temper.

"She needs to work on controlling her temper," Damian muttered aloud as he sat back in his chair, still holding the folder, "She's next in line and now temporarily the ruler of England."

"Leave that to me and Kaiden," Lord Black assured, amused. "What are your next steps?"

Damian quietly reopened the folder and reread the document, then grabbed a separate folder from the right side of his desk.

"This doesn't look right either," he muttered under his breath.

Using an ID spell, Damian opened one of the top drawers and tucked the folders inside, closing and relocking the mechanism. He didn't want anything to walk off before he could turn them over to the police and MI6. He then stood and grabbed his jacket off the back of his chair.

"Damian?" Lord Black asked as Damian put on his jacket.

"I'm heading down to the Farmer's Market," Damian replied as he zipped. "Something isn't right, and I need to follow the evidence."

A rare smile grew across Lord Black's face, though Damian didn't catch a glimpse as he rushed out of his office. He wanted to show he was the right choice for the job and was well on his way to proving just that.

✠ ✠ ✠

September 2007:

From the Journal of Lord Damian

"It is only because of Inspector Warren's do diligences that they even saved the samples," Professor Harrison said. "He knew that the technology would be better. Each new machine processed a sample smaller than the one before it."

Professor Harrison clicked the PowerPoint for the next slide. The image of blood spatters caused others to shutter; however, all I could do was stare with fascination. It told a story of desperation, speaking only for the victim when no one else could.

"The Richter Case was the case that never left the Inspector and has been solved because the technology finally caught up with the suspect," the Professor continued. "Some of the blood in this spatter pattern didn't belong to the victim, and because of the timing of when they interviewed the suspect for the first time, their injury had already healed."

⸸ ⸸ ⸸

"We're here, Lord Murrian," Damian's driver reminded him as the SUV pulled to a stop.

Damian glanced up from his phone, noting the time was 12:30. It took longer than it should have to arrive after sudden lockdown protocols were put into place. As he looked out the window, officers were all around, talking to patrons and vendors. He hastily pocketed his phone and opened the door to the chaos.

"Good morning, *Lord Murrian,*" a man with greying dark hair and sharp blue eyes greeted, holding out his hand. He wore a slightly dishevelled suit with a white dress shirt half tucked in, and his shield hung from his belt. "I'm Inspector Henry Warren."

"Hello, Inspector," Damian returned as he took a few steps to shake the older man's hand, "Are you alright?"

"Hum? Oh! I just got off from a case," Warren exhaled, pausing as he took a moment to look more presentable. "I reached the locker room moments before the reports about King Arthur started coming in."

"And why did they send you?" Damian asked curiously as they started moving down one of the paths. "Surely they should have let you get some sleep before giving you such a big case."

Warren shook his head, "Normally, I would have had a break. However, this is all hands on deck, and you can check my record..."

Damian hummed, "No, I know your work. I studied one of your cases for a university class of mine a few years ago. I just don't want you getting burned out."

"Aha, they still use the Richter Case for forensic classes?" The Inspector questioned.

Damian nodded, "The insight you had on that case is something we're all going to need for *this* case. What have you been able to gather so far?"

Warren shook his head. "Not me." As they drew near, he pointed to the centre booth ahead, *"Them."*

Damian followed the pointed hand to see a well-built for his age older man with a small older woman working in tandem. The silver-haired woman was writing in a notebook while the tall man was pacing a line that had been formed down a different path. He looked like he was making sure that everyone stayed in line.

"What are they doing?"

Warren chuckled, "Our job."

Damian looked confused, "Why is that a good thing?"

"Because that means Black never lost his skills."

"Who?"

The Inspector stopped, "Are you telling me you've never met King Andros'—*may he rest in peace*—grandparents? Haven't you lived in one of those palaces for ten years?"

Red made its way to Damian's face, "Mother kind of banned them once we moved in. The Royal Twins treated trips to the Black farm as a retreat from her craziness. Grandmother doesn't like competition either."

Warren shook his head as he started walking again, "That is why most of the population can't stand your family. The whole country will be watching your every move from this point. This is your trial by fire. Now come, I need to reintroduce you to the Queen Grandmother and Lord Security."

Wait... "That's *my* title."

Warren rolled his eyes, "That title has belonged to a Black for the past seventy years. You just happen to have it now because of your mother's power."

Damian wanted to be insulted. But he knew, deep down, that the Inspector was right. He only had this job because of the power Mother held among the Traditionalists in Parliament and the House of Lords.

"Ahh," Queen Grandmother (*Hennain*) greeted as she looked up from her writing, "*Rwy'n gweld eich bod wedi dod o hyd i'r cariad.*"

Damian looked at the older woman as his mind translated her words from Welsh to English: 'I see you found the lover'. *What does she mean by that?*

"Oh, good, you're both here," Grandfather Black (*Hen Daid*) said as he joined them at the top of the line, "*Mae gennych chi hwn, Cariad?*"

'You have this, Love?' Damian's mind translated again. *How do I even know that?!*

She nodded before continuing in English, "Show them what you found, and I'll finish up here for them."

"This way, boys," Grandfather Black gestured to the right, "He was heading to the PRIDE table."

They fell in step with the elder Black, walking past the gossiping line. The words Damian managed to overhear told him what happened without having to interview anyone.

"Those three guards were acting weird…"

"The fourth guard got attacked when he tried to interfere…"

"The King was suspicious…"

"My cell phone and tablet couldn't connect to either the network or internet to make calls or perform credit transactions while the king and the guards were at the market…"

"Services returned a few minutes after those guards took the king…"

Damian clenched and unclenched his hands. He wasn't sure what to do with this information. *Why didn't they go back to the Queen Grandmother and Grandfather Black?*

"Lord Murrian, Damian?" Grandfather Black asked, "Are you all right?"

Damian shook his head to clear it, "I'm sorry, what did you ask?"

"If you were all right?" Grandfather Black repeated.

"I will be," Damian replied with conviction, "Especially after we locate Arthur."

Grandfather Black stared into him for a moment, and Damian gulped. *What is this man thinking?*

"How long have you and Arthur been together?" Grandfather Black suddenly asked.

Damian went wide-eyed and looked around in a panic. Thankfully, no one was paying attention. Even Inspector Warren was busy giving orders.

"Don't…" he tried to get out, "Please don't do that…. I'm not *with* anyone…"

Grandfather Black used his right hand to mimic a zipping motion against his lips. "He wanted to get a gift for *someone* who wasn't sure about themselves. I sent him this way…"

Damian now understood, "You feel guilty about this."

The elder looked away briefly before looking into the alleyway, now blocked off by caution tape.

"He and Anya are all Isolde, and I have left of our son, Philip. It hurts knowing I could have helped someone take my great-grandson."

Damian reached up to squeeze Grandfather Black's shoulder. He felt a kinship with the man now that he knew he held the position of Lord Security before Lord Black did.

"You didn't assist in anything they weren't already planning on doing. They would have lured the King to this alleyway regardless." Damian said before looking down the alleyway. "Now, did anything stand out to you that you think we should know about?"

Grandfather Black thought momentarily before nodding. "I found Matthew at the far end of the alley, but..."

"But what?"

"I found something towards the end of the alley that would indicate Matthew shouldn't be there. He has a defence mechanism built into his powers that leaves traces of this behind."

"And what's that?"

Grandfather Black looked toward a CSI, collecting a shimmery, powder-like substance nearby, before turning back at Damian. *"Glitter."*

Chapter 3: Processing the Evidence

4 October 2001:
Nine Years Before the Kidnapping...
A Journal entry of Damian's private thoughts

A dark haired woman on the TV had on gloves and was using tweezers to put a fibre strain into...

"Papa Andros, Uncle Aaron, why are they pulling those items in plastic bags?" I asked, confused as we watched a United States-based T.V. show set in Las Vegas.

Uncle Aaron chuckled, "They're collecting evidence. Those bags protect any identifying factors like fingerprints or hairs that don't belong to the victim."

"Oh," I whispered in awe, "I think I want to do that one day..."

Papa Andros, with his dark blonde hair and blue-grey eyes, gave the boy a small grin, "You can do anything you put your mind to. Just continue to work hard at it."

"Can I work with the CSIs one day?" I asked, wide-eyed.

"Of course," Uncle Aaron assured, "But I want you to work with me first. I get to work with them sometimes."

"Why you?"

"Well, keeping the Royal Families safe is a full-time job," Uncle Aaron explained, "Andros has Dylan doing something important and you're showing interest..."

Papa Andros laughed, "Way to introduce him to your job, Uncle!"

"But your safety is important, Papa Andros," I grumbled, crossing my arms over my chest. "It's not a laughing matter!"

"Of course not, my Phoenix," Papa Andros said as he ruffled my dark hair, "But doing what you love is important too, that's why I have Dylan working with patients who need extra support with being their true selves. They have a big heart and love to help others."

"Oh," I breathed. "So if I want Uncle Aaron's job, we should convince Mother that's okay? She's going to want me to be some big politician."

"Of course she does," Uncle Aaron muttered, "She would sell her soul if she thought it would get her what she wanted."

"Uncle!" Papa Andros yelled as he moved to cover my ears. "Don't say that!"

"But he's right, Papa Andros," I protest as I dodge the King's hands, "I'm only important to her when she needs my help with something!"

Papa Andros shifted to kneel in front of me "Then we will work hard to prove that this is an important job, especially when it comes with a title."

✠ ✠ ✠

2 October 2010:
Twenty-Four Hours After the Kidnapping...

Damian approached the New Scotland Yard building, flashing lights from photo cameras following his every step. He tried to block out the press core's questions, not knowing any more than they did. All he knew was there hadn't been a ransom call yet.

"Have you moved the princess or the other royals?" One yelled from behind the metal police barrier.

"Are you keeping them on lockdown?" Another question.

"What's the update on the guard that was left behind?" That was the final question Damian heard as the door closed behind him.

Lord Black was walking ahead of him. He'd always been awestruck by the older lord and sometimes wished to be him. Lord Black was the epitome of *'Keep Calm and Carry On,'* especially with everything life has thrown at him since he first stepped onto the palace grounds as a teenager over fifty years ago. He ignored all questions, not faltering his steps or turning around to pay them any mind.

Damian was just happy to be away from Buckingham Palace, even if it was only for a little while. He could only take so much tension from Princess Catherine before he had to start dodging flames outside the training grounds. He wasn't sure if she was merely angry with him because Arthur was still missing or upset about something Mother, Aunt Karen, or Grandmother had done or said to her.

His extremely opinionated family members always tried to tell the Princess what she could and couldn't do. They seemingly nit-picked her over almost everything. Luckily, that only happened when they thought they could get away with it.

Most of the time, Lady Black ran interference between the princess and Mother. With one glare, she could at least put Mother and Aunt Karen in their place. However, Lord Black always had to interfere when Lady Black and Grandmother got into a shouting match. There were many things that Lady Black didn't agree with that his female family members wanted. Those fights would usually go in Lady Black's favour.

"Are you alright, Damian?" Lord Black asked, concerned, pulling Damian to the present.

"*Yeah,*" Damian replied as he finally made himself move, "Just catching my bearings from the onslaught of questions."

Lord Black's lips twitched like he wanted to smile but didn't.

"You did well with ignoring them," Lord Black praised, "I had trouble when I was your age. That's why I was sent with my late brother and my late sister-in-law into hiding. Then, it was a pain that I was sent to babysit them."

"Now?"

"Now, I wish that Philip was here to deal with this madness," Lord Black muttered, "But I'm happy I got to see them fall in love. I'm one of the few who can say they saw it first hand."

Damian desperately wished he could have met them. Every little bit Lord or Lady Black would slip was a glimpse into the past that slim to none had heard about. He wondered what Prince Philip would have done with his grandson missing.

"*Great!* You're both here!" Inspector Warren exclaimed as they approached him. He was more clean-cut this time around and looked like he had gotten some sleep. "Guard Matthew Evers wants to know why we're still holding him. He wants to help find the King."

Damian took a moment to study the grim profile of Lord Black. The lord seemed to know something everyone else on the opposite side of the room didn't. While Lord Black's face was blank, his eyes told a different story: *a storm was coming.*

"Can anyone tell me Dylan's ETA?" Lord Black suddenly asked.

"They're about five minutes out, Sir," an agent replied after getting confirmation from his *Bluetooth* device.

"Why do you want to know about that?" Warren asked, confused, "Heir Black can't do much more than we have. I don't know what you're looking for!"

Damian couldn't keep a blank expression as confusion flooded his face.

"What can Heir Black do that we *can't?*" The Inspector

continued, "That man in there has been dodging every question, insisting he's innocent and we don't know what we're doing."

"Dylan will be able to get through to him," Lord Black said assuringly. "Just give them a chance."

Inspector Warren took a few deep breaths and then opened his mouth to continue, but the door slid open before he could.

The moment Ze Dylan Black stepped into New Scotland Yard, everything changed. Looking every bit the heiress they were, they wore their curly dark hair pinned back in an elaborate bun with a diamond-studded barrette holding their bangs off their face, and a flowing blue dress tastefully hid evidence of their biological body. All hints were of rebellion to piss off the Murrian Women: their pride–their joy—*their beard*.

In many ways, Damian was both jealous and amazed by the older heir. Being widely accepted by their family and the people, Heiress Black could be their true self. And this angered Mother, as she *hated* anyone like Damian and Heiress Black.

While Damian was firmly in the closet, Heiress Black flaunted their truth and didn't care what people like the Murrian Women thought, from what Damian had seen, especially with the fights that broke out between them. Mother always lost.

"*Helo, Tad,*" (Hello, Father), Heiress Black greeted as they approached the older lord.

"*Helo, Dylan*", Lord Black replied as he kissed his child's cheek, "I'm so sorry to do this, but things aren't adding up, including Matthew's reaction."

"Where is he?" The Heiress requested, confused about the situation, "What happened?"

"He didn't recognise your *Taid* (Grandfather) and is acting passive-aggressive yet respectful to me."

They nodded thoughtfully, "Should I prepare myself for the worst?"

Lord Black gave a sharp nod.

Heiress Black stood a little straighter as they approached the Inspector. Warren blinked before offering his arm to them, which they took gracefully. He then led the Heiress down the hall to one of the interrogation rooms.

"Sir, do you think this is wise?" Damian asked after a moment, "Why would you put them in danger if you suspect something is wrong?"

"Dylan will be able to get a reaction out of Matthew, whether he's in shock like the doctors are claiming or not," Lord Black assured grimly, but not going into further detail.

"What's going on?" Damian started to ask, but a commotion from the end of the hall kept him from asking anymore.

Bobbies ran past the two men. Damian moved to help them; however, a hand on his shoulder kept him from following. He turned back to protest, but the words failed to leave his mouth when he saw Lord Black shaking his head.

"Watch and wait," Lord Black soothed. "The officers are trained for this."

The bobbies reappeared a few minutes later, dragging along a suspect, flickering similarly to the false guards. What startled Damian the most was the swearing and—

"You bloody poof! You bloody well stay away from me, you— you *freak!* I don't *need* your bloody help, and I'll *never* help you!" The suspect spat.

Heiress Black stood motionless in the doorway. They were pale but otherwise calm as one could be for the homophobic slurs directed at them. Their light brown eyes flickered from something that Damian couldn't identify, but they seemed to harden in front of him.

"You may not want or need my help. However, whoever you hired won't be coming to your aid any time soon," Heiress Black warned. "I may not be as powerful as Matthew or whatever being you compelled to cast your illusion. But Matthew taught me enough defence magic to reveal you aren't who you claim to be."

"W... *what?"* The man asked, startled that his words

couldn't shake Heiress Black. Instead, he was the one who appeared off-kilter.

"Your disguise is *flickering*," Heiress Black pointed out, "You're exposed even if I'm not powerful enough to remove the illusion altogether. You also forgot two crucial things."

"*And what's that?*" The man sneered.

"The first thing is Matthew wasn't some recently hired newbie; he's worked for the English Royal Family for over twenty years. He was Queen Eve's guard first, coming with her when she married my cousin. He's been King Arthur's guard for the last ten years."

"And the second?" The man demanded.

A small smile came onto Heiress Black's face. Damian couldn't tell if the heiress was going to troll the man. Only that, despite the tension, the older being could smile and make him wonder what was about to happen.

"Matthew is bisexual and loves every part of me," the Heiress revealed. "We've been together for fifteen years, married for ten of those."

The man suddenly tried to lunge at Heiress Black. They stood their ground as the officers holding him gained a better grip and pulled him out of the room to keep them safe, even though Damian had witnessed the Heiress take Matthew down in a sparring match.

Damian stared at the Heiress with wonder before turning to face Lord Black. The lord was pensive. *Did he know this would have been the reaction?* Damian thought. Matthew had always been loyal to the royal family, though his marriage wasn't common knowledge, or Mother would have had a conniption.

"How did you know?" Damian finally asked.

"Mind you, I truly wanted to be wrong," Lord Black murmured, "But my *Tad* told me he was being too formal with him, causing warning bells to go off. No matter how proper Matthew is in public, he's never that way with my parents."

"Why?"

Lord Black paused as if seeing if he could speak. Some relief came to his face as he answered, "Philip and I aren't royal. We're the sons of a guard-turned-blacksmith and a lady-in-waiting-turned-seamstress. Matthew sees my *Tad* as a fellow guard while he sees me as his boss first and father-in-law second."

Heiress Black quietly made their way over to the two men. They were doing their best to hide the hurt from the words coming from someone who looked like their husband, though Damian knew it would have been much worse if it had been Matthew who said those things.

"Dylan, why don't you go home? We've got it covered here," Lord Black suggested, "We'll find them. Matthew set off the beacon spell before they knocked him out."

"But that spell goes straight to his... *oh*," Heiress Black brightened. "Whoever took Matthew and Arthur are in for a surprise."

"In more ways than one if Arthur wakes up first," Lord Black agreed.

"Um, can you let me in on this?" Damian asked, confused and frustrated.

Any information they have that can be used to help locate King Arthur and Guard Evers... Black faster, and they're talking in riddles! He thought miserably.

"Da...I mean—*Lord Murrian*, Lord Black, you should see this," CSI Jayde Bradson, a dark-haired woman with light green eyes in a lab coat, interrupted before anyone could answer Damian's question.

"Be safe," Lord Black wished. "Go to your *Mam* and Anya. Let them know what's going on with the person pretending to be Matthew."

Heiress Black nodded. They took a deep breath, preparing themselves for the onslaught of yelling from the press corps right outside those doors. They turned and glided away, their guards following.

Damian hummed as he realised that some of the guards that were with Heiress Black had returned from retirement to keep Lord Black from losing his mind. These men and women have been working with or for Lord Black since he had been a guard himself. The older man needed people in places he could trust with the royal family, but there weren't enough *vetted* guards. One of the other things that Damian has to do... multitasking, was a great ally...

"This way, please," CSI Bradson requested as her words pulled Damian from his thoughts.

Damian tried his best not to stare at her. She was familiar to him, and he couldn't, for the life of him, figure out why. She seemed to know him when she started to use his first name, so she must have known him from a different part of his life.

The two men began following Bradson further into New Scotland Yard. The main room was busy with the video surveillance pulled from the city and displayed on the flatscreen. However, what *wasn't* in the footage caught Damian's attention.

"What are we looking at?" Lord Black asked, confused. Half the time, Damian wondered how much the sixty-two-year-old man understood about technology and how much he pretended to know.

"According to eye-witness accounts, a white van left the Farmer's Market and was erratically weaving in and out of traffic," CSI Bradson explained as Inspector Warren joined them, "However, the security footage is trying to make us believe they weren't there at all."

"They must be using a spell or technology to keep us from seeing it," Warren summed up.

Bradson nodded, "But they didn't do this at the right time of day."

"It's midmorning traffic on a Friday morning," Damian breathed. "Right?"

She nodded again. Her light grin showed she wasn't

angry over the interruption... she looked... *excited* that he was contributing to the conversation... adding to Damian's confusion. He didn't allow his face to show his thoughts as she continued.

"The spell they're using would have helped them and hindered us if the kidnapping happened at nighttime when there's not a lot of traffic."

She then took a laser pointer and made circles over looped footage showing a missing vehicle.

"Drivers in several of these clips wouldn't maintain a distance if something wasn't already there and in the way." She moved the pointer to a different set of footage. "This car keeps hitting its brakes because of something we can't see in what should be nearly bumper-to-bumper traffic."

"How far have you been able to trace the missing van in the security footage?" Lord Black asked thoughtfully, "Can it lead us to a location?"

"That's the ultimate goal," Bradson agreed. "We still have tips and footage to process, and more are coming in. Right now, the footage of the phantom van brings us to the edge of the city."

Lord Black nodded, staring intently at the images of the three impersonated guards that were up on a whiteboard. "What did the guards have to say about what happened?"

CSI Bradson's face scrunched up before quickly changing to a more neutral expression, "They've been at the hospital with various degrees of food poisoning from the night before the kidnapping."

"And based on the interviews I've had with them," Inspector Warren continued, "They have been going to the same place to unwind after work. I think they got too comfortable, and someone took advantage of that."

Damian pinched the bridge of his nose.

"If you're keeping them on hire, someone must retrain them," Lord Black muttered.

"Most definitely," Damian agreed, "They need to be on their toes at all times, even if they're off the clock. We can't have this happen again. Either they get with the program, or they can go."

The Inspector looked between the two of them with confusion, unsure of how to continue.

"We do have a clue that Guard, I mean Great-Grandfather Black, thought we should take a closer look at," Bradson inserted herself, "I don't understand it, but it might be the one thing that can tell us where to start looking for the King and Guard Evers."

"What clue?" Lord Black asked, curious. He hadn't gone down to the Farmer's Market yesterday with Damian.

Bradson grabbed a small jar before returning to them, "They found this in a pile at the end of the alley closest to the market."

She passed the container to Lord Black, who looked like he was trying to keep himself from chuckling. He then passed the container to Damian, who accepted it before holding it up to the light to see what had the CSI puzzled and Lord Black wanting to laugh despite the circumstances.

"Is this..." Damian paused, *"Glitter?"*

Bradson nodded, "We haven't determined what type of glitter it is. It doesn't match any glitter currently in stores within a 30-kilometre range, though one of the other CSIs does believe that they have seen it before."

"They *have?*" Lord Black asked, his curiosity still piqued.

Bradson nodded again, "The CSI thinks this type of glitter appears around late November, early December. However, none of these stores know where they get it shipped from. They're claiming that it just...*appears* in their stockrooms."

Damian wanted to call out Lord Black, who still looked like he was trying to keep himself from grinning. However, beeping from a computer kept him from asking Lord Black what was going on.

Bradson rushed to the computer.

"All right, gentlemen, the computer has managed to narrow down the van's path to an area half the size of London.," she reported after a few clicks and typing. "The best the computer can do is suggest several abandoned harbour district warehouses. We don't have any footage from that area yet. But that might be because there may not be any working security cameras."

"That's fine," Inspector Warren promised as he pulled out his flip phone. "I'll be back. I'll try to get the warrants for any buildings we come across as we explore the grounds. It might take a while. The earliest that I can predict is tomorrow if I'm lucky."

"It looks like you should at least get six or seven warrants to be on the safe side for each building," Bradson suggested as she tried to make the satellite image bigger. "I can't tell from this footage how many buildings there are or even if this is updated footage."

Warren nodded before leaving them to make the call.

"You should go with them if they're cleared to go today," Lord Black suggested quietly. "I can see if I can follow up on the glitter."

"That's all right, Sir," Bradson interrupted before Damian could answer. "I've got six techs working on the glitter follow-up."

"Then, is there something that I can help with?" Lord Black requested.

She pondered before nodding, "Can you get me an alternative schedule for the King? The schedule we have seems to be... *incomplete*..."

Damian tuned everything out as a memory drifted over him.

✠ ✠ ✠

May 2010:
Five Months Before the Kidnapping...

"*I don't know whether to trust you or not; as you know, your history with these things isn't the best,*" *a female voice commented.*

Damian gulped before turning to see his younger stepsister in the doorway leading to his rooms. Princess Cathrine's blonde-red hair was braided and snaked over her shoulder. It was messier than usual, too.

"*Did you and the King switch again?*" *Damian observed.*

Her mouth dropped, "*How did you know?*" *She hissed.*

"*Your hair is messy, and it's not from a workout,*" *he shrugged.* "*You're the only one with animosity toward me. The King's usually willing to work with me. Did he even know I was going to be there today? He was nice to me while he was dressed like you.*"

She shook her head, "*I...I don't think so. I still can't go to the Maham Exhibit,*" *she admitted,* "*It still hurts...*"

He nodded, "*Your little brother is still a huge part of your life even if he hasn't been physically here. Have you talked to anyone about it?*"

"*Who would be willing to listen to me without judgment or have what I say end up in the papers the next day?*"

Damian shrugged again, "*You could ask your Auncle; they seem to have a knack for finding the right people that won't betray the Family. Now, if you excuse me, I'm late for an appointment with Lords Black and Wales.*

The Princess could only stare as Damian moved past her. He walked away with a shaky breath as he shook his head.

✜ ✜ ✜

"They were planning on bloody *switching!*" Damian growled, pulling out of the memory as he returned the evidence container to Bradson.

Lord Black started chuckling, unable to hold back anymore, "They're a security nightmare! Woolf and Evers don't help the bloody situation; they practically encourage it!"

"Lord Black?" Bradson asked, confused.

"The twins switch places when they don't want to attend certain events," Lord Black answered, amused at Damian's rant, "My Dylan helps them pull off the switches on a semi-regular basis."

Damian was only half listening, distracted by his phone, as he searched for the guard's schedule to see where they were supposed to be. Only a handful of people knew about the Royal Twins switching places; Something must have come up to keep them from trading places.

"He wasn't supposed to be at the Farmer's Market," Damian breathed.

"What?" Lord Black and Bradson asked together, not expecting him to interrupt them.

"King Arthur *wasn't* supposed to go to the Market yesterday," Damian snarled, frustrated, "The first thing he was supposed to do was meet with Parliament, which he usually sends Princess Catherine to do dressed as him."

"How do you know that they switch places?" Lord Black asked, still amused. "Dylan does a great job at hiding their true genders when they switch. I have to do a double-take every time, and I helped raise them."

"Princess Catherine doesn't like me," Damian replied sheepishly, "When she's pretending to be the King, she has a hard time hiding it. But, on the other hand, King Arthur can't carry the same animosity toward me. I even have a hard time with keeping up the animosity when he's pretending to be Princess Catherine."

Lord Black smacked his face with exasperation, "Those two are going to be the death of me! How did they find the one person who could tell the difference between them?"

Damian could feel the way the older man looked. The Princess wasn't very good at keeping things to herself when she had a problem. It usually ended with fire everywhere and her guard putting out the flames. However, Damian got better at dodging over time because of her temper.

Meanwhile, Bradson handed the glitter container to another CSI. This CSI shifted their hat for a moment, causing Damian to do a double-take. He could have sworn this new CSI hid pointy ears under their hat.

"Damian, are you alright?" Lord Black questioned.

"Huh?" Damian sputtered, nearly bumping into the older lord as he moved back to the entrance of New Scotland Yard.

They were still away from the press corp cameras, and Lord Black must have maintained his amused look from before. "You were in your head for a little bit there. You need to keep your focus on this role."

"Yes, Sir," Damian gulped, "I'm just... *worried.*"

"We all are, but we must trust the system and Arthur."

Damian tried to keep his face neutral, "Why have trust in the King?"

A small grin made its way onto Lord Black's face. "Arthur was training to join the military," he said, his voice full of pride. "Per the tradition of the Royal Families, that training included kidnapping simulations. Whoever has him is in for a nasty shock. The first thing he's going to do is assess the situation."

"And what's the second thing he's going to do?"

"He's going to locate Matthew," Lord Black continued. "If Matthew didn't find him first or eradicate those who took them. He's not picky about the order but will try to avoid them for as long as possible."

Chapter 4: Finding the Right Warehouse

3 October 2010:
Forty-Eight Hours After the Kidnapping...

The CSIs were able to pinpoint the location of the missing van within a 30-kilometer radius. Five large warehouses in the area looked creepy enough in the daylight that Damian didn't want to know what they looked like at night. The overgrown plants and crumbling buildings made the scene appear more like ruins than a bustling business district.

Back in New Scotland Yard, the CSIs were trying to determine who the buildings belonged to. They kept finding shell company after shell company. Of the five buildings, one belonged to *Prince Holdings*. While this company had one owner, figuring out ownership would be easier than tracking down the owners of the other buildings...

"Lord Wales," Inspector Warren greeted stiffly, pulling Damian from his thoughts to listen. "We weren't expecting you."

Lord Wales moved determinedly across the parking lot and approached them grimly. He was a similar age to Lord Black. His once brown hair was more grey than brown. He was dressed more for the office in a three-piece suit than exploring crime scenes.

"My secretary contacted me about a warrant for one of my buildings," Lord Wales replied.

The Inspector started, looking like he was about to argue. "Are you here to stop us?"

The weary-looking lord shook his head. "I wanted to suggest that Prince Antonio and his bodyguards explore it and bring it down once it's cleared.

Damian grimaced. The building must be in really bad condition for Prince Antonio to be the one to stabilize and clear it. The Spanish Prince's earth powers were well-known

47

to the Nobles and staff members. Prince Antonio and Princess Catherine's duels were the stuff of legends.

The Inspector winced, "That bad?"

Lord Wales nodded, "I bought it a few months ago and had hardly any time to see it myself other than the first time. I've been trying to help Lord Black with everything which takes up much of my schedule."

Damian had to look away at that comment. Mother and her allies were the sources of the time interruption. King Andros' cancer diagnosis and death happened so quickly, and recently, it had only caused trouble.

The *'Traditionals'* tried to name Mother as Queen Regent until Arthur was old enough to be officially crowned. Some newer laws passed within the last century didn't allow a young royal to accept the crown until they turned twenty-one. This way, they had time to complete their education without worrying about making critical decisions before they understood what those decisions were.

Damian still couldn't get a straight answer as to why Lord Black kept the Head of Security role for so long. He also didn't understand why the older lord had to give it up this time around. The older man had been both while King Andros was growing up... However, he had this gut feeling that it had everything to do with Mother and her multiple schemes.

Inspector Warren looked at Damian.

"We cleared Prince Antonio if you approve of his help," the Inspector suggested, bringing Damian back to the conversation. "If this building is as bad as Lord Wales claims, the Spanish party should be sent over as soon as he comes."

Damian nodded as he pulled out his phone. Prince Antonio was training to take over Lord Black's duties within Parliament; he was working with Lord Black since Heir/ess Black had little to no interest in the government itself other than keeping the rights of all people front and centre. Prince Antonio intended to stay in England as long as his mother was the Queen of

Spain. He was preparing for the day that his sister became the Queen of Spain.

"*Hola, Sir.*" a voice greeted.

"Hello, Prince Félix. Is Prince Antonio able to come to the Warehouse District?" Damian requested, hastily starting the conversation, "I know how much his schedule changes."

"*Let me check, Sir,*" the older Spanish prince on the other end promised, followed by some faint muffled voices and a scuffle.

After that, Damian heard a different voice—

"*Why do you want me there?*" Prince Antonio demanded.

Damian huffed. The Spanish prince's hostile attitude, no doubt, stemmed from the Princess. However, it could also sprout from the fact Mother accused the Spanish Prince of trying to take the English throne for himself.

"Lord Wales has requested your presence," Damian said calmly, resisting the urge to pinch the bridge of his nose with frustration, "We have to check a building he's claiming is too unstable without someone with Earth powers."

"*And he wants me to come and check it out for you,*" Prince Antonio completed for him, calming down a little.

"Yes."

"*Alright,*" the prince sighed into the phone; the following was faint: "*Here, I'll go get ready.*"

"*Sir?*" Prince Félix's voice asked.

"Lord Wales requested Earth-powered people to come and help with an unstable building, which he's surprised is still standing. He thought it would have collapsed by now."

"*Understood, Sir. We'll be there within the hour.*"

"Let them know I'll be waiting for them by the Main Gate," Lord Wales offered. "I'll bring them to my building once they get here."

"Did you hear that?" Damian asked into the phone.

"*Sí, sir,*" Prince Félix replied, "*We're meeting with Lord Wales to help find King Arthur. Good luck.*"

"You too," Damian said, ending the call and putting the phone in his pocket. "They should be here in an hour."

Lord Wales nodded, "I'll meet you over there later–good luck hunting."

"Ready?" Inspector Warren asked.

Damian huffed, staring out over the buildings, "As I'll ever be."

⹋ ⹋ ⹋

September 2007:
From the Journal of Lord Damian

The first lab of the class was different than I thought they were going to be. The practicals I completed in secondary differed significantly from those I was currently taking.

My lab partner, Jose, and I got to fingerprint each other. Then, we needed to use powder to lift fingerprints off the table and other objects to see how different surfaces worked.

The superglue diffuser exposes fingerprints on paper!

The powder lifted prints off the glass!

The tape also collected fingerprint oils!

"Are you done geeking out?" Jose asked, fascinated by my reaction.

"No!" I replied with a wide grin, "Mother can't stop this, and Stepfather is encouraging everything!"

"Are you thinking about joining the Academy when you graduate?" A dark haired, green brown eyed lab tech asked as she joined them.

She was shorter than him and was wearing very practical sneakers that somehow didn't make a noise. He didn't know what outfit she was wearing as a white lab coat covered her street clothes. Her dark hair was tied in pigtails. "You certainly have a knack for this."

I started hopefully at the supplies before shaking my head. "The only way I could ever get away with that is if Stepfather makes me join the Academy in an order. Mother hates the fact that this is a University requirement."

"Your stepfather has to make it an order?" The woman questioned, confused.

Jose nodded. "They'd force Lady Murrian to listen to the King's orders if Damian asked him for help."

She nodded as she realised who I was. I think that the staff was going out of their way to undermine Mother. I wonder what tricks she has up her sleeves to help me achieve what I wanted by first getting out of Mother's control. She would do what she could do to help.

"Let me know when you talk to His Majesty about that order; I can write a letter of recommendation to show you're getting in on the merit and skill." She said.

I light up. "Thank you, Professor Bradson! I appreciate that!"

⁜ ⁜ ⁜

The first building they approached was crumbling in some places, not something that could come out of a horror film. It was stable enough to enter without waiting for Prince Antonio and his guards. For the last twenty-four hours, thermal imagery picked up activity that appeared to be movement. Oddly enough, there was active power in the supposedly abandoned building.

The noise of metal grinding excited and worried Inspector Warren and the officers.

Damian looked at the Inspector with confusion. "Are you okay? You look like you're going to vibrate out of your skin."

The Inspector nodded, almost smiling like a madman.

"If this is what I think it is, it would explain why no one has dumped the van yet!" He then rubbed his hands together with anticipation, "We just might catch those bloody thieves in the act!"

The Inspector then left the young lord to give orders to the officers. Damian thought for a moment before it dawned on him: Luxury cars had been disappearing overnight. The cameras were useless as the cars were in their spot one moment and then gone the next morning.

It would also be a great place to get rid of a van used in a kidnapping.

Damian stood back and let the Inspector and officers do their job. He knew that even the smallest thing could mess up any evidence that could be collected and tagged. But he always enjoyed watching the process of CSIs. He knew that he could potentially cause trouble if he got in the way. He didn't want something thrown out of court that could have helped convict someone. He desperately wished that he had applied to grad school for forensics before King Andros had died.

"*There's a van here!*" Inspector Warren called out, pulling him from his thoughts. He blinked as he saw that the other bobbies had been leading out the car thieves and mechanics in either handcuffs or zip ties. "*Somebody bloody get me one of those CSIs to process it! We need to know if it's the one we're looking for!*"

CSI Bradson then hustled past Damian, throwing him a pack of gloves as she passed.

Catching the gloves with ease, he stared at them, startled, before looking up at Bradson. *"What?"*

"I know that you're itching to help," she declared. "You were at the top of the class. You know everything we need to look for, and I may have registered you as my assistant when you left New Scotland Yard yesterday. Now keep up; we've got things to do."

Pulling on the other glove, he finally figured out where he'd seen her before.

The woman was the tech in charge of the university's science lab, where he went to lectures that, if they hadn't been mandatory for his studies, Mother would have had a fit over him attending, seeing it had nothing to do with the political science degree she was forcing him to pursue.

They were fortunate the mechanics hadn't started taking apart the van yet. Maybe they didn't know that it had been used in a crime other than transporting them to their luxury car targets. Either way, Damian hoped this would be the break they needed.

CSI Bradson opened the driver's side door. She was assigned to look for evidence of a technology blocker of some sort. Not only was it illegal, but it could also help prove that this van was used to take both King Arthur and the high-end cars off the streets.

Damian opened the sliding backdoor. He vaguely noted there was a bench seat on the driver's side of the van. The rest of the van had the seats removed but had some sort of device rigged into the floor and the ceiling of the van. There was some rope tied to the device that was rigged into the floor.

He carefully crawled into the van to examine the rope more closely. Something shiny nearby caught his attention, so he took a pen from his pocket, shifted the shining object to the pen, and raised it to get a better view.

It was a wristwatch-like bracelet with a red asterisk, and two silver snakes curled around a staff in the centre. Damian didn't have to flip it over to see who it belonged to; he already knew.

"Found something!" He declared at the same time as CSI Bradson.

She looked over the driver's seat, "What did you find?"

"King Arthur's medical bracelet," Damian grinned. Despite the situation, it proved the King had been in the van at one point. "You?"

"The illegal military-grade cloaking device these bozos *shouldn't* have access to," she muttered before turning back to take a picture, "Alright, let me come around to get a photo of the bracelet."

She hastily left the driver's seat, where a different CSI took her place. She circled the van and climbed in the back with Damian. He held the bracelet up to the camera with the pen. A flash later, Bradson lowered her camera.

"Was it in a pile of... glitter?" She asked, confused.

Damian bit back a groan; this glitter would drive them over the edge with all the questions it left behind.

✠ ✠ ✠

1 hour later...

Inspector Warren and the offers were ready to move to the next warehouse. Bradson left behind a few of her trusted CSIs to finish processing the first warehouse and the van. The medical bracelet was a great find in trying to locate King Arthur. The van's presence in the first warehouse gave them hope that they were on the right path. They just weren't expecting what they would find in Warehouse Two.

The CSIs back at New Scotland Yard gathered evidence of heat sources and active power in Warehouse Two. They also found a purchasing agreement and an application of sorts. They weren't able to find out what the application was, only that it was being fast-tracked. The CSI that found it didn't have a high enough clearance to find anything further.

Rounding the corner, Damian blinked—the brightness coming from an array of warming lights was overwhelming, though it didn't seem to bother the finger-like, star-leaf plants slowly growing beneath them.

"Please be careful," a high-pitched voice pleaded. *"They're in a delicate growing stage!"*

"We have all the right papers," another voiced. "Please don't destroy them! We don't even know what you're looking for!"

The officers looked at each other and then at Warren before backing away. They didn't want to cause trouble if they truly had the papers. Even so, the warrant called for a search of the building, not the destruction of everything in their path.

Inspector Warren hastily pulled out his phone, located the correct contact, and hit the call button. He only had to wait a moment.

"This is Warren; we've hit a snag here. Were you able to find out what's going on with the application?"

Damian heard some faint voice come from Warren's phone as he nodded a few times. After a brief pause, Damian heard the Inspector say, "Alright, thank you. I'll let them know."

He then looked at the young man and woman standing tense and defensive protectively in front of the plants. Based on their size, they'd been growing them for a while.

"Stand down," Warren ordered.

Damian wasn't sure if the Inspector meant the bobbies or the couple. However, both groups managed to relax a little. The Inspector's focus moved between the two groups before returning to the officers.

"The building inspector is apparently on his way for the final walkthrough to make sure that everything here is up to code," he started as the couple tensed up again. Warren then turned to the bobbies, "Can I get some of you to help them get this place ready while you *carefully* look for King Arthur?"

The couple stared at them with confusion.

"King Arthur is missing?" The young woman asked quietly. "We don't have a T.V. to keep up on the news."

"Is there anything we can do to help?" The man asked as some of the bobbies left the building. The couple would give the remaining five officers their orders in a moment.

"Are you the group that's staying?" Warren asked the bobbies, who nodded in agreement.

"This way," the woman motioned, "I need help cleaning the storage room."

The bobbies followed, leaving her partner with Inspector Warren and Damian.

The Inspector turned back to the man, "Mister..."

"You can call me Rori; my partner is Amy."

Warren nodded, "Mister Rori, can you think of anything out of the ordinary when you leave this warehouse?"

Rori pondered, "No one goes near the warehouse next door. It's too unstable. Another door down does have people coming and going from it. I don't know why; I've never wanted to cause trouble, so I've never asked. The last building is too far away for me to see anything."

Warren nodded, "We're aware of the unstable warehouse, but thank you for letting us know about the occupancy of the fourth warehouse. The records show no one should be there. Please let one of my officers know if you need me."

"Thank you, Sir," Rori replied, "Good luck finding His Majesty. No one should have to be put into something against his will." He then turned to join his partner and the officers.

Inspector Warren looked at Damian, "Do you know what he was talking about?"

Domain shook his head, "Not that I can think of unless he's referring to what Mother did to King Andros; may he rest in peace."

"What did she do?"

"Well, she married the king with at least three-fourths of the population hating her."

"Ahh," Warren thought as they started moving down the hall to the entrance of the building, "Is that why everyone is watching you with interest? They want to know what you are going to do and how you're going to do it."

Damian nodded, miserable, "A Parliament meeting was in session as I was travelling to meet you at the Farmers Market. I still don't know what happened in that meeting. Mother is being tight-lipped, and I haven't seen the Princess since news started coming about the king's kidnapping for her to throw fire at me."

"T...*throw fire?*" Warren asked, startled, "Why?"

"She has a temper that she hides well unless I'm nearby."

Warren shook his head, amused, "Is it a rivalry or something more..."

"Nope. I'm stopping you *right there!*" Damian pleaded. "Nothing is going on between me and the Princess; I want to keep it that way!"

Warren held up his arms in surrender, "I get it. I understand about being between what your family wants and what you want, but be careful because your mother might not see it that way."

Damian looked away, nearly defeated and feeling drained, "*I know.*"

✠ ✠ ✠

1 hour later...

The group of slowly dwindling officers, starting to look defeated, warily approached Warehouse Three. Damian and Inspector Warren joined them a few minutes later, soon realising Lord Wales understated how condemned the building truly was.

Once a clothing manufacturing facility before World War

II, the five-floor structure now stood falling apart at the seams after the company faced hardship and couldn't keep up with maintenance. The final inspection that closed them for good was over water and fire damage. At least, that was the report Lord Wales received and what the CSIs could find.

The lower level looked fine from the outside, even with the front-facing windows boarded up. As eyes drifted up the building, it told a different story. The roof had fallen in, and several windows appeared broken. Damian wasn't sure what caused the damage, and he didn't understand why Lord Wales bought the building in the first place.

"I had hoped to convert it into housing for the people who work down here," Lord Wales commented as he joined Damian and Inspector Warren.

Damian glanced at Lord Wales sheepishly. "I said that out loud, didn't I?"

The chuckle from the older man struck a chord of familiarity with Damian. Even if he didn't know why, he resisted the urge to close his eyes and just *let* his laugh wrap around him like a long-lost blanket.

"It's not the first time it's happened, and it won't be the last," Lord Wales continued warmly, "It reminds me of my late son—he would say something he shouldn't have said out loud frequently. But he always made the King laugh."

Prince Antonio, now standing next to Lord Wales, could only shake his head, amused. Damian heard stories of their antics; the younger prince must remember his uncles fondly.

"Where do you want me to start?" Prince Antonio asked.

Lord Wales turned to examine the building closer.

"If I remember correctly," he started, "The Real Estate Agent and I couldn't get too far past the front door, and there was too much damage in the back of the building to attempt to get in that way."

The Spanish Prince nodded, "Very well, we'll start in the

front. If there's no other way safely in, then the front is the most likely path Arthur would have taken."

Several of Prince Antonio's guards had surrounded the building, placing themselves at specific points so they could touch it. Most of the building was made of concrete, metal framing, and wood, so it could be stabilised without needing to be entered. Their powers could find the dirt within those materials and manipulate it to their will.

Prince Antonio and his head guard slowly entered the building. Damian assumed it was to stabilise a walking path within. He had never seen anything like how the Spanish Prince and his guards worked together.

Damian was in awe of others when they used their elemental powers because he wasn't even sure of his powers most of the time. He didn't have any of the base powers to know which elements his powers stemmed from. Sometimes, he would get flashes of scenes or premonitions that didn't make sense until *after* the fact.

The one power that helped him the most was the spell sensor. He could sense whatever type of spell was on an object. This helped him avoid traps that Mother tried to send his way.

The one spell that he feared the most and one that headed his way a time or two was a lust spell. Grandmother actually sent that one his way. Grandmother Murrian didn't like the fact he hadn't dated any of the women she wanted him to date. He's bracing himself for whatever those women currently have up their sleeves.

Prince Antonio and his guard returned, bringing Damian to the present. The prince was grim and dirty, and the guard looked disappointed.

"He's not there," Prince Antonio reported, sounding worn down, "Nothing in there but debris and something rotting."

"Do you think it's a body?" Inspector Warren inquired, concerned.

The prince paused, looking like he was gathering his

thoughts. "If it *was*, it has decomposed for over three days. Do you still want to see for yourself?"

The Inspector nodded, "If you lead me to the spot. We need to rule it out as a possible body with a crime scene. If someone knew this building is supposed to be demolished—"

Understanding, the guard returned the nod. "I'll take you. Once we're back, we should take down the building. It's taking a lot of power to hold it up and let someone around safely inside." The guard then turned to Prince Antonio. "You are not allowed to follow, your highness. Your mother would have some choice words about this adventure with both of us..."

"And might fire you if I go back in there," Prince Antonio finished, rolling his dark eyes. "You say that all the time, yet you're still here."

"That's because you've never had the urge to follow me back into the building until now," the guard replied dryly, "I have instructions to let you be a boy—now a man—first and a prince second. You're allowed to make mistakes, but I get to interfere the moment I think you're making the same mistake twice. Do you understand?"

Red crept onto the prince's face, "*Sí.*"

"Good." The guard turned back to Warren. "This way, Inspector."

The two hastily entered the building, leaving Prince Antonio with Damian and Lord Wales.

"Why did he speak to you like that?" Damian asked after a pause. "Don't you have more power than him?"

The prince huffed, "He's my uncle, one of my mama's older brothers. He might not have a title, but he is overly protective of his family. He knows the need for protocol and when he can cross that line. It usually happens when I'm being, well, *bratty*."

Lord Wales shook his head, looking entertained, "That sounded like something my son would do. He worked as King Andros'—may he rest in peace—guard until his death. The King looked up to him like an older brother, one he wanted but didn't have. My son would put the King in his place if he felt he needed to."

"I think I remember that," Prince Antonio admitted, "He was a tall man who would throw Auncle Dylan over his shoulder in a fireman hold when they didn't do what he wanted."

Lord Wales smiled fondly. However, before he could continue, Prince Antonio's uncle and Inspector Warren returned.

"Inspector?" Lord Wales asked, "Is there something I should be concerned about?"

The Inspector shook his head. "It was just an animal unfortunate enough to get trapped. They can take down the building."

"*Gracias*," Prince Félix replied with a bow. He then turned and ordered the other guards, "*¡Derriba el edificio!*"

Thank you, Damian's mind translated, *Take down the building.* He shook his head to clear it. *How in the world am I doing that!?*

The other guards nodded before carefully pushing against the lower level's walls. As they fell in, the rest of the building shifted downward to the ground rather than collapsing, allowing the guards to dismantle the walls floor by floor.

Damian stared in disbelief, having only ever seen earth powers used in fights, not in construction. This would explain how the Spanish could complete the framing and most of the walls of a new building faster than any other country.

With the building demolition safely complete, Damian and Inspector Warren left the guards and their charge to clean up the rubble. Glancing over his shoulder, Damian caught a glimpse of the debris floating off into a large dumpster. Part of him wished he could use his powers like that.

1 hour later...

Warehouse Four wasn't abandoned as the CSIs thought, especially after what the Inspector learned from the marijuana grower. Its condition wasn't as bad as Lord Wales' building either; however, the windows had boards over or behind them regardless of their condition.

"Hello," Lord Black greeted from the entrance.

While they weren't expecting Lord Black to show up, one of the CSIs called him when they learned he owned the building. It seemed that he and Lord Wales had the same idea to turn the building into affordable housing for the dock and warehouse workers who didn't want to travel far for work or were having a hard time getting to work because of the location of the warehouses.

But, unlike Lord Wales' unstable building with no one in it—

"I think people live in the upper levels," Lord Black greeted. "I would like to go in with you to help them prepare to move."

"Where are you moving them to?" Inspector Warren wondered aloud. "They can't leave until I've interviewed them."

"Several of them are moving to the family Farm to help my parents," Lord Black replied calmly. "This has been in the works for a while."

"And the ones that *aren't* moving to the Farm?" Damian asked.

Lord Black grinned, "They are stubborn, out-of-work construction workers who want to help build their new home."

"And you know how to deal with stubbornness," Warren muttered, "Alright, let's find out if they've seen anything out of the ordinary the past few days."

Lord Black nodded as he gestured for the Inspector to follow him.

Damian wondered if he should follow, too. That was until CSI Bradson appeared by his side. He nearly jumped out of his skin in the process.

"PROFESSOR!" he exclaimed, slipping back into his old name for her. His right hand over his heart, "Why did you do that?"

"I have to keep you on your toes somehow," she grinned, holding out a new pack of gloves, "Now come. We've found some tyre tracks. We need to see if they match the van's tyres and the ones we found at the Famer's Market."

"Yes, ma'am," Damian returned the grin as he took the gloves. He wasn't about to let the casting plaster pick up anything that might be on his hands and destroy evidence.

✠ ✠ ✠

5 hours later...

"Have you determined if the tyres match?" Inspector Warren asked from behind Damian, making him jump.

"What is this?!?" He demanded, making Bradson and Warren laugh, "Are you *both* trying to kill me through a heart attack."

Bradson stood, "Not yet. You know I have to return to the lab and run comparisons. Please try not to give Lord Security a heart attack. We still need to figure out who took King Arthur."

"This last building is our last hope," Warren muttered, "The group of homeless people here reported something happening there within the last ten days. They also report seeing a van drive this way two days ago."

"Has anything happened since then?" Damian requested.

"Not that they have been able to see," Warren reported, "Ma'am, are you staying with us?"

Bradson nodded, a determined glint in her eyes, "One of the other CSIs is coming to get the tyre impressions from me. I have to see this through to the end."

The three slowly approached the fifth warehouse, meeting several officers sent ahead to the slowly decaying building. This warehouse was bigger and had more closed-off rooms inside the building than the others—a sudden commotion from within made Inspector Warren and CSI Bradson bolt into the building.

Damian took his time as he slowly moved up the hallway. He didn't receive clearance to explore all of the rooms. So he would just take in the rooms from the hall, hoping to memorise them and see if something could be potentially out of place. He stopped further down the hallway after noticing weird patterns on the floor. Kneeling closer to examine them, it reminded him of something—

"Can someone *please* get Prince Antonio or his uncle?" Damian requested as he hastily stood, not wanting to touch the pattern of upturned pebbles that only occurred when someone with earth powers made a certain move. "They should be able to confirm if I'm right about what this is."

The officers looked at each other first before nodding to Damian. One of them turned and rushed out of the building. He needed to catch Prince Antonio before he and his group left the area.

Warren stuck his head out of a nearby room, "I've got three slip-ups in here. What did you find?"

Damian gestured to the pebble pattern, "They slipped up in more ways than one if this has anything to do with the missing King."

"What do you mean?" The Inspector asked, curious, as he came out of the room and approached Damian.

Before Damian could answer, they heard with accented English, *"What do you need me for now?"*

The two looked to the end of the hallway that led back to the Main Entrance. There stood a frustrated Prince Antonio and a frazzled officer. Damian wordlessly gestured again to the rubble pile on the concrete floor.

"This looks like the remains of a manoeuvre that I've seen you do in training." Damian did his best not to say who he had seen pulling this move off.

Prince Antonio had heavy steps, angrily indenting the ground, *"I have..."*

He trailed off as Damian made a hand signal with his hand that the Inspector couldn't see. The prince realised the other man didn't know of his cousin's powers with that signal. The prince and Damian knew whose favourite move was to go underground if needed. The prince hastily knelt, almost moving to touch it, but stopped when a pack of gloves suddenly appeared in his line of vision. Damian tried not to laugh at Bradson.

"Thank you, ma'am," the prince continued as he stood and took the packet from her. He opened the pack, put on the gloves, and knelt again, pointing to the rock patterns, "Lord Security is right, though. These are the aftereffects of a defence manoeuvre made by someone with earth powers and years of training."

"That would explain the first room that is being processed," the Inspector muttered as he was able to read between the lines, "There's shattered remains of iron cuffs. The idiots in the room behind me deserve how we found them when very few people knew about this location."

"How did you find them?" Damian asked, curious.

"They were pretty dirty and banged up," Warren continued, "And they couldn't get out of that room very easily, nor could we get in very easily. We had to break down the door."

"Do you need the Lord Security," Bradson asked as she handed Damian a new pack of gloves.

Warren shook his head, "Just working on processing the prisoners."

"Good, we need him in a room further down. There's something there that has his name on it," Bradson then bowed to Prince Antonio as he stood again, "If you can help reconstruct what happened here, it will be extremely helpful."

Prince Antonio nodded, "Anything to help find my cousin.

But considering what we've found so far, we might not find Arthur here."

The Inspector's eyes narrowed, "How can you tell that?!" He nearly hissed.

"One, you found shattered chains and cuffs," the prince started a list, "Two, these are remains of a ground defence attack. Three, the tied up... um... *idiots*. And four..."

"*Four?*" Damian interrupted as he pulled on a glove.

"Four depends on the amount of glitter you find in that room," Prince Antonio finished.

Bradson's eyes narrowed this time as she seethed, "Just how much do you know about the glitter?"

"Papa leaves glitter everywhere during a fight or training match," the prince shrugged, "It's one of the defensive powers that he shares with others from his home country. If the man down in New Scotland Yard isn't *Tio Matheo*, he would have left behind that glitter."

Damian's mouth mimicked a fish for a few moments before he was able to get out: "When we're done here and back at the palace, we're going over *all* the powers in the family that have nothing to do with either fire or earth."

Prince Antonio nodded, "I'll write up a report for the Inspector and the CSI, too."

"Thank you, Your Highness," Bradson said as she pulled Damian with her, "Let's see how much glitter is in the last room."

She and Damian went to the room furthest away from the Prince and Inspector. As they entered, a CSI, whom Damian hadn't met yet, handed him the note that had his name on it. He turned it over in the gloved hand.

"Did you open it?"

The CSI nodded, frustrated. "*We* opened it," she started as she gestured to the others in the room who were currently taking pictures and gathering evidence. "I couldn't read it. We were hoping you could understand the words."

Damian started at the note for a moment. *Who in the world is trying to get a hold of me?* He unfolded the note to find—

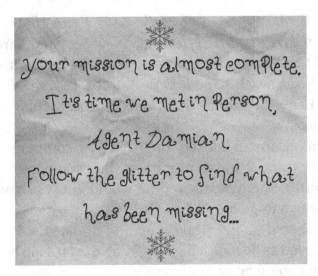

What is with the 'agent' part? Why do I have to follow the glitter? He thought as he looked around the room at several piles of glitter.

Chapter 5: The Godparent Rites

Damian tiredly shuffled into New Scotland Yard as he followed CSI Bradson. She insisted he come back with her to the lab. Needing all hands on deck to process the evidence, Bradson had a few things she wanted his help with.

"*Damian?*"

"Huh?" Damian looked up from the computer he sat himself in front of in his numbness. Bradson handed him a cup of coffee. She remembered he would always show up to her lab with a to-go mug.

"You should go get cleaned up and update the Princess," she suggested as he took a big sip, "You've been a big help with everything going on around here."

"But there's still more to do!" He protested as he lowered the mug.

She gave him a small smile, "And I can't have you compromising anything that we can pin on those three idiots that the *King* so nicely caught for us and the Big Boss that thought he could pretend to be Ze Black's partner. You're ready to fall asleep. I bet you haven't pulled any all-nighters in a while."

Damian shook his head, "I never needed to pull any all-nighters at university, not even for your class. Secondary school, on the other hand, was the first time I was away from Mother most of the time. I thought I could get away with sneaking out to parties."

"Did it work?"

"The parties, yes, the sneaking out, not so much," Damian grinned, "Papa... I mean, King Andros sent me to the parties with a guard who trained under Lords Wales and Black. He was always one step behind me, with a mindset similar to Prince Antonio's uncle; he let me make my own mistakes, but never twice." He then shook his head to prevent himself from recalling the past, "Now, what should I tell the Princess?"

"You should tell her about the glitter," Bradson suggested, "Princess Catherine might have more of an idea about where the glitter was coming from, *especially* if Prince Antonio thinks it has to do with a defensive power that runs through members of the royal families."

He nodded before slowly taking another sip of his coffee, feeling the caffeine wake him up a little.

CSI Bradson's smile hadn't left her face as she fidgeted with her leather bracelet, "I'm glad you were able to figure out a way to do what you love while making Lady Murrian think you were following her orders. Good luck with them."

Damian took another sip of his coffee as she turned and walked away to gather her things. He hummed, thinking that she was taking her advice for him. She was right; there was too much going on in this case to make a mistake that could throw all the evidence out the window.

✠ ✠ ✠

1960...

A younger Lord Aaron Black watched his sleeping nephew while Lady Melanie Black sat beside the cradle. She was humming a lullaby that she had heard her queen hum over the course of the pregnancy. It was hard to believe that Philp and Eliza were gone for a few months...

"I think we both want the same outcome," Lord Llew Wales commented vaguely from behind Aaron, "Let's make a deal."

Aaron turned and eyed the older man with silver hair, with confusion."Why do you want to help me? If anything, you benefit from gaining custody of Andros."

Lord Wales shook his head, "You have a closer claim," he assured. "Besides, I'm too old to raise another child until adulthood."

"Then what do you suggest?"

"The Godparent Rites."

Aaron paused. **The Godparent(s) Rites** *were a very sacred event. Few understood the process, and even fewer knew that the English Royal Family had invoked* **the Rites** *for centuries.*

"How do you know about that?" Melanie, Aaron's redhead wife, hissed as she stood to protect her nephew, "Only the Royal family..."

"My great-great-great-great-great grandmother was Queen Alexandra."

"Oh," Melanie deflated, the righteous fury leaving her as quickly as it came.

She hastily resettled herself next to Andros' cradle. She didn't worry about waking the sleeping baby king. There was a unique spell that had been added to the cradle that was only active when there was a baby in it. The baby wouldn't be disturbed while in the cradle, but a caregiver could hear when the baby woke up on their own.

"And unlike the lords who gained their title from someone who married into either the English or the Scottish Royal Family, your line was **born** into it." Aaron realised. "You have every right to not only know about **the Rites** but use them as well."

Lord Wales nodded.

"Who do you suggest we use?" Melanie asked, looking up at the older lord.

"I would like to suggest my son, Liam," Lord Wales motioned for his son to come forward. The dark-haired man around Aaron and Melanie's age bowed.

"I'm looking forward to helping you," Liam continued as he stood up.

"Help... helping me?" Aaron questioned, "You mean you won't take Andros from us?"

Lord Wales and Liam shook their heads.

"I would never go against my cousin's wishes," Liam assured, "She wanted you and Melanie to raise our little king the same way that you and Prince Philip were raised, humble and with honour."

✠ ✠ ✠

15 October 2010:
Two Weeks After the Kidnapping...

"Damian, are you alright?" A deep voice asked as Damian dropped to the floor a photo of Lords Black and Wales together, pulling him from a vision.

"Y–yeah," Damian started as he bent down to grab the photo.

Sometimes, his powers would bring him memories of events that were tied to different objects. Some that he would remember and others that he didn't. This was one of the few times that it happened with another person nearby...

"Erm–" Damian continued as he stood, unsure what pronouns to use with the Black Heir next to him. Hair tied back in a messy bun, they wore an androgynous ensemble neither wildly masculine nor feminine.

Heir Black chuckled, "I'm feeling male today, but you have permission to call me Dylan."

"Are you sure?"

Dylan nodded, "I know that it's hard for me to keep up with what I'm feeling on most days. My closet rivals Anya's and Arthur's on a good day. I can't imagine how you're feeling."

Damian gave them a tired nod.

"What's wrong?" Dylan asked.

"How can you be so calm?" Damian blurted out. "I have all these clues that don't make any sense. I can't even tell where Arthur is now that his phone's been recovered from the warehouse. We don't even know if he's still alive!"

"They found his phone?" Dylan asked as Damian nodded, "When?"

"Sometime after the first round of looking for clues," Damian muttered, "I think it was hidden in the same place that they found the henchpeople. Why do you even trust me?!"

Scanning Damian up and down, Dylan shifted onto their back foot and crossed their arms coyly. "Do you *love* Arthur?"

Damian blinked as his cheeks reddened, *"How–"*

"I watch, and I listen. Most around here think you were born to be the villain because of your bloodline. As you've gotten older, you are clearly leaning toward the side of good. Now, I understand more about what goes on around here than most people realise; why do you think I get into those fights with your mother?" Dylan continued. "I wanted to let you know that you have a safe place near my rooms when you're ready to come out of the closet. So, do you love Arthur?"

Damian nodded mutely, feeling a weight lift off his shoulders. He may not have admitted it out loud, but it felt right for Dylan to know the truth.

"W—*why* are you telling me this now?" Damian squeaked, more stressed than ever before, "I *just* mess things up; I don't even want to rule like Mother wants. All I've wanted to do is help solve crimes!"

"Whoever your father was is more important than we know, despite any secrets that *Gwrach* is trying to keep," Dylan replied.

Damian stared off momentarily, "She's determined to take the secret of my father's identity to her grave."

"What about a DNA test?" Dylan suggested, "Those for sale to the public are getting more refined and may help you discover the truth."

"And what," Damian started, "Hope he's in the system somehow? What if he's in prison somewhere?!"

Dylan pointed out, "He could have worked for the Government. Government agents are required to provide updated dental records, photos, and DNA samples in case something goes wrong so they can return to their families."

Damian went quiet, "I don't know where to begin."

"Well, for *right now,* you should go to your favourite section of the library," Dylan suggested. "It should have information about *The Godparent Rites*, though they may have it locked behind a ward. Let me know, and I'll give you access."

"W–what's so important about it?" Damian requested, knowing his vision of the two lords wasn't coincidental.

"I always know where Ayna and Arthur are because of those *Rites*," Dylan said, "That's how I know Arthur is still alive." They moved their hand to their chest, "I would have felt it here if someone killed him."

"*Ze Black!*" A staff member called from the top of the hall, "Can you help us with Princess Cathrine's hair and makeup?"

"*Coming!*" They replied before turning back to Damian. "Let me know if you need help with any clues. Matthew's family can be tricky and difficult when trying to protect the ones they love."

Dylan then left the young lord to think about what he had just learned. Are the clues only leading him in circles?

✠ ✠ ✠

22 October 2010:
Three Weeks After the Kidnapping...

Hiding in the library's history section, Damian scanned the report Inspector Warren and CSI Bradson sent him. Neither of them could find where the damn glitter came from, and Lord Black appeared to have some idea behind its origins; however, it seemed as if he was holding his tongue for a reason.

The two Inspectors were still trying to set up a time to interview Prince Antonio's father, the Prince Consort of Spain. However, this was proving to be an impossible task. Many securities of the Royal families around the world have put their charges on lockdown, as the real mastermind of the kidnapping hadn't been caught yet.

The other thing confusing him was the note he had found in the room where they discovered Matthew. *Who* in the world considered him an *agent*? He didn't like this mystery was getting more complicated with each passing day.

He put down the report, pulled over a notebook, grabbed a pen, and began writing.

Mystery of who currently has Arthur:

The being pretending to be Matthew, distracted Arthur and Matthew long enough to be grabbed by henchpeople pretending to be guards.

The henchpeople were attacked, likely by Arthur, in an attempt to escape

We're calling them 'henchpeople' as someone scrubbed their identities from all government systems, and they still won't give their real names:

They still refer to themselves by the names of the men they switched with.

While the henchpeople were left behind, Arthur and Matthew had disappeared from where they originally had been taken too.

Glitter, which usually only appears around the winter holidays, has popped up around the crime scenes in early October.

This is at least one month before any winter holiday supplies start showing up in every country, even ours.

✠ ✠ ✠

27 October 2010:
Three and a Half Weeks After the Kidnapping...

The one area that had brought him comfort in the past was now giving him a headache. Back in the history section, Damian had found a book about the Godparent Rites. He's determined that he shouldn't even have been able to read the book about them.

He ran his hand over the spins of the books, hoping that he could get a vision from one of them... helping him... He felt a powerful spell on several books that wouldn't let him pull them off the shelf. There was one that moved but wouldn't let him open it.

The book that he could move and pick up but couldn't open, was a thick, red leather book that had a trifecta imprinted on the front. He could feel it was important but didn't think he could leave the room with it to find Dylan. He could sense a protection spell was ingrained into the book. That usually meant that an object with this type of spell on it couldn't leave a specific area.

"*Damian, have you—*"

A voice stopped short as Damian turned to greet the speaker. His eyes widened as he realized it was Dylan.

"Oh!" They exclaimed happily, "You found it!"

"Yeah," Damian muttered, "But it won't let me open it."

"I'm surprised it even lets you pick it up," Dylan admitted as they joined Damian by the table in the centre of the room, "It's picky about blood. Someone outside the family usually has to get keyed in."

"Well, it won't let me open it," Damian grumbled as he put the book down on the table, "It must sense my Murrian blood."

"Maybe that's what's keeping you from opening it, but whoever your father was must have been from an approved family for you to even pick it up off the shelf."

"***Rituals, Protections, and Rites,***" Damian read aloud, "Is this the coveted spellbook of the Royal Family that everyone thinks exists but can't prove?"

Dylan nodded, "It hides from those with unkeyed blood. I think as long as I'm holding it, you should be able to read the pages."

"Why is this so important?"

Dylan gave him a slight, tired grin.

"I'm Anya and Arthur's Godparent," They moved a hand to their chest, hovering over their heart, "I would have felt it here if someone had killed Arthur. The bond would have snapped, which would knock me out as a punishment for not protecting him from someone with dark intentions."

Damian's mouth dropped, "Y...you're saying that the *Godparent Rites* exist?"

Dylan nodded, "Papa and Uncle Liam did the *Rite* for Andrew, Andros and I. The bond keeps its strength until the child in question is when their last power is known to come in at eighteen or when they can fully protect themselves." They then turned to the *Ritual* itself.

As Dylan rifled through the pages, Damian felt a power radiating from the magical tome. He itched to touch it for himself, though he was afraid the pages would go blank if he tried.

"Are you able to read what it says?" Dylan asked once they reached the correct section, "The writing style stays the same, but magic updates the words to the way that the reader would understand the words, especially since the way we write and talk has changed over the years."

"I think as long as you're touching the book, it should be okay," Damian admitted, "I think I can see the history of the *Ritual.*"

✛ ✛ ✛

October 1488

The Godparent Rites:

This rite wasn't used in early Anglican history. The term 'Godparent' was meant to sponsor the spiritual learning and development in Christianity. While the first of the known Saxon Kings, Alfred the Great, was baptised in 878. He was the first known royal to need this Godparent or sponsor once he converted from Paganism.

However, it wasn't until the disappearance and assumed murders of King Edward V and his little brother, Richard of Shrewsbury, Duke of York, that the Godparent Rites were created. Their sister, Queen Elizabeth of York, worried what happened to her brothers could happen to her children.

While the Rite, mixed with Paganism and Christianity, the goal was to ensure the Godparent, usually an uncle, could never turn on their royal charge.

It would cause the Godparent to feel pain if something happened to their young royal charge that wasn't a natural death or an accidental death. The backlash from an underage royal being killed will knock out the Godparent. If there was either an attempt to successfully kill the underage royal by or on the order of the Godparent, the Rite would also claim the life of the Godparent in retaliation...

1502

Queen Elizabeth of York may have commissioned the Rite and placed her children under it. However, she didn't live long enough to pass the information about the Rite to her children. I have put it here in hopes of protecting it.

Princess Margaret and Princess Mary have inquired about the Rite for their children, having some vague memory of it...

High Priestess Melinda

1547

I found this book in the library. It explains why Lady Jane Gray survived and the man who was named her Godfather did not after he conspired to have her executed. The backlash of this spell killed him.

Additionally, Mary (31), Mary of Scotland (7), Lady Jane (11), and Elizabeth (Me, 14) are forced to work together to stabilise England and Scotland after the dragon refused to choose Edward (10) as the next king.

The Marys were raised Roman Catholic, while Jane and I were raised Protestant. However, Jane thinks we need to look more into Paganism. It seems that religion just saved her life and we need to understand it better, especially since the dragon spirit should be from the Paganism religion.

Mary is looking into marrying and Cousin Jane is engaged, though that might change too. Cousin Mary has been hiding in France. Her council put her there to protect her from Father's ideas. Her half-brothers have been in communication with Mary.

Mary also has been looking to see who she can betroth us to with the dragon's approval. They are thinking about using the Rite for any children they can hope to have. Edward is uncertain about the world that he was being raised to rule but can't. The dragon said he was too young for her to even consider him as a choice. She's sad that she feels that she can't trust the last of the male Tudors as Father has betrayed her and the other women in his life for the dragon to feel comfortable with a male ruler again.

The dragon has chosen Mary, for now, with orders she has to work with us Tudor ladies to stabilise the isles. If we can't work together, the dragon will turn to other blood heirs. Mary has learned that she cannot completely change the religion back following the Roman Catholic Church. There's too much at stake to be quarrelling over something like this, and the dragon could choose someone else in the end if we don't follow her requests...

✠ ✠ ✠

"Have you managed to read the whole thing?" Damian asked, his eyes finally pulling away from the book as he reached the end of the entries and looked up at Dylan. "What is this about a dragon? I never heard Papa... I mean... *King Andros,* talk about a dragon."

Dylan nodded, "It only gets more interesting from there. Queen Mary I eventually married. However, she couldn't carry a child to full term. The dragon eventually chose Queen Elizabeth I to be Queen Mary I's heir, and I'm not sure how her partner fits into the story. It seems to be blurred out. Her only child to make it to adulthood was a daughter who was chosen by the dragon. The reason why you wouldn't have known about or heard Andros talk about the dragon spirit is that she hasn't shown herself since my aunt was still alive."

"Blurred out?" Damian asked, "How can an entire history be blurred out?"

Dylan shrugged, "I don't know what's happening, but I know I can't read parts of our history. There's also something keeping Papa from telling me anything about my aunt and her family."

"Oh," Damian paused for a moment, "Do you know anything else about the dragon?"

Dylan shook their head, "Sadly, the dragon has never tried to communicate with me, even though Andros called me his chosen sibling. Is there anything else I can help you with?"

Damian thought for a moment, "Yes, there is something that could help me with. Is there anything you can tell me about the glitter?"

"What type of glitter?" Dylan requested slowly, "Besides the fact I'm still finding glitter in clothes I haven't worn since the twins were little."

Damian huffed, "I meant *defensive* glitter."

"Ahh, you mean Matthew's powers," Dylan hummed. "The one thing I know about it is that it works like a beacon. Why do you want to know?"

"Matthew activated his power twice, but you never said anything about his location."

"I wouldn't know about his location."

"What?" Damian asked, startled, *"Why?"*

"Matthew's beacon still goes right to his brother. If anything, they have a faster response time than we do."

"Ze Black," a guard interrupted before Damian could ask anything else. "Your father is looking for you. He says you're late."

Dylan closed the book and handed it back to Damian. They then looked at their watch with a groan. "I'm not late, but he knows me too well. I hope you find what you're looking for."

"Me too," Damian muttered as Dylan left the room.

Ring, ring.

Damian hastily fished for his phone. He didn't want to face the wrath of the librarian for having a phone not on silent or vibrating in the library. It may be a royal library, but the librarian still ran it as if it was still public, which it was when neither English or Scottish royal families were in residence at Buckingham Palace.

His phone screen read: *Professor Bradson.*

"Going to have to update that—" Damian pushed the answer button and put it to his ear, "Hello?"

"*Damian,*" Bradson chirped as a greeting, "*We're interviewing one of the henchpeople. Do you want to be here for this?*"

Damian's mouth went dry, "Y—yes, I'll be right there."

"*Please take your time,*" Bradson said, "*The public defender can't get here until after lunch.*"

Damian looked at his watch. **10:45 am.**

"That's fine. I have to get Lord Black; he's meeting Heir Black for something."

"*We called him first,*" Bradson admitted. "*He'll also get here as soon as he can.*"

"Thank you for letting me know. Do you need me to bring anything to you guys?"

A pause. Then he heard a faint conversation on the other end of the line, unable to make out most of the words.

"*Warren wants to know if you can bring some of Mrs Carmichael's food if you have the time to get some.*"

Damian chuckled. He's only learned recently that the kitchen manager, Mrs Carmichael and Inspector Warren were siblings. They definitely fought like siblings.

Damian smiled into his phone, "I think I can convince her to give me a picnic basket for those trying to bring one of her favourite people home. Do you have any requests?"

"*Just her brownies,*" Inspector Warren practically yelled so Damian could hear. "*She uses our Grandmother's recipe. She's the only one that gets it right!*"

"*Did you hear that?*"

"Yes," Damian replied, "So whatever she made for lunch

here and the brownies she keeps stocked for Lord Black's sweet tooth. I'll be there soon."

"Thank you," Warren yelled again. *"She keeps threatening me over the phone when I try to put the request in."*

"Bye, Damian," he could hear the eye roll in Bradson's voice. *"See you soon."*

"Bye, Professor."

He hung up the phone and took a deep breath before hastily cleaning up. Mrs Carmichael was going to get a kick out of this request.

Chapter 6: The Vision of the Past

25 October 2010:
Three and a Half Weeks After the Kidnapping,
2 pm...

Inspector Warren entered the interrogation room hyped up with all the sugar that could send a toddler running around. He mostly only ate his sister's *magical* brownies she'd make just for him. Damian half wanted to ask what exactly she put in the Inspector's brownies the next time he saw her; the other half just wanted to leave it for Arthur to figure out when he finally got to learn from the older woman in the kitchens.

Closing the door behind him, Damian and CSI Bradson stood by the one-way glass, studying those inside. However, they still couldn't see the facial features of the person of interest. A court-assigned lawyer was sitting next to them.

"Why did you take the King?" Warren asked.

"It was just a job," the suspect smeared, their voice a little distorted from the spell. *"One I wouldn't have taken if I knew his royal Bratness didn't have fire powers."*

"Why does that matter?" Jotting notes down, Inspector Warren hid his confusion behind a blank face.

"Because he is tainted. He should be bloody living with his bloody cousins!" The suspect shouted as his cover flickered.

"Wow, this Rothbart knew how to pick them," Bradson commented offhand to Damian, who nodded, pensive.

"It doesn't start with where we were supposed to bring him," the suspect continued, *"Why they wanted to take him to Camp is beyond me."*

Damian paled, "D...did he say 'Camp'?"

"I would have been better to... that... that whelp..." The lawyer suddenly elbowed them, *"What was that for!"*

"Do not say anything else!" The lawyer hissed.

"What is he talking about?" Bradson asked her former and

possibly favourite student, as she helped him to one of the nearby chairs, "Why are you so scared?"

He gulped, trying not to heave, "They're not talking about a summer camp with nice themes like music, theatre, or even Scout camp."

Bradson went quiet as fury built in her eyes before she calmly asked, "Those... types of *camps* still exist?"

He nodded miserably. "Not everyone is as accepting as Papa Andros was. If Mother wasn't so determined to get Princess Catherine and me together, she could sent me there for not dating any girls or women. The only time I've gone out with a girl or woman was when a closeted Traditionals' daughter needed to make it look like she was with a male."

"Did that happen often?"

He let a dry chuckle escape. "Only when the heiresses were desperate and needed help. Mother would then yell at me for not being *faithful* to the Princess."

"What?" Bradson asked, confused, "But you aren't with anyone, let alone the Princess."

"*Exactly,*" Damian agreed, frustrated. "And then, Grandmother would scold Mother, saying that no man is expected to go into a marriage without experience. Royalty has double standards as the Princess is expected to remain pure and...*moldable.*"

He stared off for a moment, trying to recollect his thoughts.

"Do you need to go?" Bradson asked, "I understand, so will Warren."

"I think... I think I need to burn off some energy," Damian admitted, feeling wired up. He blinked as he realised she had her cell phone out, "W—who are you texting?"

"*Kaiden Woolf,*" she replied, "He and the Princess will meet you at the Gym if you want to fight someone. He thinks that it would help you."

"What does Lord Black suggest?"

"*The same thing,*" Lord Black snarled, coming up the hall

and stopping beside them. He was barely masking his fury. "They might even have some ideas about how to *break down* some of those horrible locations."

"I think you should go with him," Bradson suggested tightly, "I know you usually have a handle on your emotions, but this affects your family. Go hold your child or see if Kaiden or one of the Spanish guards can give you a challenge."

Aaron nodded sincerely, understanding. He moved to help Damian stand and went out the back way together so the press couldn't see how much this round of integrations affected them.

✠ ✠ ✠

2 hours later...

Damian shook as he entered the private gym scarcely attended by anyone other than the King, Princess and their main guards. He couldn't believe that the henchpeople had been taking Arthur for someone who knew the truth about Arthur and his sexuality. And that they hated that truth. They wanted to punish the King for something he had no control over.

"*Damian?*"Damian forced himself to look where Kaiden stood with Prince Antonio and Princess Catherine.

"Are you alright?" Kaiden continued, "Bradson didn't go into details about what happened. She only said you needed a way to burn off energy."

"We have a good idea about why they took the King," Damian began, but he couldn't talk further. He just wanted to curl into himself. Instead, he started backing up. He didn't think he could continue...

"*We got you,*" Ze Dylan's voice broke through the brain fog. Damian felt their arms wrap around him as they sat down on the floor. "*They can't hurt you here.*"

"*What's happening?*" Damian heard Princess Catherine's plea.

"*Concentrate on my voice,*" Ze Dylan continued. "We figured out how to take them down. Those close-minded bigots have no place in the royal court. Just like those *Camps* have no place in our country."

"Did…did Auncle Dylan say *Camps?*" Damian heard Prince Antonio ask, voice hardening. "*Tío* Félix "

"*Me estoy contactando con tu mamá*" (I'm contacting your mama,) *Tío* Félix interrupted, "*Necesitas su permiso para ir encubierto en un lugar … así. Se sabe que esas ubicaciones rompen a alguien.*" (You need her permission to go undercover in a place… like *that.* Those locations have been known to *break* someone.)

"*¡Por eso tengo que irme!*" (That's why I *have* to go!) Prince Antonio insisted, "*Apuesto a que no tienen idea de que están esperando un rey. Creo que sus expectativas son un príncipe o un niño rico en mal estado.*" (I bet they have no idea they're waiting for a *king.* I think their expectations are either a *prince* or a *spoiled rich kid.*)

"NO!" Damian finally blurted out as he somehow could understand what the Spanish Princes were saying, "I-I can't let you! I wouldn't wish that place on *anyone!*"

Prince Antonio knelt. He wanted to be in Damian's line of vision. He took his hands and squeezed them reassuringly.

"*This is my choice,*" he assured with heavily accented English, "This type of place simply existing is hurting my *familia.* Even the word is hurting you. How many others have been hurt because they don't have an understanding, loving and supporting family like *Tío* Andros loved Auncle Dylan? He put protections in place so everyone can be themselves and be with the ones they love."

"*But–*"

"But nothing," Princess Catherine interrupted, also kneeling. She was pale and shaken by his reaction to something that could greatly harm her brother, "Papa did his best to shield you from Stepmonster. I didn't understand that until now. You are the most courageous man that I've ever come across. Let us help you."

She reached out and took Damian's hand from Prince Antonio. At that moment, his world began to spin. He closed his eyes as the view in his mind eye changed to the past...

✠ ✠ ✠

1514...

"I'm not leaving you," I quietly promised as I approached a young woman dressed elegantly but in mourning clothes, "The King is honouring Art's final wish. I'm remaining with you as long as you're the Princess of Wales."

"How do I still have that title?" She asked as she turned away from me to look out the window, "Wouldn't that go to whoever married Prince Henry? Why are you still guarding me?"

I shake my head, "His Highness cannot be named the Prince of Wales; he is only a male child of the next generation, so only a male child of Prince Henry will next have the title Prince of Wales. And I promised to continue to guard you for the rest of our lives."

She continued staring out the window in silence before turning back to me and continuing. "My father is trying to convince the Pope I'm still pure enough to marry Prince Henry when he comes of age."

I swallow, "You know, I've been part of this world my whole life, and I still don't understand how it works."

She gave me a tight smile, "That's how this life works; I have no say as long as I'm useful to any crown. They raise most princesses with the knowledge that we will bear the next generation of royals and stay quiet if my husband, a fellow royal, takes as many mistresses as he desires.."

"Art wouldn't have..." I start.

"Daniel," she interrupted as she crossed the floor, reaching up to touch my cheek, "I've grown to love you the same way I would have

grown to love Art. You wouldn't have been an affair to me, but a missing piece that would have made life bearable for the both of us."

She pulled her hand away, pushed up on her toes, and kissed my cheek before turning to leave.

The room began spinning again before I could follow...

✠ ✠ ✠

Damian blinked a few times, "C... *Catalina?*"

He asked as he tried to focus his eyes on the *Princesa* in front of him. Her hair was blonde, her face was the same, and she was dressed in gym clothes, not an elegant black dress...

The *Princesa* also blinked, "I... don't usually go by that name. Tonio only calls me that when he's annoyed with me. I've always gone by Anya. Are you okay?"

"I... I don't know," Damian said as Ze Dylan continued to hold him. He needed something solid to keep him grounded. "T... that... hasn't happened to me before."

"What?" Prince Antonio asked.

"Getting a vision while awake and remembering it," he whispered.

Someone nearby took in a sharp breath. But Prince Antonio and Princess Catherine were blocking his view.

Princess Catherine looked over Damian with confusion. "Auncle Dylan, are you alright?"

Clearing their throat and still holding Damian against their chest, Auncle Dylan replied, "That's how it started for Andrew. My older brother's dreams were filled with important events that he couldn't remember until after they happened. However, the ones that he really needed to know started showing up when he touched something or someone."

"W... what..." Damian said, "What does that mean for me?"

The royal cousins looked at each other before glancing at Dylan behind him.

"*We don't know,*" Princess Catherine began.

"But we'll figure this out together," Prince Antonio finished as he put a hand on top of Princess Catherine's.

She never let go of Damian's, and together, their hands radiated a soft glow, sealing the promise.

4 November 2010:
Four Weeks After the Kidnapping...

Halloween came, though no one wanted to celebrate. Even Princess Catherine refused to come out for the party planned for her and Arthur over the past months. Mother was furious until most guests who had R.S.V.P. before the King's kidnapping and disappearance pulled out. Then Damian, with the backing of Inspector Warren, Lords Black, and Wales, informed Mother that there wouldn't be any party at all, with the massive security nightmare it would have been.

Mother threw a fit. Damian had been half-hoping she would say something revealing about the kidnapping. However, Grandmother Murrian managed to reel her in before she could do that. He was successful in not showing his disappointment in front of them. Instead, he expressed his anger in private.

"AHAAH!!!" He finally exclaimed.

The papers fell victim to his anger as he pushed them off his desk. He took a few deep breaths, hoping to bring down his anger. Suddenly, a sharp knock was on the door, *"Come in!"*

Jose quietly opened the door before calmly closing it behind him, "Are you alright, Sir?"

"Why?" Damian slumped into his chair, *"Why* is this so hard?"

"Because you care," Jose replied as he bent and picked up the papers, "Those women might even say you care too much, that you wear your heart on your sleeve as they seem to have roles of the Evil Stepmother, the Queen of Hearts, and Drucilla covered."

Damian pinched the bridge of his nose. Sure, compared to *them,* he did wear his heart on his sleeve. On the other hand, Princess Catherine was more emotionally expressive towards him, even after recovering from his panic attack a few days ago.

"Have you gotten any updates from Inspector Warren or

Professor—er— *CSI Bradson?*" Jose asked as he placed some papers on the desk, "Um, have you seen this?"

Damian looked up to see Jose holding a thick envelope with his name on it, written in rapid formula script. Jose passed it to the young lord. He hastily took it and threw it into a nearby trash can. He turned away from the trash can as he brushed his hands together, satisfied.

"Uh," Jose started, "I wouldn't celebrate just yet."

Damian turned back just in time to see the bloody letter *lifting* itself *out* of the trash can. His mouth mimicked a fish, *"What the hell?"*

"Someone *really* wants you to listen to them," Jose muttered. "How many letters has this been?"

"Twenty," Damian grumbled.

Jose blinked, "Twenty throughout..."

Damian's face firmed, "Twenty in the last week alone. It's been happening since we found the first letter in the Warehouse."

"Why haven't you responded?" Jose asked, wide-eyed.

"Because they are as vague as hell and want me to go—" he gulped, *"North."*

"And why haven't you listened?"

"Y-you think I should?"

"If someone sent you twenty letters in one week, I'd say they desperately want your attention about *something*. What's keeping you from this?" Jose asked dryly.

"What's keeping me from the letters?" Damian retorted tiredly, "Mother and her brilliant ideas about a birthday party that no one, including one of the Guests of Honour, wants to celebrate. I also have to deal with the security nightmare of protecting Princess Catherine and other royals. And, and... I *still* don't know where Prince Harry is—"

"He's with his military troops out of the country," Jose interrupted. "This happened under Lord Black and is his last assignment."

"It is a *'need to know'*," Damian nodded. "Did he at least tell Inspector Warren?"

Jose nodded, "It was agreed that you wouldn't be told for safety reasons."

"The less people that know about security movements of a royal, the better," Damian waved off, "At least, he's nowhere near here to be in danger of the madness."

Damian completely missed the change of expression on Jose's face. His old friend knew more than he could say, though Damian would find out soon enough.

✠ ✠ ✠

26 November 2010:
Eight Weeks After the Kidnapping...

Damian was tired and frustrated. He kept getting notes only he could read and missed his self-imposed deadline to find Arthur by his 18th birthday on Halloween. This was how he found himself walking with his favourite Professor turned Lead CSI lab tech, Bradson. They were heading to observe Inspector Warren make another attempt and interrogate one of the henchpeople.

"His name is still not available to us," Bradson grumbled. "He gave a generic name, but at least he no longer looks like the guard he was impersonating."

"What name did he give?"

"John Doe."

"How original," Damian replied dryly.

"The other two are listed as *'None of your business'* and *'I'm not telling,'*" she continued with a shrug as Damian stared at her in horror.

"Please tell me you're kidding!"

She shook her head, "The officers report they look disgruntled every time they call them that, too."

"Now I don't know if I should laugh or scoff," Damian

muttered as they reached the interrogation room, "Because they have brought that upon themselves. Now, who are we interrogating today?"

"*None of your business,*" Bradson replied with a straight face. "And no, the one who referred to the *Camp* was John Doe."

"Oh goody," Damian grumbled, "At least this one won't trigger me—"

"Well," Inspector Warren started as they joined him, "This one is just as bad as John Doe," Warren replied, "They have been using a photo of Ze Black for dart practice."

"You better not let Lord Black know that," Damian said.

"Too late," Lord Black grumbled as he joined them.

"It might be better to go over those letters you keep submitting finally," Warren continued.

"First, why and what letters? I didn't submit any letters." Damian asked, confused.

"Ah yes," Lord Black hummed, "I've been submitting them for you when they show up on my desk after you binned them! We should go over those letters you keep ignoring, Damian."

"Why is everyone interested in those damn letters?" Damian requested as Bradson led him and Lord Black away from the Interrogation Room.

"Because it took *years* for Matthew to trust me with information about his birth family," Lord Black replied wearily. "His brother desperately tries to get your attention in fifty letters in three weeks. I barely got that many in the fifteen years Matthew has been in our lives."

Damian blinked.

"*Wow,*" Bradson said. "That's desperate. Why does he want you?"

"He...wants to meet me," Damian admitted.

Lord Black crossed his arms. "And?"

"And he wants me to '*follow the glitter*'."

"Now, was that so hard?" Lord Black said playfully, grinning. "The glitter part—"

Ring, ring!

Lord Black hastily pulled out his phone. His grin disappeared as he read the number. "Excuse me for a moment."

He stepped away as Bradson dragged Damian to the lab station and made him sit beside a pile of letters. There was a new letter sitting on top of the pile.

"Why won't you do what this person is asking?" She finally asked.

Damian groaned, "Not you, too?"

"It's a simple question," She replied, "Let me guess, Princess Catherine's security?"

Damian nodded, "She and Mother have been clashing more as she goes stir crazy. It is helping that Kate and Prince Wills are trapped there with her, though now that Prince Antonio is preparing for a crazy mission–"

"What mission?"

"Oh," Damian paused, "I… I don't think I can say."

Bradson nodded, "Of security reasons, right?"

Damian nodded, too.

"How about I help out?"

"How?"

"Would you feel better if I stayed where Princess Catherine and Prince William are?" She asked. "I can easily coordinate with Warren, and both Lords Black and Wales have already cleared me."

"Are you sure?"

"I wouldn't be offering if I wasn't sure," Bradson pointed out. "Besides, Princess Catherine would burn anyone who tried to take her, but it doesn't hurt to have extra protection."

"Okay," Damian said, feeling some weight lift off his shoulders. "Do you think these letters have other clues of where I need to go?"

"Oh, I hope so," she grinned. "Matthew must be more important than the main villain must have known for someone to be sending you so many letters. Do you think Lord Black will be going with you?"

"I think he would if he didn't have one last mission to look after," Damian replied, "Should I open the newest one?"

She nodded, "It just got here. It's as if this person knew you would be here today."

"Okay," Damian grumbled as he lifted the heavy envelope and opened it.

He took out a sheet of old-world parchment, processing what he held as Lord Black rushed to the workstation. *"Sir?"*

"I won't be coming," Lord Black muttered, a little wide-eyed. "Prince Harry's been compromised. He'll be meeting up with you instead."

"How was Prince Harry compromised?" Damian demanded.

"How else?" Lord Black deadpanned, "It's a necessary evil of our job."

"The press has figured out where Prince Harry was?" Bradson guessed as Damian groaned.

Of *course*, it was the Press.

"Well, this letter makes a lot of sense now," Damian muttered as he held it up for Bradson and Lord Black to see. "Whoever sent this said I should ask Prince Harry for help."

Damian returned his attention to the note to study the words more closely. In the process, he missed his two mentors doing a double take with each other.

Chapter 8: Giving Report?

1 December 2010:
Eight and a Half Weeks After the Kidnapping...

Damian breathed in the frozen air as he looked around in awe. The snow-covered buildings reminded him strongly of a village or small town in Northern Scotland or Norway. It had features similar to those of the oldest village in Norway. He half wondered if this village was built around the same time. He passed a sign that read:

The Giving Village.

Harry led him to the largest, most elegant building in the village. It reminded him strongly of a town hall or a very small royal residence. As they approached, a familiar woman emerged from the double doors.

She spotted them and started waving. Her braided dark hair fell down her shoulder. On her head was a fluffy white hat. Her body was covered in an equally fluffy white coat.

"Who is that?" Damian asked, confused, "Why is she waving at us?"

Harry laughed again as he slapped Damian's back, "I wish you luck."

"Why?" Damian asked, "Wait, where are you going? Why can't you tell me who she is?"

"I've got to check in with Lady Mina, the Head Healer; she'll want to make sure I didn't get injured while serving in Afghanistan," Harry continued, "And you know *exactly* who she is. It will come to you."

Damian blinked a few times after Harry had left him standing at the entrance of a bigger version of a Christmas Village. He wasn't sure why the Scottish Prince was being cryptic. Why hasn't anyone been able to give him a straight answer for the last few weeks?

'All this snow and glitter is finally getting to me,' he thought bitterly.

Damian had to stare at the woman real hard. *'Where have I seen her before?'* He questioned himself. He found himself trying to hold his hands up like a frame as she smiled...

His heart dropped to his stomach. Has he had his whole life up to this point been for nothing? The familiar woman was someone Damian had only ever seen in photos and official portraits Mother desperately wished she could get rid of.

"*Damian?*" The woman asked as he approached, concern in her tone. "Are you alright?"

Damian could only stare for a moment before he started imitating a fish, taking a few tries to find the right words... "Queen Eve?"

A small smile came to her face, "Yes, Damian?"

"How... how are you *alive?*" He croaked out.

"Your journal saved my life."

"My... *journal?*"

She nodded, "The one you started over ten years ago."

"But that was to Santa..." he trailed off as an older man with white hair and a white beard joined them.

Damian couldn't tell if the rosy cheeks were from the cold or were natural. He was dressed in a red coat, hat, and pants. The coat and hat happened to have white fur on the edge...

The older man chuckled, sounding like *ho, ho, ho,* pulled Damian from his thoughts.

"I understand you don't believe I'm real anymore," the Jolly man said with a little grin.

Suddenly, he was tackled from behind. He tried to do everything to keep standing up.

"Damian."

"Arthur!" Damian exclaimed as he turned, accidentally forcing Arthur to let him go, "How are you here?"

Arthur grinned; he was also in five to six layers, "The elves will do anything to protect Grandfather Christmas' family."

Damian blinked, "Grandfather Christmas? Do you mean *Santa*, like the immortal jolly old man that delivers gifts to little boys and girls that believe in him?"

"There are different ways to be immortal," Arthur replied with a barely visible shrug, "Simply making *Santa* a title makes it look like he's an immortal, jolly old man. Every version of *Santa* that exists has a little bit of every *Santa* that has been *Santa*."

Damian turned back briefly to look at Arthur's grandfather. He eyed the older man for a moment before turning back to Arthur.

"Where's his... belly?" Damian asked quietly, trying not to offend Arthur's grandfather.

"Damian!" Arthur hissed, "That is some ad for Coca-Cola in the United States that has been around since the 1930s! It takes a fit man or woman to use powers to burn through sugar like water. Then, Grandfather Christmas' whitish blonde hair comes with his powers."

Damian's silent processing before declaring loudly, "You're telling Anya about this. I don't have it in me to let her use me for target practice anymore!"

Arthur shook his head as laughter from Queen Eve and Grandfather Christmas washed over them. Arthur quickly grabbed one of Damian's gloved hands.

"Hi," Arthur greeted, "Welcome to the North Pole, or *the Giving Village*. It just depends on who you ask."

"Thanks," Damian said, unsure if his heated cheeks were from the cold or embarrassment, "Um, I have something to say."

"Me too—" Arthur started as he started moving closer.

"Excuse me," a voice beside them said. "I'm so sorry to interrupt, but I need to talk to you, Agent Damian."

"Were you the one responsible for all the notes?" Damian finally asked, masking his frustration about not getting to kiss Arthur.

"Yes, Agent," the... *being* replied. For the first time, Damian noticed his ears, which he knew were associated with the legend of elves, "I need your help with the missing parts of the story, and we need to collaborate with what the others have found."

Damian nodded before reluctantly pulling his hands away from Arthur's.

"Come find me in the kitchen when you're done," Arthur urged. "I'll be helping Grandmother Christmas getting cookies and cocoa ready."

"Of course," Damian agreed, "The kitchen would have been the first place I would have looked for you anyway."

"Where's the second place?" Arthur asked.

Damian grinned, half turned away, "Our favourite place in the world. I would have asked where the nearest library was and found you in the History Section, trying to ensure history doesn't repeat itself."

Arthur returned the grin, as he was exactly right.

✠ ✠ ✠

2 hours later...

The man... being... *The Elf* that interrupted what should have been his first kiss with Arthur turned out to be one of the most important beings behind the scenes. This being was, well, *him*, for the North Pole/Giving Village. This is how he has found himself being led into the office of an *elf!* The nameplate on the front of him read *Alfred Lightfeather*. Matthew Evers Black was already sitting in one of the chairs.

"Matthew!" Damian exclaimed as he sat in the open chair, "You're alright!"

The older man nodded with a grin, "My mother patched me up nicely. Are you ready for your debriefing?"

"Debriefing? Is that what we're calling this? How am I one of your agents?" Damian asked, so tired that he wasn't giving them time to answer, "I've never met you before, and I don't know how Matthew fits into this whole mess."

"We've gotten many, many letters over the years from

children worldwide, Agent, but never an entire journal," Alfred explained as he knocked on a familiar book on his desk, "A journal that warned us Lady *Queen* Eve and Heir Nathan are in danger."

"M...*my* journal?" Damian asked again as memories slowly washed over him

⛨ ⛨ ⛨

12 May 1999: Eleven Years
Before the Kidnapping...

Jose could only stare at the boy he had been asked to help with reading and writing. The twelve-year-old rubbed his eyes tiredly, hoping he hadn't heard Damian wrong. The two of them were sitting in the school library, as it was the only safe place Damian could think of without exposing his new friend to Mother, Aunt, and Grandmother.

"You don't know who Santa Claus is?" Jose finally squeaked.

*"I just said that," Damian muttered, confused and tense, "Mother doesn't believe in anything **magical**, so why would I know anything that has to do with myths or magic?"*

"So, you don't celebrate the holidays at all?" Jose muttered.

Damian nodded, confused.

"Not even Easter and Halloween?"

"Not even those," Damian confirmed, "I think it has to do with Grandfather Murrian being in prison for crimes against the Crown..."

"Your Grandfather was Henry Murrian!" Jose exclaimed.

"Shh!" Damian hissed, "Please don't get us thrown out! This is my place of sanity away from my family."

Jose nodded as he zipped his mouth.

*"Mother had given up on **magic** a long time ago when every prayer and wish to **release** Grandfather didn't work. Not when he's considered a traitor to the English Crown."*

"Is that why you were homeschooled before this?"

Damian gave him a weird look before nodding, "But what does that have to do with anything?"

"*Everything!*" Jose muttered, "*While I think your mother might have been protecting you from disappointment, you saw my reaction about your grandfather.*"

"*Unfortunately,*" Damian replied, exasperated, "*Now, everyone just looks at me with pity. I'm always getting lumped into Mother's schemes, and this happens to be the newest one.*"

"*Do you know what that scheme is?*"

Damian nodded bitterly, "*There's a rumour going around among the nobles that King Andros and Queen Eve will be sending Princess Catherine and Prince Arthur here in the fall.*"

Jose smacked his face, "*So she wants you here for good, old-fashioned, brown-nosing.*"

Damian snorted, "*I didn't think about it like that.*"

"*Well, then I know how I can justify adding magic, myth, legend, and Santa Claus to our tutoring sessions,*" Jose declared with a grin.

"*And how's that?*"

"*One, the royal twins always have a Halloween-themed birthday party,*" Jose continued, "*And two, the Royal Family goes all out on their Christmas parties. Besides, you should have been exposed to the existence of Santa Claus at five, even if she didn't do anything earlier. If this is your first year going to school instead of private tutors, then it makes sense that you're learning about it now!*"

"*Oh,*" Damian replied, relaxing, "*I guess. Can you tell me more?*"

☩ ☩ ☩

15 May 1999: Eleven Years
Before the Kidnapping...

Damian quietly entered the one room in the house that Mother would never willingly enter. The library had become his haven on that principle alone. She would even send a servant looking for him if she needed him for something.

In part of the library, there was a desk that no one used and he had claimed as his own. He sat down at the desk with a dark brown leather journal he found stuck between the shelves. It spoke to him for some reason.

Damian stared at the book for a few minutes. He honestly didn't know what to write about or if he had the guts to add the title 'Dear Santa'. All he knew was that the paper would never leave the journal.

That was when he heard: "It's all set to happen within the next week, Milady."

The dark, slimy voice sent shivers down his spine. It was the voice of the one who did all the family's dirty work.

Damian stood quiet. Slowly, he tipped-toed his way to the partially open door leading to his Grandmother's office. Neither Grandmother nor this slimy, dishevelled man she was talking to realised that the door was ajar and that he was listening in.

"Wonderful," Grandmother replied, glee evident in her voice, "Is the plan still to use the cover of the upcoming storm?"

"Yes, Ma'am," the creepy man continued, "I'll make sure the car carrying the Pretender and the Royal brats crashes, and I'll make it look like an accident so the King and his freaky family would be too upset to think otherwise."

"My daughter will make an excellent queen," Grandmother gushed. Then her tone turned darker as she warned, "Make sure no one catches you. I won't be able to help you if someone does, Wilhelm."

"I won't be caught! My plan is foolproof!" Wilhelm boasted, "Nothing will be able to stop this!"

Damian backed away from the door. He hastily grabbed his journal and retreated deeper into the Library, unknowingly choosing the History Section. He settled himself on a window bench and started writing:

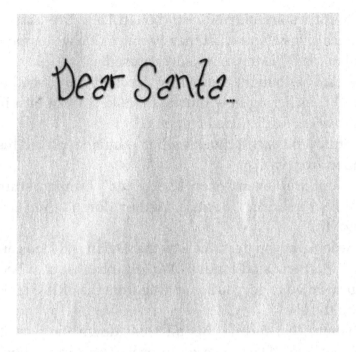

✣ ✣ ✣

Miles away, elven magic created a casting of a book with a likeness to Damian's journal. Pages started appearing, filling out with concerns of a little boy. Ella, a blonde elf maiden on duty, rushed out to find Alfred.

A storm was coming…

✣ ✣ ✣

Damian's face flushed as he came out of his memories. He realised what he might have written in the journal in more recent years. He wasn't prepared to talk to Alfred, the Head of Security for the North Pole, about some of those entries.

"How does that work?" Damian finally asked, trying to deal with his embarrassment, "What about anything… *explicit?*"

"The magic doesn't let us see anything private," Alfred assured hastily, not understanding why Damian was blushing.

"Many entries are blurred out, though Lady Eve has drawn her conclusions about what may or may not have happened."

"Like *what?*" Damian asked, confused.

"Well, she thought the two of you had been together for a while, considering how much you talked about him in the entries we *can* see," Alfred continued.

Matthew bit back a chuckle when Damian repeated his fish imitation from earlier.

"B- but we haven't even kissed yet!" Damian stuttered before backtracking. "Besides, Arthur doesn't even *like* me that way!"

"He looks at you the same way that Dylan and I look at each other," Matthew said fondly, "We fell into that trap because Arthur wanted to get you something from the PRIDE table just beyond the alley."

"B–but...that means this all went down the way it did because of me!" Damian tried to protest as Alfred shook his head.

"Don't blame yourself, Agent," Alfred soothed. "Those men would have gotten my brother and King Arthur without the change in his schedule. As long as those goons and that head goon had your grandmother's protection, we could do nothing to get them."

"And now?" Damian croaked, feeling overwhelmed.

Alfred grinned, "The head goon lost that protection when he chose to stay behind, pretending to *be* Matthew. His arrogance was his downfall. He also didn't have enough information."

Damian's eyes widened, "Like how he didn't know how close Matthew actually was to the English Royal Family and who he was to them when they weren't in the public eye."

Alfred nodded, smug, as Matthew's face was bright red.

"I like *some* privacy." Matthew protested.

"And that helped us catch the one man keeping the rest of the English Royal Family from going home," Alfred assured his brother. "We just need to get the rest of the schemers before-"

"There's *more* schemers?" Damian groaned. *"Wait,* don't tell me. Mother, Aunt Karen, and Grandmother Murrian."

Alfred nodded again, "I have worries about others, but those three affect you and have direct contact with you."

Damian sighed, "Honestly, this is just one more thing they're going down for. I've been working with both CSI Bradson and Inspector Warren to figure out what other misdeeds they have committed over the years. CSI Bradson is an old professor who loves mothering others. She practically moved into Buckingham Palace when I was hesitant to leave for this mission even though Princess Catherine has a protector in both Ze Dylan and Kaiden Woolf."

"And Inspector Warren?"

"Before this, I only knew him by reputation," Damian continued, "We studied several of his cases in the informational side of CSI Bradson's class. One of the things I got from those case studies was that he doesn't give up, and if something is out of place, he picks it up and keeps working with it until it fits the information he has."

"Do you have any questions?" Alfred asked.

Damian nodded before turning to Matthew, "How did you and Arthur get here?"

Matthew grinned, "Let's get Arthur. He knows more about the rescue as I was… *out of commission."*

Alfred snorted, "That's putting it lightly."

Matthew rolled his eyes, "You can't wait for this story either."

"Of course," Alfred agreed as they stood, *"Mor* (Mother) forbade me from asking any questions until after Damian got here. She always knows when our matches come or back into our lives."

Damian stared at them, *"Matches?"*

Alfred chuckled as Matthew's grin widened.

"Mor has a type of sight that allows her to see the person you'll end up with," Matthew continued as they started moving

out of the office, "If you end up under her care, she *sees* more than what's in front of her."

"Prince Harry left me to find her," Damian muttered, "Is that a good thing?"

"It is when you've been in a warzone like he was," Alfred explained. "She's able to rebalance energies. She would go to him over the holidays if he couldn't get here. She'll be working on his energy for the next few hours."

"So he won't be joining our story," Damian said.

"At least not right away," Matthew continued. "Now, where's Arthur?"

"The kitchen," Damian replied as Alfred looked amused. "I can't wait to have some of his cookies and hot chocolate."

"Ahh, Grandmother Christmas rarely lets anyone into her kitchen," Matthew agreed, "Arthur and Lady Eve are the only ones who are truly allowed in there without any supervision or to help her out."

Damian stopped short, and his mind reset.

"*Sir,*" Alfred asked as he also stopped, "Are you alright?"

"The children of Santa Claus and Mrs Claus are Nicholas and Eve... for *Christmas Eve?*" Damian questioned as the brothers laughed.

Matthew nodded, "Grandmother Christmas has been teased many times over the years for that."

"But I wouldn't have it any other way," Grandmother Christmas commented as she entered the kitchen, "Why don't you boys take the cookie trays? Damian, can you grab the hot cocoa?"

"Yes, Ma'am," the three respond together.

Grandmother Christmas then turned to Arthur, "You can take the tea for your mother."

"Yes, Grandmother Christmas," Arthur replied, "Are you joining us?"

"But of course," Grandmother Christmas replied as she took off her flour-covered Chef's coat and threw it in a nearby hamper. "Healer Lady Mina just cleared you, and your partner is here to listen to the whole story. I wouldn't miss hearing about Matheo's folly."

She grinned as Matthew groaned, "Are you *all* going to use that against me?"

"*For the rest of time,*" Alfred teased.

"Where are we bringing these, Ma'am?" Matthew asked, trying to avoid his brother.

"The main living room," She replied, "Where Noel should *not be trying to light a fire without supervision!*" Her voice got louder with every word, "*NOEL MARIE!*"

"*I didn't do it!*" A young girl's voice protested back.

"Noel?" Damian asked Arthur, "Who's she?"

Arthur grinned, "My little sister."

Damian grimaced, "She has fire powers?"

Arthur nodded, "At least this one doesn't have the urge to throw a fireball at you."

"*Yet!*" Damian muttered, "Just wait until your sisters meet. Your uncle is going to be asking Alfred for a permanent Elf Agent—*wait...*"

Alfred laughed, "Don't worry; I already have a list of volunteer agents who would like to keep an eye on the young princess."

"Oh *goodie*," Damian replied dryly, "Just feeling the tension between Kaiden and Princess Catherine was *hard* to keep from saying anything."

"*Mor* should be able to give you an idea of where you should start looking for Noel's match," Matthew pointed out as they came to a big living room where there were already four others.

Damian recognised Queen-Lady Eve and Santa, who was no longer wearing his red coat. He could only assume Prince Nathan and Princess Noel were the others in the room. Prince Nathan had features like Santa, while Princess Noel looked more like a much younger Princess Catherine.

"Umm," Damian started as he entered the room. He moved

to the centre of the room to put down his tray on the coffee table. He could feel two sets of eyes burning into him, *"Hi."*

Suddenly, the young prince and princess tackled him from the front. All he could hear over the laughter was: *"Thank you, thank you, thank you!"*

It was then that it hit him… he had saved *three* lives… with his *journal*. He pulled them closer. He couldn't save their father, but he would do everything in his power to keep these two safe from his insane family.

"Okay!" Arthur exclaimed, "Let's settle on the couch."

"I claim one side!" Noel demanded as she pulled away and ran to the couch. "I want to sit with my protector!"

"But-" Nathan and Arthur both protest.

Damian felt warmth spread over him. A Drago girl that *actually* liked him! He followed, dragging Nathan and Arthur with him. He had an idea, and the young princess squealed as he had Nathan and Arthur sit on the couch before he picked her up. He then sat down between the two princes with the princess on his lap. His left knee was touching Arthur's right.

"How's that?" Damian asked as the other adults laughed.

"Good!" The three siblings exclaimed together.

"Alright, *Lille Bjørn,*" Lady Eve continued, "Do you want any cocoa before story time?"

"Umm, just a cookie for now," Arthur replied as Noel settled on his and Damian's laps.

"Damian?" She asked.

"Both, please," he requested.

Lady Eve nodded as she poured the hot chocolate. She then passed out the hot chocolate, cookies, and tea before settling in her chair. Once Arthur finished his cookie, he began to speak.

"Alright, I think I need to start before the kidnapping took place—"

Damian closed his eyes as the events began drifting through his mind…

Chapter 9: Arthur's Great... Escape

24 September 2010:
One Week Before the Kidnapping...

Books were scattered all over the floor in the History Section of the Royal Library. He couldn't, for the life of him, figure out why he could see the information required for his first major history paper for his last year of school... and no one else could. The Royal Librarian, Lady Belle, would cringe and kick him out if she were to see the mess he made—king or no king, no one harms her precious books, not even Arthur, who was ready to pull his hair out with frustration.

Arthur sighed as he closed yet another history textbook, pushing it away from him. He couldn't use anything in it nor tell anyone what he learned. All he knew was that this spell was affecting his teacher and classmates. The professor had kindly given him an extension to rewrite the paper.

"Arth fach?"

Arthur looked up, relieved, when he realised that Uncle Aaron stood at the entrance of the History Section and not Lady Belle. The older man has been a lifeline for him and Anya for the last few months. He would run interference between them and Stepmonster. He was also training them to rule together.

Uncle Aaron stared at him momentarily before hastily crossing the room to the table.

"May I please read your paper?" Uncle Aaron requested. His voice had a weird tone Arthur had only heard a few times. It was like a mix of hope and apprehension.

"Sure," Arthur shrugged, not expecting that Uncle Aaron would be able to read the whole thing. He handed over the typed paper.

Uncle Aaron sat down across from him. Arthur watched quietly as a small smile slowly made its way across the older man's face. This was a true smile—one that lit up Uncle Aaron's grey eyes.

Confusion rushed through Arthur with every page that Uncle Aaron turned.

"Uncle Aaron?" Arthur spoke up after a few minutes, "Are you okay?"

The usually calm, cool, and collected older lord had tears silently rolling down his cheeks while maintaining his smile. He put down the paper. Their eyes met.

"How could you find, let alone see, the information about the women of your family line?" Uncle Aaron asked after a moment.

"I don't know..." Arthur trailed off, "Wait! You were really able to read my paper?"

Uncle Aaron nodded as he whipped away a stray tear, "I just don't understand how you could read the original information, as there was a spell cast to keep your father ignorant about his mother and grandmother."

"But you can!" Arthur exclaimed, wide-eyed, "Does it have to do with Grandmother and Grandfather's deaths happening around the time Papa was born?"

Uncle Aaron nodded, a little happier than Arthur had ever seen him.

"Your grandfather and I weren't born into royalty, but he married into it," Uncle Aaron continued, looking relieved that he could explain, "Your grandmother was a descendent of a long line of Queens, and there were and still are people among the nobles who didn't like that."

Arthur tapped his knuckles on the book in the centre of the table, "But that doesn't explain why my professor can't read the pages in this book or parts of my paper."

Uncle Aaron's smile turned grim and tight. "They call themselves 'Traditionalists', but they are menaces and don't remember that if you go back far enough in their family lines that they had humble beginnings. The only reason why they're even considered nobles is because someone far enough back from their family married the Queen of England. They're using your grandparents' death to change the narrative back to a patriarchal line."

Arthur gulped, feeling the weight on his shoulders getting heavier. "So, they used a spell to rewrite history, essentially censoring several generations–including the Royal Family. Leaving them ignorant of our true history, making me their heir and king in the process!"

Uncle Aaron nodded tiredly.

"For what?" Arthur groaned, "Why in the world would they put on a... a... gag order!?"

"Control is my best guess. The Traditionalists want to control the power of the Royal Family and who marries into it. Their worst nightmare is a strong, independent woman who only marries the royal bodyguard that can keep up with her."

Arthur blinked, processing what Uncle Aaron said. "Wait, is that how my grandparents met?"

Uncle Aaron's face relaxed as his grin returned. Memories must have danced through his mind as he briefly went silent. Arthur couldn't remember a time when Uncle Aaron looked so—relaxed.

"U–Uncle Aaron?" Arthur quietly questioned, regretting having to retrieve him from his memories.

"We graduated from the military university with high marks," Uncle Aaron finally continued, leaving his memories. "The Lord Security at the time thought one of us had a chance of keeping up with the headstrong princess that was your grandmother."

Arthur felt happiness rising in his chest, excited to learn more about his family's past. "Is that why you hired Kaiden? He's the only one that has been able to keep up with Anya."

Uncle Aaron's smile grew as he leaned in, "Hopefully, they admit their feelings soon, or I'm getting Kaiden's work partner to lock them in the corner room down the hall."

Arthur felt a grin come to his face, "That should be fun. But something drastic has to happen to get them to admit their feelings, especially with Stepmonster's feelings toward romancing the 'help'." He then looked down at the book again, seeing it differently than before. Arthur thought quietly for a moment before looking back at Uncle Aaron. "Do you think the spell is losing its power?"

Uncle Aaron shook his head. "I can't tell your Auncle or sister the truth. Anyone born after your father won't discover the truth until Anya comes into her final power."

"What power is that? And how do you know it's Anya?"

Uncle Aaron stood. He carefully moved around the scattered mess of literature on the floor to the shelf of historical legend books. Running his hand over the hardcovers, he stopped at a deep blue book, pulled it off the shelf, returned to Arthur's table, and placed it in front of him.

"Legends of the Royal Family Lines and Animal Spirits," Arthur read aloud before looking back to his uncle. "What is this?"

"I believe this will explain how I know about Anya and what her last power will be," Uncle Aaron replied, "Your cousin has already come into her last power because of her life-threatening illness. The rules on how the next ruler is chosen are different for each country."

"And Dad?" Arthur asked, "Did he ever transform?"

Uncle Aaron shook his head, "Your father was the only ruler of his generation who never gained the final power but was chosen to rule by the people. That was because he wasn't the right gender."

"And Papa wasn't non-binary like Auncle Dylan," Arthur finished, using a term he'd overheard Kaiden use as he opened the book, "What are you going to do?"

"I'm going to learn more about the spell used on the gag order. You shouldn't be able to see anything about the female rulers of our family," Uncle Aaron replied, eyes sparkling with excitement. "Before you get settled, you might want to pick up these books lest Lady Belle finds out and bans you for the rest of your life."

Arthur gave his uncle a sheepish look, "Erm, oops?"

Uncle Aaron chuckled, "You're so much like Andros. Lady Belle's father was always after him to clean up after one of his research binges."

Arthur squirmed in his seat with excitement, "Can you tell me more about them later?"

"I would love to," Uncle Aaron nodded. "They would be so proud of you and only want you to be yourself."

"Even if it goes against every tradition?" Arthur asked worriedly. "I can't... bring myself to be with a woman, not even for an heir... that I'm gay..."

The older man reached across and squeezed Arthur's hand,

"Your father would be putting up the rainbow flag as we speak. Your grandmother would be trying to hug all the doubt from you. Your grandfather would be trying to help you figure out what you need to be yourself. And your mother... well, your mother's best friend is now married to Dylan, so..."

Arthur grinned at his uncle's assessment.

"Now, I've heard Anya has challenged Kaiden to yet another sparring match. I want to witness that," Uncle Aaron said, his tone laced with mischief.

Waving at Uncle Aaron as they simultaneously shook their heads at each other, Arthur looked down at the new book on the table, deciding he'd clean up his mess when he finished.

As Uncle Aaron turned to leave the alcove, unbeknownst to them, someone had overheard their entire conversation. They slipped away just in time, ready to tell their Lady what they heard.

☩ ☩ ☩

1 October 2010:
Twelve Hours After the Kidnapping...

Arthur groaned, head pounding. He blinked a few times, trying to will the headache away. He's *never* letting Antonio convince him to go on a drinking bender with him again.

Why the hell did that memory play through my head? Arthur thought as a weird clicking noise kept ringing in his ears. He moved his hand to try and rub his eyes.

Cold metal against his skin caused him to blink a few times with confusion. His eyes adjusted to the semi-darkness as he pulled his hands away from his face, only to realise they were locked in iron mittens with chains. He shifted his legs to realise they were bound in metal as an attempt to keep him in place.

If these events were happening to anyone else, it would have been a great time to panic...

"*Fools,*" he whispered.

Arthur closed his eyes, concentrated on the shackles, and

pushed the dirt particles out of the iron. The shackles weakened enough that when he clapped his metal-covered hands together, they simply *shattered* like glass.

He cringed, certain the noise was bound to bring whoever took him captive running to the room. He hastily bent over to pull the broken shackles off his ankles before shaking the iron dust particles off his body, noticing his missing socks and shoes. But bare feet only made his earth powers stronger, not weaker.

Arthur quickly crossed the concrete floor to the only door to the room, using the shadows to hide along the wall. He listened for a few minutes, hoping his half-brained kidnappers didn't come investigating.

When they never showed, Arthur inched his way along the wall. He carefully grasped the doorknob and turned it.

Locked.

Okay, the kidnappers weren't completely stupid.

However, this wasn't a problem for Arthur. Placing his hand on the knob, he checked to see if he could unlock it from his side, finding the keyhole a moment later. He crouched to peer through, hoping to see something on the other side, though he saw only darkness.

Knowing he should leave the door intact in case his kidnappers came back as he explored, Arthur returned to where he was shackled.

Arthur still had to find Uncle Matthew; he couldn't leave behind one of the few people who knew his mother. Holding out his left hand, he summoned the slightly broken ankle shackles to him. Once in his hands, he took the thicker cuff and broke off the chain, letting it fall to the ground as he lightly *pushed* the broken cuff with his powers—the dirt particles started moving under his grasp, then shifted into the shape of a key.

Arthur then returned to the door to try the key, turning it to the right and prayed to the spirits that his makeshift key would work.

CLICK!

He did a little jig at that most wonderful noise, then cautiously pushed the door open and stuck his head out slightly. He looked left, then right, pushing the door open more once he knew the hallway was clear. Grinning, he noticed the hallway floor was also cement.

Most people would cringe at the thought of walking on cement ground in the middle of a construction zone. However, this only worked to Arthur's advantage. Not only did the cement keep his footsteps silent, but he could also 'see' where other people were in the building without having to turn on any lights, like a metal detector or ground-penetration equipment. He moved his way down the hall to where he could determine what room his kidnappers had been camping out in.

"When is Wilhelm going to be released?" Arthur heard one of the henchpeople whine, *"We didn't rough him up enough that he'd have to stay in the hospital overnight!"*

"Hopefully soon," another replied, *"I don't know how much longer we can keep His Bratness from waking up without causing more head trauma. He must be in one piece for Proof of Life and delivery to the next location."*

"Bratness?" Arthur whispered. *"Where have I heard that before?"*

"Your Bratness!" a third henchperson yelled as they appeared from around the corner, swinging a flashlight widely.

Arthur hastily dropped *into* the cement. The ground gave him perfect cover to hide from the idiots who had no idea he had earth powers. Thank the gods that Tio Félix and Promo Tonio taught him this move.

The other two came running into the hall. They each were carrying flashlights. They flashed them up and down the hall. The power wasn't turned on in the building in some places.

"Wait, where did he go?!" the person who stumbled upon Arthur demanded as they swung their flashlight again.

The first of the henchpeople approached. "You let His Bratness escape?! You were supposed to be watching him!"

"Those bloody chains were fireproof! *You* didn't put them on tight enough!"

As the two argued, the henchperson trailing behind knelt. Their light had caught on something: a pile of pebbles Arthur left behind when he hid in the ground. "Hey, guys—"

"What?!?" The other two snapped together.

"His Bratness doesn't control fire…" The one examining the pile said as they started to stand in a panic. Their jaw dropped as Arthur reemerged from within the cement, appearing behind the others, who quickly turned to see what was behind them.

"I don't *have* any fire powers," Arthur finished, his arms extended and hands curled as he forced iron-like vines to twist around the three henchpeople. He then used the vines to push them back into the room they had come from and pulled the door shut. Then, he grabbed a rock and slammed it down onto the doorknob, jamming the lock and rendering it unusable.

"Well, that was anticlimactic," Arthur muttered with a shrug before moans from two rooms away had him running to it. *"Uncle Matthew!"*

This time, he didn't even bother with using the makeshift key he made for himself. His powers only sensed those three people on the premises anyway, so he had no reason to hide his escape now. He hastily grabbed the knob, slid his hand through it as if it weren't even there, and opened the door from the other side.

Uncle Matthew was tied up on the floor, looking worse than Arthur felt. He rushed over and shook him.

"Uncle Matthew?" He questioned, "Are you alright?"

Matthew slowly opened his eyes, startling Arthur. His uncle's ordinarily blue eyes were now *gold,* and his ears were—*pointed?*

Arthur pulled his hand away, confused.

"*Uncle Matthew?*" He asked again, "W-what happened?"

Before Uncle Matthew could answer, the room suddenly filled with smoke. Coughing, Arthur tried to turn back to the door. He must have missed something.

His eyes began to burn and blur as he fell to his knees.

The last thing he heard before blacking out again was: "*It's the prince! We found them!*"

Chapter 10: Where am I now?

Two-year-olds Anya and Arthur giggled as they ran *away from their Auncle. They had a mission: They desperately wanted two of their favourite people in the world together.*

The goal was to lead Auncle Dylan to Uncle Mattie.

And Mama and Papa were in on it! All Anya and Arthur had to do was lure Auncle Dylan to the room. Mama and Papa were supposed to get Uncle Mattie and meet there.

"Come back here, you little troublemakers!" Auncle Dylan exclaimed as they chased the Royal Twins down the hall. "Your parents are going to kill me if you make more glitter messes!"

Whilst their Auncle was napping, the twins had "accidentally" covered them all over with glitter. The terror twins were also supposed to be napping, but thought this would be more fun.

However, the glitter was only part of the plan. Mama was hiding behind the door that the three of them went through. She closed and locked it behind Auncle Dylan.

The Royal twins ran through the Jack and Jill ensuite their parents suggested, not stopping. If they did, they would have accidentally gotten an eyeful of something they wouldn't understand until they were older, as Matthew was getting ready for his own shower from getting covered in glitter.

As soon as they ran through the door they were supposed to, Papa closed it and locked it from the outside. He then scooped up his little troublemakers and casually strolled away with his 'captives' giggling. He picked up his pace when he heard Auncle Dy's and Uncle Mattie's screams of shock.

"You two did good," Mama said before kissing their cheeks, then kissing Papa over their heads. The twins continued to giggle at their parents.

✠ ✠ ✠

2 October 2010:
Thirty-Six Hours After the Kidnapping…

Arthur slowly came to; this time, he was startled to find himself on a bed instead of on the ground. His mind quickly cleared from the childhood memory, now embarrassed that Uncle Matthew might have been naked as he and Anya ran through his room. Then, the events of the past few days came flowing back to him, overriding that embarrassment.

The last thing he remembered was looking into Uncle Matthew's golden eyes. Some muffled yelling arose, and then he blacked out again.

He carefully sat up in the all-too-comfortable bed and rubbed his eyes; this time, his hands were free from the iron mittens and cuffs. However, some unexpected scratchiness made him pull his hands away. Arthur's eyes adjusted to see white bandages wrapped around his hands and wrists.

He looked warily around the room. The moonlight was filtering through the window on the far wall. The walls were a lighter colour that had round splats around the walls that vaguely reminded them of ornaments. In a way, it reminded him of his childhood room at his grandparents' house.

Pushing off the covers, Arthur slowly moved to the edge of the bed before he cautiously stood and moved to a full-length mirror. His eyes widened, realising someone had taken the time to change him into pyjamas with penguins on them—

Wait… Penguins? These pyjamas were more familiar than he realised…

They were supposed to be this year's holiday pyjamas… in three months. Pyjamas that he had just sketched on paper. He just had gotten the fabric for *Hennain* to work on.

Arthur suddenly twisted and rushed to the closed door next to the bed. He didn't know what made him choose to go to that door. If the room setup was anything like his rooms at the many palaces in England… it should be the closet…

He jerked it open as he flicked the light switch on the wall outside the door. Rows of clothes easily caught his attention. He drifted into the closet, running his hand over the clothing, mostly tailored dress shirts and pants, both familiar and foreign, as there were some warmer dress shirts he wouldn't wear in England. It doesn't get cold enough to need some clothing lined with *fur*.

The panic started rising in his throat. In the corner of the closet was a dress. Designed to make him or Anya look incredible, the teal floor-length gown hung gracefully on a mannequin. However, this was a copy of his dress, something that only he and Auncle Dylan knew about and were going to work with *Hennain* to make it for the holiday season. Auncle Dylan wanted to be prepared if the twins needed to switch at the last minute for a more formal dinner party during the holidays.

Arthur started heaving, trying to remember to take deep breaths to keep a panic attack at bay. He was about to curl up a ball on the floor when a noise behind him kept that from happening. Instead, his fighting instincts kicked in.

He closed the door behind him before diving deeper into the walk-in closet. If this closet had the same clothes in it that were in the closet in Buckingham Palace, down to the dress, then his polo mallet *had* to be somewhere in there, too. Hopefully, in the same place that he kept it in, or this would be a very short attempt at self-defence.

After finding the mallet at the back of the closet, Arthur returned to the door and put an ear against it. He strained to hear any potential movement on the other side. His grip tightened around the pole so much he thought he made it crack.

Then, he heard a door from the other room open. A woman spoke, her voice full of amusement: *"Arthur, please come out. I'm not going to hurt you."*

"That's what they all say," Arthur muttered to himself,

unwilling to take the woman's word, before yelling back, *"Prove it!"*

He heard some light chuckles.

"You used to pretend to be Ash Ketchum and tried to catch Pokemon," she replied, muffled by the door, *"Anya wasn't happy with you when you dressed her bunny up like Pikachu as she liked Pollyanna much better."*

Arthur nearly froze. Only three people knew that information; out of the three, only one should be alive. He took a few calming breaths. Then he hastily yanked open the door. He swung the polo mallet, only to be met by the woman's raised arm, stopping it in its tracks.

"Who are you?" Arthur demanded as he tried to force the dark-haired woman back.

He had to push her either back into the bathroom or into the closet to get past her. He vaguely noticed that she had turned on a light so he could see her better.

She was too relaxed for someone who was getting rushed at. She was standing her ground. She didn't move her other arm into any fighting stance, like with a clenched fist or shifty feet.

"Why did you take me?" He continued, "I was so close to escaping—"

The tired woman was dressed in green fleece pyjamas that also looked familiar— like someone he knew once wore something like this before. His memory from childhood was a little hazy. She scanned over him sadly.

"You don't remember, do you?"

Arthur's face was filled with confusion as she released her hold on the mallet, and he lowered his arm.

"Remember what?"

"You were almost seven the last time we saw each other," the woman continued. "I've always regretted having to leave you and Anya behind."

Arthur's confusion lessened as the familiarity of her soft voice began registering in his head.

"Mum?" Arthur hesitantly asked as the polo mallet dropped to the floor.

Eve Evergreen Drago, the Queen of England, nodded as her half-a-head taller son nearly tackled her with a hug.

"My *Lille Bjørn* (Little Bear)," she whispered into his ears as she reached up and petted his hair. *"I'm never letting you go."*

Arthur's small bubble of a world just popped. He never thought he would see his mother again, at least not in this lifetime. Her voice was the long-forgotten whisper making its way through his memories.

"I'm not so little anymore," Arthur muttered, not wanting the hug to end.

Her laughter started to mix with faint laughter, and the squeaks of sneakers running through the halls through the closed bedroom door reminded him of something.

"Is Nathan here, too?" Arthur asked, hopeful, as he pulled away from the hug.

They moved to sit on the bed as she nodded.

"Who's the other person he's playing with?"

"Your sister," Mum replied. "Though they should be going to bed soon."

"They got Anya too?!" Arthur said with his voice cracking. His hands flew to his mouth, cheeks redding, realising his voice cracked. That hasn't happened to him since he was thirteen.

Mum shook her head, amused by both his assumption and his voice.

"Mum?"

"That's your little sister, Noel."

Arthur's hands and mouth dropped.

"Your boyfriend's actions saved us from a fiery death," Mum continued. "We can't wait to meet him—"

Arthur could only stare at her as his mind tried to catch up to what he was hearing.

"Mum?" He tried to interrupt her continuing babble.

"Yes, *Lille Bjørn?*"

"What boyfriend?"

Now it was Mum's turn to be confused, "You and Damian aren't together?"

Arthur felt his jaw drop as he tried to find the words. He felt his cheeks redden, too.

"MUM!" He exclaimed, "How...why...*why* did you assume that?! How did you know that I'm-"

She gave him a tired smile. "I always knew, especially since you followed your Auncle Dylan around. You always wanted to be like them. You're the reason why they and Matthew got together."

"Mum!" Arthur nearly whined, trying to get her to focus, "How do you know about Damian!?"

"His journals saved our lives," she replied. "When he started writing to your grandfather, the first thing he wrote about was someone hired to hurt me and what *should* have been the four of us."

Arthur blinked owly. *"'Four of us'?"*

Mum nodded as she raised her hand to ruffle his bangs out of his face. "You would have been with Nathan and me if you hadn't wanted to stay with Anya since she was sick that day."

Arthur stood and started pacing, "This means that no good, she-devil of a stepmother wanted all of us gone!" He paused, "That explains so much and leads to more questions."

"Arthur?" She asked, confused.

He felt her eyes tracking him and shifted to look in her direction.

"How did Grandfather get a hold of Damian's journal?"

"I honestly don't know," she admitted. "All I know is that his words saved our lives. The one who would know more is your Uncle Alfred."

He blinked, *"Who* is Uncle Alfred?"

Mum's eyes lit up, "You get to meet the rest of Matthew's

family! Alfred is his older brother and the head of security here."

"Now?" Arthur squeaked, staring out the window at the darkness.

"Of course not," Mum gestured to the bed, "No one has cleared you to leave the bed, let alone the room."

He wearily made his way back to bed, as all the adrenaline left him more tired than he thought. She lifted the covers as he shifted to lie down. It felt surreal to have Mum tucking him in after ten years.

"Mum?"

"Yes, *Lille Bjørn?*"

"Who has to clear me?"

"Matthew's mother, Lady Mina. She's the main healer and matron here," she replied with a small smile, "She's the only woman your grandfather listens to willingly when it comes to his health. He goes to her after he eats too many cookies."

Arthur chuckled—more tired than he realised—as a distant memory of eating cookies alongside his grandfather ran through his head as he closed his eyes, finally allowing the rest of the adrenaline to leave his body.

Mum hummed a long-forgotten lullaby as she kissed his forehead. She clapped twice, causing the room to plunge into darkness with the moonlight coming in. She settled back into the large armchair near the bed, helping to keep an eye on Arthur and his head.

Chapter 11: A Celebration
in the Mountains

December 1999:

"Now, what happened?" *A dark-haired, golden-eyed woman knelt to get a good look at Arthur's knees.*

"I fell," the seven-year-old prince replied as he tiredly rubbed his bloodshot eyes, "It throbs, and the rocks weren't even nice to me."

"Well, let's get you cleaned up," she continued, "Do you think you can push out the stones?"

Arthur bit his lip and closed his eyes. He heard the small pebbles fall, hissing and shuttering as she ran water over his knees.

"Shh, Your Highness," she soothed, "Can you open your eyes? You'll want to see this."

He opened his eyes and they widened as a white light appeared from her hands. He held his breath as the scrapes on his legs disappeared.

"How did you do that?" He whispered in awe.

She smiled brightly, "Magic."

☖ ☖ ☖

6 October 2010:
Five Days After the Kidnapping...

Arthur couldn't bring himself to stop staring at the healer who was examining his head. He knew this woman, but from where, as the last time he could have seen her... her hair must have been brown.

The now short silver-haired woman smiled warmly, "Your grandfather calls me the Drill Sergeant."

Red crept onto Arthur's face, "I said that out loud again, didn't I?"

She smiled, her golden eyes sparkling, "Something you did as a child."

"I'll have to work on that," he muttered, "I might give away something that I shouldn't."

125

"Like your feelings for Damian?"

Arthur's mouth dropped.

Mum chuckled from the other side of the bed, "He's been living in Egypt and not in England this entire time."

"*MUM!*" Arthur protested, cheeks now bright red as the two women laughed together. "This has nothing to do with the Nile!"

"Well, you're healing nicely," the healer commented after a moment as she lowered her hands, "You might remember me as Madam Mina."

"Wait," he breathed as it clicked, "You helped me with my knees!"

She nodded, "But *you* helped me get those rocks out. And now you're strong enough to hide *within* concrete."

Arthur grinned, "Those three *idiots* had no idea what I could do. They put me in fire-proof chains!"

Mum shook her head in amusement as Madam Mina turned and pulled out an ice pack from her bag. "I want you to use this if you start feeling a migraine. The Heir or the Saint can refreeze it for you later."

Madam Mina put some loose bandages back into her bag, closed it, and picked it up as she stood, "You can join the family for activities."

"Thank you, Madam Mina," Mum replied as she bowed before retreating and closing the door behind her.

"Mum, who is the Heir and the Saint?" Arthur asked after a moment.

"Those are the names the elves use for your brother and grandfather," she replied as she, too, stood.

Arthur pushed off the covers. "Why?"

She was quiet as she moved around the bed, looking thoughtful, "I really don't know. I haven't been able to figure out why."

"Oh," Arthur replied, missing the glint in Mum's eyes, not realising she knew more than she was saying.

"Are you ready for breakfast?" She asked, "The Madam of the Hospital is impressed with your body's defences. You don't have to stay in bed."

"Yes!" He exclaimed, jumping out of bed. Habit taking over, he bolted to the closet. He needed to change before going down for breakfast.

A giggle stopped him from opening the door to his closet. He turned back, "Mum?"

"Things are very different up here," she said as she linked an arm with his, gently leading him to and out the door, "Here, we eat breakfast in our pyjamas."

✠ ✠ ✠

Arthur was excited to be cleared to move around the house. Madam Mina was worried about the redness from the chains on his wrists, hands, and ankles and the gravel he walked on. However, his body was so used to the dirt and metal that the redness was more pink than red when he woke up earlier.

Mum led him down a bunch of halls. He was pretty sure that he would need a map if she didn't help him get back later to change into day clothes. He grinned to himself as Mum led him to a bright, airy kitchen.

Mum led him to a table in a breakfast nook of his dream kitchen! He couldn't wait to add some private kitchens to the royal residences around England.

"Choose whatever seat you want," Mum suggested, "Your grandmother loves cooking and has been cooking all morning. She made some of your favourite breakfast foods from your childhood, which I bet you haven't had in a long time."

Arthur's mouth was salivating as he stared at some cinnamon buns he knew were made from scratch, "As long as she teaches me how to make her cinnamon bun recipe! Do you think she'd even allow me in her kitchen?"

Mum laughed, "More so than your grandfather or Nathan.

The Elf fire department has to be on standby. They've been known to burn water."

Arthur blinked, "That's supposed to be impossible."

"Yet, somehow, they both have done it several times," Mum shrugged, "Get settled; the Gang should be down in a few minutes."

"Do they know I'm here and who I am?" Arthur asked as he sat down on the bench near the wall and started spooning some scrambled eggs onto his plate.

"They know that someone is here but don't exactly know who you are," Mum replied as she placed a large cinnamon roll onto his plate, then one on hers. "Although, they think it's just Matthew because Alfred and Madam Mina have been in a tissy the last few days, worrying about him."

"Why would they be worried?" Arthur asked, confused as he picked up his cinnamon roll to pull it apart. "You told me about Alfred being Uncle Matthew's brother. What about Madam Mina besides healing his head?"

"Madam Mina is their mother," Mum replied as she poured herself some milk. "She misses Matthew so much and is excited that you're both here."

"Hey!" A young female voice exclaimed from the entrance of the kitchen. *"What'ch stop for!?"*

Arthur looked up to see a white-blonde fourteen-year-old frozen in the doorway, staring at him for a moment. He was wearing the same penguin pyjamas Arthur had on.

A small, dark-blonde girl who looked about nine years old appeared as if she wanted to punch the teenager she bumped into. She was also wearing penguin pyjamas and was carrying a little stuffed animal shaped like a dragon.

"Are you okay, Nathan?" Arthur asked with a wince.

"Hey!" The young girl exclaimed as she stomped fully around Nathan and crossed her arms over her chest, "Who *are* you? Why do you get to question me?"

"*A-Arthur?*" Nathan asked hesitantly as he confused the girl, slowly making his way to the breakfast table, "Is that you?"

Arthur gulped as he nodded. The older prince had seen the updated photos of him and Anya in the room where he woke up. Those updated photos must be in other rooms of the house.

Nathan rushed to Arthur and tackled him. Arthur laughed as he almost fell from his seat, suddenly feeling thankful that he was on a bench, not a chair.

Nathan buried his nose into Arthur's chest. "You still smell like dirt and plants."

"And you smell like pine trees and sugar cookies," Arthur whispered as Nathan plopped into his lap, wrapping his arms around him like a baby koala. "I've got you, and I'm not letting you go."

"*Who are you?*" the girl asked again, a little nicer this time. Her head was tilted, and her grey eyes narrowed at the older teenagers with confusion. She had never seen Nathan behave like this before. He was always the one comforting her. "*Mummy?*"

"Come here, Noel," Mum replied as she pulled out a chair and sat down, the girl approaching her for a hug. "Do you remember the photos in my room?"

The girl nodded before it dawned on her, "That's my biggest brother, isn't it?"

Mum nodded as she tucked Noel's hair behind her ear. "The Elves thought he was safer in England until now."

"Oh," Noel whispered, looking over at them, "Is that why Anya isn't here yet? Is she still safe there?"

"For now," Mum agreed before settling to watch her boys, "*For now.*"

"This is the best surprise ever!" Nathan sighed happily into Arthur's chest, "Nothing can top this!"

✠ ✠ ✠

15 May 2010

Hey Nate,

I went to a new museum exhibit that opened today and saw these neat art pieces. I thought of you when I saw them. The last time I saw you, you were into bugs, spiders in particular. We used to use these spiders to freak Anya out. I think that's why she sent me to the opening as her. You were too young when we last saw you, but Anya and I can switch places for events that we don't want to do, with some help from Auncle Dylan. This way, she wouldn't have to go. I don't think she would have gotten out of the car. The exhibit was by Lousie Bourgeois. Her spiders were outside and inside the museum. These spiders were huge! Some were even taller than me, and I've gotten taller!

The spider outside the museum is the only spider Anya can tolerate for one day of the year, your birthday. This one's taller than me, as we can walk under its body and through its legs. This one isn't the only spider that is in London permanently.

Papa had commissioned Mrs Bourgeois to build what she calls Mamon, the spider, for your fourth birthday. He intended to have it placed in our portion of the garden for you to play under and around it.

When you and Mum died, he had the artist place her Maman outside the Science and Art Museum that has since been named after you.

Maman is special to Mrs Bourgeois as it represents and honours her mother. Her mother had been a weaver and restored weaving projects. I think Papa liked the idea of having Maman for you as you're close to Mum and she was always working on a yarn project.

It's hard to tell what materials Mrs Bourgeois used to make Maman. The main body is weirdly spun so that sunlight can filter through it. I bet you would have known what materials she used Mrs with your passion for building things.

Mrs Bourgeois and the Museum board wanted to do something for your birthday. This is how I ended up here, opening an exhibit all about spiders. So, happy birthday, baby brother. I hope you have found those ice spiders that you were obsessed over.

Your big brother,

Arthur

✠ ✠ ✠

Arthur happily found himself wrapped up in a blanket in front of the fireplace in the main living area as Nathan and Noel snuggled into his sides. He was watching the flames before Noel broke the silence.

"Are you as boring as Nate?"

"Noel!" Nathan exclaimed as he pulled away from Arthur to glare at her.

"What?" She gave him a side-eyed stare. "All you do is work with the elves! I want to play with someone who isn't involved with making the toys first!"

Arthur smiled at them as Nathan's glare lost its power.

"Okay," he relented with a shrug. "I'll give you that. What can I say? I like what I do."

"He accidentally gives me the chills sometimes, too," Noel continued. "He uses his ice powers to cool down the room when he's too hot."

Arthur blinked as a memory nagged at him…

✠ ✠ ✠

July 1996:

Fourteen Years Before the Kidnapping…

"Can I hold Nate?" Arthur asked quietly as he observed the squirmy baby lying in a big bed with pillows all around him.

"Of course," Mummy replied as she crossed the room to help Arthur onto the bed.

He crawled to the top, and she took a pillow from Papa's side and put it down next to Arthur on his left, then took a pillow from her side and put it next to his right.

"Hold out your arms, Lille Bjørn," She continued as she moved to pick up baby Nate. "You'll need to cradle his head to keep him from hurting his neck."

"Okay," Arthur wondered. "But why pillows? You and Papa don't really use them."

Mummy gave him a small smile, "They're here to help you hold

Nate if your little arms tire. Nate weighs more than the little weights that your aunt gave you to get used to your powers."

"Oh," Arthur replied.

"Are you ready?" Mum asked.

"Yes, Mummy," Arthur replied.

She lifted baby Nate, one hand under his head, and cradled him close as she moved to the top of the bed and carefully placed him into Arthur's arms, and he studied the small baby in his arms for a few minutes.

"Mummy, why is Nate's hair white?" Arthur asked, his eyes not leaving Nathan's blue ones as he cradled his little brother.

Mum gave him another small smile. Her ash-brown, curly hair fell forward over her shoulder as she sat down next to her oldest son. She kissed Arthur's forehead as Nathan made a little noise, sucking his fist.

"That's because he takes after your grandfather. You know how you don't have the same gift as Anya?"

Arthur nodded, wondering why she started with that.

"Well, Nathan's gifts are different too. That just means his path is different from yours."

"Like what?"

"Look."

Arthur's eyes widened as small snowflakes started falling lightly.

"It snows all the time?" Arthur asked, amazed.

His mum nodded.

"That's so cool! Can I help?"

She chuckled as she pulled both her boys close to her.

"Always, Lille Bjørn," she continued, "He'll need all the protection he can get as these aren't normal powers in England."

Arthur hummed, "Okay, Mummy, I'll help keep him safe."

✠ ✠ ✠

"You have ice powers, right?" Arthur questioned.

"Yeah, he has ice powers," Noel answered for Nathan, "I have fire powers. What powers do you have?"

"I've got earth-based powers," Arthur replied. "Did you light the fire today?"

Noel nodded.

"She's also a walking space heater," Mum said as she entered the room with a tray of cookies and hot chocolate. "Your father was like that."

"Where are Grandmother and Grandfather?" Arthur asked as the three of them each took a cup from the tray.

"They're taking care of the reindeer," Mum replied as she placed the tray on the coffee table. She then took that last cup and settled on the couch on the other side of Noel. "They're joining us later."

Arthur nodded as he inhaled the hot chocolate's steam, bringing back memories from his childhood. He remembered playing here with Anya and Nathan. Anya had helped Father set a fire in the fireplace as she learned to control her powers.

"So, what do you like playing with that *isn't* something Nathan made for you, Pipsqueak?" He finally asked his little sister.

"'*Pipsqueak*'? What's with big brothers and nicknames?" Noel huffed, annoyed.

Nathan laughed into his mug.

Arthur turned his attention back to his brother. "What do you call her, *Shadow?*" he asked, disregarding Nathan's laugh, which sounded more like '*ho, ho, ho*'.

Nathan stopped laughing as he lowered his mug, "'*Shadow?*'"

Arthur nodded with a goofy little grin, "You were always following me around as soon as you could walk."

"Neat!" Nathan exclaimed, "I've got a nickname!"

Noel rolled her eyes, "You know, you would *not* be this excited about a nickname if we grew up with him."

Arthur gave her a grin over his cup, "Let me enjoy this for now, Pipsqueak. So what does Nathan call you?"

Noel grumbled something under her breath after sipping her hot chocolate.

"*I didn't hear you,*" Arthur teased.

"Short Stack," Nathan said under his breath.

Arthur twisted to stare at Nathan before exclaiming, "Are you trying to get yourself beat up?! That's one of the 'no-nos' you must follow regarding women. You never ask a woman's age, height, or weight!"

"And *Pipsqueak* doesn't fall into that category?" Noel demanded as a small ball of rightful fury.

"A Pipsqueak is a small cute animal that lives in England," Arthur replied with a straight face.

"Ho, ho, ho! I haven't heard about a pipsqueak in such a long time!"

The three looked to the kitchen's entry as jolly laughter filled the room. Arthur's mouth dropped. As Krystopher and Isma Kringle-Evergreen entered the room, dressed in red, things began falling into place.

Mum let a smile drift onto her face as her children squabbled as if Arthur had been there the whole time. Everything was going to be okay—for now.

16 May 2010

Hey, Nate,

Mrs Bourgeois just doesn't make spiders! There's a googly-eyed rock you would have given me a whole story about! Heck, you would have been helping her! I hope she would have been okay with that. I don't know if any of this artwork was made recently.

I didn't have to go back to the museum today, but I wanted to. This time, I went as myself though. The opening day/your birthday was a big hit. I shook hands with more people than I thought I would. Uncle Aaron ended up joining me today. He wanted to see what I was so excited about. Anya said she would think about it. I might need to unleash Aunt Melanie on her soon since there are more than spider sculptures here.

But back to the rock. It looked like it could either be a monster hiding in wait or a rock that was in a losing battle with the elements. Hey, you know what? I like the idea of the rock in a losing battle better. Monsters are more in the shape of a woman who wants something that doesn't belong to her...

Sorry, I didn't mean to bring Stepmonster into this, but no real choice. She's annoying Anya and Damian again. She wants them to get together and marry when Anya and I turn 18. That will never work. Anya has a crush on her guard and hates Damian's guts. Stepmonster is just upset that she couldn't get pregnant while Papa was still alive.

Okay, end rant

Something weird happened, though: Mrs Bourgeois was asking me how long I had been with Damian. Uhh, I don't know how to explain that. First, she has to be, like, almost 98. How can she tell that I even like guys? Second, I don't even know where the Damian part comes in.

She just gave me a warm smile and told me she's an ally of the LGBTQ community. She originally agreed to bring Maman to the palace because of Papa's stance on rights for the LGBTQ community, even if not everyone agrees. Auncle Dylan was a big reason why Papa made sure that the LGBTQ community here had those rights.

I hope you're having a huge party with Mum and
Papa right now. I'm sorry that we couldn't keep
Papa here any longer. I'm surprised that he had made
it as long as he did.

I miss you.

Your big brother,

Arthur

✠ ✠ ✠

Halloween, 2010:
Thirty Days After the Kidnapping...

"Happy Birthday, Arthur!" Noel exclaimed, hyped up on sugar from Halloween candy and treats. She chose to dress up as Sally from *The Nightmare Before Christmas*. Grandfather got a jolly laugh from that.

"Nate's got something for you! I'll go get my gift from my room!" She continued before running off, excited that she was getting to celebrate a special birthday with a sibling she didn't grow up with, even if he'd only been with them for a month.

Nathan shook his head, 'forced' to dress like Jack Skellington to match his sister. He handed a green and purple wrapped gift to his older brother. The last birthday they celebrated together was Anya and Arthur's sixth birthday. Nathan and Mum had to go into hiding by the time of Nathan's fourth birthday the following May.

Arthur unwrapped the paper around the rectangular object, revealing it was a book.

Its cover didn't have any words; instead, it had two images. One was a dragon's egg with a sun, a symbol he'd grown up wearing on special occasions since he was the heir, and the other was a snowflake, one he'd seen on Nathan's clothes.

He opened the cover, and the first two words on the top page read: *Dear Arthur...*

Arthur looked up to see his brother smiling at him from across the coffee table.

"Nate?"

"Those are my responses to your daily letters," Nathan replied shyly. "Do you know how hard it was to keep up with you? Especially when I could only respond to your letters with Elven or Norse artists."

A smile came to Arthur's face, "I'll have fun learning about them. We can go-"

"After New Year's," Nathan finished for him. "Nothing *fun* is open around here until *after* January First. Everyone comes to help Grandfather Christmas with his many toy orders."

Arthur nodded, completely understanding why the businesses in the Giving Village would either be closed or redirected to helping Grandfather Christmas. 'The most wonderful time of the year' was very important to everyone around here.

Chapter 12: Elves?

"Arthur, do you want to help me make cookies?" Grandmother Christmas asked as she stood, brushing flour off the bodice of her long red dress. Her greying hair, mostly hidden by a red cap, sat above a pair of gold-rimmed glasses falling to the tip of her nose, causing her to adjust them constantly.

Arthur nodded as he marvelled at how much she looked like the depicted version of her. Grandfather Christmas, on the other hand, *didn't*. Even though he enjoyed all the milk and cookies left for him year-round at home, his powers kept him from gaining the belly that the Legend of Santa Claus always depicted in the Coca-Cola ad from the 1930s. He kept his beard nice and tight to the jawline, and his hair was still white-blonde with some grey.

However, Grandmother Christmas had another reason for covering her hair, which came from her upbringing; he just didn't know what it was called. He knew the religion she was raised under was Islam, but that was it. He never thought to ask what the head coverings she used were called.

What Arthur didn't know was that the older she got, the more relaxed the different scarves and headpieces that she would wear. With a baby living here full-time, Grandmother Christmas needed something that would keep her curious granddaughter from pulling at the cloth. She only started wearing the cap full-time about ten years ago, shortly after Noel was born.

"So, when was the last time you made gingerbread?" She asked, shaking Arthur free of his thoughts.

"I made gingerbread last holiday helping the cooks," He said, "But with another family member? The last holiday that you and Grandfather Christmas were there in person."

Grandmother's brown eyes blinked now, trying to keep from tearing up, "Oh, Arthur, what about Anya?"

"She remembers making gingerbread with Mum, and it's just too hard for her to come do it with me," Arthur continued, picking up a ball of dough and starting to knead. "Papa just liked watching. I would look up to find him with either a digital camera or a video camera. He loved recording all the quiet moments the public wouldn't get a chance to learn about unless we released the information."

She smiled as she picked up a rolling pin.

"I wasn't too sure about both of my twins coming into such a public life when they married into two royal families," she said, rolling the dough thin enough to use the cookie cutter. "My parents attempted to arrange a marriage with the Murrians for power."

Arthur squeaked.

"*It didn't work,*" she assured. "Your grandfather and great-grandfather interfered. In their quest for control, my parents forgot who truly held the power within the family. Your grandfather was already speaking to my grandfather for my hand in marriage, per my culture and faith traditions, as he was the head of the family at the time. However, I went to my wedding day thinking I was marrying a Murrian from my country."

"You're from the royal family of the Ottoman Empire if I remember correctly," Arthur commented, "Uncle Matthew told me that a few years ago."

She nodded, "The First World War almost tore the Ottoman Empire apart. It didn't because the animal spirits of the countries grouped under the Ottoman Empire only went to those who swore loyalty to the head. It didn't help that a herd of Arabian horses represents the empire."

"Why a herd of Arabian horses?" Arthur asked, confused. He never knew which spirit animal represented the family on his grandmother's side.

She gave him a toothy grin, "Arabian horses are strong enough to survive the desert. They're also fast enough to help the next leader return to the capital when the previous one dies."

"I bet many spirits put their rulers in their place."

"More than most of the public realise," Grandmother continued, picking up a gingerbread man-shaped cookie cutter.

"I think some of those movie ideas of *'what if there weren't soul animals?'* or *'myths were myths'* coming out of Hollywood are interesting. What could have happened if there weren't any spirit animals or worse, everyone *ignored* them."

Arthur shuttered. He may not have access to the dragon since the soul protector of his country hasn't chosen him to be the next ruler, but he did his best to respect the spirit protecting his family and country for *generations*. He couldn't *imagine* a world where nobody listened to the spirit animals.

"And truthfully, my father was lucky he wasn't born *into* the family, not after my great-grandfather died," Grandmother Christmas shook her head, "All sons of the passed emperor must rush back to the capital. Whoever got there first won the right to rule, and the losers should have died, killed through execution."

"Your grandfather changed that law, right?" Arthur asked as he grabbed the rolling pin next. "His coming to power coincided with the end of the first war, and several of your great uncles and great aunts were showing up to the capital with the horse spirit."

Grandmother Christmas nodded as she pushed the cookie cutter into the dough. "The ones who arrived with the horse spirit were from different territories of the empire that have since reclaimed their ancient names. They now have to see the first ruler who makes it back to the capital as the overall leader, but they rely on those ruling the territories or countries to represent them to those areas."

"How did Great-Great Grandfather approve of Grandfather

Christmas marrying you?" Arthur asked after a moment. "I mean the man that is essentially Santa Claus and is associated with the birth of Jesus Christ."

Grandmother Christmas gave him a slight grin. "Your grandfather is quite good at negotiating. He introduced himself as my pen pal—though he essentially *was*. I had heard of *Kris Kringle* and started writing to him, thinking I was writing to *Santa Claus*. I accidentally started writing to their *son*, Krys Kringle, because elven magic requires a name for the letters to be passed to the right person."

Arthur stared at her for a moment, "How did you even hear of either, though, when you were raised in the Islamic faith."

She shook her head.

"You forget how tightly *entwined* the European royal families have been for centuries as yours managed to escape that nightmare," Grandmother Christmas pointed out, "I might have been born and raised in the Islam faith, but many of my cousins were not born and raised that way. Because of them, I knew about every possible version of Santa Claus. My great-grandmother was Queen Victoria of Scotland. Great Grandfather Albert was the one who brought the concept of a Christmas Tree to Scotland and was adopted everywhere else."

"Oh," Arthur said, loving the history lesson he was getting. "Do you know why Papa's family didn't get further *entwined* after Queen Catherine of Spain and Queen Mary I?"

Grandmother Christmas stopped cutting the gingerbread and stared at him, thinking, "I thought it had to do with the dragon spirit. She always seemed to have a *say* in who heirs marry. Your mother said she always heard a faint purring when she held hands with your father."

Arthur's eyes narrowed curiously, filing the information in the back of his mind... *Purring*?

26 December 1995:
Fifteen Years Before the Kidnapping...

Arthur quietly played at Mum's feet with his toy trucks that he had gotten from Grandfather Christmas. The tree had been decorated by the family rather than staff, as it had homemade crafts for ornaments and paper chains. It was also one of the few times that the family had chosen to stay at Buckingham Palace instead of heading to Sandringham House.

Arthur didn't know why they didn't go to see Great Aunt Lizzy and the rest of his cousins. He was listening to Mum and Uncle Mattie talk above his head, not understanding what was being said, only that it was important...

"What made you say yes to His Majesty?" Uncle Mattie asked, suddenly, "Why did you agree to this crazy life?"

"Besides the Lists to Christmas Eve?" Mum asked.

Uncle Mattie nodded.

"He's funny, loyal, sweet, kind," Mum started, "Above all, I could hear his family's dragon, and he can't."

Uncle Mattie hummed, "Prince Felipe Drago could hear the dragon once he married Queen Elizabeth, even though she wasn't chosen to rule England until after Queen Mary I had died."

"How..." Mum started, "Wait, Madam Mina sent you to protect him, didn't she?"

Uncle Mattie nodded again, "Well, it was your greatest grandfather, but she encouraged it. I'm still waiting for what she wants for me. She told me that I would find the person I love in the English Royal family."

"And have you?"

"I think I have; I want to ask Dylan to marry me," Uncle Mattie said as he settled in the chair across from Mum. "But I can't subject them to my... elven heritage and being young until we find a soulmate."

"Matthew," Mum said, finishing her last stitch. "Have you looked at yourself in the mirror recently?"

"N... no," he replied, his voice filled with confusion. "W...why is that important?"

"You haven't been using your illusion spell for a couple of years now," she pointed out as she put down her crocheting. "You've been ageing—"

"What?!" Uncle Mattie exclaimed as he hastily stood, rushing out of the room.

Mum and Arthur heard a loud "Reveal!" from the other room, followed by a glee shout. Uncle Mattie came rushing back with a huge grin on his face.

"I'm finally aging!" He exclaimed as he sat back down. "They're the one!"

"Of course they are," Mum agreed, "Madam Mina is the one who told Alfred you needed to come to live with me full time. You know she would only do that if she knew your soulmate was somewhere in the palace."

His mouth dropped, "Is that why the four of you set me and Dylan up?!"

She grinned, "A lady never tells her secrets."

Uncle Mattie snorted.

"Well, when it comes to important secrets," she replied as she rubbed her stomach. "Mor and Far (Mother and Father) will be so excited to learn about this little one. But let's get back to you. Do you have a ring yet?"

Uncle Mattie nodded as he started patting around his clothes for something."Ah!" He exclaimed as he pulled out a small square box from his pants pocket and opened it. "What do you think?"

Arthur huffed as he realised he didn't have the right angle. He wanted to see what Uncle Mattie wanted to give to Auncle Dylan.

"I wanna see the ring too!" Arthur finally exclaimed.

Uncle Mattie chuckled, "Of course," he said and approached Arthur, squatting to be at his level. "What do you think?"

"Who made it?" Mum asked before Uncle Mattie could show Arthur the ring.

He stood, picking up Arthur in the process.

"Your husband did," Uncle Mattie replied as he placed Arthur on the couch with Mum, "He knew Dylan the best."

"And did you ask Lord Black for his blessing?"

"And Lady Black, Lord and Lady Wales, and I talked to Heir Wales' gravestone," Uncle Mattie continued, "That last one was a little awkward, especially since I'm not supposed to officially know about Heir Wales' being the unofficial big brother."

"Oh, yes, family secret," she nodded, "What wisdom did my husband give you?"

"That Dylan can be stubborn to a fault but has a big heart," Uncle Mattie said. "However, I already knew about them. It was Lord Black who gave the best advice."

"And what's that?"

"I have to keep working for it," Uncle Mattie replied, "The growth of a relationship continues after we say 'I do'."

"Uncle Aaron told Andros that too," Mum replied, "That's why we are trying to have a date... Ohh, quickly!"

She grabbed Arthur's hand as Uncle Mattie hastily moved to sit on the other side of her. Taking his hand, too, she put them on her stomach. Arthur felt something hit his hand before he pulled it away.

"The baby kicked me!" He whined.

"They're supposed to move around," Uncle Mattie chuckled. After a certain point, the baby doesn't have a lot of room to grow, so they move around to get comfortable."

"Oh," Arthur replied as Uncle Mattie picked up the ring box and put it into his pocket, "Wait, I didn't get to see the ring!"

"It's a surprise," Uncle Mattie replied with a wide grin. "Besides, Auncle Dylan would want to show you and Anya together."

Arthur pouted, causing Mum and Uncle Mattie to laugh.

☩ ☩ ☩

26 November 2010:
Eight Weeks After the Kidnapping...
Arthur followed Nathan into the Workshop. The Workshop came straight out of every tale that he had heard, read, or seen about Santa Claus. There were long tables and benches.

The tables were covered with toys, all in different stages of production. He also saw some beings working on developing computers and smartphones further down.

Arthur moved to introduce himself to some of the beings that work with Nathan. They were along the benches Nathan was leading him to. He blinked with uncertainty. Could his stories be right about this one?

"Um, Nathan?" Arthur asked as he almost walked into his little brother.

"Yeah," Nathan replied as he turned back.

"Are those...*elves?*"

With confusion, Nathan stared at his older brother, "You've figured out that Grandfather is the fabled *Santa Claus*, and you don't think we would work with elves?"

"Yeah, well, most stories about Grandfather Christmas say that he's an immortal, jolly old man with a belly from too many cookies."

Nathan laughed. Arthur will always be amazed at how much it sounded like *ho, ho, ho*.

"Okay, I'll give you that," Nathan gestured to the elves, *"Come meet my big brother!"*

Arthur suddenly found himself surrounded by elves of all shapes and sizes. Every story that has ever been told about elves was right in some form. They all have a place in the Workshop or the Giving Village.

"Where are the adults?" Arthur asked awkwardly, as he realised that many of the elves looked to be in the range of Fourth Graders to Tenth Graders.

"You mean we're not old enough for you?" One of the elves, who looked to be around Nathan's age, asked slyly, "I'll have you know I just celebrated my two hundredth birthday."

Arthur's eyes widened as other elves joined in with different ages. Only a few were in their mid-twenties. The rest were a hundred or higher.

"What did I just get myself into?" He muttered as Nathan's

ho ho ho started echoing, "Please tell me that you're just pulling my leg!"

"Nope," the 200-year-old elf continued gleefully; they don't usually get people they can *troll*. "We just look young until we meet our soulmates. Most of us don't even get to meet them unless we're willing to adventure beyond the Giving Village."

"Then how old is Uncle Matthew?" Arthur paused. "Actually, some of his grumbling when he's annoyed with us makes sense now."

"Like what?" Nathan asked, confused, while the elves just grinned.

"Like how he keeps comparing Anya to one of our ancestors as if he knew her and how long it took to get anywhere by horseback," Arthur continued, "The horseback one always comes out when we say, *Are we there yet?*"

"Who's the ancestor that he compares Anya to?"

"He keeps calling her '*Kat*' but doesn't clarify the full name," Arthur complained. "The only ancestor I can think of is '*Catherine of Aragon*', but I don't know how she can be our ancestor when her only daughter didn't have any children."

Nathan's mouth dropped, "You mean the mother of Greatest Grandfather Felipe Drago?"

"What, who?"

"You don't know the name Felipe Drago?"

"Um, there's been a lot of control going on that has been rewriting our past," Arthur replied sheepishly, "I'm surprised that you know that much information."

"The censor spell doesn't reach up here; we have access to information that others may not. My brother is meticulous at keeping historical records," Uncle Matthew said, having heard a bit of the conversation and finally entering the room, causing the younger-looking elves to scatter. "And yes, I've been comparing Anya to Catherine of Aragon. And you are everything like the man they describe Prince Arthur to be. I didn't meet them until after his death."

Nathan blinked, *"Them?"*

Uncle Matthew nodded, "Queen Catherine and her loyal protector, David Drago. David once was Prince Arthur's protector and lover."

"W... what?" Arthur asked, startled, "I never found anything about that."

"You wouldn't," Uncle Matthew shrugged, "Besides the spell being active, the queen and their protector were very careful with who they told the truth, especially when she died trying to keep her youngest child's existence from her ex-husband. She was rightfully worried that he would try to claim him as his son."

"How did you find this out?" Nathan asked with wonder, he also didn't know much about his father's side of the family.

"Because I was there," Uncle Matthew replied with a grin, "Queen Catherine wished the baby for the protection of St. Nicholas when King Henry VIII came around before she could send Felipe to her sister-in-law. At the time, The Saint sent me to get the young prince as the king would ignore a child servant. I brought the baby to his aunt and went back to tell them. That's when they told me the story that is your family line's foundation. Now, are you ready to show Arthur around?"

Nathan nodded as he started pulling a confused Arthur around the Workshop.

✠ ✠ ✠

1 December 2010:
Eight and a Half Weeks After the Kidnapping...

"Have fun with your woodworking!" Noel exclaimed as she watched Arthur bundle up in the main hallway of the Holly Manor, "Grandma and I will be working on hot chocolate and cookies for your return."

She then turned and skipped down the hall as Arthur stared at Nathan.

"Where's your coat?" Arthur finally scolded as Nathan moved past him, "It's gotta be below zero out there. Not even Anya or Noel's powers can keep up with that much cold!"

Nathan chuckled, again sounding like *ho ho ho*. "My powers make it feel like it's spring out there. Besides, I'll be finishing the inside of my first big project that is on my own. I won't need my coat, I'll get overheated working on it. Hopefully, this will be very helpful to others."

"If you say so," Arthur mumbled as they left the manor.

Nathan led Arthur past the reindeer barn and to a garage.

"What the bloody hell is *that?!*" Arthur exclaimed as they approached a bright red truck with a small building attached to it.

"*It's a shed sleigh,*" Nathan replied with a grin, "What do you think?"

"Wow," Arthur whistled, amazed. "You came up with that?"

"Yep," Nathan continued pridefully, "I wanted to make it easier to get supplies to people stuck in the snow."

Arthur shifted his glance from the shed sleigh to his brother. The grin had almost taken over Nathan's entire face, and Arthur couldn't help but let a smile spread across his.

They returned to the courtyard from the barn a few hours later, tired but happy, to a commotion that made Arthur perk up—*Damian had found his way to the Giving Village.*

Arthur ran across the courtyard to Damian. He couldn't believe that Damian had finally made his way to the one place that was the safest for everyone...

Chapter 13: First Kiss and Going Home

1 December 2010:
Eight and a Half Weeks After the Kidnapping...

"And that's how we got here," Arthur concluded, trying to keep red off his cheeks, remembering the conversation with his Mum.

Damian reached over Noel and grabbed Arthur's hand, "Your Auncle knows about me and my feelings."

"And those are?" Noel asked as she slid off their lap to look at them.

"Erm," Arthur and Damian simultaneously said as they stared at each other.

"Noel," Mum warned as she stood. "Don't pressure them."

"But I want to know!" she whined, "I want my protector as my big brother too!"

"I know that," Damian said as he leaned forward and grabbed her hand, "But Arthur and I haven't even had a first date yet, and it sounds like all the places up here are closed until after the New Year."

Arthur also leaned forward and grabbed her other hand, "It wasn't safe to say anything before. His..." He paused.

"My rather unpleasant mother," Damian finished for him, "Has gained enough power that could have had me arrested or..."

He looked over to Alfred, who stood up straight. They had missed something in their debrief from before...

"Or?" Noel urged.

"Send me to a place that's not nice and is known for breaking people," Damian carefully explained, glancing at Alfred and hoping he could read between the lines. "Arthur isn't safe to come home yet. Your cousin, Antonio, is quite determined to destroy such places."

Alfred nodded and hastily retreated from the room. The older elf wasn't going to let the other descendants of the Saint

151

be endangered. The Spanish Prince was going to need all the help he could get…

⊕ ⊕ ⊕

3 December 2010:
Nine Weeks After the Kidnapping…

"Are you ready?" Harry asked as Damian joined him at the edge of the Giving Village.

Harry and the Elven guards that had come with them were packing up the red truck Nathan had been working on. This would get them home quicker than it took trekking up here in the snow less than a week earlier. There was so much Damian had to do once they got home.

Damian sighed, "As I'll ever be. I just wish…"

Harry nodded, "You want more time with him."

"And I have some loose ends to tie up before the Evergreen family can come home," Damian said, trying to keep his voice steady, "I need to lay a trap for *my* family."

Harry reached across and squeezed his shoulder. "If you need any help, let me know. I can't return to the front lines for a while anyway."

"And you would like to hide from any wedding planning that Wills and Kate might try to rope you into now that you're back in the country," Damian added.

Harry chuckled, "Am I that obvious?"

"You willingly volunteered to freeze your butt off in an adventure that our country will think for a while didn't result in anything for me," Damian pointed out as Harry grinned.

"Go say *'see you soon'* to Arthur," Harry gestured, "If you two kiss, I promise to look the other way."

"*Hey!*" Damian protested, and Harry laughed, pushing him toward a very bundled-up Arthur who was coming up behind them.

"You thought you could leave without saying goodbye?"

Arthur asked as the others did their best to give the two of them some privacy.

"Not intentionally, there's so much I have to bring back," Damian shrugged, "I like you...*oof!*"

Arthur crashed into him. He grabbed Damian's head, hands entwining into Damian's raven hair as he stood on tippy toe to kiss him.

"*WHOOO!*" Came from the direction behind Damian, who reached back to give them a rude gesture.

Arthur laughed as he came up for breath a few moments later; their foreheads met, and they stared into each other's eyes.

"Harry will be insufferable for the whole trip down," Damian said. "When I return to the UK, I'll do my best to catch my mother in her lies."

"I don't think she wanted me at that camp."

"W... what makes you say that?"

"I remembered something when captive... I think someone who works for your grandmother might have overheard me and Uncle Aaron talk about me being gay," Arthur continued, "I think I can describe him..."

"Was he slimy looking, with greasy long hair and crooked teeth?" Damian asked.

Arthur's mouth dropped as he pulled away. "How the *hell* did you know that?"

"Because he's shown up in my memories, too," Damian replied as he grabbed Arthur's gloved hands and squeezed. "Do you remember me talking about Professor Bradson and how she was trying to help me get into the Academy before Papa Andros died?"

Arthur nodded.

"She is the CSI working on bringing you home."

"*Brilliant,*" Arthur beamed, "The bonus is that she knows how to put your mother in her place and help you do what you love."

Damian chuckled, "She's thrown packs of gloves at me and Antonio."

"Why Antonio?" Arthur asked, confused.

"We needed his help identifying one of your favourite moves without letting Inspector Warren in on the truth."

Arthur burst out laughing.

"What?" Damian asked, confused, "This isn't something to laugh about."

"Inspector Warren knows that I have earth powers."

"He does?"

"He's Mrs Carmichael's only sibling, and she doesn't keep many secrets from him," Arthur continued. "He's one of the good ones who helps protect me when I need to escape your family."

"Oh, good..." Damian said, though he was interrupted by Harry seconds later.

"*Come on, you love birds!*" Harry shouted, "*We've got to head out!*"

Damian huffed, "I should leave him to Kate's mercy and Wills' misery."

Arthur shook his head, "Don't do that. He's one of my favourite cousins."

"How are they related again?" Damian requested, "I thought the English Royal family managed to escape the cousin intermarrying."

"*Officially, yes,*" Harry yelled across the yard as he approached.

"*Unofficially?*" Damian turned to Harry's general direction, not letting go of Arthur's hands.

"Unfortunately, the men in my family line are not good at keeping it in their pants," Harry continued as he rejoined them, "My great-grandparents wished they knew where Arthur's great-grandfather was when he was an infant as they would have claimed him to be Queen Mary's son with Prince Albert."

"The one that died of an illness before he could marry Queen Mary?" Damian asked.

Arthur and Harry nodded.

"Huh," Damian said as Arthur squeezed his hand. "And I thought my family was complicated."

"She still hasn't told you about your father?" Arthur groaned.

"Nope," Damian muttered, "But mail-order DNA tests are improving. I'm considering doing that to see if I can track down my father."

"Oh, good luck," Arthur replied, "Maybe you could find out by Christmas. I know that you've wanted to know for a long time."

"Only if we get back sometime soon!" Harry yelled as he moved away again. He was trying to help the elves with gathering the rest of the supplies needed to head back down the mountain.

"Hold your horses!" Arthur yelled back, "I'm almost—"

Damian interrupted this time by kissing him. His gloved hands entangled in Arthur's golden hair, making his handmade hat skewed. The group waiting for Damian whooped again.

Arthur reluctantly pulled away, *"Go—before I mess up the plan."*

"By keeping me here?" Damian whispered, *"I wouldn't mind, but I still have to tell your sister the truth."*

"Just make sure Kaiden is nearby for water duty."

"I wouldn't have it any other way," Damian continued, *"See you soon."*

Arthur grabbed his hands again and held on tightly, *"See you soon."*

Damian nodded as he reluctantly let go...

Chapter 14: Coming Home...
What Wedding?

10 December 2010:
Ten Weeks After the Kidnapping...

Damian returned to Buckingham Palace to find everything turned upside down... The staff were even stiffer and angry with him as he was brought to his Mother's office as soon as he entered the palace doors.

Her office was a part of the apartments she was assigned to when they moved to the palace. She wasn't upset, as historically, the king and queen have had separate households. His rooms were nowhere near her, something he was always thankful for.

Until now, Damian had to get to the other side of Buckingham Palace when he was just cold and tired. All he wanted to do was shower and crash into bed.

Damian couldn't process what she was saying. He could only stare at Mother. She was currently looking like the cat who swallowed the canary.

"*There* you are," she greeted, "Are you excited?"

Damian blinked, "About what?"

"Now, don't be coy," she continued as she shuffled papers from one pile to another. "Now that you're back from that pointless trip," she said, showing she knew more about what was happening than he realised. "We can move forward with the plans since you failed to find the king."

"What *plans?*" Damian asked, having a sneaking suspicion he had just walked into a trap.

"Your impending nuptials to *Princess Catherine*, you daft boy," Grandmother sneered as she entered the ornate office from one of the side rooms, "The Princess needs protection and a firm hand to keep the throne from falling apart. The *only* way to do that is for you to marry her and name your mother the Regent personally..."

156

Damian listened with disbelief. He had only been gone for a week, and now his overhearing Mother and Grandmother making plans for the rest of his life made his skin crawl. How does he share the same blood as them? He would never do as they were planning.

The simple thought of being with a woman was something he wanted nothing to do with. He battled his need to bolt from the room as he connected it was Catherine they wanted him to marry, which made no sense. She barely tolerated him on a good day and couldn't stand him on a bad day. They were working on it, especially since Damian left to locate Arthur, but he didn't think it would be enough to have a physical relationship with the young woman.

Damian now understood why half the staff seemed ready to rebel. The other half of them were either giving him glares of disgust or looks of pity. He couldn't blame them for reflecting what he felt inside.

Damian retreated from the office once Mother and Grandmother finally dismissed him. He was suddenly feeling more awake than before he got home. He rushed to find Princess Catherine.

The Princess' hiding place was in the Library. This was the worst kept secret among the Palace staffers and courters. He never felt the need to go there, never wanting to intrude on her space.

He took a deep breath as he lifted an arm to knock on the door to the library. However, it opened before he could. His fist was inches away from accidentally punching a startled Kaiden in the nose.

Damian hastily lowered his arm as the American shifted his body to look at the princess. She was sitting at a new desk against a wall across from the windows overlooking the Gardens.

"Well, it looks like Damian knows where to find you, after

all," he commented tiredly before turning back to Damian, "I was *just* about to come get you."

Kaiden shifted out of the doorway so Damian could warily enter the room.

"I'll be outside," Kaiden continued. "Remember, this is the library, *not the gym*. There's only so much water I can carry with me."

"*Kaiden!*" Princess Catherine groaned, cheeks inflamed. "I can handle myself!"

Kaiden gave her a small smile before saying, "*Good luck.*"

He then pulled the door closed behind him. Damian blinked as he saw a flash of light travel around the room's walls. The Muffle Spell was only used for private offices.

"That's new," he commented, impressed.

The Princess nodded, "Auncle Dylan and I added it when we turned this into my office."

"Ahh," he gestured to the desk. "I knew something was different; I just didn't want to bring it up. The library has always been your safe space away from us."

"Kai...*den*," she corrected herself with a shrug, now leaning against the desk, "*Kaiden* says I'm here enough that it just makes sense to make it my office. Now, what can I help you with?"

"Mother's current scheme, Your Highness."

"Oh," the princess said, deflated, "You've heard about that."

He nodded, "Why didn't you tell me about it?"

"You were so focused on finding Arthur, and it would only come into play if you *didn't* or *couldn't* bring him home," the princess stressed. "I figured I would let you keep your focus on Arthur, and I would deal with Stepmonster's scheme."

"What can I do to help get out of this mess?" Damian asked.

"*Besides calling me Anya,* nothing," she replied, finally permitting him to use her family nickname.

"That's all?" He repeated, dismayed, "Are you sure?"

Anya nodded again, "That bloody contract is air-tight.

Antonio and I have gone over the stupid thing with a fine-tooth comb. We have no choice but to get married."

Damian could feel his throat tightening. He gulped, trying to clear his throat. "Can we add anything?"

"Like what?"

"Like using science to get you pregnant when you're ready for children. We will have the perfect marriage in the public's eye and history books. But behind the scenes, I will never touch you sexually. I can't; it's making me sick just thinking about it."

"Gee, *thanks*," she muttered, "I guess that's my fault?"

Damian shook his head. "No, it would be the same with any woman. You just have a better understanding of the situation. Can it be done?"

"I think so," she sighed, understanding what he wasn't trying to say, "I can also see about adding something discreet about a male partner..."

"No," Damian interrupted, "The one person I've ever been interested in and love has always been Arthur. If we're going to do this, then I'll be there one hundred and fifty per cent. No matter what, I'll be loyal to you and our children."

And with that, Damian felt like he could breathe again. He didn't mean to admit his love for Arthur out loud to someone other than him like this. At least it was Arthur's twin...Anya *seemed* like she would understand.

"*Oh, Damian...*" she finally whispered as she stared at him.

"If anything, add something for you and Kaiden," he continued, hoping he had read the situation correctly. "One of us should be happy."

Anya bit her lip before shaking her head, "I can't do that to him, and he won't be staying here anyway. He has to leave by the end of the year."

Damian's jaw dropped, "Why are you sending him away? Is it because of Mother?"

"*I'm* not sending him away, and if we could, we would be openly defying Stepmonster," Anya assured, "He has to go back to Hawaii by his twenty-second birthday because he isn't in a traditional university or trade school. He'll have to stay there if we aren't together. You'll have to ask him why, though; it's his secret to tell."

Damian heard the pain in her voice, but he couldn't voice his pain to her and explain he understood what she was feeling. It took every fibre of his being to leave Arthur with the others, even though the young king was safe at the North Pole under the protection of the Elves.

Instead, he nodded, resisting the urge to wrap his arms around himself for a self-hug, knowing he must remain strong like the young woman before him.

"Is there anything that you need me to do?" He asked.

A tight grin made its way to her face, *"Distract your family."*

He grimminced, "I was afraid you would say that."

✠ ✠ ✠

Once he left Anya and Kaiden, Damian retreated to his hiding place in the Library. He made his way to the shelf housing journals of numerous royal family members.

He ran his hand down over the spines of the more decorative books. The book he was searching for, he'd placed an illusion spell on to make it appear more elegant than it was. Silently, he removed the spell, which helped to hide it in plain sight as he ran his hand up and down the book three times...

Damian was unaware of the other secrets the room held. The Murrian blood in his veins kept him from reading other journals and the true history of the nation. The spell that Ze Dylan had told him about protected these journals from Mother's blood. He could pick up the journals but couldn't open them.

It was also where Arthur and Lord Black had their heart-to-heart before everything began. Though, he didn't know that either.

He took the journal off the shelf and hastily crossed the room to the nearby work table, grabbing a nearby pen and taking a seat before flipping to an empty page towards the back. Damian then put the pen to the paper:

Alfred, there's even more trouble stirring here than we realised. Mother and her allies have created a magical contract that Anya and I may not have a way of getting out of very easily...

Damian hated leaving Arthur behind for the moment as there wasn't enough evidence to catch the true mastermind. He needed a way to contact the North Pole— and this was it. This contract blindsided him. He wouldn't even have a way to protest because of how binding it was.

He just hoped Arthur would be alright with everything currently playing out and not come rushing back and blow up the plan...

✠ ✠ ✠

15 December 2010:
Ten and a Half Weeks After the Kidnapping...
Damian was pulled into wedding planning by Mother as Anya wanted *nothing* to do with the nightmare she was

creating. Jose and *Modryb Fawr* (Great Aunt) Lady Melanie Black were his two allies in this fiasco.

Anya insisted the wedding, regardless of the year, *must* be on Christmas Day so her grandparents could be there. She also refused to let Mother have any say in the wedding dress.

Mother agreed to the date request—as long as it was *this* Christmas. The wedding would be in less than two weeks.

"Are you sure about this?" Anya asked Antonio as Damian approached the room they were talking in.

"Hey, I'm more than okay with it!" Antonio replied with a grin, *"I get out of being your Man of Honour..."*

"For now," Anya finished.

"What?"

"You're still going to be my Man of Honour when I'm cleared to marry Kai," Anya continued.

Damian guessed Antonio's mouth dropped since there was a beat of silence. He wasn't close enough to the room to see Antonio's actual reaction. He was looking for Anya to give her the folder he had found in his office...

"But Arthur should be back by then," Antonio whined.

"As Kai's best man." Damian heard a smirk in her words.

"Why can't you use Damian?" Antonio demanded as Damian got to the doorway.

"We're not that close," Damian answered mindlessly as he finally entered the room, reading from the folder. He closed it as he looked between the cousins. "Now, what are you two arguing about?"

They answered with silence, and Damian shrugged. "Alright, I'll leave you two to your planning. I'm off to distract my scheming, wicked family so that you can figure a way out of this."

"What does Stepmonster want *now?*" Anya groaned.

"We're supposed to be going over tablecloth colours," Damian grumbled.

Anya looked sick, "She still thinks that shades of orange are appropriate for a Christmas Day Wedding, doesn't she?"

"Apparently, to go with your powers," Damian said with a shudder.

"Isn't she expecting both of you to be at this wedding planning meeting?" Antonio wondered aloud.

"Yep," Damian replied with a bitter grin, "What colours am I countering with?"

"Green, red, blue, and white," Anya replied as Antonio nodded, "Those are my family's colours."

"Then, why are you having Anya stay away from the meeting?" Antonio asked, not knowing of Anya's request from earlier in the week.

"I promised to distract my family, and Anya doesn't need to lose her temper with them," Damian shrugged. "I also intend to give those *witches* a piece of my mind. They aren't being fair to either of us, and everything in my life has always been about how I could *satisfy* her wants. Papa Andros did everything he could to give me something resembling a childhood."

Damian then turned from the doorway to continue on his path.

"Do you think that Papa was drugged?" Anya asked suddenly, causing him to stop and turn back to them.

"Well, the older I got and learned about drugs and potions in health class, the more I suspected something was wrong," Damian admitted. "I could never prove it—those b...*witches* are too good at covering their tracks."

"Now?"

"Now, I've gotten some help proving what has occurred and their involvement," Damian's grin lost some bitterness. "Your grandparents are overprotective and have done everything possible to keep the family safe. Please excuse me; I'm going to be late."

He had to pull himself away before accidentally giving

away Arthur's secret in a place where ears were everywhere—Grandmother Murrian had other spies in place.

As he walked away, Damian managed to hear:

"Where did he meet Grandmother and Grandfather Evergreen?" Antonio asked with confusion in his voice.

"I... I don't know," Anya replied faintly.

✠ ✠ ✠

30 minutes later...

*"Where is that **ungrateful** girl?"* Grandmother bellowed as she paced the main dining room where she and Mother had set up samples for Anya to go over.

Damian watched them out of the counter of his eye as he tried to focus on the task in front of him—making the day a wedding he would want. Anya's few requests meant he'd have to make up the rest. Even though he and Arthur had not spent much time together as a couple, he wished they could have talked about a wedding themselves.

However, if Damian had known what was on the line before travelling north over both land and sea, he might have approached the North Pole differently than he did or, for his sanity, chose not to return home at all.

Either way, Damian would need to make a lot of guesses regarding what Anya and Arthur would have wanted in a wedding.

He desperately wanted to ask Ze Dylan's advice, though they weren't about to *willingly* step into a room with Mother unless they needed to defend Damian.

Right now, Damian was holding his own with a bit of help from *Modryb Fawr* Lady Melanie Black. He was pleasantly surprised she was in the room when he arrived.

"Arthur would have liked this," the regal redhead Lady Black whispered as she pointed to a sample of a snowflake garland twisted with a pine garland decoration. "Anya would agree to

it because snowflakes are important in their family. They're sentimental that way."

Damian concentrated on the sample on the table in front of them. He nodded. He knew that it would have been a reminder of Prince Nathan. The powerful young man's gifts had only grown in his time away from England. He couldn't tell Lady Black her nephews were safe but would do everything he could to listen to her advice.

Lady Black also seemed to know his preference for Arthur or at least her child's protective nature for him, keeping Mother and Grandmother from looking too closely at his life. He also preferred her over his aunt. When Damian was younger, he wished Lady Black was part of his family. She was more loving than all three Murrian women he shared blood with and showed it to him when they were too busy being caught up with themselves.

Like right now—

"Do you know what shades would go well with the colours Anya wants?" Damian asked quietly.

"You mean something *besides* orange?" Lady Black replied dryly as she lifted the linen and napkin samples from different tables. "It looks like our options are either pumpkin or tangerine."

"What about something that honours Papa Andros and Andrew Wales?" Damian continued.

Lady Black gave him a small smile. Her blue eyes twinkled with the laughter she couldn't express without angering Mother and Grandmother. Mother would do everything *not* to honour the past.

However, Papa Andros needed to be honoured, being the late king. However, not many people know that Andrew Wales was raised alongside the late King and Ze Dylan. Of the three, Ze Dylan was the last royal of their generation who was still living. Lord Black was overprotective of his child for a very good reason.

"What colours were you thinking about?"

"I was thinking blue, sliver, green, and red," Damian continued, "To honour all the family Anya has lost over the years."

"I think that's a perfect idea," Lady Black replied, "It's one that both Anya and Arthur would have done for their weddings, and it fits with the public's expectation of lots of symbolism."

"We wouldn't want to disappoint the public," Damian said jokingly.

"Of course not," Lady Black said with a grin, "It would be one more thing to annoy your mother and grandmother with, and there's nothing they can do about it. Do you want me to tell them?"

Damian shook his head, "It should come from me."

He then cleared his throat loudly, getting the attention of his squabbling relatives. The women turned to him with a disdainful look. He stared back as he gathered his courage.

"We will go with the blue, silver, red and green," Damian hastily interjected.

"That's not how it's done," Mother protested.

"No, Mother, arranged marriages in the 21st Century aren't how things are done, and look at where we are," Damian reminded. "You will leave the planning of this... *sham* of a wedding to Anya and me. The colours Anya likes are blue, silver, red, and green. You've already taken her power to choose her life partner. You will give us this if you want to get anything out of this."

Mother pouted, and Grandmother frowned. They hadn't expected him to stand up to them. He was going to throw them for a loop after the wedding. He couldn't wait to see their faces when they realised the only Regent he and Anya would name until she was twenty-one was her Great Uncle...

Chapter 15: The Bachelor Party?

17 December 2010:
Eleven Weeks After the Kidnapping...

Damian needed to get out and away from Buckingham Palace. He was going stir-crazy. Anya was still on lockdown from before he left, even though Inspector Warren and Lord Black determined she wasn't in danger of being taken. It was *Mother's* twisted idea to keep her locked in the palace.

However, Mother would regret the decision when both the Scottish and Spanish Royal Families converged on Buckingham Palace. It was the only exciting thing he was happy not to have missed.

Anya, Kaiden, Damian, and Jose all stood. Anya curtsied, and the others bowed as a tall, elegant woman entered the room with a shorter but equally elegant older woman with her. Queen Rosa, was *Tía* Rosa to Anya; her dark hair was tied back in a bun at the base of her neck. Her designer clothes of an elegant skirt and a short-sleeved blouse only showed off her scars from the car accident that caused her to earn the title Queen of Spain. Queen Elizabeth II, the Queen of Scotland, joined her. She was dressed in one of her signature long raincoats and a matching hat, which was red for the upcoming holidays.

"Please come with us, *sobrina* (niece)," Queen Rosa requested, "Queen Elizabeth and I would like to start your heir training."

"Are you sure?" Anya nearly squeaked, "What about Arthur?"

The Scottish Queen nodded, "He'll get his training when he returns, but we promised your father to help the two of you. Lady Murrian has interfered long enough."

Anya looked back at her guard and Damian. Jose hadn't raised his head to see she was looking at him, too. Kaiden nodded as Damian gave her the shooing movement with his hand.

"Kayla and Prince Charles are going to be there," Queen

Rosa said, "Prince Charles just wants to help the two of you and knows the only way to get past your Stepmonster is to involve me and Queen Elizabeth."

Anya took in a deep breath, nodding. She then turned to Kaiden.

"You don't have to come," she commented, "We'll only be down the hall."

"Are you sure?" Kaiden asked.

She nodded again. This time, with a smile, "*Tía* Rosa and I can protect Queen Elizabeth if we get attacked in here."

She followed her *tía* and Queen Elizabeth II to the rooms permanently assigned to the Scottish Royal family when visiting Buckingham Palace. Kaiden and Damian bowed as the queens left the room. After they were gone, Kaiden made a face.

"Can I relax now?" Jose asked, his head still bowed.

Damian smacked his head; he was surrounded by goofs!

"How is it you *still* don't know how to follow protocol?" Damian asked.

"King Andros wasn't too big on the protocol in private when we were growing up," Jose replied as he finally straightened up, "I didn't start working as your assistant until *after* King Andros died."

Damian could only shake his head as Kaiden let out a tired laugh before getting caught off by a high screech, followed by:

"WHY ARE THOSE TWO... *BUSYBODIES* HERE!?" Mother's angry voice floated up several flights of stairs to the room they were in. "THIS ISN'T EVEN THEIR COUNTRY!"

Damian groaned as he moved to the doorway. He was going to have to intercept Mother. However, he ran into the Scottish Princes: Wills and Harry, before he could get further than the door.

"*Come,*" Wills practically demanded as they entered his office. "We're heading out. Granny and Pa have your mother in a right tizzy, and she won't notice if we escape for the next few hours."

Damian looked to Jose and Kaiden, who nodded.

"The timing is right," Jose agreed, "And Professor Bradson wanted you to stop by New Scotland Yard."

"What about you?" Damian asked Kaiden, "Are you coming with us?"

As a smile tugged at his lips, Kaiden shook his head, "I'm going to help protect the Royal leaders from your mother's wrath. Not that it would help her."

"Huh?" Damian asked, confused.

"I would have to protect her from Princess Anya's flame," Kaiden started, keeping a straight face. "But who's to say anything about my aim."

He then left as Damian shook his head. Jose smacked his face as the royal brothers laughed. Damian suddenly didn't want to be there when Mother screeched about being wet.

Damian sighed, *"Alright."* He turned and grabbed his coat off the back of his chair. "Where else are we going?" He asked the grinning brothers as he put on his jacket and started moving with them out the door.

"We wanted to take you on a Stag night, and we cleared it with Lord Black," Harry explained. "He said as long as we take the Inspector with us, he's okay with us having some fun."

Damian blinked, "Why does he want Inspector Warren with us?"

The brothers glanced at each other before looking around.

"I think he wants us to share with the Inspector what we found in the north," Harry continued in a low voice after Wills signalled no one was around. "He knows you haven't been able to leave to give your report."

Damian nodded, suppressing a grin. Who knew the Scottish royal brothers would make such great accomplices?

They moved from the room, and Jose felt safe enough to return to his work in peace.

10 minutes later...

Getting to New Scotland Yard would take a little longer than anticipated. On the way, they ran into Katie and her brother, James. Katie had been looking for Wills to see if James could accompany them.

"That's really up to Damian," Wills said, "It's his Stag Night."

"And I'm more than fine with that," Damian assured, thinking Katie would turn to plead. "I think this should be something for Wills, too. One of us should appreciate this night."

"That will also throw the press off when Wills has *his* Stag Night with other friends," Harry grinned. "And Damian can feel like he's not alone in this."

"Are you sure?" James asked, "I mean, I'm just a nobody..."

Damian shook his head, "You're going to be Wills's brother-in-law, and if things were different, we could have gone to the same university, even if just for a little while."

"Okay, let me go get my coat!" James exclaimed, rushing to the guest apartments they were staying in.

"Thank you," Katie murmured, "He was getting bored with the wedding talk, and being cooped up in the apartment has also started to drive us stir-crazy."

Damian just blinked, "Didn't the rest of your family just get here?"

Katie shook her head, "James was with me when Lord Black sent some men to get me. He's been exploring when I was doing something with Wills or meeting with Princess Anya. I also think he's been getting lessons from Mrs Carmichael in baking."

Then an idea came to Damian, "Do you think he would want to help her make a wedding cake?"

"What?" Wills and Katie asked together; all the while, Harry started grinning.

"Anya would be on board with that," Harry pointed out.

"And it seems that the two of you are going out of your way to piss off your mother even more."

Damian nodded, "My thoughts exactly, and if he's already helping in the kitchen, Mother can't exactly put a stop to it."

James returned a few minutes later after retrieving his coat, huffing, and putting on a hat. He also had a bag hanging from his arm.

"*I'll never get used to being in a place like this,*" he grumbled, "How did the three of you grow up here?"

"It grows on you," Damian replied with a shrug.

"And Harry and I only come to visit," Wills responded a second later, "As it's Granny's primary residence when in London."

"Have fun, guys," Katie said as they started moving away from her, "I'll see if Lady Black can help me with a few things…"

✣ ✣ ✣

1 hour later…

The stop-and-go traffic made driving much more tedious when there wasn't a full-out security team leading the way. The Scottish Royals wanted this to be under the radar for as long as possible, and with the English and Scottish Royal family on lockdown, no one was paying attention. That also meant London traffic wasn't being diverted.

This gave Damian time to think. He wasn't sure what *exactly* he was going to tell Inspector Warren. He hadn't been able to find any evidence around Buckingham Palace that could prove someone in his family was involved with either the kidnapping of Arthur or the disappearance of Queen Eve and Prince Nathan.

Damian was jolted to the present as the SUV pulled to a stop behind New Scotland Yard.

"Are you ready?" Harry asked as Wills and James got out of the vehicle before them.

"As I'll ever be," Damian muttered, "What are they going to do while we do this?"

"It looks like James has a goodie bag of some sort," Harry grinned, "I think his impromptu apprenticeship will benefit the Inspector."

Damian shook his head. He has acted as a delivery boy for Mrs Carmichael in the past. She wanted to ensure that her brother ate while working on cases.

"We come bearing gifts!" James called as he entered the back entrance of New Scotland Yard ahead of them, "Where's Inspector Warren? I've got goodies from his sister, a Lord Security, and a Scottish prince for debriefing."

"How many times has he been sent over here?" Damian asked as Harry shrugged.

"Whenever he's driving Katie and Mrs Carmichael nuts," Wills replied, "Which has been a few times a week. He's one of the few that can leave Buckingham Palace without the press realising he's even there."

"About *time* you got here," Antonio commented, stopping Damian from asking more questions.

"You're back!" Damian exclaimed as confusion set in. *"Why* are you back?"

Antonio glared at him, *"Someone* informed my Grandfather's Head of Security of what I was about to do. I got as far as a van ride before I was switched out with *Agent Bat* himself. What did you *do?"*

Harry chuckled as Damian's expression faded to astonishment. Wills was confused; they had no idea what happened in the north.

"All I said is that you would need some help," Damian protested. "I didn't want him to overtake the investigation!"

"Thank you for saying something," *Tio Félix* (Uncle Félix) said from behind. "Rosa was about to take my head off. *Hermanitas* (Little sisters) can be annoying and overprotective when it comes to *familia.*"

"I was sure Lord Black would have as well," Inspector Warren said dryly as he joined the group. "James, you and Wills can put my treat on my desk. I have some papers for you two to get and bring back to Buckingham's kitchen."

"Yes, Sir," the two future brothers-in-law said together before taking off to the left. Wills followed James down the more familiar path.

"Now–I understand Lord Security Murrian and Prince Harry have stories to tell, and I have a space where no listening and curious ears can hear," Warren continued as Damian and Harry nodded, "Bradson will finish what she's doing soon, and join us there shortly. Prince Antonio, Prince Félix, they will be out within the hour."

"Oh, goodie," Prince Félix muttered, "More time babysitting the royal boys."

"*Tio!*" Antonio hissed as Damian and Harry started following the Inspector down the hall to the right so they didn't hear any more of the Spanish Princes arguing with each other.

Damian suddenly paused. Harry stopped with him. Harry followed Damian's stare through the one-way window.

"Damian?" Harry said, "What's wrong?"

"*Inspector–*" Damian called to him, gesturing to the window, "Have you figured out his identity yet?"

The slimy man's features were no longer blurred to him. His hair still looked grimy and was longer than he remembered. He was very pale, as if he were allergic to the sun. His face was now… *normal* and showed his dark, cruel eyes that burned into Damian when he was a child.

However, he was no longer as afraid of this man as he had been when he was a kid.

"*No,*" Warren replied. "The spell is still strong–"

"But I can see him," Damian interrupted, confused.

"You *can?*" Warren and Harry asked simultaneously.

Damian nodded, "He's got dark eyes, crooked teeth, greasy hair, and a blotchy red face."

Warren looked through the window and grinned before turning back to Damian and Harry.

"That worked. The spell is gone, and I can see everything you just described!" Warren exclaimed. "How is this possible?"

"We're still trying to figure that out," Harry said dryly. "I think Damian has emerging powers that might have come from his father's side of the family, as the Murrians don't have any powers."

"Ahh," Warren replied. "That would explain Bradson's request to get a blood sample from you. She's trying to prove something. But, what's *his* name?"

"I think I heard Grandmother calling him *Wilhelm*," Damian said thoughtfully, "But, I was, like, nine when I overheard the conversation through the crack in the office door—*I've just never forgotten his eyes.*"

"Does he have a last name?" Warren requested.

"Not that I can recall at this time," Damian admitted, "Grandmother only called him by this name."

"We can still work with that," Bradson said as she joined them from further down the hall. "Warren, why don't you start the interview with Prince Harry? I'll bring Damian to you once we finish."

"Of course," Warren replied as he bowed his head, "This way, Prince Harry."

"Good luck," Harry said to Damian as he went by, "She's looking a little like a vampire right about now."

Damian rolled his eyes and went to follow Bradson.

"What do you need my blood for?" He asked as they moved to the lab.

"Well, I can do this whole process without your blood. Warren's used to asking for blood but forgets I can get DNA in ways other than drawing blood. Besides, I'm not set up here to draw blood," she replied. "But the idea is there. I just need some of your saliva."

"That I can do," Damian grinned, "I was looking into doing a DNA test through one of those new public companies."

"I bet I can get results a little bit faster than them," she promised. "Alright, get comfy—the longer we take, the longer it'll be until you return to Buckingham Palace and back under your mother's thumb."

Damian laughed; It was clear she was determined to make his life a bit brighter by giving him a chance to try his hand at his passion.

"Alright," Bradson started, with her gloves on and a test tube at the ready, "Have you drunk or eaten anything in the last half hour?"

"No, Ma'am."

"Then you're ready for this," she said as she passed him the tube.

"As I'll ever be," he muttered before he spit into the tube. "When will you know anything?"

"The processor will take time," Bradson replied, taking the tube back and sealing it. "And if your father's in the system for *anything*, it doesn't matter if it's criminal or government, I'll get an answer."

He sighed, "Okay, well, wish me luck."

She smiled, "Always. You're in good company; they'll keep an eye on you."

"Yeah, they will," he agreed, "They snuck me out of Buckingham Palace to see you and Warren."

"Do you know where you're going next?"

He shook his head with a slight grin. "Wills and Harry have the plans. I'm just along for the ride."

"Good," she continued. "You need some fun in your life. Now, why do I have an *'Agent Alfred Lightfeather'* contacting me?"

Damian pinched the bridge of his nose, "Apparently, he's my boss."

She blinked, "How's that possible?"

"Queen Eve's parents are still alive and well," Damian said

quietly, "They're protecting a huge secret regarding the event that Wilhelm was part of before attempting to kidnap Arthur. Wilhelm conspired with Grandmother to do something to Queen Eve and Prince Nathan."

Her lips tightened, "Are you sure?"

Damian nodded before pausing, "Has someone from the Ottoman Empire tried to contact you recently?"

She opened her mouth to talk but paused before speaking, fiddling with her leather bracelet, "You know, I think the Ambassador for the Ottoman Empire has been inquiring a little bit more than the others. But I thought it was because members of the Royal Family were putting him up to it."

"You're still right about that," Damian muttered, "One of their older princesses, Princess Isma of the Ottoman Empire, is Queen Eve's mother."

"Oh," Bradson whispered before her lips twisted into a grin, "That explains why the Ambassador has been hinting about possible extradition for line theft and kidnapping. But I don't know how that could work with Arthur being an heir of England."

"I don't think it has to do with Arthur," Damian hastily shook his head, "I think it has to do with Queen Eve and Prince Nathan's disappearance."

She nodded, "This *Alfred* said he could help extract information, but only after Christmas."

"That sounds right," Damian murmured, "This is a hectic season for the family, and then, on top of all that, the wedding on Christmas Day."

"Are you going to be okay?"

He was quiet for a moment. *Will I be okay?* He thought to himself. He swallowed before answering, "I will be. I have to be. Anya and I will work it out."

She reached out and squeezed his hand. *Hopefully, she didn't hear the pain in my voice.* Damian's mind wandered as they stood in silence.

Chapter 16: The Wedding that Shouldn't Be Happening...

Christmas Morning, 2010:

Damian desperately wanted to disappear into the ground and was utterly jealous of anyone with earth powers. Grandmother had firmly planted herself in the living room of his apartment in Buckingham Palace. She ordered the staff about and was there to ensure he got ready for this *stupid* wedding and couldn't run.

She wasn't happy about the Scottish Princes springing him last week. At least Damian returned when he could have simply gone to the *Giving Village*, not that she knew *where* he ended up. All she knew was that he had gone *north*.

He could hide from Grandmother's eagle eyes in his dressing room. Jose rushed around him, hoping to make him presentable for the next few hours. Cameras and eyes from every nation were going to be on him and Anya.

"Your scary relatives will kill me if I can't get you looking somewhat like a happy groom and not a prisoner walking to his execution!" Jose muttered as Damian buttoned a white dress shirt, "For some reason, they think I can get you to behave for their bloody schemes!"

Damian snorted, fidgeting with the sleeves, "I no longer care. The only person I'll be helping after this is Anya. Whatever power Mother thinks she's gaining will be minimal."

"What is your—" Jose began as a knock from the far wall interrupted him. "Uh, what was that?"

Damian perked up as he moved to the wall and knocked back a sequence. The wall swung open, revealing a hidden door, and the concerned face of Lord Black peered into the dressing room.

"I'll go distract Madam Murrian..." Jose said as he hastily retreated, not wanting to know anything Grandmother could

grill him over. He pulled the door to the main rooms closed behind him.

"You'd think he'd be less afraid of me now," Lord Black commented dryly.

"Well, you're still the boss around here no matter what Mother and Grandmother think," Damian replied, just as dry, fidgeting with his other sleeve. "So, what's with the back entrance?"

"Madam Murrian has your rooms locked down until you need to go down for the ceremony, and your mother is keeping an eye on Anya, " Lord Black said, amused, *"She's paranoid you'll run."*

Trying not to grimace, Damian looked away from him for a moment to stare at himself in the mirror. His heart ached from the visualisation of his facade of happiness—and he was wearing it in front of the man he learned how to mask his emotions from. After a pause, he forced himself to turn back to Lord Black.

"I wouldn't have returned from the Giving Village if I had known about this nightmare *before* I left," Damian replied. "Please come in, Lord Black. You're better company than Grandmother and her minions."

"Thank you," he replied, "And please, call me Uncle Aaron. You're about to become my great-nephew-in-law. I can't get my son-in-law to call me Dad, Papa, or even Aaron. I don't need that from you either."

Damian gave him a modest, bashful grin.

"Now," Uncle Aaron picked up a red strip of cloth, "Let me help with your bowtie."

"Okay," Damian replied as his hands shaky lifted the dress shirt collar, "I've never been able to do it right."

Uncle Aaron hummed as Damian bowed his head so Uncle Aaron could see where he was putting the bowtie. Damian stretched his neck out so the older man could tie the bow. They were so close in height that it wasn't too uncomfortable.

"And *I'm* helping," the voice of Lord Wales said as he appeared a moment later and entered the walk-in closet before pausing, *"Oh."*

"All set," Uncle Aaron said before Damian lowered his head to look at Lord Wales.

"Are you alright, Sir?" Damian asked as Uncle Aaron turned to take a navy blue vest off a hanger.

"I haven't truly gotten a good look at you since Andros died, and you are looking so regal," Lord Wales said wistfully as Uncle Aaron helped him put on the vest.

"Please button that up," Uncle Aaron requested, "I don't know how much time we have with your friend distracting Madam Murrian."

Damian nodded. He was suddenly thankful that these buttons were larger than the ones on the white shirt. He didn't think he could get those buttoned with Lord Wales staring so intently.

"I see why you thought I should be here, Aaron," Lord Wales commented, "I feel like I just went back in time when we were helping King Andros get ready for his wedding."

"It's the hair, isn't it?" Damian asked as he moved his hand to flatten his hair, "I don't know why I even bother; I can't get it to behave on a good day."

"Andrew couldn't get his hair to work for him either," Lord Wales replied tiredly.

Damian stopped as he lowered his hand, "Lord Wales?"

"Please don't be mad at me," Lord Wales said, "I may have asked CSI Bradson to help me with something."

Damian swallowed tightly, *"W–what's that?"*

Lord Wales looked pensive, "I asked her to check my DNA against yours."

"I see," Damian said quietly as he sat on a nearby bench. "And does she have the results already? I only just got to her last week."

Lord Wales nodded, "I gave her mine before the kidnapping.

I've always felt that Andrew had a child out there somewhere. At least a quarter of your DNA matches mine."

Out of everything he wanted or didn't want to happen today, he wasn't expecting to receive the greatest gift on one of the worst days of his life.

"A... are you sure?" Damian asked as his throat suddenly dried.

Lord Wales nodded and smiled.

"That explains a lot," Uncle Aaron muttered, causing the two to look at him.

Damian raised a brow. "Like what?"

"You have a lot of mannerisms Andrew had, and you're growing to look more like him every day that passes," Lord Wales continued for Uncle Aaron, "On another note, I gained access to his last case before he died—"

Damian leaned forward, excited to finally learn something about his father, *"And?"*

Lord Wales knelt to look the younger man in the eye. "His last case was getting enough evidence against your grandfather, Marcus Murrian."

Damian blinked again, "That would be why Mother has never told me anything about Father. Do you think Grandmother knows that?"

Lord Wales hesitated, "I can't be too sure. I only know Andrew died the same way that Anrdos did, from cancer."

Damian remained quiet about his suspicion as Lord Wales suddenly pulled something out of his inner jacket pocket by his chest before he could say anything.

"I want you to have this."

Damian looked closely at a closed jewellery box. His hands shook as he accepted the small box. Carefully, he opened it, then looked up in surprise.

"A... are you sure, milord?"

"First, please call me Liam if it's too early for you to call me any form of Grandfather," Lord Wales suggested, "Second, this should have been yours from the moment Andrew died or you turned eighteen."

Damian exhaled sharply as he looked back down at the box. Inside was a male heir ring with a large ruby in the centre deep within the metal. He pulled it out carefully and slid it onto his pinky finger.

The ring flashed three times before tightening on his finger. He let out a breath he didn't realise he was holding. It would have stayed loose if he wasn't the true heir of Lord Wales. The families of the nobility have always had ways of proving bloodline. He already had gone through it for the Murrian ring.

Lord Wales allowed a faint smile to come to his face. Damian felt his stare on him as he glanced back up and was startled to find a set of eyes similar to his own. It now made sense he was related to the older man, and Damian wondered if some of his powers came from the Wales line.

"Does the power of sight..." Damian started to ask.

Knock, knock.

"Are you almost ready?" Jose asked faintly through the door. *"Your grandmother might break down the door if you don't come out soon."*

Damian sighed as they stood.

"You should get to Anya, Uncle Aaron," Damian suggested. "The only reason Grandmother would be so impatient is if Mother is no longer distracted by whatever she had planned for Anya."

Uncle Aaron nodded as Lord Wales moved to do something unexpected. Damian felt himself pulled into a hug. One that he just *melted* into.

Was *this* how it felt to be hugged by a grandparent? Grandmother never showed this type of affection, even in private. He never met Grandfather Murrian. That man had died before he was born.

"You are wanted, and you are loved," Lord Wales whispered

into his ear before letting go, "My door is always open for you no matter what happens."

"Thank you," Damian whispered as Uncle Aaron led Lord Wales out of the room through the hidden entrance, ensuring it was shut tightly behind them. Damian then opened the main door to face Jose.

"Are you ready?" Jose asked.

"As I'll ever be," Damian muttered as he rubbed the new ring, "Let's go get this over with."

"Wait!" Jose exclaimed, "You forgot your tuxedo jacket!"

Damian paused as he looked down at his white dress shirt, covered with the vest. "Oh, I didn't mean to."

Jose rushed past him to the far side of the closet. He returned with a navy jacket that matched the vest. It didn't look warm enough for an outdoor wedding in December, but enough spells were stitched into it for him to know that he would feel *too* warm.

Damian took a deep breath before turning. He allowed his friend to help him put the jacket on him. It settled heavily on his shoulders...

✠ ✠ ✠

3 pm...

Damian rubbed his hands together to try and keep the cold off. The spells stitched into his jacket for warmth couldn't do anything for his hands unless he pulled the sleeves over. He stood at the altar waiting for his *bride*. Next to him stood Jose, Harry, Wills, and James. The Scottish princes and the Middleton son were becoming his friends the longer they were stuck at Buckingham Palace and hung out together.

They agreed to be his other groomsmen with Anya's approval. Damian wanted her to feel more in control than she was, and he didn't have anyone else he'd like to stand beside him, anyway. The last-minute decision threw Mother for a loop. She kept quiet because she didn't want to face Queen Elizabeth II any more than she needed to.

Damian accepted nothing more could happen to prevent the wedding. Mother's final round of scheming paid off as he waited for Anya to walk down the aisle. The contract was so magically binding that it would only cause havoc on Daiman's and Anya's lives if they tried to break it now.

However, Mother was fuming about a few things that were happening at the wedding. For example, Ze Dylan was the officiant. Prince Antonio Evergreen Oso was the maid of honour. Jose was his best man. and Anya's refusal to wear the monstrosity of a dress Mother and Grandmother wanted her to wear.

Damian honestly had no idea *where* the dress in question came from or if and *when* Mother had worn it. *Not that he was too interested in the details.* It was all puff and lace, something even he would have taken apart just for it to work. He also never saw photos of her in this dress with either Father or King Andros. He didn't know if she was ever married to Father, knowing now the so-called marriage to King Andros wasn't legal as Queen Eve was still alive.

He was so distracted by his thoughts he didn't see Noel come down the aisle dressed like a little security guard, holding a pillow with rings. He also missed the Spanish cousins coming down the aisle, with Antonio looking more comfortable with being *maid of honour* than he should have been.

Damian stood at the end of the makeshift aisle in the courtyard of Buckingham Palace. Behind a mask of happiness, he was a mess of emotions. He was angry with Mother and sad that Anya covered herself in a flowing red velvet cloak with white fur on the edge, making it so he couldn't make out her wedding dress. It happened to be similar to Grandfather Christmas' red jacket. He couldn't make out any emotions as her entire face other than her eyes were hidden by a thick red veil draped over her—he guessed it must have been Grandmother Christmas' veil.

Hurting Anya was the last thing Damian wanted to do, especially since he had finally gotten on her good side in his quest to find her family. He planned on taking her to the Giving Village after telling the public they'd go to Norway for their *'honeymoon'* to reunite her with her mother and siblings.

Uncle Aaron stood tall next to Anya; she was taller than him, even taller than normal. *They must have convinced her to wear heels.* Damian thought for a fleeting moment.

Mother sat smugly adjacent to where he was standing. She saw that as a *fix* for something she had *failed* at gaining complete control of the royal family through an heir she had given birth to. Mother must be thinking about the child that he and Anya would have to have together per the contract.

Uncle Aaron and Anya stopped once they got closer to Damian. He had never gotten a read on the older man, but this time, he caught a glimpse of a shine in his grey eyes. Uncle Aaron held both of Anya's hands and squeezed them before she lifted a white-gloved hand and gently dried off an escaped tear.

Damian couldn't hear Anya's words, but Uncle Aaron's response was audible: *"I know."*

Uncle Aaron then took her hand and kissed it. He then finished escorting her to Damian. It felt odd that Uncle Aaron didn't lift the veil. Anya must have chosen to honour Grandmother Evergreen with her veil remaining on until it was time for them to kiss.

"Take care of them," Uncle Aaron requested as he placed Anya's gloved hand onto Damian's.

Damian nodded before he led Anya to be in front of her second cousin, Ze Dylan, who agreed to officiate the ceremony, even if it was just to piss Mother off. Mother didn't see Ze Dylan as a person most of the time, nor did she use the correct gender pronouns. The protections for the LGBTQ+ community that King Andros put in place could only change by the hand of the next ruler of England. Damian and Anya would have to be extra vigilant to ensure Mother wouldn't have any influence over any children they would have together.

"*Lord Damian?*" Ze Dylan asked as Anya's hand tightened in his.

"*I'm sorry,*" Damian said sheepishly, "Can you repeat the question?"

"Of course," Ze Dylan replied. "Do you take your partner to have and to hold from this day forward as long as you both shall live?"

"I do," Damian replied as hastily as possible, mouth dry as a bone. He had to hide his sadness that they were already at this part of the ceremony. That meant Kaiden didn't try to interfere.

"*Your Highness,*" Ze Dylan continued, twisting to talk to their niece, "Do you take your partner to have and to hold from this day forward, as long as you both shall live?"

"*I do,*" Anya replied, voice muffled through her veil.

Ze Dylan nodded, "Then, with the power vested in me by the late King and the spirit of this great Nation—I now pronounce you partners for life. You may seal your promise and union with a kiss."

Damian let go of Anya's hand. The two turned to each other. Damian shakily raised his hands to lift the veil. The veil slowly revealed Anya's face, eyes sparkling. *Wait... sparkling?* Damian thought as he leaned in to kiss her softly, only to be startled when the kiss suddenly deepened.

He wasn't expecting *that* to happen.

Then, a tingle of true love magic washed over them...

Wait—

Whiskers? Was his last thought as he was pulled into a vision...

Damian's Journal...

Alfred, there's even more trouble stirring here than we realised. Mother and her allies have created a magical contract that Anya and I may not have a way of getting out of very easily...

✠ ✠ ✠

10 December 2010:
Ten Weeks After the Kidnapping...

At the North Pole, Alfred's eyes widened as Damian's journal started recording a new entry. He hastily faced Matthew, who stood a little straighter, knowing the situation was about to get worse.

"Get Prince Arthur, Lady Eve, and the Saint," Alfred ordered, "We must read them in on this new problem!"

Matthew nodded before turning and rushing out the door—they'd need to plan if the elves were to get Prince Arthur back to England in time to crash a wedding. Thankfully, one thing that the Saint loved to do—which has passed to his children and grandchildren—was to make an entrance.

✠ ✠ ✠

2 hours later...

"*What's the plan?*" Matthew and Arthur requested at the same time.

The Evergreen-Kringle family gathered in the conference room located in the main workshop. It was a spacious room, much too large for the six people currently using it. However, it was the only location in the North Pole with a large whiteboard and projector that Alfred needed to present the mess Damian had sent them through the journal.

Usually, two weeks *before* the biggest day of the year, the Saint would sit at the head of the table with Nathan on his left and hold meetings with the other elves. Each department's head would come to speak with the Saint and his heir.

However, today was different; the meeting was to share what Alfred found. Grandfather Christmas the Saint, his wife, Mrs Claus, and Arthur's mother, Lady Eve, had chosen to sit in the seats near the projector.

Damian explained in the journal that the mess, for lack of better words, was the marriage contract. Arthur had a few choice thoughts for Lady Kendra Murrian and her allies within the government the next time he saw them. He would no longer call her their *Stepmonster*, as she was never actually married to Father. This information meant New Scotland Yard could potentially charge her for *Line Theft*.

Arthur then rose from his seat and walked up to the screen, wanting a closer look at the words. His confusion grew as he read, and Matthew joined his nephew and brother.

"*What do you see?*" Matthew asked, curious.

Arthur paused. "Does Damian know who wrote this?"

"It wasn't Lady Murrian?" A confused Matthew raised a brow.

Arthur shook his head, "The wording doesn't align with how Lady Murrian writes. She's so homophobic and controlling she definitely would have used improper names and non-gender-neutral terms."

Alfred looked down at his notes, "Agent D seems to believe Lord Wales might have had a hand in drafting the contract."

"Well, that explains the wording," Arthur murmured.

"What do you mean, *Lille Bjørn*?" Mum asked as she stood and moved closer.

"Look at most of the terms," Arthur touched the wall and was pleasantly surprised he could digitally mark up the projection. He highlighted lines like *'Member of the House of Murrian'* and *'Member of the House of Drago'*. "This is vague and filled with loopholes, loosely worded enough to apply to any gender. Then, if it weren't for the section about children." He gestured to the newest grouping of words, "They could have put off this contact for generations."

Mum read the child clause closer. A smile slowly came to her face, "*Lille Bjørn*, the child clause was written with you in mind."

"What are you talking about?"

"She's right," Matthew said, "Lord Wales was your father's and Dylan's Godfather. He would have done everything in his power to protect you and Anya. Including tricking that woman into thinking she won."

"And I think Damian had this part added about children," Mum pointed out, as she highlighted a few lines, "Like using the IVF for Anya to get pregnant when she's ready to carry a child."

Arthur re-read parts of the document about the day of the wedding. His eyes widened.

"*The dress!*" He exclaimed.

"What dress, Arthur?" Grandfather Christmas requested with confusion, "Why would you want to wear a dress?"

"Anya and I switch regularly," Arthur shrugged, "If Anya was expected to wear a dress, then I would wear a matching one in her place."

Matthew started laughing. Arthur knew he had connected the dots. The others just looked confused.

"Auncle Dylan's unused wedding dress may have appeared in my closet, which seems to be magically linking my room at Buckingham Palace to my room here," Arthur explained as Matthew settled into grinning. "From what I remember, the dress was made *in case* they felt feminine the day they were going to get married."

"And Dylan felt like dressing more masculine that day," Matthew remembered fondly, "Andros rewrote the traditional vows to officiate us; he felt they were too... *set in the old ways* for a progressive country."

Mum grinned, "He enjoyed being the officiant even if the Church of England hated that he did it... you know, I don't understand *why* the Church of England claimed him as their leader."

"That headache goes back to King Henry VIII when he wanted to divorce his second wife, Anne Boleyn," Matthew snorted. "She gave birth to two sons that either died before or shortly after they were born. The king wanted to try again, but the Roman Catholic Church wouldn't resolve a second marriage."

"King Henry VIII created the Church of England and the Protestant dominion for the Christian faith as the response," Alfred continued, "That is why the Church of England still claims the current ruler is the head of the Church of England."

"Even if they don't follow their version of the church?" Mum asked, dismayed.

Arthur shrugged. He had never heard that part of the story before. He wondered if it had to do with the censor spell.

"*Come with me,*" Grandmother Christmas suddenly whispered into his ear, pulling him out of his thoughts, "*Let's go make that dress yours.*"

Arthur turned to her, "What do you mean?"

"I don't think Dylan would be upset if we made their dress fit you better," Grandmother Christmas said. "Besides,

189

Melanie deserves to see her hard work worn by *someone* in this generation."

Arthur nodded before turning to Matthew, "Are you okay with us changing the dress?"

Matthew nodded, "Dylan wouldn't have put it in your closet if they didn't want you to change it. It deserves its day in the spotlight.

Arthur then turned to Alfred, "Do you still need me?"

"I think Matthew and I have this covered, Your Highness," Alfred replied, "He knows the ins and outs of the palace."

"And with you still missing, Lord Black won't allow the wedding to be anywhere lacking security," Matthew continued, knowing his father-in-law. "So, instead of going to Sandboruam or being at one of the traditional churches around England, he would push to keep it at either Buckingham Palace or Windsor Castle."

"Mum, Grandfather?" Arthur asked.

"Alfred is good at what he does," Grandfather Christmas assured. *"Eve*—why don't you go with them? You were always worried you couldn't help Arthur or Anya prepare for their weddings."

Mum smiled, *"That's a great idea."*

Arthur then left the room with Mum and Grandmother Christmas as he heard Matthew suggest, *"We should sneak back in right before the wedding..."*

✠ ✠ ✠

1 hour later...

"Oh, Arthur!" Mum exclaimed with awe, sitting on the bed behind Arthur, "You look so beautiful."

Arthur stood before a floor-length mirror, running his hands down the long sleeves clinging to his arms. The dress was white with a high neck and buttons up the front. The lace was the same colour as the dress. It was simple and tasteful.

When he walked forward, he was just the right height not to rip the hem accidentally.

"There's another piece," Grandmother Christmas said as she returned to the bedroom from the closet.

"What is it?" He asked as she came up beside him.

"I think it's a cape," She continued, "Can you lower yourself a tad so I can help you put this on?"

"Of course."

He dipped his body so he was at least a head shorter, allowing Grandmother Christmas to wrap a simple red cloak around his shoulders. She clipped it closed in the front before smoothing the fabric down. She then stepped back. Arthur returned to a standing position and looked in the mirror again.

"*Oh!*" Arthur and Mum gasped together.

"Melanie did a great job making Dylan feel feminine with that gown," Grandmother Christmas praised, "That cape and fabric cut make you look like you could be Anya."

"Until you get to my head," Arthur grumbled as he carefully twisted to see the back. "But it does hide my shoulders and chest enough to make Lady Murrian think she's won. Can we add something to the dress?"

"Like what?" Mum asked.

"Red and white flowers, similar to the Tudor Rose," Arthur replied as he carefully turned away from the mirror to face his mother and grandmother. "And I want the two of you to be the ones to put them on. This way, all four women who raised me have worked on this dress. I recognise some of the stitch work from *Hennain*."

"Oh, Arthur!" Mum exclaimed as she stood up and, whilst not wanting to damage the dress, carefully pulled him into a hug, "I'm so proud of you! You're taking this in stride."

"*You don't know,*" Arthur said quietly into her ear.

She pulled away with confusion, "I don't know what?"

"I don't mind wearing dresses because Anya and I switch all the time. We mostly do this to trick Lady Murrian and her allies," Arthur explained as he rubbed his hairy chin. "This stubble is the most I've let it grow since I was a teen. I keep my face clean-shaven so Anya and I can switch at any given moment."

Mum giggled, "You mean you found someone you've successfully tricked into thinking you're Anya and vice versa?"

Arthur nodded, "Papa always knew but never said anything. He just had this little smile that encouraged us to keep switching. Auncle Dylan has been helping us since ageing makes it harder."

"Of course they would," Mum grinned, "They live for chaos, and making Kendra Murrian angry has been their favourite thing since they were young."

"And to tie more family in, the red is my inspiration from Grandfather," Arthur said as he ran a hand over the cloak. "It looks like it could be Grandfather Christmas' if we add the white fur..."

"We're putting the white fur on, and I have the perfect veil!" Grandmother Christmas excitedly chimed in.

"Grandmother, what do you mean?" Arthur asked, curious.

"I mean, it's perfect if you don't want to shave everything off," she continued. "My veil will work. Your grandfather and I fell in love through letters despite never meeting officially until after we said *I do*. To follow my cultural beliefs, they made my veil to completely conceal my face except for my eyes."

"Do we know when the wedding is going to be?" Mum asked. "If it's near Christmas, you can use my red headpiece."

Arthur's face lit up, "Mum, you're *brilliant!*"

His mum and grandmother glanced at each other before looking back at Arthur.

"What did I say?" Mum asked, confused.

"Anya would want the wedding to be on Christmas Day or after that, so Grandmother and Grandfather can attend. And knowing Lady Murrian's impatience, she would have it be *this*

Christmas," Arthur said as he gathered the gown up at the knees and scrambled for the door.

"Where are you going?" Grandmother Christmas asked.

"I'm sending for Uncle Matthew and Uncle Alfred."

He pulled open the door to find his temporary guard, Ella Garland, a dark-haired elf who has worked closely with Uncle Matthew and Alfred. She helped to bring Mum and Nathan to safety. This was why she was assigned to him while Uncle Matthew was still in a meeting.

"*Milord?*" She asked, concerned, "Are you alright?"

"Can you get your boss?" He requested, "I think I know *when* we have to be home."

⳾ ⳾ ⳾

Winter Solstice, 2010:
Eleven and a Half Weeks After the Kidnapping...

The day that the elves took time to celebrate was December 21st, the Winter Solstice and Yule, as a way to renew themselves. The elves were pagan and respected the changes of the seasons. The Saint and his family used the time to rest and refuel.

The Saint's busiest day of the year was December 24th, followed by sleeping all day and most of the night on the 25th. They celebrated *Little Christmas* on January 6th, giving them time to get gifts for each other from the *real world* without relying on making them.

However, this year was different. Arthur was in attendance, and the elves felt like they needed to do something extra special. They even seemed to know it was the same day as a similar party was *sprung* on Anya back in England. They knew about Anya's shower because Alfred had other agents working at Buckingham Palace.

"Um..." Arthur said as he was pulled into the conference room they used the week before, now redecorated with shades of blue and white streamers and balloons. "What's going on?"

"We thought you would appreciate this better than the Princess," Ella said, "We even intercepted some of the gifts so Princess Anya doesn't have to open them."

Arthur heavily sat down in a decorated chair, realising what was happening. The elves were using their holiday to give him a *wedding shower*. He was quiet for a few moments before asking, *"Why?"*

"You're family. We get to watch the Saint and his family grow. We want to celebrate with you," Ella continued with a grin, "Princess Anya will get a do-over when she marries her chosen partner. I know you weren't expecting this today or even at all."

"I never thought I would be able to marry my preferred gender, let alone—" Arthur trailed off as his eyes widened upon seeing his mother enter the room, *"Mum!* You're here!"

"Lille Bjørn!" she exclaimed happily as she came forward and pulled him into a hug. "This is so exciting! I never thought I would get to do this for either of you!"

"Mum!" He said as he pulled away, "There *never* would have been one for me."

She stared into his eyes briefly, still smiling, "When we gave one to Auncle Dylan, you were so happy helping them with everything. I knew then that we would give you one just to see that smile again."

Chapter 18: Homecoming...

Uncle Matt coordinated with 'someone' back home to get Arthur to the palace, although Arthur heavily suspected that someone was auncle Dylan. The downside was that they had to wait for Christmas Eve when the Holiday Magic was strong enough to activate the fireplaces around the world for travel..

Usually, Grandfather Christmas would use the reindeer for local trips or locations that didn't have fireplaces, using the fireplaces for everywhere else. The belief in his legend made them need to change how the gift delivery worked as the popularity of Santa Claus grew so he could get to all the children in one night.

Lucky for Arthur, Grandfather Christmas's blood ran through his veins. He might not have the same powers as Nathan or his grandfather, but he could use the fireplace to leave the North Pole and enter Buckingham Palace, where Anya was in lockdown.

The one night where the holiday magic was the most powerful? Christmas Eve. This was why he was carelessly spat out through the fireplace in Anya's hiding place, sliding across the floor. It was the best option because no one but Anya should have been there. The other reason why choosing her hiding place over any other fireplace in Buckingham Palace? They didn't want to give the plan away until it was too late.

"Am I in the right place?" Arthur asked, sitting up on the floor, as Anya laughed. Well, at least she wasn't startled by someone being spat out of the fireplace. "When did this room get redecorated?"

The last time he was there, the couch was in the centre of the room, in front of the fireplace. It was now off to the side, under a window overlooking the gardens. Anya's favourite armchair sat next to the couch, and a stack of books was on an end table between them. The other wall, which had no windows, now had a desk of a good size in front of it. A comfortable computer chair was pushed up against the wall, waiting for someone to sit there.

"You went missing, and I needed a safe place to keep all my papers from landing in the wrong hands," Anya shrugged as she held out a hand, "Auncle Dylan had the idea to make the place where I already hide into my secondary office. Spies must go through Kaiden to find me here and loyal Librarian Staff when I'm not here."

"Huh," Arthur said, grabbing her hand as she helped him stand. He then brushed off the soot and glitter from his clothes, "That was a trip; I wouldn't suggest travelling like that unless you have to."

Anya nodded, amused, "Noted; the glitter alone will take forever to get out of here."

"Doesn't it always?" Arthur asked, "So, where are we getting ready for this thing?"

"We're getting ready in my rooms," she replied tiredly, "You'll pretend to be Kaiden while he stays here until Uncle Matheo can get here to smuggle him out of the palace, which he's quite good at doing."

Arthur nodded, "He's used to smuggling members of the royal family out of palaces. Where will Uncle Matheo be taking him?"

"The United States Embassy."

Arthur blinked, "The United States Embassy? Why does he need to go there?"

"I'll be returning as a diplomat for Hawaii with the current US President," a dry voice came from the couch.

Arthur's eyes moved to the corner he wasn't paying attention to. Kaiden emerged from the shadows, looking amused. It was like he knew something that Arthur didn't. Arthur's eyes narrowed.

"Am I *finally* allowed in on the secret now?" He asked the older man.

Kaiden nodded, "I'm the missing prince of Hawaii. The current president was born there. This is why I would be coming with him."

Arthur's mouth dropped, "How the hell did I miss that you're a prince?!"

"And guess when he chose to tell me that he was a prince from the Hawaiian Kingdom State?" Anya interjected.

Arthur looked between them.

"No," he realised, as his eyes trailed back to the older prince, "You waited to tell her about you being a fellow royal until I was bloody taken?!"

"It wasn't intentional," Kaiden protested, "I was *going* to tell her on your eighteenth birthday. I was supposed to reveal my true identity then and ask her if she would go out with me."

Arthur stared at him momentarily before asking, "Why am I suddenly happy for my kidnapping?"

"That's because it was a stupid plan, and I would have said no, feeling betrayed that he's been pretending to be this simple guard," Anya said, crossing her arms, "I think Uncle Aaron would have killed him for messing up his plans."

"Plans?" Arthur asked, "What plans does Uncle Aaron have for the two of you?"

"Something about Drago women following their path and needing someone equally stubborn to keep up with them," Kaiden continued vaguely, "Believe me, you could tell he was out of practice when he tried to recruit me to be one of Anya's guards."

"Why did you agree anyway?" Anya asked, "Especially since your sister didn't let you leave the country without your guard."

Kaiden shrugged, "I was bored with the job options I had. Your temper made it worth staying; it became more endearing than a nuance. We challenged each other to refine our powers because you craved freedom, and I was the only one who could keep up with you." He then pulled off his coat. "Now, Lady Murrian knows I'm assigned to a room near Anya in case she needs me in the middle of the night," he continued, "She has decided that she needed to post one of her spies at my door to act as a guard."

Arthur's eyebrow raised as Kaiden handed him the coat.

"So, she doesn't know that all the rooms connect by the staff hallways?" Arthur asked.

Anya snorted, "Oh, she does. She just thinks she's clever enough to keep us apart. She also believes *we* don't know about the hallways. However, the staff spies don't realise our rooms have a hidden door in the closet, connecting them. I think Uncle Aaron had him put in those rooms on purpose. Those rooms were designed to allow for a royal married couple to sleep separately if needed."

"We believe she plans to keep me in my rooms," Kaiden reported, "She doesn't want anyone interrupting the wedding. She sees me as a threat to the power she wants to keep."

"You mean the power she never had," Arthur muttered.

"What?" Anya demanded, "What are you talking about?"

Arthur blushed, "I wasn't supposed to say that out loud— *it's a surprise.*"

Kaiden's eyes narrowed, "You found something more than your grandfather being Father Christmas."

The fireplace flared again before Arthur could answer, and more bodies flew out. Arthur moved out of the way to avoid being knocked over. He wasn't the only one navigating the travel system for the first time. Arthur hastily helped to catch Noel. He was somewhat jealous that Nathan managed to land better than either of them.

Then, Anya could only stare as Mum emerged from the fireplace as if the painting above it came to life. Her darkened hair had some new streaks of grey running through the strands, but other than that, she still looked like a dead ringer to the portrait.

"M... *mummy?*" Anya whispered. She turned to Arthur, "Is this happening? Is it her?"

"Do you remember Uncle Mattew's stories about elf ninjas?" Arthur asked.

"Those are **real?**" Anya said with awe.

Mum nodded.

"They're the security detail for Grandfather Christmas's children and grandchildren, these ninja elves," Arthur continued before Mum could, "Uncle Mattew's brother is the Head of Security for the North Pole."

Anya was quiet for a moment. Arthur could see the wheels turning in her head. Then, a moment later, she tackled the older woman in a hug. Arthur helped Nathan and Noel to the couch, he realised everything would work out...

☩ ☩ ☩

"*Why* are we doing this again?" Arthur whined, having snuck back into Anya's room. "And *why* is Auncle Dylan here, drinking like a fish?"

Anya handed him his first official legal drink from the cooler. The one she handed him happened to be one that Antonio picked out for him over the summer.

"Stepmonster needs to think her bloody plan is working," Anya hissed, frustrated that he wasn't getting it. "And that includes a Bachelorette Party I've been putting off. She already has guards outside of Kaiden's doors and made an appearance here, so—"

"And I'm here, *not* having a reunion with my husband because he's still working," Auncle Dylan pointed out with a wide grin, nearly drunk off their ass. They raised their wine glass, "We also like trolling the Crazy Lady, especially when she has no idea it's happening!"

"You're making me participate because I have nowhere else to go with Uncle Matheo playing the sleeping body in the bed next door?" Arthur retorted. "What's in it for me?"

"We're doing this for you as your last night as a free man and to celebrate our eighteenth birthday," Anya continued, also with a grin, "Now that you're here with Mum, secrets are about to be revealed."

"Isn't it weird that I'm here?" Mum asked after she sipped her Strawberry Daiquiri in a glass bottle.

Anya and Arthur shook their heads.

"It would be if it were normal circumstances," Arthur muttered. "But nothing about this is *'normal circumstances'*. I would've liked to have dated my husband-to-be before marrying him."

"Who, by the way, still believes he's marrying *me*," Anya grumbled, "I would *rather* jump off London Bridge if I thought I could escape. I'm thankful he found you, even if he doesn't realise we're doing the ultimate switch."

"I can't wait for this," Auncle Dylan rubbed their hands together, "This is our speciality."

"Can I have an update?" Mum asked, "How has the switching been working with Arthur's hair short and Anya's hair long?"

The grin that grew on Auncle Dylan's face would scare most people. "Now, let me see," They thought for a moment. *"There was the time that we bonded over hair…"*

✠ ✠ ✠

2007: Three Years Before the Kidnapping…
Anya, a fifteen-year-old princess, pulled off the shaggy blonde wig and placed it on the wig stand. She looked at herself in the mirror of her vanity. She desperately wished that switching with Arthur had gotten easier, not harder, as they got older.

"Do you need help?" Auncle Dylan asked as they came up behind her.

"Please?" She requested as she sat on the stool before the vanity.

They nodded as they took the wig cap off her head and put it on the vanity. Then, they started pulling bobby pins out of her hair. "You have the Council completely fooled?"

"Of course," Anya scoffed, "They're always fooled, except for Lord Wales, Papa and Uncle Aaron. They don't count."

Auncle Dylan chuckled, "I think that's because of Lord Wales' five times great-grandmothers."

Anya hummed before looking at her Auncle in the mirror, "Wait, what great grandmothers?"

"They were identical twins who ruled and raised their families together. No one could tell them apart except their husbands, children, and most of their grandchildren," They pulled the elastic off the end of Anya's hair before handing it to her and then started undoing the braid. "Now, how did Arthur style his wig today?"

"A braid," Anya giggled as Auncle Dylan's face dropped with dismay.

"Why didn't you stop me?" They whined.

"It's messy, and I made a fishtail."

"Huh," they looked closer, "So you did. Alright, pass up your brush."

Anya grabbed the brush with her right hand, passing it over her left shoulder without turning around. Auncle Dylan took the brush and started running it through her hair.

"I've got to find a spell that will keep yours and Arthur's hair the same length," they muttered. "No wigs required."

"How about you? Why do you keep your hair short?" Anya asked as Auncle Dylan's eyebrows arched, causing her to giggle again. "Men having longer hair can pull off the man bun, this new concept among the commoners, and I know how much you **love** to piss off Stepmonster. Having a man bun would be something you would have to piss her off."

"Matheo and I have been talking about it," Auncle Dylan admitted, *taming her hair before parting it into three sections, "He likes playing with my hair, but it's too thick and curly to put it up without getting a headache. Now, let's get your hair fixed to switch you two back."*

✠ ✠ ✠

"The best part of the whole thing was Andros knew the whole time and heavily encouraged it!" Auncle Dylan exclaimed, almost falling out of their chair.

"Okay," Anya said as she took their beer bottle. "You shouldn't have anymore. When did you start drinking?"

"On and off for the last decade," Auncle Dylan admitted, "Mostly because I was trying to keep your father from doing something even stupider than bringing home the she-pack of social climbing witches. The only thing that was good about that event was Damian."

Arthur swallowed; he didn't know his Auncle could be so chatty.

"Why was that a good thing?" Arthur found the courage to ask.

A smile came to Auncle Dylan's face, similar to what Arthur remembers on Papa and Mum's faces when they talk about something he and his siblings did. Something that they were proud of.

"I've always wanted to take him home and bundle him up away from the world," Auncle Dylan droned on, "Lady Murrian hurts him with her conditional love when all he wants is someone to love him for who he is not for what he can do for them."

Arthur nodded as Anya looked away from Auncle Dylan. Arthur knew what she was still dealing with up until Damian left to find him; she hated Damian for being like his family. She has since learned that he was nothing like Lady Murrian and the other women.

"He's accomplished so much," Auncle Dylan continued,

"Papa and I have been working with one of his old professors to ensure he can do what he loves."

"Wait," Anya gapped. "You and Uncle Aaron encourage Damian to work with Inspector Warren and CSI Bradson?"

Auncle Dylan nodded, a little loopy, "We needed to carry out Andros' plan. We just didn't expect a kidnapping to jumpstart Damian's career at New Scotland Yard."

"What else did you set up?" Arthur asked, curious about this new side of Auncle Dylan. He's never actually seen them this drunk before... Come to think of it, he had *never* seen Auncle Dylan drunk before.

"Well, I didn't set it up," Auncle Dylan started, "It was something that Papa did that Andros approved."

"And that was?" Anya asked, leaning in.

"That Kaiden would be Anya's perfect match," they replied as they tried to stand, "Oh, I don't think I should have done that." They fell back to the couch, *"Wake me up tomorrow."*

Arthur and Anya looked at each other as their Auncle fell asleep. Mum cannot stop herself from laughing at her cousin-in-law. The twins then look at her.

"Is this..." Anya started.

"Normal?" Arthur finished.

Mum nodded with a grin, "I knew if I wanted to know anything was to get some alcohol in them. That's how I knew that your father was going to propose before he proposed. It drove your father nuts."

"Can you tell us more?" Anya asked quietly.

"Are you sure?" Mum asked, consurned, "Arthur, this is supposed to be your last day single."

"Nothing about this is normal," Arthur pointed out, "We're leaving our drunk Auncle to sleep out their one-person party. I shouldn't even be having one of these, as no one knows I'm gay other than everyone here. I will be coming out to the world with this wedding."

Mum leaned forward and put her drink down.

"The first thing that you need to know about your father is that family for him always came first," she continued, "I was introduced to your Auncle Dylan and Uncle Andrew before I met his aunts and uncles."

"Who is Uncle Andrew?" Anya asked, confused, "Why have we never met them?"

"He was your father's older cousin through a different branch of the royal family," Mum hummed, "Lord Liam Wales is his father. You never met him because he died before you two were born. I think he might have died before Damian and Antonio were born, to tell you the truth..."

Arthur closed his eyes and allowed Mum's voice to wash over him. He had missed her storytelling. He couldn't wait to hear those stories again.

He didn't realise that he had dosed off at one point. He briefly opened his eyes to see Uncle Mattew's face. He just didn't know why. He closed his eyes again...

Chapter 19: Getting Ready

Christmas, 2010, 9 am...

Nothing was going to plan. Arthur woke the following day, head pounding. He must have been more tired than he thought. He didn't think he drank enough to black out... yet he barely remembered going to bed. He thought he had fallen asleep in Anya's room. But here he was, waking up in Kaiden's bed he's used for the last three years...

Arthur had a gut feeling something was wrong. He sat up and stretched his arms. The curtains were still closed, and the digital clock on the bedside table read 9:30 am. He knew Kaiden was usually up before even Anya was...

"*Shit!*" He exclaimed as he hastily pushed off the covers.

He scrambled across the room to the closet to borrow some clothes Kaiden would be known for wearing. He was supposed to pretend to be Kaiden until he and Anya could switch. But he didn't know how Lady Murrian's people planned to keep Kaiden distracted until after he had dressed and tried the door.

It was locked from the outside. *Well, this is very familiar.* He thought bitterly.

"*Your services are no longer required, Mr Woolf,*" an aloof male voice said from the other side. "*You will be released and escorted off the premises after the ceremony. Any ideas of interfering are over.*"

Arthur then made his way over to the measly breakfast that he didn't realise had been left out for him. It was on a desk on a wall across from the bed. He discovered a not-so-nice note the staff wrote, informing him, in so many words, that the back entrance was also locked, thus cutting off his way of escape.

Eventually, the noise of something getting knocked over and some swearing from the closet pulled him from his thoughts and measly breakfast. He quietly entered the walk-in closet with Noel trying to pick up some mannequin she knocked over. He tried not to laugh as it was taller than her.

"Are you going to help me or *not?*" Noel demanded. "I think I could have woken the dead with that thing!"

"You're being dramatic," Arthur replied as he helped her lift the mannequin. "Why are you here, anyway? Anya said she'd come to get me."

"Oh, Lady Nutso decided she was giving the blushing bride a spa treatment," Noel said, "Auncle Dylan says they need time to style your hair wig." She paused. "What do you need a wig for, anyway?"

Arthur chuckled, "Auncle Dylan is recovering from indulging at the party and probably didn't even notice how much my hair has grown. I didn't have the same pressure of keeping it short as I did here."

"That's due to Lady Nutso's pressure, no doubt," she said with a little huff and a roll of her eyes, "And I *know* what alcohol is."

"Good to know," Arthur returned the eye-roll, "Lady... Nutso and her noble allies wanted me to be more manly."

"And what would *manly* mean to them?"

He knelt a little to look at her in the eye, "When I figure that out, you'll be the first to know. Now, let's get to Auncle Dylan before they burst in here themselves."

Noel giggled. "I like them. They remind me of Ms Ella, a diva."

"It's called being a *Queen* in my case, *darling,*" Auncle Dylan greeted from the doorway as Arthur stood. "Oh my, Arthur, you've made this both easier and harder for me with your new beard, but you'll rock the bearded lady look."

"Thanks, Auncle Dylan. You sound and look better today," he replied.

"Why thank you," Auncle Dylan preened. "You know your Uncle Matt is my impulse control. He gave me his hangover elixir. But I thought your new face fur was part of my imagination."

Arthur laughed, "Do you need me to shave?"

Auncle Dylan stared at him for a moment before a smile settled on their face, *"Arth fach,* what's one more bee in Murrian's bonnet? She's about to get what's coming to her; might as well make her uncomfortable, too. I might trim your beard a bit, but I think it's coming in nicely. What made you grow a beard?"

"There aren't any razors in the North Pole, and some of the elves aren't even physically old enough to need to use razors," Arthur grinned as he passed Auncle Dylan, who simply blinked before bursting into laughter.

"You know, I've heard that complaint before," Anucle Dylan replied, "It's usually coming from Matt."

"Why would Uncle Matt complain about that?" Noel asked, confused, as they made their way through the closet to Anya's room. "The male elves can't wait to grow facial hair."

"He thinks I pull it off much better than him," Auncle Dylan shrugged, "I think he's been young for so long that he just grew used to *not* having a beard and just preferred *not* to grow one."

Arthur laughed, "It's not that."

"Oh, enlighten me, why does my husband dislike growing a beard?" Auncle Dylan requested.

"It grows in patchy," Arthur replied, "You didn't see because he headed straight to the bathroom as soon as we got here before pretending to be Kaiden in the bed last night."

Auncle Dylan suddenly grinned as they approached the bathroom, "I'm going to hide the razors while we're on paternity leave. I want to see this."

Arthur blinked, "Paternity leave? Did it take? Is Lily pregnant?"

"Yep!" Auncle Dylan exclaimed. "Her appointment to confirm the pregnancy was the Monday after you and Matt were taken. I've gone with her to every appointment. You'll see her later; she's still doing Anya's hair despite the Murrians."

"Brilliant!" Arthur grinned.

He knew that Auncle Dylan and Uncle Matthew had been

wanting children for a while. Lily had been Anya's hairstylist for the last few years and adored Auncle Dylan's quest for stylish tips. She didn't mind giving them or learning how to help maintain other hair types among the royal family.

"Now, let's get you in the shower," Uncle Dylan continued, "I need wet hair to work with, and there isn't a hair sink in this room."

"Yes, Auncle!" Arthur gave a cheeky salute before dashing into Anya's bathroom, leaving Noel to ask Auncle Dylan any questions to her heart's content.

"What is *'pregnant'?*" Arthur heard Noel ask before he closed the door. He let himself cackle; too bad he couldn't hear Auncle Dylan get themselves out of that question.

✠ ✠ ✠

1 hour later...

This was how Arthur found himself sitting in front of Anya's vanity with Auncle Dylan behind him with a brush. Noel was sitting behind them, watching and learning. She seemingly was content about whatever answer Auncle Dylan could give as she wasn't asking any questions now.

"Now that your hair has been washed, trimmed, and straightened, let me send a photo to the hairdresser..." Auncle Dylan started as they pulled out their smartphone.

"What are you doing?" Arthur squealed as he tried to cover his head with his hands, "No one is supposed to know I'm here until it's too late!"

"Relax," Auncle Dylan soothed as they squeezed Arthur's shoulder, "I'm just sending it to Lily. She's just going to cut and style Anya's hair. Then I can copy the process on you."

"Oh," Arthur whispered as he lowered his arms and relaxed.

"So, how was your time up north?" Auncle Dylan asked as

they opened some apps to text the photos of Arthur's hair to the hairdresser.

"It was frigid; I don't know how Grandfather and Grandmother can live up there full time," Arthur replied with a reactive shiver as Noel grinned. "It's warmer here, even with it being cold right now."

Auncle Dylan snorted, "That's the same answer Matt gave me. How about you, *darling*? Are you excited to be in a new place?"

"I just wish there was something for me to do," she moaned, "Our youngest cousin already got the part of flower girl, and I'm sure Nathan's been given the role of ring bearer."

Arthur grinned, "Actually, Nathan's busy with snow production; I think you having the role of ring bearer would be perfect."

"And would fit with the fact that Antonio is the Maid of Honour," Auncle Dylan said as they brushed the shoulder-length locks again.

"No," Arthur gasped, astonished, "She did it! She actually did it! Anya's been threatening to make him '*Maid of Honour*' for years!"

"Oh, yes," Auncle Dylan grinned.

"I bet that went over well," Arthur snarked.

"Both Antonio and that Bi…"

"*Lady Nutso*," Noel chimed before they could swear.

"Ahh, I like that name too," Auncle Dylan cooed. "Anyway, Antonio and *Lady Nutso* threw a conniption. At least *Da* could talk Antonio into taking the role, especially when it's one more thing to annoy Lady Nutso with. It's fun to watch her right eye twitch."

"*Which is something you have mastered,*" Uncle Aaron commented from the doorway, making his way into the room before kneeling in front of Noel, "Now, I understand you want to be in the wedding."

Noel nodded, nearly bouncing out of her seat.

"Well, I think between the women of the house, we can whip something up for you," he stood and held out his hand, which she took, "Let's go find them and leave these two gossipers to catch up."

Both Arthur and Auncle Dylan let out groans of protest, and Uncle Aaron chuckled. "If little ears aren't around, you can swear," he reminded.

Arthur saw Auncle Dylan's cheeks redden in the mirror.

"Besides, you have to get ready at some point today," Uncle Aaron continued.

"I'm only wearing my robes today," Auncle Dylan replied after a moment. "I'm officiating this wedding as Spiritual Leader Black today."

"Ahh," Uncle Aaron hummed, "That will surely annoy the Murrian women just as much as attending the wedding in a dress."

His commentary got a laugh from Auncle Dylan as they nodded. Then Uncle Aaron moved to lead Noel out of the closet.

"Wait," Arthur called out.

"Yes?" Uncle Aaron paused.

"How did you get Antonio to calm down about being the 'Maid of Honour'?" Arthur asked.

"Before Matt contacted us?" Uncle Aaron asked as Arthur nodded. "I told him at least Anya wasn't making him wear a matching bridesmaid's dress. Although, I think he might be off the hook for that role now that you're here."

"Anya's plan," Arthur commented, understanding, "She's going to pretend to be him so she can be next to me to stop anything from going wrong."

Uncle Aaron nodded before turning to lead Noel out of the enormous closet.

"Alright, now that the Snow Princess..." Auncle Dylan started to say.

"Fire," Arthur interrupted.

"Huh?"

"Noel has fire powers like Anya. Nathan has snow powers."

"Not water?"

"Nope, it's snow powers," Arthur continued. "I've seen him use them enough to know the difference."

"Does that mean he's—" Auncle Dylan said as a **Ding** cut them off. They hastily dove into their pocket for their phone."

"Ahh, Lily is done with Anya's hair. Let's see what she did." They manoeuvred themselves so Arthur could see, "She sent a video, too."

"Is that a braid made into a bun?" Arthur asked as Auncle Dylan handed him the phone, tilting it so they could copy the style.

"It looks like it is a braid to a bun. But is that silver clip okay? What tiara are you using?"

"The one Papa made for Mum, the ruby and gold lace-like tiara."

Auncle Dylan paused and looked him in the eye through the mirror, "You were able to find it?"

Arthur nodded, "Grandfather Christmas had it hidden up north. The elves took a few of Mum and Nathan's things to protect them from Lady Murrian."

"That makes sense," Auncle Dylan said as they tucked a few bobby pins into Arthur's hair. "Let me know if I'm hurting you."

Arthur shrugged, "It's nothing I'm not used to."

"Do you think you'll stop switching after this?"

"We'll keep switching if Uncle Matt provides a spell to allow Damian and Kaiden to switch, too," Arthur admitted, "It would be weird if they didn't. Kaiden would take it in stride, but I think Anya and Damian still have to work through to get along."

"True," Auncle Dylan agreed with a few more poking of bobby pins. They went around Arthur to find a hair barrette similar to the one the hairdresser had put in Anya's hair, yet in the same gold colour as the tiara. They picked it up and helped it up for Arthur to see, "What do you think?"

"It's close enough," Arthur scrutinised, "Besides, Lady Bitch won't be able to see anything once the veil's on."

"Oh?"

Arthur nodded, "Grandmother Christmas gave me her red veil to use. The fabric is thick enough to cover my identity completely."

Auncle Dylan's face fell, "Why didn't you stop me from doing your hair?"

Arthur's cheeks reddened. "I like it when you do things like this. You were the real mother figure that Anya and I needed after Mum went into hiding for her safety."

"Thank you," Auncle Dylan fanned their face, trying not to tear up, "I would do anything to protect you and Anya. Why aren't you calling her *'Stepmonster'* anymore?"

"Mum's still alive," Arthur pointed out. "I don't think Papa would have remarried even if the Traditionalists wanted him to, and the legal magical document he signed with Mum would have prevented him from signing a new one. We're missing something on why Papa thought he had remarried Lady Murrian."

Auncle Dylan was quiet, trying to process what Arthur told them. Arthur wondered if he should turn to check on his shell shocked Auncle. He couldn't see their face as their head was down.

After a few moments, Auncle Dylan finally looked up and said, "That makes a lot of sense now. I wished we had looked deeper into everything back then. Andros had left to find something. He wouldn't tell anyone what he was looking for. Then, he returned with that yapping she-pack and Damian; we didn't even question why they were here."

They then grabbed a hand mirror and reflected into the big mirror so Arthur could see the back of his head. He could see that the braid that Auncle Dylan had done was pinned to the side of his head as a bun.

"Now, what do you think about your hair?" Auncle Dylan asked.

"You've outdone yourself again." Arthur said in awe, "You even made it work with this mess on my face."

"Are you sure you want to keep your bread?" Auncle Dylan asked, " You look so different with it on."

Arthur nodded, "Damian needs to know who he's kissing. Now, does Anya have a beanie or slouchy hat lying around?"

"Why do you need one of those?" Auncle Dylan asked mournfully, "All that hard work would destroy it!"

Arthur stared at them in the mirror, "I need it to pretend to be Kaiden before I put the dress on."

"You didn't stuff pillows under the covers to make it appear someone is sleeping in the bed?"

Arthur quirked his head, "Should I, even in the middle of the day?"

Auncle Dylan nodded as they laughed, "Oh, you have so much to learn and so little time to teach. Come, let's go trick those dirty rascals into thinking they won their little game."

☧ ☧ ☧

2:30 pm...

Arthur once again found himself standing in front of the full-length mirror. It was free-standing near the entrance of the closet. His family moved behind him, helping to get the last-minute things in order.

His dress had a new feature—long gloves. Mum had the idea when she realised the December wedding was outdoors in a place with some of the world's most inconsistent temperatures.

The red and white Tudor roses were important to the family legacy. The roses were for the Tudor Queens who worked together to save the kingdom from the conflict between religions that King Henry VIII had left behind when he died. The red for the Saint and his role in many lives, including Arthur's.

The red cape was already on his shoulders, feeling a little heavier than it did less than two weeks ago. Grandmother Christmas and Mum added the same white fur they used on the red jacket Grandfather Christmas was best known for wearing to help keep Arthur warm as he went to meet his future husband.

"Can you please sit?" Grandmother Christmas asked, shaking Arthur from his thoughts. "We should get the veil on you in case that... that... *eahira* barges in here."

"She's already been next door to gloat," Anya grumbled from a nearby seat as Lily again tried to fix her hair, "I'm going to punch her the next time if this keeps happening. How did I get the role of pretending to be Kaiden?"

"Because you're the only one free, and hiding pillows in the bed under the blankets isn't an option when Lady Nutso wants to gloat to your face," Arthur pointed out dryly.

Anya was known to act differently depending on her mood at the time, and Arthur rolled his eyes at his sister. He moved to the chair from earlier and faced the mirror to see what Grandmother Christmas was doing.

"I had chosen this veil at the time of my marriage because I was going into it blindly. I did not know your grandfather would be waiting for me at the end of the aisle," she explained as she laid the veil over Arthur's head, confirming it would perfectly hide his face. "We chose words over looks, and I've never regretted that choice. I learned to be myself and raised two children to find love independently."

Grandmother backed away, and Mum took her place, carefully lowering the ruby and gold lace tiara onto Arthur's head. She blinked back tears before leaning in.

"Your father created this out of love for me and our future together," she reminisced, "It was new then but old now, but out of all the pieces I've worn over the years shared with the Scottish royal family, I love this one the most because he had made it himself. Your father wanted to be a jewellery maker if he didn't rule a kingdom."

Mum pulled away as Uncle Aaron appeared out of the corner of his eye, this time kneeling on the floor. He had a shoe box in his hands.

"Uncle Aaron?"

The older man smiled up at him, "I've gotten to work with my father a few times now. However, this isn't just from the Blacks. It's also from the Osos."

Uncle Aaron pulled off the top of the box. He reached in and pulled out a pair of white flats. "These were made with you and your powers in mind. This way, you can always see even if you're blindfolded."

Arthur lifted the bottom of the gown slightly so Uncle Aaron could put the shoes on him similar to how the prince put the glass slipper onto *Cinderella*. They went on smoothly, and as soon as Arthur's first shoe-covered foot hit the floor, the vibrations of the palace made their way back to Arthur.

Uncle Aaron stood.

"Your grandfather got away with not having to deal with the Drago women and their craziness," he continued, getting a few laughs from the others as he backed away. "If you have a daughter, I wish you the best of luck, as I'm finally retiring from public life. Your grandmother and your sisters have been a handful. Another woman added to the Drago tree will be one too many for these old bones to handle."

Aunt Melanie smacked Uncle Aaron's arm but nodded with agreement as Nathan and Noel approached Arthur.

"We have something for you," Nathan said. "Your *'something blue'* normally wouldn't fit with the rest of your theme, but I hope this is an exception."

Nathan held up a blue snowflake charm. It was small enough that no one would think that it was very important in protecting Arthur. It was something that he would be able to hide as a pin on his clothes after the wedding.

"It clips to your flowers; you can use it as a pin once this is over. Please hit it when you're taken again; it's a way for the elves to watch you and help with your damsel-in-distress routine."

Arthur snorted, "I won't get kidnapped again for a damsel-in-distress routine to happen."

Nathan's eyebrow rose, "You can't promise something like that. Can you please take it for peace of mind?"

Arthur held his hand out. Nathan dropped the charm into his palm, "I hope I can rescue myself, but if I cannot do so, I will make sure to hit it for backup."

"That's all we ask," Noel whispered, looking handsome in her little security outfit. *"We can't lose you now that we've found you."*

Instead of waiting for his flowers, Arthur moved to pin the charm to his chest, near his heart. He then pulled his younger siblings into a hug. Anya hastily stood and joined the hug.

"We'll be protective of each other until it gets too much," Arthur promised, "And even then, too much will never be enough."

Anya pulled away first, blinking back tears, "You're going to make me cry!"

Arthur chuckled, "That wasn't my intention,"

"Just a few more minutes," Antonio called from the other room, *"Lady Murrian is getting antsy!"*

"I can't wait to give her a piece of my mind," Mum grumbled before yelling back, *"We're coming!"*

Arthur let go of his younger siblings, "You should go follow the Osos into place. I won't be too far behind."

"Okay!" Noel exclaimed before leaving to catch up with her cousin.

Nathan lingered for a moment before giving Arthur one more hug. He then rushed out the door behind his sister.

Uncle Aaron then helped him stand, "It's amazing what you did to the dress," he commented.

"I like it too," Arthur replied, his grin hidden by his veil, "All my mother figures worked on it, so it's extra special."

Lily then handed him a bundle of flowers that Damian had hand-picked from one of the greenhouses.

"Thank you, Lily," Arthur paused momentarily, looking over her glowing presence, "How much longer?"

Lily smiled as she rubbed her growing stomach, "Just a few more months, you should be back in time to meet your little cousin."

"Are you excited that it worked this time?"

She nodded, "I'm excited to help Matt and Dylan. Matt hasn't seen the progress yet, but Dylan is overprotective of me. They snap at Lady Murrian when she's near and look at me the wrong way."

"It's amusing to watch," Uncle Aaron commented as he held up his arm, "There are times I question Dylan about having an inner dragon because of all that growling. But then I remember they don't have the royal blood the way you do. Are you ready to get married?"

Arthur took a deep breath and exhaled as he linked arms with his uncle. "I'm ready as I'll ever be."

"Wait!" Uncle Matt called from the hallway. He almost missed them.

Arthur and Uncle Aaron stopped and waited for Uncle Matt to catch up with them.

"What's wrong?" Arthur asked, confused. "Did I miss something?"

Uncle Matt nodded, "I have one last spell for you and Damian. It will help keep the illusion of you being Anya *until* it's time for Damian to kiss you."

"How does it break?" Arthur asked, "I want him to know that it's me he's kissing, not Anya."

Uncle Matt grinned, "The spell breaks with True Love's kiss, or in this case, Love at First Sight's kiss."

Uncle Aaron chuckled, "That's perfect! It will keep Lady Murrian from finding out too early about you under the veil and not Anya."

"But it will startle Damian when he suddenly feels hair on his lips," Arthur protested lightly.

"But it will also ground him in the moment," Uncle Matt assured, "It will be everything that his heart is wishing."

"Okay," Arthur agreed, "All of your spell work has never led us wrong before."

Chapter 20: The Royal Wedding

Christmas 2010: 3:30 pm...

Anya and Damian did their best to create a wedding that they could handle within a two—to three-week window. Kate and Wills also did what they could to help. However, their wedding was a love match in a different season. Damian was waiting for an arranged bride.

The wedding would begin at sunset. The gardens of Buckingham Palace were more of a lawn with little to no flowers. Everything had to be brought in: decorations, seating, even the snow in some parts of the garden. The flowers that were added were the Cuetlaxóchitls imported from Central America.

Lady Murrian was the first to go down the aisle. Lord Dudley, her ally in this affair, escorted her down to her spot. They have been allies since she came to court ten years ago. The rumour was that his ancestor was Lord Dudley, with whom Queen Elizabeth I had a possible relationship before she married Prince Felipe. He also seemed to be trying to claim the power his ancestors had missed out on.

It was fun witnessing Lady Murrian get redder and redder. She had *no* explanation for the young girl playing the role of ring bearer. Nor could she figure out how it was lightly snowing on what should have been a cold but sunny without a cloud in the sky. There was no time for her to demand an explanation, as most of the wedding party came down just as the wedding was supposed to start.

Lady Murrian also had to keep her mouth shut if she didn't want to face the anger of the Spanish Queen. It was her children who served as the bridesmaids and flower girl for the bride's side. They had gone down first. But Anya was the last to go before Arthur; she was disguised as Antonio.

Auncle Dylan had gone down the aisle first. They now stood in front of the bridal party at the top of the aisle near the makeshift altar. The guests and bridal party were waiting for the wedding march to start.

But all of this was a blur to Arthur. He barely heard the wedding march begin as he had focused on Damian. His nervous groom didn't know that the bride was Arthur and *not* Anya. This was going to be the greatest day of their lives.

Uncle Aaron walked Arthur down the aisle, knowing everything would be fine once Damian realised Arthur was under the veil. No one let him in on the secret because of how much he ended up under either Lady Murrian or Grandmother Murrian's watchful eye.

Earlier, Arthur thought they weren't going to pull off the ruse. But thanks to some loyal staff and a few stubborn Drago women, they were able to make this possible. He loved that his family actively looked for ways to piss off the women making their lives miserable behind closed doors.

Arthur vaguely noticed that Kaiden was sitting with American President Obama and First Lady Obama. They have been placed closer than normal because of Kaiden's position in security. Uncle Aaron knew it was better that Kaiden was ready for any *explosion* that might happen.

Once they got close to the end of the aisle, Uncle Aaron stopped and lifted Arthur's hand. He then kissed Arthur's gloved hand. He then lowered their hands but kept them held.

"I'm not going to lift the veil. Those who remember your grandmother's story would know that only your groom can do that," Uncle Aaron explained quietly.

Arthur nodded slightly. He reached up to wipe a tear off Uncle Aaron's cheek. Uncle Aaron chuckled.

"These are happy tears," the older man assured so Arthur didn't have to ask, "Let's make Damian yours before Lady Murrian figures out that you pulled another switch."

Arthur nodded again before Uncle Aaron placed his hand on Damian's. Then, he and Damian walked the rest of the way to Auncle Dylan. Arthur quickly took his time to look over Damian.

His soon-to-be husband looked every bit of the prince he was about to become. He wore dark pants, a grey vest, and a dark red tie beneath a navy blue jacket. Damian's powers helped regulate his body heat in the cold weather, making his ensemble less heavy than others around him.

The last time Arthur saw Damian, he had a beard beginning to form from his extensive investigation. Now, he was clean-shaven, and Arthur couldn't wait to touch his face. He liked that Damian did have a clean-shaven face. But it might have to do with the fact that he hadn't seen him any other way.

"*Lord Murrian?*" Auncle Dylan asked, and Arthur regained his focus. "Lord Damian?"

Arthur squeezed Damian's hand to get his attention.

"*I'm sorry,*" Damian replied sheepishly, "Can you repeat the question?"

"Of course," Auncle Dylan said lightly, slightly worried the plan could fall apart at any moment. "Do you take your partner to have and to hold from this day forward as long as you both shall live?"

"I do," Damian replied as quickly as possible, trying to hide the sadness that they were already at this part of the ceremony.

Arthur knew Kaiden couldn't interfere, not with the steps Lady Murrian took to keep him otherwise *occupied*. She had no idea of his true identity and that he was part of the delegation representing the United States as a diplomat.

"Your Highness," Auncle Dylan shifted slightly to look at their hidden nephew, "Do you take your partner to have and to hold from this day forward for as long as you both shall live?"

"I do," Arthur replied, hoping he sounded muffled by the veil. He also hoped the spell could help hide his voice. He thought both were successful because Lady *Nutso* didn't try to stop the wedding.

Auncle Dylan nodded, "With the power vested in me by the

late king and the spirit of this great nation, I now pronounce you partners for life. You may seal your union with a kiss."

Damian let go of Arthur's hand. The two turned to each other. Damian shakily raised his hands to lift the veil. The veil slowly revealed Arthur's face. He leaned in and kissed Arthur hesitantly but stiffened when the kiss suddenly deepened. He wasn't expecting that to happen.

Then a tingle of magic washed over them...

✠ ✠ ✠

"NO!" Damian heard Mother exclaim angrily. He pulled away from the kiss in confusion, only to find himself staring into Arthur's sparkling eyes. He gingerly touched Arthur's bearded cheeks.

"Arthur, is... is it *you?*" Damian asked, shocked.

A chuckle left Arthur's glossy lips, "Yep. Love always wins."

"How?" Damian asked, true happiness bleeding through in his voice.

"That's what we want to know!" Lord Dudley interrupted angrily. The wild-haired man looked ready to attack. He was so close to gaining the power that his ancestor failed to get.

"Loopholes!" Ze Dylan declared gleefully, "For some homophobic, unpleasant people like yourselves, you neglected to put genders in the legal document!"

"Why, you little bas-" Mother started as she moved to rush the bridal party, fire encasing her fist...

Suddenly, Kaiden and Anya were at the altar in front of the three with a water shield in place, courtesy of Kaiden. He had run up from where he had been sitting near the President of the United States when Mother started screeching. Anya's fists held flames, and a wig was on the ground where Damian thought Antonio was standing.

"Stop hurting my family!" Anya growled.

She then started changing before their eyes. Kaiden moved

out of the way as Anya's regal clothing ended up on the ground in tatters. A blue and gold spotted dragon with scales grew to be as tall as the two-story face of the palace. Wings then grew out of her back, stretching the span of two cars.

This mystical, majestic being stood in place of Anya, towering protectively between them and Mother. From Damian's vantage point, he saw the Traditional Nobles and Mother run off, only to be caught by Inspector Warren and his co-workers. The other guests were either backing away or ducking behind chairs.

"ANYA!" Kaiden yelled from beside her, trying to get her attention.

It worked, as the next thing she did was bend down and snatch Kaiden up.

"HEY! I'M ON YOUR SIDE!" Kaiden continued yelling as Anya deposited him onto her shoulder.

"Boys," Ze Dylan said from behind them, "We should retreat into the palace. Anya won't regain her mind if she thinks you're both in danger. Kaiden can only do so much."

Arthur and Damian nodded and hastily followed Auncle Dylan through the grand palace doors in hopes that Anya would start working with the dragon and change back to human form. A small group stayed behind to help Anya as they headed inside.

"This way!" Arthur called as he led Damian up the staircase. His dress was dragging behind them, and his white flats peeked out of the long gown.

"How the hell are you running in a dress with ease!" Damian asked, "Where are we bloody going?"

"We're heading for the infamous balcony," Arthur replied gleefully, *"I want to see Anya barbecue them!* As for the shoes, I dressed like this to get past your mother's eyes, and they're specially made. Uncle Aaron knew that I would have to run at one point. Auncle Dylan also helped. This was their dress. I'm just used to wearing ball gowns."

223

"Wait," Damian pleaded, breathless.

"What?" Arthur whined, "Anya's going to maim someone, and we're going to... *umf!"*

Damian hastily kissed him as they backed up against the wall leading to the balcony, unable to hold back any longer. Arthur clenched Damian's jacket, dreading that he would pull away any moment.

Damian reluctantly broke the kiss to breathe.

"We have to see this," Arthur insisted, flushed. "Once your mother and her allies are rounded up–"

"We can truly love openly," Damian finished, "You'll have to help me understand how you ended up under the veil. My visions could only show me so much."

Arthur grinned, *"Later!* Anya needs to explain her side of the plan, too. Come on, I don't want to miss this!"

Arthur then grabbed Damian's hand again and continued to pull him along, reaching the balcony and pushing the doors wide open just in time to hear:

"ANYA!" Uncle Aaron called proudly from the ground, *"EVERYONE IS SAFE. LOOK TO YOUR LEFT!"*

Her head twisted toward the balcony. Arthur, still in his beautiful gown, reached out and fearlessly touched her blue snout. Damian was behind him, smiling as he knew what was about to happen next.

"MAY I INTRODUCE QUEEN CATHERINE EVERGREEN DRAGO, LONG LIVE THE QUEEN!" They heard Uncle Aaron declare, loud and proudly.

"LONG LIVE THE QUEEN!" The guests cheered as they came out of hiding, realising that this... *dragon...* was only mad at a select few people. Those people in question were being rounded up by guards and police from New Scotland Yard.

"THAT'S IMPOSSIBLE!" Lord Dudley raged as he tried to throw off the guards attempting to take him in. *"THE LAW CLEARLY SAYS–"*

"THE LAW DOES NOT CONTROL THE WILL OF THE

SPIRITS!" Uncle Aaron snarled as Anya slowly regained her mind. Arthur could see her eye colour changing from gold to grey. *"THE DRAGON SPIRIT HAS ALWAYS CHOSEN A WOMAN FROM THE DRAGO BLOODLINE!"*

"Can you put me down, Your Majesty?" Kaiden asked in awe. "You should be in human form to confront them."

'Fine,' She huffed, speaking into their minds, which Damian didn't know she would be able to do, *'We're talking about this when everything settles!'*

"Of course," Kaiden hastily assured, loud enough that Damian and Arthur could hear from the balcony, "Especially since Antonio and I can now share the legends of our cultures without the gag spell interfering."

'Gag spell?'

"Put me down and find out," he replied.

'Okay, but I'm putting you with them.' Her left-clawed hand grabbed him again and moved to place him on the balcony next to Arthur and Damian.

"Anya!" Kaiden exclaimed, now pissed, *"I'm supposed to protect you!"*

"Give up," Arthur warned with a chuckle. "She's going to hold this over our heads for the rest of our lives."

Kaiden glared at Arthur, this time making Damian chuckle.

"That's the problem," Kaiden muttered, "I'll have two overprotective Spirits looking over me. You're lucky that you'll only have one overprotective Spirit looking out for you."

Damian just listened to his *husband* and possible brother-in-law descend into bickering. He pulled out his phone and looked up a quick number. He hit the call button.

"Yes, Damian," Lily greeted over the phone.

"I know you're doubling as a Lady-in-Waiting for Anya," he started as Arthur stopped bickering to pay attention, "Can you bring clothes for Anya?"

"Wh..." she started to ask. *"Never mind, I see the huge dragon. Lord Black must be excited."*

"What makes you say that?" Damian asked, confused, "Can you hear him all the way from her rooms?"

"No, but I know my county's past," Lily replied. He could hear her moving around through the phone, *"The Gag spell only affected those who had fire powers, the ideal English person, whatever that means. I'm also Welsh, not English. Matt is here. You'll see me in a moment."*

She then hung up the phone. He stared at it for a moment before a loud noise forced the three of them to look into the gardens. Damian's eyes widened.

"He could have come back at any time?!"He exclaimed as he realised that Matthew could do a form of teleportation.

Arthur shook his head, "Uncle Matt's range is the equivalent of Buckingham Palace. It's a power that was unlocked after he met Auncle Dylan, and it's only useful for bringing him wherever Auncle Dylan is located."

"But…" Damian started before shaking his head, "I need an updated list of powers from *everyone*! I need to know who can protect themselves and who I can put on their security teams that can help boost them!"

Kaiden gave him a side look, "Why would you do that?"

Damian snorted, "The Queen of England can transform into a *Bloody* dragon! She'll need a protection team that will protect her back, not try to stifle or control her actions."

"And me?" Arthur asked, "What will you do with me?"

"I will work with Prince Félix and Matt to make sure that I have the right people with the situational training needed to be your security!" Damian growled, "Those three idiots got replaced because they had the same patterns outside of work!"

"I think the elves that came with us are staying," Arthur said as he looked over Damian's shoulder.

Damian turned to see a female elf that was friends with Matt. She waved at him before stepping back to be in the shadows. He barely saw her once she did that. He turned back to Arthur and Kaiden.

"You two are convincing Anya about elven protection," he muttered.

"Lord Black had such an *easy* time with getting her to accept me," Kaiden said sarcastically as he looked out into the garden, watching as Uncle Aaron tried to convince Anya to switch back. "I had to bribe her into proving she could beat me in order for me to *go away* like she wanted. However, by the time she beat me, she *didn't* want me to leave."

"I have my work cut out for me," Damian grumbled, "That isn't even including security for Nathan and Noel. But I suspect that Alfred has a few ideas for them."

Arthur grinned before leaning in to kiss Damian...

Chapter 21: Dragon Tales

28 December 2010:
Twelve Weeks and Three Days
After the Kidnapping...

Four generations of the English Royal Family, three significant others, a Spanish Royal cousin, and a Lady-in-Waiting gathered around the breakfast table on the private side of Buckingham Palace. The Spanish Royal Family was out exploring London. Meanwhile, the Scottish Royal Family had gone to the Sandringham House after the chaotic wedding and its dramatic conclusion.

Damian knew that he needed to rethink his honeymoon plan, as everyone from the North Pole was on the other side of the table. Mum, Noel, and Nathan were sitting across from them, and Grandfather Christmas and Grandmother Christmas were at one end of the table, while *Hen Daid* and *Hennain* were at the other.

Uncle Aaron and Aunt Melaine were next to Mum. They didn't want to let her leave their sight. Auncle Dylan and Uncle Matheo were on Nathan's other side, with Lily between them. Liam, who was well on his way to becoming *Taid*, was next to Damian.

Anya admitted she could hear the dragon purr in the back of her mind every time she pulled Noel into her arms. Noel could be a dragon if Anya didn't have any daughters. She also has a sharper memory of their grandparents' true identity.

"Can we get the missing pieces?" Noel pleaded between waffle bites. "We know Arthur ended up in the North Pole and how Damian tracked him down. But how did you guys pull off the greatest switch of your lives?"

"I want to know that too," Damian admitted. "I've been in the dark since leaving the North Pole. Some agent I must be."

Uncle Matheo shook his head, "There are times we have to

limit what information gets out to protect long-term undercover operatives, and this was one of those times."

"And I think I should start," Liam said, "Though my part begins *just after* the kidnapping."

✠ ✠ ✠

1 October 2010:
One Hour After the Kidnapping
Westminster British Parliament...

Parliament and the House of Lords called an emergency meeting, gathering a few hours earlier than scheduled, as soon as the news of King Arthur's kidnapping from the Farmers Market broke. The large building was a sanctuary for Liam, who was well-versed in hiding behind a mask. He worked for years to keep his emotions off his face, a blank slate. He never wanted his political enemies to be able to use his feelings against him.

Liam never wanted to see the country revert after it had made such strides for women, people of colour, and the LGBTQ+ community. It became one of his chosen jobs to help Lord Black protect the English Royal Family from the Traditionalists. Luckily, nothing could be changed if the next ruler was underage.

His father, the previous Lord Wales, had evoked an old law that kept the Traditionalists from interfering with the raising of King Andros. The familial law kept the Child King with Lord Black.

However, right now, all the enemies would see his annoyance. Liam never understood the ridiculousness of the nobles who referred to themselves as 'Traditionalists'. He just couldn't wrap his head around the fact they wanted to go back to a time when women were 'controlled', a male-led royal line, and homosexuality was illegal altogether. These were all guesses about what they wanted to talk about... or what the meeting should have been about.

Liam was pulled from his thoughts as he felt the floor shift under his feet. He hastily moved to place a grounding hand on Prince Antonio's shoulder. He then gave a slight squeeze.

"Don't let them see your anger," he instructed quietly. "Besides, this building isn't earthquake resistant."

The Spanish Prince closed his eyes and took a few deep breaths. Liam felt the floor settle as he took a few more deep breaths.

"Are you feeling better?" Liam asked.

Prince Antonio nodded before shaking his head.

"Why are they even debating about Anya's eligibility to get married and who she marries?" He questioned. "Doesn't something like this fall to Anya or Lord Black trying to get Anya and Kaiden together?"

Liam shook his head. "We only have a final say, and even then, Parliament can still override if they're scared and determined. And right now, they're scared that there's one heir left to the English thrown in their near direct control. So that will make them determined to keep that control in any way possible. It will be better to work with them than against them."

The prince swallowed. The English Royal Family hadn't practised arranged marriages since the 1500s. "Anya isn't going to be happy about this..."

✠ ✠ ✠

28 December 2010: Twelve Weeks and
Three Days After the Kidnapping
Buckingham Palace...

"Wait," Anya interrupted, fingers interlaced with Kaiden's. "How many people knew about this plan of Kaiden and I?"

"Plan?" Liam snorted. "It always falls to the Lord Security to find the right guard for the Crown Princess. It just happens that Aaron has been Lord Security since your grandfather died."

"But what happened after that?" Noel demanded, listening to the story of the edge of her seat. She looked annoyed at Anya and Arthur for interrupting.

"Oh, yes, where was I?" Liam asked.

"A tradition resumed," Nathan added with a grin.

"Ah, yes," Liam hummed, "Lord Dudley started ranting..."

✠ ✠ ✠

1 October 2010: One Hour After the Kidnapping
Westminster British Parliament...

"We should have paired the Prince-King off ages ago!" The greying Lord Dudley bellowed, from the Traditionalists' side of the room, "Or at least heavily encouraged him towards an heiress of our choosing. What about the Princess? Has she shown any interest in the heirs?"

"Hoping to push her toward your son," Liam muttered, loud enough to cause Lord Dudley to turn red in the face, "It wouldn't be the first time your family has made a move for the throne."

"Says the man whose claim to the English Royal Family is through a bastard," Lord Dudley sneered, trying to recover from Liam's zing, "At least Queen Elizabeth I made the right choice in the end."

Prince Antonio looked between the two English lords in confusion, but Liam understood why. The **Gag Spell** *didn't affect the Spanish Prince as it did Lord Dudley. Prince Antonio knew that Liam wasn't a descendant of a royal bastard, just that his ancestor was a male.*

"As entertaining as this is," Lady Murrian interrupted, amused, "We need to secure the princess so she won't disappear, too."

"And how do you suggest that we do that?" Liam requested, "She's strong-headed like the grandmother she never met."

The slow shark-like grin growing on Lady Murrian's face sent shivers down Liam's spine. The last time he saw that grin was four months ago, right after King Andros had died. The Traditionalists had overridden the King's will to place Lady Murrian as the primary guardian of Prince King Arthur and Princess Anya, claiming they needed a woman.

However, this backfired as the Royal Twins never went to her for anything. They always went to either Melanie or Dylan. It was fun to watch Princess Anya hold herself with more tac than the

Traditionalists whenever she appeared in Parliament looking like Prince King Arthur. She could also hold her temper better when she pretended to be the Prince King.

"She will be eighteen at the end of the month," Lady Murrian continued, "She'll be old enough to marry off as it would be socially acceptable that not even those Americans would protest, especially to someone older than her."

Lord Dudley stood a little taller, happy someone was finally entertaining his idea. "My son would have agreed when I proposed this a year ago. But now he's engaged himself."

Lady Murrian shook her head, the grin never leaving her face, "There's another one closer in age and can wear the crown as soon as they're married."

"Your son," Liam interrupted as a shiver went down his spine, "You want to marry your son off to Princess Anya?" He paused for a moment as she nodded. "Have you lost your damn mind?! They can't stand each other on a good day! The Princess picks fights with him every chance she gets."

"They'll learn to love each other. The King and I certainly did. Besides, it isn't like she'll be marrying her brother because of the amount of arguing between them."

Liam could only stare at the woman. She was a piece of work, though he hadn't realised how genuinely horrible she was until now.

"She's that desperate for the throne," Prince Antonio whispered only loud enough for Liam to hear. He was in attendance solely to report back to Aaron since he couldn't make it.

Liam bit his lip to keep himself from replying aloud. He must manoeuvre the situation to his advantage to maintain control.

"You should go warn Anya and Kaiden," Liam said quietly to Antonio. "I can tell Aaron the rest. The princess shouldn't be caught off guard by Lady Murrian."

Prince Antonio nodded before hastily retreating. Liam needed the prince out of the building to keep things from blowing up in their face, literally.

Liam knew he needed to help Lord Damian, and the young man's *secret could still be protected without Lady Murrian finding out about it until it was too late for her to do anything about it. He just hoped he could help word any marriage contract that Lady Murrian could think about in a way that could make everyone happy…*

✠ ✠ ✠

Damian's mouth dropped.

Arthur reached under the table and grabbed his hand, squeezing it before asking, "So, how many people in this family knew of our feelings before he found me at the North Pole?"

His and Damian's cheeks reddened when almost every hand went up except Noel's. Nathan even knew about it because of the letters Arthur had accidentally sent him.

"*I didn't want to admit it,*" Anya sighed, "I knew you preferred men. It made it easier for me to flirt with them when we switched places. I just didn't want to find out you liked Damian. He's the only one I *couldn't* get along with."

Kaiden blinked, "Flirted with other men? Arthur never *flirted* with anyone *but* Damian. *You* hated Damian so much he knew when the two of you switched."

"You *knew?*" Arthur asked as Anya's face flushed.

Damian nodded, "Kaiden's right; she couldn't remain neutral whenever I was near. I wonder if Mother thought we were compatible because you were too nice when pretending to be Anya."

The others laughed as Arthur pouted. He thought he did better pretending to be Anya.

"Can we please get back to the story?" Noel whined, "I want to know how you guys figured out you could switch out Anya and Arthur!"

Anya, Kaiden, Auncle Dylan, and Antonio exchanged grins.

✠ ✠ ✠

Halloween, 2010:
Four and a Half Weeks After the Kidnapping...

"*What a rotten birthday this is turning out to be!*" *Anya muttered, pushing away the paper she was reading. Nothing made sense anymore. The last arranged marriage in the English Royal Family was back in the 1500s. There was no law* **against** *it yet, and every generation since Queen Elizabeth I Tudor-Drago — the woman behind the change of tradition— married for love over any alliances that also asked for marriage, unlike other royal marriages that worked more like transactions than for love.*

How did they do that? She thought.

"*I've got it?!?!*" *Auncle Dylan exclaimed as they rushed into the library-converted office for Anya.*

"*Oh, thank the Spirits,*" *Anya said as she brushed the hair away from her face.* "*Nothing about history makes sense. I don't understand Arthur's fascination with it.*"

"*That's because it isn't the official betrothal agreement,*" *Auncle Dylan grinned, holding up a scroll,* "*Lord Wales was considerably helpful. He understands what's at stake here.*"

"*He's being weird, too,*" *Antonio grumbled from beside Anya,* "*He and Uncle Aaron have been conspiring about something. I think he knows about you and Kaiden.*"

"*Why didn't he bring it up to the other lords?*" *Anya asked, confused as she took the scroll,* "*Isn't he on their side?*"

Auncle Dylan shook his head, "*He has always been on our side. He just couldn't help any more than he did; something was stopping him.*"

"*Do you think it has to do with why passages and pages from your history books are blurred??*" *Antonio asked,* "*But when I read it, I can see the true history; no matter which book, I can see what you can't. The spell is still powerful enough, though; I can't tell you anything about what I read.*"

"*Lord Black thinks it has everything to do with the spell,*" *Kaiden said from the doorway as he closed the door.* "*He also thinks we can see it because our abilities aren't fire-based. That's the only way I can explain why your cousin and I can see the truth, but you can't.*"

Anya hummed as she opened the scroll. Both Kaiden and Antonio had a point. Something was keeping her past from her, and she wanted to know why. She also wanted to find a way out of this arrangement to marry her stepbrother.

"Have you looked this over?" She asked.

Auncle Dylan nodded, grin growing, "Look how Lord Murrian worded the beginning."

Anya unravelled the scroll and read aloud:

"An arrangement between the House of Murrian and the House of Drago..." she trailed off, frustrated, "This doesn't help us in any way! This still keeps us together!"

"Wait," Antonio said, "Does it really say 'between the houses'?"

"YES!" Ayna growled, exasperated, "I can't change these words no matter how hard I try!"

"But there's nothing there about names or genders, right?" Antonio questioned, excited for his cousin, "Words and names have power when magic is involved. We can twist this in our favour! Arthur is alright wearing dresses, right?"

"We switched places for our sanity when we were younger," Anya replied, "He would do it again to get what he wants. He just needs to be found."

"When you were younger?" Auncle Dylan smirked with a raised eyebrow, "I helped the two of you switch just days before Arthur was taken!"

"And Damian is close to finding Arthur," Kaiden continued, "We can't include Damian in this because he still has to deal with the Murrian women once he returns."

"The look on his face will be worth it," Anya declared, feeling better about the situation.

✠ ✠ ✠

"I should have read the whole bloody contract," Damian groaned, interrupting the story, "How did I not read the whole bloody contract?!"

"You *did* read the whole contract," Anya assured. "The gender-neutral wording wasn't in the draft version where we added the part about getting me pregnant later when we were ready. Uncle Liam had changed that *after* your mother and her allies approved the contract. It was the only way to get them on board with the document."

"You wanted this for *me?*" Damian squeaked.

Anya nodded, "The day you had that bad panic attack, I knew you could never be part of the arrangement. When we realised Uncle Liam had added a way for Arthur and me to switch without any magical consequences, we had to get the others involved. I just didn't know Auncle Dylan knew *where* Arthur was.

Damian snorted, "I'm pretty sure everyone who knew about Matthew's true powers knew where to find Arthur; even *Prince Harry* knew where we were going. But I don't think they told you we found glitter in two places. I think the other person kept in the dark was Kaiden."

Her eyes widened, "That was the blacked-out piece of information?"

Uncle Aaron nodded, "You're not mad we kept it from you?"

She shook her head, "We still have staff loyal to the Murrian women."

"It makes sense to keep a piece of information hidden, and why not the one clue used to lead you straight to Arthur," Kaiden said as he squeezed her hand, "I'm proud of you."

"Wait," Nathan exclaimed, "Why are they calling you 'Kaiden'? Isn't your name *'Kailoa'?*"

"How did you know that?" Kailoa and Anya asked together.

"North Pole magic," Nathan and Grandfather Christmas replied simultaneously.

"But I don't celebrate Christmas the same way you guys do," Kailoa protested, "My culture follows gods and goddesses like the Ancient Greeks and Romans."

"Same as the elves," Grandfather Christmas replied, "But

you wrote a letter to *Snegurochka Anastasia*, the granddaughter of Santa Claus."

"Anya's Snegurachka Anastasia?" Kailoa squealed as his cheeks reddened.

"Does that mean you're *Kai?!*" Anya exclaimed as she stared at him. "I mean, *Kai* from my pen pal letters. You've been letting me call you Kai for a while now."

He nodded, "It's my family nickname, which you can call me." Then his eyes widened, "But that means we've been dancing around each other longer than Lord Black came looking for me!"

"That would explain why Matthew suggested I go as far as Hawaii to find the one guard who could keep up with Anya!" Uncle Aaron exclaimed. "I swear Matthew has been one step ahead of me for years!"

"Well, I had to be to protect the descendants of Queen Catherine of Aragon and Wales," Uncle Matt shrugged, "it was her last Christmas wish to protect her son from her ex-husband."

"How is that?" Anya asked, confused, "You're the same age as Auncle Dylan."

Auncle Dylan laughed, and Uncle Matt shook his head.

"We only told you that because I look like I'm the same age as Dylan," Uncle Matt said, "The truth is I'm over six hundred years old."

"How is that possible?" Kai asked, "You can't look this young and yet be so old."

"Elves age differently than most humans," Uncle Matt replied, "We will look like teenagers for years unless we meet our soul mates."

"And it took this one forever to realise he started ageing without the help of an illusion spell," Auncle Dylan said as they poked Uncle Matt. "We could have been together from the moment he entered the grounds with Eve. instead, the Royal Trouble Makers helped to play matchmaker."

"I'm sorry," Uncle Matt retorted as he glared at his partner. "i've always been slow in the romance department. Ella has been telling you stories."

Auncle Dylan nodded, "You shouldn't have brought her home if you didn't want me to learn things about your childhood."

"I didn't have much of a choice when she's here to be Anya's guard," Uncle Matt grumbled. "My mother practically forces us to leave the North Pole when she feels it's time for us to meet our soulmates."

"But it sounds like you've been leaving the North Pole longer than Auncle Dylan's been alive," Anya said. "Why's that?"

"Queen Catherine made a plea to 'Matheo', not 'Matthew', which was the normal name for Santa Claus then," Uncle Matt said. "The thing is, names have power. Her letter and plea came to me instead of the Santa of the time because my birth name is Matheo. My mother seemed to know I would eventually marry into the English Royal Family because she encouraged me to reply to the Queen."

"Names have power," Damian snorted, "I feel that's what has either saved some of the royal family or brought lovers together."

"*In more ways than one,*" Lady Eve said under her breath.

The Evergreen-Drago kids all stared at their mother.

"Your father accidentally wrote a list titled '*Christmas Eve: these are the things I would like to do,*" she continued, her cheeks reddening, "My true name is *Christmas Eve*. We started writing back and forth when we were in Primary School. He couldn't believe my parents named me Christmas Eve."

"You were supposed to be our third child," Grandfather Christmas said softly, and she nodded, seemingly knowing something the others didn't. "We named you that for the destiny we thought you still had."

"And if my brother and sister-in-law had survived to have

more children," Uncle Aaron picked up, "We would be in a very different situation."

"Like the dragon choosing someone else," Arthur continued.

"Exactly," Uncle Aaron said. "Dragons like this only appear when something goes wrong. The dragon always came to help the Queen of England's aid when she needed it the most. However, that usually happens *after* their eighteenth birthday."

"What if Anya needed her before then?" Arthur asked as Anya stared off into the distance momentarily, "What if Anya was kidnapped instead of me?"

"She's saying that she would have emerged early," Anya spoke before Uncle Aaron could, "She said that's what she did to protect Elizabeth of York from her uncle."

"Queen Elizabeth of Scotland?" Nathan asked, confused.

She shook her head, "Queen Elizabeth of York was married to King Henry VII. They were the beginning of both our royal lines. His claim to the throne was through his father's older half-brother and not through a previous king. Elizabeth's line was in control during the War of the Roses. There were rumours that her uncle, King Richard III, was responsible for the disappearance of Queen Elizabeth's younger brothers, King Edward V and Richard. My dragon, Sofia, also seems to think the uncle was going to move to marry Elizabeth before he was killed."

"Were her brothers called *The Princes in the Tower*?" Damian asked suddenly.

Everyone nodded.

"Then the Godparent Rites that Dylan and Matheo went under were created on her request," Damian continued, wide-eyed, "It was in a book I could read but couldn't touch without Dylan's help."

"I bet you will be able to read it now," Dylan grinned, "Uncle Liam was excited to yell at Lady Nutso when he figured out you were his grandson."

"Does the dragon always choose the next ruler?" Arthur

asked. "She never chose Papa, and while it would have been interesting to be the first county with a gay king with a Prince Consort, I'm relieved she didn't choose me."

"She would have if she could," Anya said after listening quietly to her dragon. "Her faith in men to rule with common sense was greatly shaken by King Richard III and King Henry VIII. She would have had you and Papa in the running. However, I think it has to do with the fact we were raised by a very loyal bodyguard in the form of Uncle Aaron."

Uncle Aaron snorted, "The dragon calls me *a 'very loyal bodyguard'*?"

Anya shook her head as a grin appeared, "She calls you *'Uncle Loyal Bodyguard'.*"

That caused everyone around the table to laugh.

Chapter 22: The History of the Dragon...

31 December 2010:
Thirteen Weeks After the Kidnapping...

"The King died, and the Queen died of grief," Arthur read aloud from a history book written *after* their father had been born. He was sitting on the couch in front of a window overlooking the garden. Anya was at her desk.

A small group had gathered in Anya's office without the North Pole crew. They had returned to Holly Manor to get some things for Noel. She would be living here with Anya full time, with the others coming to visit as much as possible.

He looked up to Uncle Aaron. He had never seen his great-uncle look so furious, "I take it this wasn't what happened?"

"These terms are wrong," Uncle Aaron said, now able to speak the truth. Anya's dragon could override the **Gag Spell** that the nobles placed on him when Andros was a few days old, "The oversimplified sentence about your grandparents should be: *'the Prince Consort died, and the Queen died of grief'.*"

Anya and Arthur looked over their great uncle. He's always been a proud man. But at this moment, he looked like he was twenty years older. He had been carrying this burden for a long time.

"The truth is your grandfather got hit with a bullet meant for your grandmother. She died after giving birth to your father," Uncle Aaron continued as Kai entered the room, carrying something. "But what we didn't know at the time was the bullet that killed your grandfather was enchanted."

"It's known as *the Soulmate Curse*," Kai continued as he held up the object, showing it was a journal from the History Section. "You figured out that whoever wanted Queen Elizabeth II wanted to punish Prince Consort Philip."

The aged lord nodded, tired. His anger slowly bled away

the more he spoke his truth. He leaned against Anya's desk, relaxing now that he knew everyone was safe.

"I haven't updated the journal, but it was Marcus Murrian who killed my brother and sister-in-law. He pursued Eliza before Philip and I joined her security team and decided that no one could if he couldn't be with her. But that is how your father was England's first king since King Henry VIII by default."

"Did this Marcus Murrian have a plan for Dad?" Anya asked, concerned.

"I believe he wanted to raise Andros alongside Kendra and Karen. I think they wanted to ensure Andros would end up with one of them," Liam interjected as he stood next to the fireplace, helping Uncle Aaron explain some of the missing history. "My father interfered with the family rule that kept Andros with Aaron. My part was to help raise Andros and only take over if something happened to Aaron and Melanie."

"How do you fit into the family rule?" Arthur asked, not realising how close he was to Uncle Aaron.

Liam grinned, "Aaron ended up raising Andros from the beginning because he was Philip's brother. I was next in line to raise Andros as Eliza's cousin. We shared a set of Great-Great-Great-Great Grandparents. I'm a descendant of Prince Kaiden, and Eliza was from his younger cousin, Queen Alexandra."

"How did he have enough power to get the **Gag Spell** put in place but still get arrested?" asked Damian. "They mustn't have found him right away as Aunt Karen was born *after* Papa Andros, and she looks a lot like him. He was with them long enough to influence much of their decision-making."

Arthur squeezed his hand. Though strange, Lady Murrian 'marrying' Andros was the best thing that could have happened to either of them. Andros was part of the reason Damian could survive the last ten years.

"It's been twenty years since Marcus Murrian was finally arrested," Uncle Aaron said. "The files and recordings Andrew was able to get can become public soon."

"Wait, Uncle Andrew brought Marcus Murrian down?" Arthur asked as he squeezed Damian's hand again.

Liam nodded, "He started his mission a year before Damian was born, but who seduced whom? I don't want to know."

The others laughed as Damian winced, "I don't want to know either," Damiam grumbled, "I really wouldn't put it past Mother to try to get pregnant any way she could, especially if she knew that my father was to be the next Prince of Wales."

Uncle Aaron hummed, "I think you're why he brought the four of you here. Andrew would have had Andros be your godfather. The moment he met you for the first time, the protection magic sealed it into place. Your mother might have thought she succeeded this time in claiming him, but—"

"Papa was just trying to bring Uncle Andrew's son home," Anya finished for her uncle.

Uncle Aaron nodded, "And now, Damian has brought home our missing family members."

☩ ☩ ☩

7 January 2011: Fourteen Weeks After
the Kidnapping, Pre-Dawn...

Damian woke up, sweating and confused. He tried to orient himself as he pushed himself up into a seated position. He looked around, and he took in a few deep breaths. His cell phone on the bedside table assured him that he was in the present and not in the past...

"*Cariad*, what's wrong?" Arthur asked as the movement from the mattress shifting woke him up.

"I—I don't know," Damian replied, rubbing his eyes, "I need my—"

"*Dream journal and tea*," Arthur interrupted as he sat up. He then kissed Damian's bare shoulder, one of the few places he could reach from behind, "On it."

Arthur pushed off the blankets and leaned over his bedside

table. He ended up with the journal as Damian didn't always have a clear mind when waking up with dream visions. He hastily opened it to a ribbon-marked page and handed it to Damian with a pen.

Arthur then stood barefoot as his powers informed him someone was nearby. He grabbed a pair of sweatpants off a nearby chair, pulling them on as he quietly moved across the floor.

He then opened the door to ask the night guard for tea, only to find himself greeted by a servant with a tray of two tea cups and a teapot.

"Oh," he said.

The butler, one loyal to the Drago family, smiled slightly.

"He woke up the whole palace again, didn't he?" Arthur sighed as he moved out of the doorway.

"No, milord," the man assured. "It was such a powerful dream vision that Lord Wales had one too. He was already down in the kitchen, ordering about the early morning staff."

Arthur winced, "I'm sorry."

"Don't be, Your Highness," the older man replied, "He's still a better option than your other in-laws. Besides, we're used to the Wales abilities."

Damian half heard some of the conversation. He forced himself to contrate on the pen and journal in his hands. He placed the pen on the blank page and started to write.

⊕ ⊕ ⊕

6 January 1536: Kimbolton Castle...
He kissed her brow.

"See you in the next life, my queen, my Catalina," he whispered.

She opened her eyes and looked up at him, tired, "The baby... Daniel, is our baby safe?"

He nodded, "My sister is protecting him like he's her own. I'm going to them once you're gone."

"Will you look after Maria?"

"Always," he replied as he brushed her greying red hair off her face, *"I'll go to her once the mourning period is over."*

"Do you think Henry will keep you from her?"

He shook his head, *"He knows I'm following his father's last orders regarding you. He told me that once you passed, I could protect Maria. I think he can't handle that she looks too much like you and Arthur."*

Her laughter turned into a cough as she tried to take a few deep breaths. *"I wish my Marias could be with me."*

Knock, knock.

Startled, Daniel twisted to the door before yelling, *"Come in!"*

"My lord, it's Lady Willoughby," a servant on the other side of the door started, *"She's here to see Her Majesty."*

He turned back to Catalina, *"One of your Maria's was able to get here after all."*

"Let her in," Catalina whispered with a small smile, *"She's our biggest supporter."*

He nodded. He kissed her head one more time before standing. He then went to the door and opened it to find a greying, dark-haired lady dressed in a dark travel dress. His respect for this woman went even higher as she had been exiled from Catalina.

"Maria," he greeted, *"Thank you for coming."*

"Did I make it in time?" She requested, *"Please tell me I made it before my Queen passed!"*

"Yes, Maria, you made it before Catalina passed," Daniel replied as he moved out of the doorway, *"Please come in; she's been waiting for you…"*

"You really mean she's been waiting for both of her Marias, but I'm the only one that can truly defy a king," she replied as she began untying her cloak, *"That man has more control over the daughter he doesn't want to claim anymore simply because they won't see his new bride as queen."*

His eyebrow raised, *"You don't see her as queen either."*

"Of course not," she replied as she shrugged off the cloak, *"Where should I put this?"*

"*I'll bring it to the servants,*" *Daniel replied as he took the cloak.* "*The doctors think she could pass soon. She hasn't eaten or drunk anything in a few days.*"

"*Maria?*" *Catalina asked quietly,* "*You're here.*"

She rushed to the bed, "*Always, my queen. How can I help you?*"

"*Just stay with me,*" *Catalina whispered,* "*It hurts that I can't have my babies with me.*"

"*Can you tell me anything about our little prince?*" *Maria asked as Daniel closed the door behind him, not hearing Catalina's response.*

"*Milord?*" *The servant asked as they passed him,* "*Can I help you with anything?*"

"*Yes, can you get something to eat for Lady Willoughby?*" *He asked,* "*She came a long way with only loyalty and adrenaline driving her.*"

"*Of course, milord. Do you need anything?*"

He shook his head. "*I'm going to the nursery to check on my son and nephew.*"

"*Would you like me to take Lady Willoughby's cloak?*" *The servant asked.*

He looked down at the cloak as his world started to shift.

✠ ✠ ✠

Damian blinked as he felt arms around his waist bring him back to the present. He leaned back into the chest before wiping the tears off his face. He hadn't realised he had been crying.

"What's wrong?" Arthur asked in his ear.

"I think I saw your Greatest Grandmother, Catalina... She was dying. Why would I see that?"

Arthur gulped, "It might be that today is her death anniversary. Can you tell me what you saw?"

"It was my point of view, technically," Damian tried to think, "I was following a man that... looked very similar to me... but older."

"Do you think it could be Greatest-Grandfather Daniel?" Arthur asked, "We don't have any paintings of him, but his description from Greatest Aunt Mary is very similar to yours."

Damian smiled as he twisted to kiss Arthur. He pulled away a moment later, "That is starting to make sense. Do you know where Liam is?"

"Richard said that he was bossing the morning kitchen staff around and that he could meet me at the door with tea and crackers." Arthur gestured with his head to the table nearby. "Who else was in the vision?"

"Queen Catalina's most loyal lady-in-waiting who came with her from Spain," Damian hummed, "Who looks similar to your *Tia Rosa*. She came to be with her queen as she died."

Arthur smiled, "Thank you."

"For what?"

"You've confirmed a legend to be truth and that Greatest Grandmother Catalina had one of her Maria's with her when she died," Arthur continued, "When we refer to someone being like Maria, we're saying that they are like her, loyal to her friends and will defy anyone that tries to keep them away from their friends."

"Do I know anyone like that?" Damian asked, "I feel like you two have each other for that."

Arthur stared at him momentarily, "Anya and I refer to Jose as your Maria. His loyalty to you is just as legendary as Maria's to Greatest Grandmother Catalina."

"Oh," Damian whispered, "I didn't think of it like that. He's always just been there. He's the reason why *Agent Bat* is my boss."

Arthur looked at him, head tilted, "How's that possible?"

Damian grinned, "Jose suggested I write my journal to him because I felt silly writing *Dear Diary* or *Dear Journal*."

"And writing *Dear Santa* was less silly?" Arthur asked, trying not to laugh.

"It was because I had never done it before," Damian replied,

"And I didn't have any pre-perceived notions of writing to *Santa Claus*. And don't knock it because that journal saved three lives..."

Arthur leaned forward and kissed Damian, cutting his rant off. He pulled back a moment later. Damian was pouting.

"You can't keep winning like that!"

"Like what?" Arthur asked innocently.

"Kissing me into submission!" Damian hissed before Arthur kissed him again.

"I think you should stop complaining," Arthur said between kisses. "You like these."

"I do," Damian replied as the dream journal was pushed to the floor, forgotten for the rest of the night.

Chapter 23: Past and Present Collide

2008: Two Years Before the Kidnapping...

King Andros found himself going in and out of the same fog that Andrew did fifteen years ago. He operated the best he could. Most of his people believed he was grieving and forced into a relationship with Lady Murrian on the orders of the Firm and the Traditionalists, despite the rocky past tying them together...

✠ ✠ ✠

4 February 2011: Four Months After the Kidnapping, 10 am...

When Damian returned from his honeymoon, he found Alfred waiting for him in his office with a grim smile.

"Sir?" Damian asked, "Is something wrong?"

"Not entirely," Alfred replied, "We felt we should wait to interrogate Wilhelm until you got back. You started this; you should also be there to discover why he's doing all this."

"The Ambassador was alright with that?"

Alfred nodded, "Especially when he learned you're part of the reason Lady Eve and Heir Nathan were saved."

"When are we doing this?"

"As soon as we get down to the station."

✠ ✠ ✠

2 pm...

"When my benefactor gets me out of this hole, you're going to be fired!" Wilhelm Rothbart swore.

He was back in the integration room. Inspector Warren and Alfred were seated in front of the man who had tried to derail the monarchy. Damian was hiding in the shadows so Rothbart wouldn't see him.

"You've been keeping me here *illegally!* His Brat—*Royal*

Highness needs my help! I haven't done anything wrong!" Rothbart continued his rant.

"That's the problem, Rothbart!" Inspector Warren said gleefully, "You've done several things wrong, and that doesn't even include the reason for your capture four months ago."

"Who told you that?" Wilhelm demanded. "I mean, my benefactor assured me the spell would hold... That—"

"We would never figure out who you were," Alfred said, arms crossed, standing next to the Inspector, "That we were too dumb to figure out the plan of taking Prince Arthur to a Camp! You were going to have an heir to this county locked up and brainwashed!"

Damian continued to stand in the shadows, watching the Inspector and Alfred lay down the facts for the paling enemy. To think this man was once someone he was afraid of. He couldn't wait to see how Inspector Warren and Alfred get the information out of Mother.

"Where is my Benefactor or lawyer?!" Wilhelm exclaimed. "They promised me there wouldn't be repercussions!"

"Lady Melinda Murrian and Lord Dudley are currently in their holes for treason," Warren replied as Rothbart's fists tightened, "No one in their right mind is going to let them out on bail anytime soon."

"Besides, you and Lady Melinda Murrian have much more to worry about," Alfred said, "You tried to harm the wrong family, a family two other countries want to try you and her for treason, line theft, and attempted murder."

"And which family do you represent?" Wilhelm sneered.

"The Evergreens, also known as Osman of the Ottoman Empire."

Rothbart gulped, "W—what?"

"Princess Isma Osman Evergreen is Lady Eve's mother," Warren said, trying not to show his glee at Wilhelm's squirming, "Very few people knew a princess of the Osman family married a member of a branch of Norway's Royal Family."

"And Lady Eve and Prince Nathan are considered heirs of the Evergreen family," Alfred continued, glaring at the man, "We had to interfere to keep you from succeeding in killing our heirs! All for a power that wasn't yours to chase!"

"But it's *theirs!*" He exclaimed, unable to hold back, "The Murrians have been kept from power for too long! I was only trying to help bring the true royal family into power!"

Damian swallowed as he listened to the man of his nightmares start spilling his secrets. However, they were secrets that didn't make any sense. He tried to listen to the rambling man before stepping out of the shadows.

"Sir!" Wilhelm explained, hopeful and scared, "I—I—didn't mean to—"

Damian shook his head, "I'm not your ally here; I'm with these men. I want to know, did you help my mother, or were you only helping my grandmother?"

"What do I get for revealing anything?" Wilhelm snapped.

"That depends on the information," Alfred replied, "If you turn against your benefactor and plead guilty to the charges, you'll just have to one country's punishment. The two I represent will be content with what England comes up with."

Rothbart went quiet for a moment. It was as if he didn't want to know who the other countries were. But just being punished by one country was a better deal than having to be extradited to two other countries.

"Just your grandmother," Wilhelm replied, defeated, "And your grandfather when he wasn't locked up. But your grandmother made me get a few things for your mother."

"Would some of those things be plants?" Damian asked, "Do you remember the ones you picked up?"

Wilhelm nodded, "But I never asked what they were for."

"I never would have expected you to ask what they were needed for," Damian nearly snapped, "I don't even think Grandmother knew what they were for. The plants separated are harmless. But a skilled pharmacist or potioneer would know how those plants would work together to make a love potion or a mind-control medicine."

"What?" Everyone asked together.

"D…does that mean I could have helped to kill a … *king?*" Wilhelm whispered.

Alfred snorted, "You have no problem with trying to kill Lady Eve and Prince Nathan, but you draw the line at killing a king?"

"I wasn't trying to kill the Queen and the young prince," Wilhelm hastily denied, "My goal was to hide them until Melinda Murrian got what she wanted. That King Andros abdicated to the Murrians. But with the Queen out of the picture, Melinda Murrian decided Kendra Murrian marrying the king would work just as well."

"But why would King Andros abdicate to Grandmother?" Damian asked, "The line has been women rulers since Queen Mary I. It would have gone to Anya. Unless Grandmother is somehow related to the main line."

"*I don't know!*" Rothbart said, exasperated. "They never showed me, but Melinda Murrian had proof *somewhere* in her office."

"I'll get a warrant for the Murrain Manor," Warren said as he pulled out a phone, turning away to call the authorities. "Thank you for your help."

Wilhelm made a face. Damian did everything in his power not to snort as he turned away from the man who used to haunt his nightmares. At least he couldn't hurt Arthur from being here even if the man turned more information on Grandmother.

Alfred started following him away from Wilhelm Rothbart. They started moving down the hall as a bobby showed up to take Wilhelm back to his cell.

"Do you really think that your mother drugged King Andros?" Alfred asked quietly as they moved to Inspector Warren's office to wait for him.

Damian nodded, "I've suspected it for a while; taking the Forensic Class with CSI Bradson really drove home about the plants I asked Rothbart about."

"You need permission from the Royal Family to exhume the king's body," Alfred said to Damian. "You should get your *Taid's*, too, while you're at it."

"I understand getting permission to exhume King Andros's body and talking to Queen Anya," Damian started, "Do you think something happened to my *Taid*?"

"If you believe your mother is capable of drugging King Andros into submission," Alfred continued, "What steps would she have taken to get close to him?"

"They were using each other," Damian said, wide-eyed. "My parents were using each other to get what they wanted!"

"With Andrew's determination and overprotection of the two people he viewed as his little siblings, it wouldn't surprise me if they were using each other," Alfred replied, "It would explain many of his actions after the king met Lady Eve."

"My mother was trying to marry King Andros that far back?"

"Longer it seems," Alfred hummed, "When Lord Nico married Queen Maria was when King Andros and Lady Eve met. Your father was trying to run interference with your mother before then."

"Mother was older than King Andros?"

Alfred nodded, "By a few years. She was closer in age to your father than your—"

"Um, Papa Andros was what I called him growing up," Damian admitted. "It's safe to say if he were alive today, I would still call him that. He would have insisted on it, and Lady Eve already has me call her Mama Eve."

Alfred grinned, "She would do that."

✠ ✠ ✠

7 February 2011:
Four Months After the Kidnapping, 9 am...

Damian wasn't sure who he should approach about a new development. In the end, he went to the two men who had worked together to raise the late King Andros. He quietly approached Lords Black and Wales after a Parliament meeting.

Liam was the only one of the three with an office in the building. He led his newly found grandson and Lord Black there. Once the door shut and the soundproof spell was in place, Damian let concern come to his face.

Taid took a seat behind the desk while Damian and Uncle Aaron sat before him on the other side. This office would one day belong to Damian, something that *Taid* Wales was excited to train him to take over. He was gleefully counting down the days to his retirement.

"What's wrong?" Uncle Aaron asked, not needing to hide his worry in a private setting.

"Inspector Warren sent his newest report," Damian began after taking in a deep breath and exhaling, "He's requesting to exhume Papa Andros' body."

"On what grounds?" *Taid* asked, confused, "Everyone knows he died of cancer."

"You found the proof you were looking for," Uncle Aaron said under his breath before Damian could continue, "She's—"

"Arrogant, stupid, choose any word to fit," Damian said with a shrug, "The CSI team found her potions lab in Buckingham Palace filled with books, drugs, and ingredients that separately would be considered innocent, but together make an illegal mixture. Part love potion and part mind control. The lab techs are hoping the chemotherapy wouldn't be able to mask anything he was exposed to for the ten years we lived at the palace."

"And when you factor in Andros's not having received chemotherapy for long, it couldn't mask much," *Taid* agreed,

"Have you brought this information to Queen Anya and Prince Arthur?"

Damian was barely able to keep himself from grimacing. He and his sister-in-law were working on having a more stable relationship for Arthur's sake.

Uncle Aaron shook his head, "You came to us because you're still afraid of her."

"We've only truly been working together for the last few months because of Mother," Damian grumbled, "Half of the time, I still feel the urge to duck from her flames. We still have ten years of misplaced issues to work through. But I've come to you today as fathers, not Lords."

"Are they asking about Andrew?" *Taid* asked. "He died before you were born, trying to bring your Murrian grandfather in. However, the coroner believed he didn't have much longer to live with all the internal damage that he found that wasn't related to the gunshot that killed him."

"Liam?" Uncle Aaron asked, startled, "Are you sure?"

Taid nodded, resigned, "He was also in a fog similar to Andros. I'm surprised he could get as much information on Murrian as he did."

Damian groaned, "Mother is a damn Black Widow! She can't continue to get away with this!"

"She won't," Uncle Aaron assured as *Taid* nodded in agreement, "You have our permission to exhume the bodies of Prince Andrew Wales and King Andros Drago to help gather the necessary evidence. You just have to tell Anya and Arthur. We'll tell the Lady Eve."

"Great, leave me the hard part," Damian huffed as he stood and bowed, "Thank you for your help."

He hastily made his way to the door and pulled it open, temporarily breaking the soundproof spell. He heard *Taid's* question to Uncle Aaron: *"How many family members can a different family take from us in their quest for power?"*

Damian sighed as he walked through the door, knowing

he wondered about the same thing many times in the past few weeks. He didn't hear Uncle Aaron's response as he shut the door behind him, reactivating the soundproof spell.

He knew he had a lot of work to do, so he stopped for a moment, feeling his phone vibrate in his pocket. Taking it out, he read *'Inspector Warren'* and hastily swiped up to accept the call.

"Good morning, Inspector," Damian greeted.

"We've got the warrant to take down the protective spells on your grandmother's office," the Inspector said immediately, *"Do you want to meet us there?"*

"I'll be there," he paused to check his watch. "in a half-hour."

"Take your time, Your Highness," Inspector Warren said. *"It will take us at least an hour to get everything ready. Just think of this as getting one more step closer to the truth."*

"Thank you, Inspector," Damian replied, trying to remain calm and not show his excitement in public, "I'll see you soon."

"Of course, Your Highness. See you soon."

Damian hit the *end* button and slipped the phone back into his pocket before picking up the pace to get to the car.

✠ ✠ ✠

2 pm...

Damian was still reeling from the fact that he was standing in Grandmother Murrian's office. The closest he had ever gotten to being there was when the people Grandmother Murrian was meeting with didn't close the door all the way. He was only allowed in the office when Grandmother Murrian or Mother was there. It was usually to receive marching orders or punishment for not meeting their expectations.

It took the team of CSIs all afternoon to take down the protection and lock spells in front of the room. But it was worth the evidence locked inside. The CSIs were hoping to find more evidence that could link Grandmother Murrian to the deaths of Queen Eliza and Prince Philip.

"Can I help?" Damian asked CSI Bradson, "I need as much closure as I can get."

She nodded as she pulled out a pack of gloves. Damian's grin grew wide. He hastily grabbed the pack from her. Her laughter was music to his ears.

Something that caught his attention as a potential place to find any damning evidence was a drawer in a desk with a locking sequence requiring blood to undo the spell. Damian was willing to provide the blood, hoping his royal blood was too diluted to trigger any traps. He pulled off one of his gloves as CSI Bradson approached him.

"Are you sure about this, Your Highness?" She asked, "We can get one of the other CSIs who specialises in breaking blood spells."

Domain nodded, determined, "There's no time to get anyone before the swanky lawyers my family has on their payroll figure out a way to get us kicked out of here, even with a warrant."

CSI Bradson nodded, understanding as she knelt and pulled out a ceremonial dagger from her kit. Damian gave her the side eye.

"You casually have a ceremonial dagger in your kit," He said, trying not to freak out on her, "Why do you have something like that in your kit? I don't think it's standard."

"Oh, it's not standard on a normal CSI's kit," she grinned, "But I'm not a normal CSI; I'm a WCSI, Wiccan Crime Scene Investigator. The W is silent unless I introduce myself that way to someone. I get called in when the case has supernatural elements. Missing vans, mysterious glitter, and disguises created by magic were big parts of Prince Arthur's case."

"Oh," Damian paused, "Actually, the title of my Forensic class makes more sense now that I think about it."

"*The Magic and History of Forensics* wasn't a dead giveaway?" She asked.

"It is now!" Damian exclaimed, "The test I had to take to get into the class now makes sense, too!"

"You've been slowing coming into your powers," she continued, "You were showing signs of your gifts back then." Bradson then held up the dagger, "This is going to hurt," she warned.

"I know," Damian said, holding out his left palm, "But I've been wondering about what has made my tight-lipped family act the way they have been for the last century, and I think this drawer holds those answers."

She nodded and made a small cut in the centre of his hand as gently as she could. He winced. Bradson went to get the first kit while blood pooled into his palm. He made a fist and let the blood drip onto the desk holding the drawer.

A green light from the drawer flashed twice. Damian held his breath with both hope and apprehension. If the third flash were red, he'd better duck... The explosion would not be worth whatever was inside...

Chapter 24: The Blood
of King Henry VIII

Green.

Damian sighed with relief, never happier to hear something unlock than at that moment.

CIS Bradson returned as Damian pulled the drawer open with his uninjured right hand. He allowed her to wrap the other with gauze designed to heal cuts caused by ritual magic.

Heart pounding, Damian stared down at the contents of the drawer. Inside, on top of some other things, was an envelope bearing a Laurel reef stamp with *Royal Historical Society* written in the centre. His grandfather was the addressee, a man he never met but who seemed to have control over the rest of the Murrians from beyond the grave.

"Here."

Damian peered at Bradson. This time, she held out a larger glove than his size. He took it with confusion.

"This should fit on your left hand with that bandage on," she said, "I think that envelope might be the answer we've been looking for. Wait a moment so I can record its existence. We don't want those lawyers you were talking about to get this thrown out of court because you were impatient."

"Yes, ma'am," Damian replied as she went to retrieve her equipment. He tenderly pulled the new glove over the bandage, and Bradson returned with a crime scene camera.

Click! Click! Click!

"Alright, you're cleared to pick it up."

Damian nodded and returned to the drawer, picking up the envelope from within. He carefully turned it over as the clicking continued.

"No –" he whispered, realising another symbol was on the back: A red 'M' with a snake-like creature intertwined through the M and into a circle, *"The Order of Mordred."*

The clicking stopped, and Damian looked up.

"W... What did you say?" CSI Bradson whispered.

"This has the Order of Mordred seal on it," Damian repeated, "Please take a picture of this."

He could see her fingers were trembling as she raised the camera. A click of a moment later gave him some concern.

"Are you alright?" Damian asked.

She shook her head.

"Do you need a break?"

Bradson shook her head again.

"How do you know about the Order of Mordred?" She finally brought herself to ask, "I thought you were a toddler when they arrested your grandfather."

"I was," Damian agreed as he laid the envelope on the desk, "Mother was trying to brainwash me, but I was incredibly resistant. I only know its name and the symbol. How do *you* know about the Order of Mordred?"

Bradson swallowed as she put down the camera next to the envelope, fiddling with her thick, leather bracelet. She wore it for as long as he'd known her, so he never had a reason to ask her about it. She tugged at the clasp and pulled it off enough to show him what was hiding beneath.

The symbol on her wrist was a dragon circling a Tudor Rose. Quickly, Bradson put it back on before anyone else could see, and Damian understood.

A dragon circling a Tudor Rose represented the unknown descendants of the Knights of the Round Table. They've sworn to protect the descendants of *King Arthur* and *Queen Gwenver*, those the dragon chose to rule. They were the ones who kept the Order of Mordred from truly regaining control of the throne.

"This gives us more questions than answers," Damian moaned.

Bradson stared at the envelope, "Whatever is inside will do the same. Are you prepared for that?"

Damian scanned the envelope again before picking it

up."Ready as I'll ever be," he said, "I want all these secrets to end!"

She nodded as she grabbed the camera, understanding his frustration. She resumed taking photos of the drawer. The clicking noise returned as Damian flipped the envelope flap up someone in the past painstakingly unstuck. He carefully took out the document, holding it up to examine it before nearly dropping it.

"Your Highness?" Bradson asked in a concerned tone. "Are you alright?"

Damian moved his astonished gaze to her. "If this document is true. It will change what we know about English history!"

✠ ✠ ✠

11 February 2011: Four Months and Two Weeks After the Kidnapping, 3 pm...

Despite the situation's sensitivity, Damian couldn't see Queen Anya until the Friday after the raid. Anya found herself busier than ever, and Matthew was finishing training the new guard set to replace him as Arthur's security. Her schedule became a security nightmare for Damian, who would remain Lord Security until Queen Anya married. He hoped it would be Kai.

It was planned for Matthew to take over the Lord Security role during his apprenticeship under Taid Liam. Still, his responsibility over Queen Anya's schedule would fall to her partner once she married.

Anya could give him tea time, so long as he ensured to add it to her calendar as a meeting between them. This way, they would have daily meetings instead of working around her schedule when they needed to make a decision right away.

They were meeting in her office in the Library. It was decided that it was still the safest option compared to where King Andros had his office. Inspector Warran had found evidence of mics that had been traced back to Mother's office and lab.

"So, what do you *desperately* need to talk to me about?" Anya asked, being a little less formal than she normally would have.

They were still trying to find their groove after learning Damian wanted nothing to do with the Murrian family. Anya sipped her tea as he thought about how to approach this subject.

"Inspector Warren would like to exhume your father's body," Damian finally said, "And I would like you to submit for a DNA test."

Damian then braced himself for Anya's temper, feeling like he should fall to the floor to dodge a fireball. But it never came. Instead, she nearly choked on her tea.

She carefully put her cup down and took a few deep breaths, not wanting to blow up at him as she would have done in the past.

"You want me to do *what?*" Anya asked, shocked at the request.

"Exhume your father's body and a DNA test," Damian repeated as he put the teacup down on his side of the desk.

"I understand the request for my father's body," Anya waved off, "I've had my suspicions about my father. I didn't bring them up because of how young I was and thought my judgment was off. But *why* do you need my DNA?"

"We need to establish a baseline for who is in the royal line," Damian explained, hiding his worry.

"The dragon chooses the next ruler, no matter what," Anya said firmly, "You saw what happened at your wedding."

Damian nodded, taking out and placing the folder he found onto Anya's desk. "Someone sent this to Great Grandfather Murrian. It explains a good portion of my family's actions for the last century."

Damian observed Anya as she took the envelope with unsteady hands. Carefully, she pulled out the document and quietly read it to herself, flipping through the pages before shifting her focus back to him.

"Have you been able to get the Royal Historical Society to confirm this?" She asked.

He shook his head, sighing, "The current head of the historical society is trying to understand which historian was even able to *find* that document. I don't even know how family tree documents like that exist. Most generational potions only show four to five generations back. This is a mess."

Perplexed, she flipped through the rest of the pages until she got to the last one. "How far back are we talking about?"

"We're talking about trying to confirm for at least fourteen generations back," Damian said as Anya suddenly dropped the document.

She nearly jumped out of her seat as her facial features began to shift. Her skin became more scaly. Her nose and mouth started to merge into a snout.

"*Your Majesty*, you're too big to shift in here," Damian reminded her, trying not to panic.

She breathed in deeply before letting out smoke as she exhaled. She did this motion a few times, but the sparkly blue scales and snout stayed.

Instead, Damian was startled by a gravelly voice.

"This explains why I'm both protective and exasperated with you."

"Lady Dragon?" Damian questioned, not sure what to call her. "You can speak too?"

"Please call me Sophia, and I can't do this long," the gravelly voice continued, **"Only long enough to make sure. May I have your left hand?"**

He nodded as he held out his still unhealed hand, wrapped in merely enough bandages to protect his palm.

"Can you remove the bandage?" Sophia asked, sounding worried. **"I don't like that your sacrifice hasn't healed yet."**

Damian pulled off the bandage and held his hand back out for the Dragon Queen. It wasn't until that moment he realised that the young queen's hands were now super sharp claws. He bit his lip to keep himself from yelling and pulling his hand away as he felt a sharp prick, reopening the cut.

However, the pain didn't last long. Damian was amazed that as soon as she moved her talon away, the injury was fully healed. He missed witnessing the Dragon Queen lifting her blood-dripping talon to her snout. She hummed momentarily as the dragon's features retreated, leaving a confused human in her place.

"What just happened?" Anya asked.

"There's a lot we still need to learn about your dragon side," Damian breathed, staring at his now healed hand, "Including how many rulers she has chosen over the years. Is she explaining anything?"

Anya went quiet before shaking her head.

"She's sleeping," she said, swaying slightly.

"Say no more," Damian assured as he stood, cutting their meeting short. "I'll get Kai and see myself out. I have to find Arthur anyway."

She nodded, looking even more exhausted than before. "Will you arrange for a doctor to come?"

"Of course," he said, bowing. "Feel better."

He slowly backed away from the desk, not turning his back to her until the last minute. He then pulled open the door, breaking the soundproofing spell for a moment. "*Kai?*" He called.

Kai came running from down the hall, "Is everything okay?"

"Did… did the last Prince Consort leave any details about dealing with a dragon fusion?"

Kai nodded, "Prince Philip mentioned she would need lots of meat, steak as rare as she can handle. I can send for food now."

Damian shook his head, "I'm heading there now. I have to talk to Arthur; he has a training session with Mrs Carmichael. He's taking over baking for now."

Kai grinned, "Shouldn't you be the one doing the baking?"

"Well, unless Arthur's powers changed on him overnight,

I think it's safe to assume Nathan is Grandfather Christmas' heir," Damian quietly pondered, "Out of all his grandchildren, Nathan is the only one with ice powers."

"Huh," Kai said as he approached the door and motioned over his shoulder to Ella. "I didn't think about that."

Ella settled in the spot beside the bookshelf and saluted her boss, giving him a small smile and a nod.

"Please don't say anything about Nathan to the others," She requested quietly. "I understand why you said something to Kai because of his position within the security side, but Nathan needs to transform to be officially named the Saint's heir."

"I think that's how it works for all the Royal lines anyway," Damian said with a grin, "Let me know if their Highnesses need anything else."

"Of course," she agreed.

Damian shook his head as he moved through the library. He quietly marvelled at the changes in the staff greeting him as he passed. They weren't treating him with indifference or contempt like others had for the last ten years. Mother didn't care herself; she just gave it right back. Damian, on the other hand, was sensitive to it when he was younger and forced himself to learn how to cope with the treatment.

Looking back, Damian understood what happened. The staff loyal to the Royal Family seemed to know the events around Queen Eve and Prince Nathan's supposed deaths weren't all they appeared to be. The staff and most of the English population seemed to be operating on the chosen fact the Queen and the Prince were missing and not dead. They refused to accept otherwise until their bodies were found.

"Hello, Damian," an amused Uncle Aaron called over to Damian

"Good afternoon, sir," Damian greeted after being lost in thought.

"Good afternoon, where are you heading?" Uncle Aaron asked.

"The kitchen, I'm looking for Arthur."

"May I accompany you?" Damian nodded.

"I heard you could finally tell Anya about Inspector Warren's request. How did she take it?" Uncle Aason asked as they continued on to the kitchen.

"She wasn't surprised, actually," Damian replied, noting that the staff had left the area. They always seemed to know when they shouldn't be around. "She said she thought the changes in King Andros' behaviour and appearance were just childhood grief and imagination. That's why she never brought it to your attention."

Damian glanced over in time to see Uncle Aaron's emotionless face fall and pain reflecting in his eyes. A tear rolled down his cheek.

"Why didn't she trust me?" Uncle Aaron whispered with devastation. "I would have trusted her judgement."

Damian stopped. At first, he wasn't sure of what to say. He thought quietly before turning to look directly at Uncle Aaron.

"You had a lot on your plate from the moment Grandmother Murrian conspired with a criminal to attempt to kill off Mama Eve and Nathan," Damian said, "I didn't even know what I stumbled upon, and the only adults willing to listen to me were elves that would do anything to protect their lady and heir."

Uncle Aaron stared off into space. "Dylan and Matheo were so confused. They could feel the Godparent bond with Nathan was still active and couldn't do anything about it—"

Without warning, a loud **CLANK!** echoed through the halls of Buckingham Palace.

Damian and Uncle Aaron looked at each other.

"I think it came from the kitchen," Uncle Aaron said.

Damian's eyes widened. *"Arthur!"* He exclaimed before taking off to the kitchen. Uncle Aaron followed behind, hoping everything was going to be okay.

3:30 pm...

The Legend of King Arthur:
Similar yet different versions of this legend exist.
History/Twist:
King Arthur was Queen Alexandra I, the first queen who was known to have been chosen by the dragon.
Queen Guinevere was Prince Consort George I, the only guard who could keep up with her.
He also happened to be a noble who 'volunteered' to protect her
Sir Lancelot: a sibling of "Queen Guinevere" - not lover, always identified as male, unsure of their true identity. Prince George I's family was never really identified, but it was his brother, Liam.
Merlin: the first 'Santa' protector of the elves.
He's also the ancestor of the Kringle family.
Knights of the Round Table: protectors of the Queen and Prince, in each generation, one of the descendants could end up marrying the next queen.
As long as they can keep track of and keep up with her
Families of the Royal Prince Consort end up joining the Knights of the Round Table if they weren't part of it in the past
Morgana and Mordred: founders of the Murrian family for all European countries:
The Murrians are all part of the Order of Mordred as well as allies
England Murrians were close to gaining the throne in the 1500s in the form of Prince Edward, King Henry VIII's only surviving son and coveted heir.
They failed when he died.

Ding!

Arthur put his pen down in his notebook. His family still doesn't make any sense to him. He felt like he was missing something big, but he couldn't seem to find it.

He had been doing his schoolwork in the royal kitchen. He was getting informal cooking training under the watchful eye of Mrs Carmichael at Buckingham Palace. She was his favourite cook, allowing him to work on the schoolwork he had missed when he had to stay in the North Pole.

Rising from his place at the counter, Arthur grabbed a nearby towel and approached the big oven. He opened the door to pull out the cookie tray—

CLANK!

"*BLOODY HELL!*" He yelped as he stared at the cookie sheet now on the floor.

"*What happened?*" Mrs Carmichael asked as she came rushing around the corner from the other side of the kitchen.

Mrs Carmichael was his protector and safe haven for the past ten years. His family knew that if he wasn't in the History part of the Library, they could find him in the kitchens. It didn't matter which palace they were in; Mrs Carmichael was the head chef for the English Royal family.

"Shit, I think I made a mistake," Arthur said as the wet towel did nothing for him but give him a burn on his fingertips.

With sympathy, Mrs Carmichael shook her head as she grabbed a nearby broom and pan. She went over to him, "I've done that; I bet you didn't realise wet towels can hurt you?"

He shook his head, "I thought all towels could work to take hot things out of the oven."

"Why don't you go run your hand under water," she suggested, "I've got the mess."

He nodded and manoeuvred around her. She swept up as he turned on the cold faucet, placing his hand under the running water when the door burst open.

"*ARTHUR!*" A concerned Damian shouted.

"*Over here!*" Arthur yelled back.

Damian hastily rushed over to his side, Uncle Aaron trailing behind him. Damian took Arthur's hand and worked to inspect the small burn on his fingertips.

"How did this happen?" Damian asked as he rubbed his fingertips, trying to take the heat out of them, "You're not fireproof."

"I know; I grabbed the wrong towel," Arthur admitted, feeling the pain recede, "I was distracted by my current history paper. I'm still missing pieces to why the Murrians think we took the throne from them."

Damian froze, "Who told you that?"

"Nobody," Arthur said, "But it's easy to overhear your grandmother ranting about the dragon and how it keeps interfering with all their plans."

Damian blinked, "Where did you hear that?"

"Here," Mrs Carmichael chimed in, causing them to turn and face her with confusion. "What?" She shrugged, "Those crazy Murrian Women have many enemies among the staff. We did everything we could not to overhear their every scheme. But they made it, well— too easy to listen in."

Uncle Aaron pinched the bridge of his nose, "It's a wonder how anything gets done around here," he grumbled before ducking a towel thrown at him, "*Hey!*"

"Did you or did you not create a spy network out of the staff and homeless people?" She asked, "We're the ones most of that blasted Order ignores anyway. They always forget we have two ears, a mouth, and a working brain."

"A spy network that took its sweet time trusting me," Damian grumbled, missing the comment about an *Order*.

Arthur laughed as Uncle Aaron said, "Says the man who got the elves willing to work with him quicker than I ever could. They took forever to allow Matheo to admit he was a security elf ninja, let alone agree to answer to me."

"Alright, take your pestering outside my kitchen!" Mrs

Carmichael commanded, "Lord Damian, you should take Prince Arthur to the hospital wing to get that wrapped."

"Yes, Ma'am," Damian and Uncle Aaron said together as Arthur shook his head.

"I can handle myself," Arthur said, turning off the water.

Damian gave him a stern look, and Arthur smiled.

"Well, I can get there on my own most of the time."

Damian shook his head, handing Arthur a dry towel, "I'm starting to understand all the ranting the other Prince Consorts wrote about in their journals, but I didn't think it applied to you."

"Hey!" Arthur laughed as he dried his hands, "I'm not as bad as Anya."

"That's debatable," Uncle Aaron said. "I already knew Damian could keep up with you, and he wanted to be here; I didn't have to recruit him. However, I didn't realise he knew when the two of you switched places," he said as he looked over Arthur's notebook, "Uh, Damian, you should take a look at this—"

"Why do you want him to see the notes for my research paper?" Arthur asked as they moved back to the counter.

Mrs Carmichael had stopped sweeping and was standing next to Uncle Aaron. She was also reading the notebook with curiosity. Her eyes widened after a few moments.

"Where did you find this information about the Knights?" As she looked up to Arthur, she asked, "It's a carefully guarded secret from everyone, even the royal families, for their protection."

"The Library," Arthur replied, "Some journals in the history section that would only open for me, making it hard for me to use them as references since they were never published properly."

"How do you know about the Knights?" Damian interrupted.

Mrs Carmichael removed a thick leather band on her right

wrist. Damian could only stare at the familiar symbol he saw on CSI Bradson last week. Arthur looked at it, moving closer.

"You're a Knight!" Arthur exclaimed in awe, seeing the same mark on Uncle Aaron before. "Is that why you're so protective of me?"

She nodded as she put the band back on, "My family has sworn for generations to protect this family no matter what and that She-Devil had no right to treat you like scum because you weren't the right fit for her plans."

"Wait," Damian muttered, "This means Inspector Warren knew more than he was letting on!"

"He was testing you," she continued, "He wanted to know Bradson's assessment of you was correct."

"Did I pass?" Damian asked.

She nodded, "We weren't sure if you could join us because you're the next Prince of Wales as you're Lord Wales' grandson. We're still debating that."

"I understand," Damian replied, "Especially since we still don't know Mother's plans."

"Well, we do know Arthur was the kink in her plans," Uncle Aaron suddenly boosted, "Especially now, Damian; look, I think he's found the missing piece you were looking for."

Uncle Aaron slid the notebook across the counter, and Damian shifted his gaze. He read a few lines silently; his eyes widened as he realised Arthur had connected *why* the Murrians believed they had power stolen from them. He turned and kissed Arthur.

Uncle Aaron and Mrs Carmichael turned their heads, giving them some illusion of privacy. Damian pulled away a few moments later, and Arthur looked a little dazed.

"Not that I mind," Arthur said, "But what was that for?"

"England Murrians were close to gaining the throne in the 1500s in the form of Prince Edward, King Henry VIII's only surviving son and coveted heir," Damian read aloud, "That fits into the

271

information I found hidden in a desk drawer in Grandmother Murrian's office."

"They tried to use Prince Edward?" Arthur asked, "But history says he died without being married or having children."

"But who is to say that he didn't have sexual relations, he was sixteen years old when he died," Uncle Aaron said, "If members of the Knights can hide in plain sight like Mrs Carmichael..."

"Then, who's to say the members of the Order of Mordred didn't do the same thing," Mrs Carmichael continued, "King Henry VIII was so desperate for a male heir."

"Well," Arthur said as he reached to pick up his notebook, "As much as I would love to talk more about the craziness that comes with my family's legacy, I still have more work to do on this paper after I get the burn checked."

He then pulled the notebook to his chest and turned to leave the kitchen.

"Did you tell him?" He heard Uncle Aaron ask Damian.

Arthur glanced over his shoulder, "Tell me what?"

"Let me leave for a moment," Mrs Carmichael said as she lifted the dustpan, "The timer is about to go off."

"Could you send up some rare steak for Her Majesty?" Damian asked, remembering the other reason why he was coming to the kitchen.

"Lord Damian?" Mrs Carmichael gave him a confused stare.

"Her Majesty and her dragon temporarily merged for a bit—" Damian explained.

"*Ah!*" Mrs Carmichael exclaimed, "Say no more. The middle of the roast should be perfect to help her perk right up."

She then bowed before leaving the three men standing around the counter.

"What's going on?" Arthur asked softly,

"Inspector Warren and CSI Bradson want to exhume your father's body."

"Oh, thank the gods." Relief danced across Arthur's face. "Why do you think Anya and I overrode Lady Murrian's orders for a cremation."

"She wanted *WHAT?!*" Uncle Aaron fumed, "How did she think she could get away with that?!"

Arthur shrugged, "Anya and I had to remind her that he needed to lay In-state in Westminster for at least two weeks before being buried at Windsor. I don't understand why she even wants the throne when all she did was undermine it and throw protocol out the window when it didn't suit her."

Damian reached down and held Arthur's free, uninjured hand. Most of the time, the protocol should have kept them apart if it wasn't because King Andros was working on updating the laws and protocols for mental health and LGBTQ+ rights. His championing paved the way for a prince or princess to be able to be involved with someone of the same gender.

Chapter 25: The Legacy of the Dragon

Damian whistled on his way up to his office. It wasn't near Queen Anya's office, which was fine with him. He was near the office that Uncle Aaron had claimed once the older man had moved out of this one. After seven months, he had an office of his own as Lord Security was still surreal.

He rushed to his desk when he realised what was waiting for him. The large envelope was tan and had a few stamps in the corner. It wasn't open because it was part of his job to check for any dangerous spells or powers from the envelope that only activated once it was opened.

Damian waved his hand over it. He couldn't feel any harmful magic coming from the envelope. He grabbed a pack of rubber gloves he had started keeping in the office and opened them. He pulled them on, one at a time. Once the gloves were on his hands, he picked up a letter opener. He lifted the envelope and took the letter opener to the side of the envelope. He carefully started to slice it open to ensure there wasn't any powder that could come out of it.

He flipped the envelope upside down to let the contents fall onto the desk. He breathed easily when he realised there wasn't any powder. He shifted through the papers to find the first page.

It was the more in-depth DNA test that Arthur and Anya agreed to take with him. He wanted to find if there was any truth to the Order of Mordred's claims about the Murrian line. Damian's eyes widened as the DNA test revealed he was distantly related to the English Royal Family on Mother's side of the family.

The markers came from the same half-siblings who shared a father from the Tudor Dynasty. Every one of his fears was coming true. His imprisoned family believed the English throne was theirs. They just never considered the dragon spirit of Britannia and would always choose the next ruler.

"*Damian?*" Auncle Dylan asked as they knocked on the open door, "You wanted to see me?"

"Yes, Auncle Dylan," Damian replied, "I have some news for you."

Auncle Dylan closed the door to Damian's office before crossing the room. A flash of light signalled the privacy wards slid into place as they sat in an armchair beside Damian's desk.

"Do you remember the ritual book you showed me?"

Auncle Dylan nodded, face perplexed.

"Do you know when they added the blood spell?" Damian asked.

Pausing to think, Auncle Dylan pulled out their phone. They started doing something on it. They concentrated on the phone as they searched.

"*I've got it!*" They exclaimed a moment later, standing and handing Damian the phone.

The screen showed a picture of a painting Damian recognised as the father of the brothers who fell in love with the Twin Queens, Martin Ambros.

Martin was considered the Merlin of his time. The man depicted in the painting would have been powerful enough to cast a spell that would have tied his bloodline to the book and locked out the Murrian blood if he discovered a connection to the Tudor line.

"I want to know just how long Mother's family has been trying to gain the throne," Damian huffed as he handed the phone back to Dylan, "If Greatest Grandfather Martin Ambros did cast the protection spell, it would explain why I could lift the book but couldn't open it. The magic could sense I was a Wales Royal descendent but could also sense my Murrian blood."

Auncle Dylan nodded, "It would also explain why you can even sense the spells, to begin with."

Damian gave them a confused stare as they chuckled.

"I never knew about the spells that protected the book," Auncle Dylan continued, "Matheo is the one who told me about them. He's always been able to sense different types of magic."

"That's why he asked Uncle Aaron to make sure I was assigned to him for training," Damian's eyes lit up with excitement.

Auncle Dylan nodded with another chuckle, "His face lit up like that too. If you were younger, he would have requested your grandfather to adopt you."

"Well," Damian took out a folder from a side drawer and handed it to Auncle Dylan, "I think he still did—"

Auncle Dylan opened the folder curiously. They ran a hand over the document within and looked back at Damian.

"We had talked about this extensively," Auncle Dylan replied after a pause, "This was even before we knew you were Andrew's only son. Are you sure about this? As this something you want?"

Damian nodded, "Grandfather and I spoke. He knows I can't stand any of the Murrians. This way, they can't use *family obligation* against me if I no longer have the claim to the name or title that comes with it."

"Papa has already claimed my child second in line for the Black Lordship," Auncle Dylan warned.

Damian grinned, "That's okay; Taid named me his heir the moment he had me try on the magical heir ring. I think Alfred wants to claim me as his heir for all the work I've done to protect Queen Mother Eve, Prince Nathan, and Princess Noel."

Auncle Dylan stared at the younger man briefly, "And you're sure about being adopted into this insanity? This will make this family even more complicated."

"Arthur thinks it's amusing," Damian shrugged, "And think about Lady Murrian's face when she realises who my new parents are."

Whatever concerns Auncle Dylan had were slipping away.

The fact they could win one last fight over Kendra Murrian and protect Damian caused their grin to return.

"Alright, hand over a pen!" They said enthusiastically. "Let's get this adult adoption done!"

Damian handed them a pen, excited as he watched Auncle Dylan sign their name next to Mattew's signature.

Auncle Dylan was always someone he looked up to and desperately wanted to be. Damian wanted to be unapologetically himself, and now, he could be. He now had the family he was looking for most of his life. Who knew his birth mother tricking a king would lead him to his true family?

RING. RING. Abruptly came from a nearby red phone. It wasn't a normal phone... at least not one that connected to the outside world. This phone only worked with other phones *inside* Buckingham Palace.

Auncle Dylan looked at Damian, startled, "Why would that line call you right now? I didn't think anyone from the Scottish Royal Family was in residence today."

"I don't know," Damian said, confused, as he stood and hesitantly picked up the red corded phone. "Hello?"

"*Damian?*" Wills' voice flooded over the line. "*Can we meet you and Arthur in the history section in the Library?*"

"Who's 'we'?"

"*It will be most of the Scottish Royal grandchildren. We each got a confusing message that we wanted to make sure it wasn't an April Fool's joke. It seems only you and Arthur might be able to answer as Anya now is as hard to get a conversation with as it is with Granny.*"

Damian chuckled, " I think Arthur's there now, trying to finish his paper. I can be there in a few minutes."

"*Thank you, Damian,*" Wills said, sounding relieved, "*There might be a few more secrets we weren't prepared for. See you soon, bye.*"

"Bye," Damian replied before he put the phone down, standing in a haze.

"What's wrong?" Auncle Dylan asked, "Are you alright?"

"I... I'm not sure," Damian said slowly, "Wills thinks there are more family secrets about to be revealed."

✠ ✠ ✠

2:40 pm...

Arthur wandered through the shelves of his grandfathers' journals. He hovered his hand over his great-grandfather's journal; something different about it drew him to take a closer look.

He carefully lifted it off the shelf, and his eyes widened. Finally, he could read the name of his great-grandfather on the cover. Either this fell under the **Gag Spell** or similar, as he could never read the name through the blur of the spell previously.

There was a knock on the door frame.

Arthur looked up to see all the Scottish Royal Cousins cramped in the doorway.

"Oh," Arthur said. "Is everything okay?"

"Damian told us to meet him here, we all have letters but don't understand *why* we got them," Wills said for the Scottish Royals. There were five familiar faces all poking their heads out from behind Wills' back. "Can we come in?"

"Yeah, but let me get Anya," Arthur started, "She's going to want to hear this."

"Y...you can get time with her without scheduling a meeting?" Harry asked. "The older we get, the harder it is to get time to see Granny... I mean Queen Elizabeth."

Arthur grinned, "Get settled, and I'll get her."

They filed past him as he went out into the hall.

Psst! "Kai!" Arthur called out, "Oh, Kai! Can you get Anya? I need her help with something!"

Anya's hearing must have been getting better because she came flying down the hall before Kai could answer him. Her golden winds flared out, lightly flapping, lifting her off the floor just enough that she didn't hit her head on the ceiling. She had been working with her dragon, Sophia, to do more mixed combinations so she wouldn't be tired like she was with Damian a few months ago.

"Why do you want to switch now?" Anya growled, "You're better at history than I am, and I actually *like* the meeting that I'm supposed to be getting ready for."

"Why do you always assume that I want you to switch with me?" Arthur asked, stopping her as she came up to the entrance of the History Section.

She stared at him with a raised eyebrow.

He rolled his eyes, "I'm getting better now that you're *actually* Queen."

"That's because we don't need to switch anymore!"

"Then it's a good thing that I didn't want to switch with you today," Arthur replied. "I need your help with something else."

"Oookkkay," Anya drawled, "How can I help that doesn't involve us switching?"

"What is Sofia saying about the people inside?" he asked.

She sniffed, "Three are heirs. But what does that have to do with anything?"

"How close to the rule of the English Throne?"

She stared at him again.

"Please humour me," he pleaded.

She breathed deeply a few times before finally replying, "The fourth, fifth, and sixth heirs in the line of succession of the English throne."

There were a few gasps from inside the room and right behind Arthur. One of those gasps belonged to Damian. He had come up behind Arthur to meet up with the Scottish Royal Family. Arthur turned to Damian.

"*Helo, Cariad,*" Arthur greeted, leaning in and kissing him, "*A ydych chi yma oherwydd y Royals Albanaidd?*" (Hello, Love. Are you here because of the Scottish Royals?)

"*Helo, fy nghalon,*" Damian returned, "*Galwodd William*

fi i ymuno â'r cyfarfod. Pa gyfnodolyn sydd wedi datgelu ei hun o'r diwedd?" (Hello, my heart, William called me to join the meeting. Which journal has finally revealed itself?)

"I believe this one has ties with letters that have been coming in recently," Arthur said, switching to English, holding up the dark book, "The last name is very revealing."

"What's with our family and hidden journals?" Anya asked tiredly. "When did you find that?"

"I've always known about it," Arthur shrugged. "I just couldn't read the name of *who* the journal belonded to until now."

Damian and Anya nodded. Arthur headed into the History Section first, and the other two followed.

The Scottish Royal Cousins settled around the large table in the centre of the room. They each had a similar letter in front of them. Anya motioned for them not to stand as she found her seat.

"Please, we don't need protocol here. I'm not here as queen," Anya assured, "I'm here as a concerned sister of these two dolts."

Damian looked sheepish, and Arthur rolled his eyes.

"What is with the letters? I mean…" She began, removing a copy from her pocket, "I also received one."

Damian sighed, "They say everyone who looks into their family history will find a secret sooner or later. I just didn't realise how complicated this would get before pulling in the secrets of the Scottish Royal Family."

"And if this name is right, of how close our family has come to uniting the kingdoms of England and Scotland through marriage," Arthur said as he held up the journal.

They could read the words: *The Journal of Prince Consort James Albert Saxe-Coburg-Gotha-Drago.*

The Scottish Royals gasped at reading the very long last name. Most of the last name had been their Great-Grandfather's last name until World War I. It was changed to

Belmoral-Windsor to get rid of their very German-sounding last name.

"If Great-Grandfather wasn't hidden when Prince Albert died, Queen Mary of Teck would have been willing to claim him as her son. King George V also would have been willing to be Prince Regent if it meant having a son to do his duty better than King Edward V did."

"Great-Great-Grandmother Mary would have wanted to spare Great-Grandfather the death he had," Wills thought out loud.

Harry shook his head, "With the amount of cigarettes and cigars we heard he seemed to go through, I think he still would have died of cancer. Especially with what we know about cigarettes and lung damage."

"But why is this important?" Wills asked for all the Scottish Royals, "Besides confusing all of us."

"Because if the Traditionalist had performed the blood spell, your past, present, and future would be quite different," Damian said. "Your grandmother would have had closer claim over King Andros than Lord Wales."

"And if the Traditionalists insisted Queen Elizabeth take custody of my father as her fourth son. I wouldn't be officially crowned," Anya interrupted.

"What?" came collective voices.

She nodded, "The dragon would have named Queen Elizabeth the next ruler as she was the next female heir available."

"Are Wills and I included in that heir count?" Harry asked.

Anya shook her head, "The dragon says the current order line of succession is currently me, Noel, Aunt Elizabeth, Aunt Ann, and Zara."

"And if Granny adopted Uncle Andros?" Wills asked, "Would the kingdoms have been combined into one?"

Anya shook her head, "England and Scotland would have remained separate unless Uncle Charles would have been willing to give up his spot as heir to the Scottish throne. The order of the English Throne then would have been Aunt Elizabeth, Aunt Ann, Zara, little Savannah, Beatrice, Eugina, Me, Noel, and Lousie."

"Why would Savannah be after Zara and not Lousie?" Harry asked, curious. Peter was in between Wills and Damian. He joined his cousins in concern for his daughter, Savannah. She just had turned three months old a few days ago.

"Because Peter is Aunt Ann's son," Arthur started before Anya could continue, "It's kind of a similar situation for Aunt Ann, where she was pushed to the end of succession once Uncle Andrew and Uncle Edward were born. Even though you're the oldest…"

"The men wouldn't even be considered for the English throne unless something really bad happened as it did with Uncle Andros," Wills finished as Anya, Arthur, and Damian nodded.

"Where do we go from here?" Harry asked suddenly, "Do you want to train Zara, Bea, and Gina?"

Zara, Bea, and Gina had been sitting to his right. They sat a little straighter as he said their names. They were princesses by blood, even if only two of them had the title *'Princess'* added to their names.

"I think you three should have training with me and Noel," Anya addressed, "Noel and I are the only true heirs left of the English Royal Family. While the dragon does adore the men born into the family since King Henry VIII, she wasn't too pleased with him or King Richard III, and she said that she would keep choosing the females."

"What if you give birth to a female for Arthur and Damian when you're ready to carry a child for them?" Wills asked, "What if you don't have any other female children?"

"Then she will be my heir," Anya declared, "Luckily, by then, the Murrian women would be in prison for a long time, and they can't have any influence on her raising and the eventual decision-making that she would make alongside a child of Wills and Katie."

Arthur suddenly groaned, causing everyone to stare at him.

"What's wrong with you?" Anya asked, "That's a *good thing* that the Murrians can't access your kids."

"It's not that!" Arthur exclaimed, throwing up his hands.

"Then what is it?" Damian asked, concerned.

"I have to redo my paper again!" Arthur continued, "I've been working on that Bloody Paper for two semesters! I just want to be done with it!"

The Scottish cousins and Anya laugh as Damian just shook his head, amused.

Interlude: Arthur's Final Paper for Freshman History

Arthur Wales-Drago
Professor Daily
10 April 2011
The Dragon Queens

History is complicated and messy. Some parts are known to have been hiding the truth. Recovered documents have revealed what people of the past were hoping would never be found. The more information discovered, the more people of the current day are becoming aware. Events once deemed good now have a much deeper, darker meaning than ever before. Many rumours have swirled around the first Queens of England. Some were true, some were wrong and some have never been proven.

When Lady Mary Tudor took the crown at 31 years old, it was because the dragon spirit had the ultimate say in who the next ruler and heir to the English throne was. The dragon chose Mary on her eighteenth birthday, three years before Prince Edward was born. Mary kept the decision to herself while her father was still alive. She didn't want him to kill her in hopes of changing the dragon's mind.

The dragon was also why Queen Mary Tudor I worked with her younger half-sister, Lady Elizabeth, and second cousins, Lady Jane Gray and Mary, Queen of Scots. She was also trying to raise her half-siblings to adulthood. The dragon could technically be her most trusted advisor, as the spirit would tell her about those in her court and government plotting against her. Mary removed her siblings and cousins from those influences that could and should have turned them against her.

Mary spent the early years of her reign raising her siblings and trying to keep her country from imploding. The dragon's determination to keep Mary from using religion against her siblings and cousins, in turn, had both Roman Catholic and Protestant worshipers start to leave each other alone.

However, Queen Mary had to interfere with who Lady Jane was to marry, at least until she knew her young cousin wouldn't be used as a pole for the throne. One potential in-law, John Dudley, was one of the men prepared to rule in Prince Edward's palace until he was of age. Prince Edward's uncle, Edward Seymour, was the first person who would have been Prince Edward Tudor's Regent.

Then there was Edward's other uncle, Thomas Seymor. Even though he married the late King Henry VIII's widow, Catherine Parr, he tried to use Lady Elizabeth to get what he wanted. He also wanted to establish an arrangement between Lady Jane and Prince Edward. The dragon was not happy with either of these suggestions.

The dragon could feel Elizabeth's discomfort every time their step-uncle was near. There was also a problem with Lady Parr-Tudor-Seymor, putting the dragon on the defensive. When Queen Mary and the dragon realise that Seymor may have done something to Lady Elizabeth, they learn the then fifteen-year-old was pregnant…

Queen Mary's dragon also wanted to bring forward a young man to help protect Lady Elizabeth from their stepfamily. It was Queen Mary's young brother from her mother, Prince Fillip. He was the hidden Prince of Wales and was not related to Lady Elizabeth.

Queen Mary placed him in charge of Lady Elizabeth's protection. He had learned everything from his father, Lord Daniel Drago. She believed that if she could get her two heirs together, she could establish the dynasty that her father had longed for...

Queen Elizabeth of Scotland came to power the same year that Queen Elizabeth II of England did.

Most Dragon Queens of England came to power around the same time as the Kings and Queens of Scotland. The Dragon Queens always chose names to be close to or similar to the Scottish rulers to carry the illusion that England, Scotland, and Wales are one country, the United Kingdom...

Chapter 26: Happy Birthday, Nathan

5 October 2012:
Two Years After the Kidnapping...

The world wasn't ready for the sinister truth that unfolded during the trial of the century. In the end, Lord Damian completely abandoned the last name of Murrian, effectively ending the name in England, as his Aunt Karen never got married. He now understood his inner conflict had everything to do with his father's side of the family and was proud to be Taid's new heir.

✠ ✠ ✠

3 May 2013:
Two and a Half Years After the Kidnapping...
Arthur and Damian were going to the Giving Village for Nathan's 18th birthday. Anya was disappointed she couldn't come. However, the closer her wedding and coronation got, the more duties placed upon her. She also told them she had an appointment coming up she couldn't reschedule.

The Royal Twins were initially disappointed their mother and Nathan couldn't stay in England full-time, though they did come to visit as often as possible. On the other hand, Noal stayed at the palace most of the time, being considered Anya's heir until Anya gave birth to a girl. She didn't mind for now and liked that she got to train with her sister daily.

It was still as cold as the day they had left the Giving Village. However, Arthur and Damian could feel the excitement building in the air. Damian knew the elves couldn't wait to officially claim Nathan as their heir and future Saint.

At one point during the madness of Mother's trial, Alfred had asked him not to say anything to Arthur about Nathan's future. Not even Nathan had an inkling, even though out of all of Grandfather Christmas' grandchildren, Nathan was the only one with powers similar to those of the Jolly Old Man.

"Would you look at that," Arthur said as they came into the courtyard of the Holly Manor. "I didn't know that any of the reindeer were pregnant."

Damian hummed, "Would Nathan have told you that?"

Arthur shrugged as he stopped at the reindeer and held out a hand, "I think normal reindeer mate between September and November. I have no idea about magical reindeer."

"And this one looks too big to be a calf," Damian stood next to Arthur as the reindeer's nose bumped Arthur's hand, "His eyes..."

"Oh, happy day!" Alfred exclaimed and opened the front door to Holly Manor, "This is cause for celebration!"

"Besides Nathan's birthday?" Arthur asked as the reindeer kept trying to get him to continue to pet him.

"Oh, yes!" Alfred exclaimed, "Lady Hecate and Mother Nature have finally let the Heir transform. Can you tell your family? I have to alert the others."

"What do we tell them?" Damian asked as Arthur tried again to pull his hand away without the reindeer following him.

"Tell them that *Rudolf* is here," Alfred offered, giving Damian a pointed look, "Lady Eve knows who *Rudolf* is."

Damian nodded, "Come on, Arthur."

The reindeer grabbed Damain's jacket, not letting him go for a moment.

"Damian?" Arthur questioned.

"Go on," Damian assured, "I'll be there in a moment."

Arthur nodded before making his way into the main door of the Manor. Damian turned back to *Rudolf.*

"Please let me go, Nathan," Damian said calmly once Arthur was out of hearing range, "Grandfather Christmas should be out in a few minutes to help you change back. Will you be okay here without me staying?"

Nathan, in his reindeer form, let go and nodded.

"Thank you," Damian said as he touched Nathan's nose, "Everything will be explained to us once you change back. The elves will keep you safe until then, alright?"

Nathan nodded again. Damian rubbed his nose quickly before turning to follow Arthur inside…

✠ ✠ ✠

"Hey, Mum," Arthur greeted as he placed his and Anya's gift for their brother on one of the chairs, "Where's Nathan?"

Mum smiled, "He's the reindeer you passed on the way in."

"We only passed one of Grandfather Christmas' reindeer," Arthur said, "I think I heard the elves calling it *Rudolf.*"

Damian started chuckling, understanding what Mum was implying. He's known the truth for a while.

"What's so funny?" Arthur demanded, turning to his husband.

"*Rudolf* is Nate," Grandfather Christmas replied proudly as he entered the living room, holding his signature red coat in his arms, "Do you want to watch me coach him into changing back?"

Damian was now practically rolling on the floor with laughter at Arthur's face. Arthur paused and thought momentarily, unsure what to say without sounding like a jerk.

"Thank the gods that I'm not the next Santa," he finally settled on, "It's way too cold for me up here!"

"Good," Damian said after regaining some composure. "However, I don't think I can handle all the responsibilities that come with being Mrs Claus on top of my shared duties of Lord Security."

Arthur swatted at him as he ducked. Mum and Grandfather Christmas joined in with Damian's renewed laughter. Then, Grandfather Christmas continued to pass them with an amused look. It was time to get his youngest grandson back into his human form.

"I don't know," Grandmother Christmas started to say, flowing into the room and carrying a tray of cookies and goodies smelling of chocolate. "I think Damian would have made an excellent Mrs Claus, and he wouldn't be the first male referred to as such."

Damian stopped laughing, now curious.

"Well, he would have been the first gay Santa Claus," Mum continued for her mother, "My Grandfather Christmas was Mrs Claus to the rest of the world or Prince Sasha of Imperial Russia. My Grandmother Christmas was the Santa Claus of her time. These seemingly gendered role swaps have happened a few times in North Pole history."

Grandmother Christmas nodded, "If I hadn't miscarried my first child and Andros' parents had survived, then Eve would have been Santa Claus, and Andros would have been Mrs Claus."

"What?" Arthur gasped before turning to Mum, "Is this true?"

She nodded, "I have access to some of the Saint's powers, like knowing the perfect gift to leave and crocheting projects that I whip through nonstop. But I never transformed into *Rudolf.*

I had already met your father when my eighteenth birthday came around and on a different path. I couldn't become the next Santa Claus. Are you upset about *not* being my father's heir?"

Arthur shook his head, "Honestly, I'm relieved."

"Will you finally apply to culinary school now that you truly don't have any more duties anywhere?" Damian asked as he sat down on the couch. "Mrs Carmichael has been waiting to retire because she wants you to take her place in the kitchens."

Moving to sit next to Damian, Arthur asked: "You think I can be a Kitchen Manager?"

Damian nodded as Arthur grabbed his hand.

"You can do anything you put your mind to," Mum assured, taking out some yarn for a crochet project, "Anya may want to keep you safe; what's better than a job in the palace, and it's a job that travels between the other palaces to wherever she's located to help keep an eye on you."

Arthur shook his head with a small smile, "She seems to think that I will disappear on her again."

"Is she wrong to think that?" Damian pointed out, "Just be lucky that she trusts me and Kai with our jobs, or you wouldn't have been able to come up here..."

A small crash kept him from continuing.

"*MUM!*" Nathan called as he ran into the room, practically swimming in the oversized red coat Grandfather gave him. "Did you know that was going to happen?!"

Arthur wondered if his little brother would start wearing a pillow for a pretend middle, seeing all the growing he would have to do for it to fit him properly.

Mum giggled, "Aren't you forgetting pants?"

Nathan stopped and looked down.

"Oops," his cheeks turning rosy, "I'll be right back!"

He rushed back out of the room as he passed Grandfather Christmas, who shook his head, amused. "I think I did the same thing," he commented as he moved to the other open seat. Grandmother Christmas passed him a hot chocolate. "I didn't even realise I was the heir until I had changed into *Rudolf.* I had two older siblings I thought were ahead of me but never showed interest in the family business the same way I did. I think they felt the same way you do."

Arthur signed in relief. So he *wasn't* the only one from either side of his family who was not looking forward to a predestined life. He couldn't wait for the rest of his life with Damian and cooking for his family.

Ding! Ding! Ding!

Notifications started coming in on several phones; thanks to elven magic, they had reception even this far out.

Damian's eyes widened as Arthur read the phone over his shoulder. Arthur squeaked.

"I... *is that true?*" Mum asked quietly.

"Well, Anya did have to stay behind..." Arthur said slowly.

"For an appointment, she couldn't move—" a RING RING cut off Damian's thought from Arthur's phone.

Arthur grabbed his phone and read aloud, *"Anya."*

"ANSWER IT!" Everyone exclaimed.

He slid to answer and put it on speaker. "Anya?"

"Am I on speaker?"

"Yes," Arthur replied, "I have Mum, Grandfather, Grandmother, and Damian with me."

"So, I have some news, and I think someone Tweeted before I could tell you," she said, *"My doctor is already looking into who broke protocol."*

Damian and Arthur gulped, looking at each other.

"So the tweet is true?" Damian asked.

"Yes," Anya admitted, sounding happy yet defeated, *"I can't believe you found out this way. I wanted to tell you guys when you returned to England."*

Arthur spoke excitedly into the receiver. "So the transfer worked?"

"Yes!"

The yelling and whooping drew in the elves and Nathan, who now had pants on. Damian and Arthur hugged each other tightly.

They couldn't wait to be parents.

Chapter 27: The Dragon's Nest

Halloween, 2013:
Three Years and Four Weeks
After the Kidnapping...

Damian shifted through the paperwork on his desk. He was in his office, trying to figure out the security for the next major holiday, Christmas. He was thankful that he didn't have a birthday party to manage security for. Arthur and Anya decided they would have their official birthday celebration in June, like Queen Elizabeth of Scotland. This was started when the rulers wanted a birthday celebration in a warmer month. Anya didn't want to do it by herself... and neither did Arthur.

Instead, he was doing what he loved best: being behind the scenes. Well, being behind the scenes as much as one can get being married to the Prince of England. He and Kai, Kaiden to the rest of the world, worked together to protect the royal families.

He also worked as a liaison to New Scotland Yard. The work he did to find Arthur and uncover a plot to take over the throne was centuries in the making and helped to cement his place in New Scotland Yard. He turned over his mother, grandmother, and aunt for their place in the plot they were all willing to participate in. He was the *only* blood Murrian wanting nothing to do with the throne. This only made New Scotland Yard adore him even more.

Everyone who worked there knew he won his place among them. The head of CSI was one of his professors at Oxford. She knew he had a passion for the science behind the clues. The other techs, inspectors, and officers were willing to give him a chance while he tried to find Arthur because of her and some of the CSI elves who referred to him as an agent.

"Where the hell is my brother?!" Anya demanded as the door slammed open, Damian nearly jumping out of his chair. This time, she sounded panicked rather than angry.

Damian looked up after swallowing sharply, not knowing

where this was going. He took a deep breath as he shook his head to clear any flashbacks to the last time she barged into his office.

"He should be in the kitchen," Damian said, "Getting meals ready for you and Kai to test for your coronation and wedding in a few short days —"

"*Ugh!*" She interrupted, the wall helping to prop her up.

Damian quickly stood and rushed to Anya's side. He held out his hand for her to grab. She grabbed it and clutched it hard.

"Anya, take a deep breath, work through it," he coached like he was taught, "How long has this been happening?"

"It feels like hours. Sofia gave me wings to get to you," she whispered after the wave of pain subsided. "We'll have to postpone everything because my niece or nephew is too impatient to wait for the due date in November."

"Well, they take after their Auntie-Mama, huh?" Damian joked as he helped her to stand.

"Haha, *very* funny," she grumbled despite the pain.

The Hospital Wing was closer to the kitchen, so they could grab Arthur along the way. The plan was always to have the baby in the Hospital Wing because her father's fear passed to his kids. Queen Eliza had died giving birth to her son at the hospital, so Queen Eve gave birth at the palace, and Anya felt that she would be safe to do the same.

"How far apart are the contractions?" Damian asked.

"I think ten minutes," Anya replied tiredly, "I kind of stopped keeping track."

"I don't even think I could keep track," Damian huffed as they slowly started making their way through the palace.

Anya gave him a weak glare before she grimaced. He had no idea her dragon was rumbling in the back of her mind. He was very lucky the pregnancy threw off her powers, or else he might have been a crispy Co-Head of Security.

"She's not happy with me, is she?" Damian asked, breaking the silence.

Anya laughed despite the pain. She had to admit he was better at reading her and her inner dragon.

✠ ✠ ✠

3:05 pm...

Mrs Carmichel entered the kitchen and did her best not to laugh. Arthur was usually calm, cool, and collected. However, he was none of those things right now. Pastry bags and dirty mixing bowls covered the counter, and Arthur was coated in flour.

"Are you planning on baking yourself any time soon, Your Highness?" She finally asked as Arthur finished putting a sugar Tudor Rose on a large cake he was preparing as a double coronation and wedding piece.

"Huh?" Arthur asked.

Mrs Carmichael pulled out her phone and placed it into selfie mode. She held it up with the screen facing him. He stared, squinting for a moment before bursting into laughter. Mrs Carmichael then let herself laugh.

"I look like a kitchen ghost!" Arthur exclaimed as he pulled out his phone, "Here, can you take a photo of this?"

She pocketed her phone before she took his phone in hand.

"Thank you," he continued with a grin as he heard a few clicks coming from the phone, "You don't understand how grateful I've been for your generosity over the years. You were willing to take a grieving prince and raise him as your own."

She gave Arthur a small smile as she returned the phone to him.

"You were looking for a place to hide, and you were a curious little thing," Mrs Carmichael began as she moved to grab a towel. "You saw I needed help and jumped in. We hadn't seen you happy until then, and we didn't have the heart to stop you. We were even more determined to keep you out of that witch woman's path as much as possible. We didn't care that it didn't fit into her idea of how royalty should look. King Andros, may he rest in peace, would come down just to watch you perform your cooking magic. He said you remind him of Queen Eve."

"And the fact she was never legally married to my father had nothing to do with it?" Arthur asked as he pocketed his phone.

"Well, I heard all the rumours when there was never a royal wedding or coronation," Mrs Carhmichael said as she used the towel to wipe some of the flour off his cheek, "Some of the staff also thought something wasn't right between the two of them."

"There were days Papa wasn't paying attention," Arthur agreed as he took the towel from her before wetting it in the sink and wiping his face. "Looking back, it always happened in the middle of the month for a week, and it was usually two weeks before Lady Monster would scream and break things when she didn't get pregnant."

"Arthur! You need to come with us!" Anya's voice boomed from the kitchen entrance.

He turned to see Damian and Kai helping Anya stand. Despite the pain of a new set of contractions, she started laughing. Kai joined her laughter while Damian shook his head with a huge grin. He was used to Arthur coming up to dinner, happy and covered in whatever the dessert was that night.

"I think the cake won this round," Damian commented, amused.

"Haha," Arthur said dryly, setting the towel on the counter, "I was just washing my face. What's wrong?"

"This baby doesn't want to wait anymore," Anya said between breaths, "Are you ready to be a Papa?"

"Now?" Arthur gulped before looking around at the mess he made, "Well—"

Mrs Carmichael smiled at the royal group, "I've got the

kitchen; go clean yourself up. If that baby is like the two of you, you don't have much time—"

Without warning, a splashing sound echoed through the kitchen.

"*Guys,*" Kai said, looking at the puddle forming at Anya's feet, "We're losing time. Come on, Damian."

They left as quickly as they came. Arthur could only stare at the doorway to the kitchen, unsure of what to feel.

"*What just happened?*" He asked mostly to himself as a cleaner came over with a mop.

"Why are you still standing there?" Mrs Carmichael demanded, excited for the two princes as she took back the towel, keeping him from picking it back up, "Go get cleaned up! Your baby is almost here!"

"But, what about all of this..." He gestured to the mess on the island counter.

"This is my speciality," she started with a grin, "It brings back memories. I don't mind cleaning up after you if it prevents you from getting in trouble with your sister and your husband."

Arthur grinned as he took off his apron and threw it into the hamper. He rushed past Mrs Carmichael, stopping to kiss her cheek, then ran around the cleaner, who gave him a grin as he passed. All the staff couldn't wait for this little one.

Mrs Carmichael shook her head as she chuckled. She started stacking mixing bowls and wiping down counters as she went. Other kitchen staff came to help her as they talked with happiness vibrating throughout the room. The head chef paused as she came across the modelling chocolate Arthur left out. A smile grew on her face as an idea came to her...

⚜ ⚜ ⚜

40 minutes later...

Arthur threw his dark blonde hair up in a bun as he rushed through the halls and down the staircases to get to the Hospital

Wing. Several startled staff members dove out of the way as he passed them.

Arthur didn't care he was barefoot and in lounge clothes; he was in such a rush that he didn't realise he had passed his laughing Uncle Aaron. Unbeknownst to him, this was the same panicked walking path his father had taken twenty-one years ago.

By the time Arthur reached the designated waiting room, Kai was pacing back and forth in front of the door leading to the Hospital Wing. Pausing, he scanned over Arthur before bursting into laughter.

"I don't think Anya will be happy about the fact you don't have shoes."

Arthur rolled his eyes, "I'll get those cloth boots. Why are you out here?"

"She wouldn't let me in," Kai explained, "She wants my first time in the delivery room with any children we have together. She'd rather have you and Damian in there. So, go get those boots. I'll go back to pacing."

Arthur shook his head as he pushed the door open, and Madam Mina greeted him. She recently transferred to the palace to keep an eye on Noel when the decision came for her to live there long-term. Having worked for their family since Lady Eve was pregnant, she insisted on caring for Anya since they couldn't trust Anya's previous doctor's office.

"Dr Stevens is in there with Anya and Damian," Madam Mina said as she glanced over at him over her paperwork, "Where are your shoes?"

He hadn't met the new doctor yet. He knew that Madam Mina had hired them personally. Anya had been meeting with Dr Stevens during his hours in the kitchen.

"I have them here, Mother," Matheo said as he strolled in behind, handing the shoes to Arthur. "He's too fast for me."

Her glare relaxed once Arthur took the slippers. The prince

donned scrubs and a medical gown and slid on the slippers. Madam Mina then pointed to the sink.

"Wash up first. I have no idea what you might have picked up on your mad dash."

"Yes, Ma'am," Arthur saluted.

"Take a mask too!" She snapped.

"Of course," he said as he picked a blue paper mask from a box on the counter.

"Don't forget the hat!" She called, "Your hair needs to be covered!"

"Got it!" He exclaimed as he swiped a cloth hat next to the box of masks. He put it on, stopping a moment, ensuring he covered his hair.

She then turned to Matheo, "You can wait with Prince Kai. Let your partner and in-laws know that we've got things under control."

"Yes, Mother," Matheo replied with a grin before retreating.

"Those boys," Arthur heard Mina tut as he made his way to the furthest room, hearing faint yelling noises as he pushed the door open.

"AHH!" Anya exclaimed as she tried to push. The mist over her head was an attempt to keep her powers from acting on her emotions. The last thing the medical personnel needed was a fire to break out in the delivery room.

"Oh, thank the gods!" Damian said, "I keep forgetting how strong your sister is. I think she might have broken my hand!"

Anya took a few deep breaths.

"Your Majesty, you need to push on the next contraction!" Dr Stevens requested.

Arthur really couldn't see who was under all the protective gear. Their voice was feminine, though the gear hid all hints of gender. He manoeuvred to be on Anya's left side.

"You... took your... time," Anya huffed with sweat pouring down her face, hair looking more brown than blonde.

"Yeah, well, you would rather one of us look presentable

for meeting this baby," he joked, mask hiding his grin. He then grabbed her hand as Damian had to switch hands.

Arthur suppressed a chuckle when he realised Anya had bruised Damian's hand, "Now that I'm here, will you stop abusing my husband?"

"No… promises," she huffed before groaning.

"Push now, your Majesty!" Dr Stevens ordered.

"Ahhhh!"

Arthur held on to Anya's hand tightly. His knuckles turned white as cries reached their ears. Anya sighed in relief.

"Alright, which Father would like to cut the cord?" Dr Stevens asked as they wrapped the baby in a towel.

"You should do it," Damian urged, relieved his hands could get a break.

"Okay," Arthur replied as Anya let go of his hand.

He quickly took a pair of sterilised scissors off a tray offered to him. He leaned over, keeping his eyes on his child and the doctor.

"Where?"

"Here," one of the nurses gestured to a space about two to three inches away from the baby, "That will give us enough cord to clamp."

He nodded, carefully took the scissors to the cord, and made a cut once cleared to do so. The baby's cries started to subside as the nurse wrapped *him* up and took *him* away to be washed. Yes, *he*, a little boy, that made Arthur's hidden grin widen. In the back of his mind, he knew it would be his baby's choice on how they expressed themselves.

"Ahh! Wha…t's happen…ing?" Anya groaned as her body entered another round of pain.

Dr Stevens returned to their position, ready to catch what was next. With another towel at hand, they seemed to know that something was about to happen. Arthur and Damian hastily returned to their spots, and Anya blindly grabbed at their hands.

"I need you to push for me one more time!" They ordered, "I think the fathers are in for a surprise. Push in three, two, one—"

"*Ugg!*" Anya exclaimed.

Arthur helped as he heard a crack from Damain's side. A flash of pain in Damian's eyes let him know that Anya had broken his hand this time.

But it was another round of crying that brought confusion to the fathers.

"There was a baby girl behind your son," Dr Stevens said as they held up a crying infant, half wrapped in the towel, "Heir Wales, would you…"

"Yes!" Damian interrupted, letting go of Anya's hand.

He hastily grabbed a new sanitised pair of scissors with his unbroken hand. Keeping his eyes on his crying daughter, he was entranced by her as he carefully cut the cord in the spot he was instructed to.

A nurse then returned with their son, who was wrapped in an orange blanket with black cats.

"Who would like to hold him first?" The nurse asked.

"*Anya,*" Damian and Arthur said together before she could say anything.

The nurse nodded, handing him to Anya. The baby rested against her upper chest, near her heart. The doctor then handed the baby girl, who was also in an orange blanket but had little bats on it, to the nurse to be cleaned up.

"Why me?" Anya whispered.

"You're still their mother," Arthur replied as a nurse led Damian to get his hand checked out, "You're legally going to be their aunt and Godmother. What is your dragon saying?"

Anya went quiet as she brushed the dark blonde hair off the infant's forehead, "That our little girl has the potential to be the next ruler. However, it will all depend on the children Kai and I have together too. His blood then adds the potential for the Lunar line's spirit to claim any of our future children as their heirs if they meet the right requirements."

"Your Highness?"

Arthur looked to see a nurse approaching with his daughter. "Would you like to hold her?"

Anya let go of his hand as he turned to the nurse. The nurse carefully transferred the little princess to his arms. He then turned back to Anya.

"Do you want to hold her too while Damian gets a cast?"

"Are you sure?" She asked quietly.

Arthur nodded as he placed his daughter into Anya's other arm.

"Oh," Anya whispered as the baby curled into her shoulder.

"What?" Arthur asked, concerned, "Did the doctor miss something?"

She shook her head, "Sofia is purring in my head."

"Like a cat, right?"

She stared up at him, "Can you hear her?"

Arthur went silent. He rubbed his daughter's cheek as he heard in the back of his mind. *Hello, Prince Arthur Henry Andros Evergreen Drago.*

"How is this possible?" He asked, loud enough for Anya to hear.

Your ancestor harmed many dragons in his quest for a male heir and 'sealing his legacy'. You are more like the Arthur I wanted to choose. You have done everything to protect your family. Your Catherine might be in the form of your sister, you love all the women in your life unconditionally. You've also found your Daniel. I like that you can be yourself. That is enough for me to talk to you through your bond with Anya. You just don't get a dragon of your own.

"That's okay; Anya and I are good at sharing," he whispered as Anya giggled and nodded. "Besides, my powers would have given me a bear if I had the right blood, right?"

"Who would be a bear?" Damian asked as he returned to the room, and the nursing staff left to give them some privacy. Anya winced when she saw his cast.

"I'm sorry," she whispered.

"Don't be," he brushed it off, "This is nothing compared to what you just did for us. Did you know it was going to be twins?"

She nodded tiredly, "I wanted it to be a surprise. What are you going to name them?"

"It's a good thing that we had names for a boy and a girl picked out. We thought we should give them the names they had in the past with some names from the present," Damian said as he went up to touch their son's cheek, "This little one will be Philip Andrew Andros Drago Wales. A name for the great-grandfather and grandfathers he never met but who did everything they could to protect me from the Murrians, and an English version of the name Prince Fillip."

"And our little princess will be Mary Catherine Anya Drago Wales," Arthur continued, "She's named for the Tudor Queens responsible for stabilising our family line, and the Auntie Mama helped to bring her and her brother into the world."

"Oh, you guys!" She said as she blinked a few times, "You're going to make me cry."

"Milords, milady," Mina knocked on the door before bowing, "How about you greet the family in the waiting room while I check on Queen Anya? Princess Noel, in particular, is getting antsy."

"You should take the twins with you," Anya suggested, "They look more presentable than me; just take your masks off. You might scare Noel."

Arthur snorted as he lowered his mask, "I think it takes a lot more to scare that one."

"That's only because she's gotten better at pranking you," Damian said as Arthur carefully lifted Philip and settled him into Damian's good arm, "She hasn't forgiven you for the *Pipsqueak* comment."

"I don't think she ever will," Arthur huffed as Anya let him lift Mary into his arms.

"We Drago women tend to hold grudges when we want to," Anya reminded with a tired grin, "Can you send Mama back once Mina gives the all-clear?"

"Sure," Arthur shrugged, "Thank you so much, Anya."

"No problem," she quipped, "Kai is really lucky I want a baby of my own one day; this process could turn anyone off."

Damian shook his head as he moved toward the door, "At least Kai can heal himself if you break his hand the next time around."

Damian and Arthur could hear Anya's laughter behind them as they went toward the waiting room with the surprise twins. They stopped right before the doors to the waiting room to truly see their babies. Damian and Arthur were facing each other, standing close. Their foreheads touched as they looked over the new set of twins.

"It's a good thing we had both name sets picked out," Damian breathed in awe, "I can't believe Anya kept this from us."

"I can," Arthur whispered, "She's always had these little secrets I was eventually let in on. I thought it was because I was going to be the leader one day, but now..."

"You're not going to be involved with politics outside of LGBTQ rights," Damian finished, understanding.

Arthur nodded, "I'll leave these secrets to you and Anya."

They stared down at the new twins for a few moments before Arthur leaned forward to kiss Damian's lips before pulling away.

Damian took in a deep breath, "Let's do this. Let me go first. We should surprise them with Mary, just like Anya did."

Damian went through the door first, with Philip safely nestled into his left arm. Arthur waited, taking in his little girl. He had no idea of the destiny that awaited her. But he knew he would do anything to protect her and her brother...

Epilogue: Truths Emerge

1 October 2020
Ten Years After the Kidnapping...

It has been ten years since Damian and Arthur's world was turned upside down. Their love has only grown stronger as their family continues to grow. A typical morning for them was having breakfast together in a private dining room before starting work for the day. Arthur was still working his way up the ranks in the kitchen, now under Mrs Carmichael. Damian had a love-hate relationship with his liaison role at New Scotland Yard. He loved his job... but hated the commute.

"It's been seven months into a worldwide pandemic, and it's been nine months since the Scottish Royal Family had a massive shake-up," Damian read aloud from *The Sun* tabloid, *"The English Royal Family has been quiet—"*

Arthur snorted, "They don't know you, Uncle Matheo, and Kai, if they think we've been *quiet* about anything. Why do you read that rubbish anyway?"

Damian rolled his eyes, "So I know what mess of the Scottish Royal Family I have to help Uncle Matheo and Kai clean up."

"Those people are still following around the body doubles," Kai sighed as he joined his brother-in-laws' at the dining room table, "It's disgusting."

"Well, not every tabloid operates like Hawaii's papers do," Damian said, "How are they settling in with your sister in Hawaii?"

"Pretty well, for all the things happening in the world right now," Kai continued, "I just wish Uncle Charles could see the damage left behind when a lost family power suddenly activated."

"Wills is devastated that he can't help Harry," Anya said quietly from her end of the table, "He has never been triggered the way Harry was. But I can somewhat understand what has happened. The press has always been cruel; they always compared Aunt Diana to the other Royal women over the years, even long after her passing. Then there's everything they harp on Megan about where she grew up. Then everything they praise Katie during her pregnancies."

"The stereotyping the papers use has always been an issue," Arthur grumbled. "They barely listened to us when they learned about Kai's past. Although, the Scottish Firm hasn't done anything *not* to encourage the press."

Kai shook his head, "We didn't have to do anything but agree with the Hawaiian Press. They are so overprotective of us that the Hawaiian Press is forcing the World Press and the tabloids into line."

"How much longer is Harry training?" Arthur asked Kai.

"I'm not sure," Kai replied. "He's getting a crash course in controlling powers I've spent a lifetime mastering."

"And a wolf that he needs to master changing back-and-forth from," Anya said before blowing on her tea, "Believe me, it's hard to do when no one around us even understands how the spirit—"

"*Tad! Papa!*" Two young voices yell together, "*Where are you?*"

"*In here!*" Arthur called as Damian put the paper down.

Mary-Anya and her twin brother Phil, the next set of Royal Twins, came running into the room with their biological half-brother totting after them. The twins were one month away from turning seven years old. Their half-brother, Anya and Kai's son—legally their cousin—just turned three.

"Can you tell us a story?" Mary-Anya asked as she rushed to Arthur. Phil settled himself into Damian's side as Kai bent down to pick up his son.

"Which one?" Arthur asked as he pulled her into a hug.

"Your story," Phil said, "It's been ten years and the an... an... *What's that word again?*"

308

"Anniversary?" Damian asked as he helped Phil into one of the chairs.

The young boy nodded, "That word! Of the kidnapping. *Wait...* how can it be kidnapping if you're a prince?"

"Kidnapping isn't always gender specific. Princes' can get taken too; it just isn't as common as you think," Anya replied, "Especially one who has his rescue attempt blocked."

Arthur glared at her, "It's not *my* fault Uncle Matheo hadn't told me about the elf ninjas he still reported to."

The younger twins giggle.

"Please, Papa," they requested.

"You want to hear all about Papa's Frustration?" Damian asked as he hid the paper away from their curious eyes.

"And *Tad's* mission as a secret agent," Mary-Anya said, "Please?"

"Of course," Arthur grinned as Kai came around to bring Anya their son. "It all started with the death and funeral of your Grandpapa Andros..."

About the Author

Lorinda Kalajian writes speculative fiction. She weaves magic and romance into alternative histories. She loves creating new twists for known myths, fairy tales, and histories. Her favorite type of stories to read and work with are royal romances. Most of her novels have a royal character trying to navigate the world that they are from.

She enjoys crocheting blankets in her downtime, using her creativity to make works of art, and bringing warmth one blanket at a time. The movement of working a hook through a project also helps with the words for the novels she is writing. Her favorite type of project is making blankets that inspire or are based on the novels that she reads or writes.

She has a bachelor's in History and English, with a concentration in Creative Writing, from Massachusetts College of Liberal Arts. She wanted to be able to write accurate historical fiction. A degree in history helps with research in finding the facts that get intertwined into a creative fictional novel. She also has a Master of Fine Arts in Creative Writing from Southern New Hampshire University. One day, she would like to pursue a master's in history.